THE TURQUOISE

She was born Santa Fé Cameron; her mother
was high-born Spanish, her father an aristocratic
Scot. On her seventeenth birthday her only
home had been a slum in New Mexico; nine
years later she was married to one of the
wealthiest men on Wall Street. She had a
magnetism more memorable than physical
beauty, and extraordinary powers for good and
evil. In New Mexico some called her a saint, but
that was at the end of her eventful career.
"A tale of conflicting emotions and passionate
events. As ever, Anya Seton takes us into other
worlds, making us live for a few hours on a
grand scale."

Woman's Journal

The Turquoise

Anya Seton

CORONET BOOKS
Hodder Paperbacks Ltd., London

First published October 1946
Fifth impression 1958
Coronet edition 1960
Second impression 1966
Third impression 1967
Fourth impression 1968
Fifth impression 1968
Sixth impression 1969
Seventh impression 1971
Eighth impression 1973
Ninth impression 1974

Printed and bound in Great Britain for
Coronet Books,
Hodder Paperbacks Ltd,
St. Paul's House, Warwick Lane,
London, EC4P 4AH
by Hazell Watson & Viney Ltd,
Aylesbury, Bucks

ISBN 0 340 15700 3

AUTHOR'S NOTE

In this life story I have tried to keep the background and incidental history accurate. I am deeply grateful to librarians in Santa Fe and New York City, and appreciative of the many fine source books on the period.

All the main characters are fictional except—perhaps—Fey.

One summer day, the year before she died, Mary Austin and I drove from Santa Fe to my father's ranch. As we left Mary's beautiful home on the Camino del Monte Sol, we both looked at the guardian peak behind it. The little mountain held for her a mystical significance. We talked of that, and then she said, quite casually, "Once there lived a woman on that slope of Atalaya . . ." There was little more, a few sentences mentioning New York and strange contrast, only the hint of a forgotten legend.

I, too, forgot it, during many later visits to Santa Fe.

Then one day that rhythmical sentence came back, "Once there lived a woman on the slope of Atalaya . . ." I went again to Santa Fe to find the story. I did not find it in the museum or historical libraries or town records, no trace of it in the memory of the "Anglos."

But at last, in a crumbling adobe near the Chapel of San Miguel, I found an old Spanish-American, and he remembered a little. "It must be, Señora, that you mean 'La Santa.' It was so long ago. I was young then."

So here is the story. I do not know, but I believe it may have been something like this . . .

A. S.

1

SANTA FE CAMERON was named for the town of her birth, because her Scottish father and a distressed little New Mexican priest could agree on no other name.

This was on the twenty-third of January, 1850, while a bitter wind blew snow down from the Sangre de Cristo Mountains and darkened by contrast the adobe walls of the New Mexican capital.

In a bare two-room casita on lower San Francisco Street, the Scot, who was a doctor as well as husband, stood beside the priest staring down at the woollen pallet where Conchita Valdez Cameron had given birth to the baby three hours ago. Conchita was dying. Her dark eyes were fixed on her husband's face in unquestioning love while her already cold hand clutched the crucifix on her breast. The beautiful ivory pallor, her Spanish inheritance, had dulled to a bluish-grey as the life of her eighteen-year-old body flowed away in hæmorrhages that Andrew Cameron for all his skill was powerless to stanch.

The padre had administered the last rites; his concern was now with the feeble infant, prematurely born. It showed every sign of soon following its mother and must be baptized quickly.

"What name shall it be, doctor?" whispered Padre Miguel to the grim man by the bed, "María de la Concepción like her mother? or Juana—Catalina?" He paused, seeing the haggard misery in the other man's face tighten to resistance. "Come, my son," he said with gentle urgency, looking at the baby and thinking that the actual name hardly mattered, "this is the feast day of San Ildefonso, shall we give her that name?"

Except for the hissing of the piñon logs in the high Indian fireplace there was silence in the small room, which was whitewashed to the same glistening purity as the snow which sifted into the still calle outside. Then the baby gave a faint whimper and Andrew turned on the priest. "My child shall be named for no whining Spanish saint."

Padre Miguel flushed, his fingers, already wet with the holy water, trembled and an angry rebuke leaped to his tongue. But he checked it. He had encountered the Scottish doctor's stubborn Calvinism before, and he made allowances for the man's anguish. In a nature which showed no softness to the world, it had been astonishing to see the tenderness which this harsh stranger had always given to the girl on the pallet. Nor, to do him justice, had he interfered with Conchita's own faith. During the past months she had been untiring in her prayers to Our Lady of Guadalupe; prayers for forgiveness for the wrong she had done her family, prayers for a safe delivery of the baby within her womb.

The priest dimly understood that part of the doctor's violence came from realization that the Compassionate Mother had not seen fit to answer these prayers, and that lacking the consolation of the True Faith the man had no recourse but blind wrath.

So the padre's anger died, but he said inflexibly, "The baby must bear a Catholic name, doctor."

The Scot's jaw squared; he opened his mouth to speak, but the girl on the bed stirred, her straining eyes widened. "Please —" she whispered.

Andrew's face dissolved. He knelt on the hard-packed dirt floor beside the pallet. "Shall we name her Santa Fe, then?" he said softly. "It's papist enough, and—" He stopped, went on with difficulty. "We have been happy here."

The Padre saw the girl relax and a wistful smile curve the grey lips, so he dipped his hand again in the holy water. Santa Fe, he thought, "The Holy Faith"—well, why not? He made the sign of the cross on the baby's forehead.

In the corner of the room those two completely disparate human beings looked at each other with the great love which had bridged the gulf between them. The smile on Conchita's mouth lost its sadness. She tried to lift her hand toward the blunt face near her own, to smooth away, as she had often done, the furrows in his forehead. She gave a long gentle sigh and her hand fell to the sheet.

The baby astonished everyone by living. A wet-nurse was found for her, Ramona Torres, wife of a lazy and bad-tempered wood-cutter who lived across the Santa Fe River near the Chapel of San Miguel in the poor Analco quarter. La Ramona and her Pedro were dazzled to get three monthly pesos for so easy and insignificant a service. It was the little padre who negotiated this transaction by means of two gold sovereigns flung him by Andrew after Conchita's burial. For six months Andrew would not look at his child, nor hear mention of her. He shut himself into the room where Conchita had died. He went out to the market in the plaza only when hunger drove him to buy a little food, a handful of frijoles, or some hunks of hard, stringy mutton which he cooked himself in a pot over the fire and washed down with goat's milk.

He lived in an isolation which nobody tried to penetrate except Padre Miguel, who came back from his visits to the casita thwarted and rebuffed by Andrew's tight-lipped silences.

In July the padre tried a new plan. He sent Ramona with the baby to Andrew, saying, "If he will not let you in, tell him that the little Conchita is watching from paradise and her mother's heart is very sorrowful."

Ramona nodded, her broad peasant face showing no curiosity. She pulled her dirty pink rebozo over her head, wrapped one end of the scarf around the baby, and padded to the cottonwood footbridge across the river, her brown splayed feet raising little puffs of dust on the path to San Francisco Street.

Andrew opened the door at Ramona's timid knock. "Here —" said the woman, frightened by the expression in the bloodshot eyes that glared at her. "Your baby. El padre say Conchita very sad in paradise you no see baby." She sidled past the motionless Andrew to lay the swaddled bundle on the only table. Then she darted out of the door, murmuring, "Later I come back." And she hurried away to the delights of the plaza and a gossip with friends in the shade of the portales.

Andrew shut the door and walked slowly to the table. The baby lay perfectly still, staring at him with unwinking grey eyes.

"Grey!" said Andrew aloud, startled from the remote prison of his grief. He leaned closer. Grey as the waters of Loch Fyne, he thought. The homesickness which he had denied these two years sent a twinge of new pain into his consciousness. His daughter gazed up at him quietly, and after a while he experienced a feeling of solace. The eyes were like his mother's, the gentle Highland mother who had had the gift of second sight, and wisdom and pity for all things.

"Santa Fe—" said Andrew bitterly, and at the sound of his voice the baby suddenly smiled.

"Aye, 'tis a daft name for ye, small wonder ye smile." He repeated the name, and this time the last syllable echoed in his mind with a peculiar relevance. " 'Fey!' There's a true Scottish word will fit you, for ye're fated—doomed to die as we all are, poor bairnie."

The baby gurgled, tried to kick against the tight-wrapped

9

greasy blanket; thwarted, she protested tentatively, then fell asleep. Andrew continued to stare down at her.

When Ramona came back for the baby, she saw that the wild loco light had left the Señor.

"Bring Fey here once a week until she's weaned," he commanded in his halting Spanish. "After that I'll keep her."

"Fe?" questioned the woman blankly.

Andrew pointed at the baby.

"Ah!" said Ramona, and shrugged her fat shoulders. She picked up the little bundle, tucked it again into the fold of her rebozo, and pattered off down the street.

Andrew shut the pine door and walked to the back room. He looked at the corner where Conchita had died and at the carved blue-and-gold figure of Our Lady of Guadalupe which stood in a small niche in the wall as Conchita had placed it. From this figure he averted his eyes. They rested on the cowhide trunk which had accompanied him from Scotland. Inside the trunk, long untouched, lay his dirk, sporran, and kilt woven in the rose, blue, and green of the Cameron tartan.

He knelt beside the trunk, opened it with a key from his watch chain, and slowly lifted up the kilt. The soft wool fell to shreds as he touched it. It was riddled with moth holes. He let the trunk lid fall.

He walked into the front room, where he pulled his leather instrument case from the floor of the carved pine cupboard.

The contents of the medicine bottles had evaporated or dissolved into gluey masses, but on the instruments there was little rust; the dry New Mexican air had preserved them. He laid them out on the table—knives, probes, scalpels, and forceps—then picked them up one after the other, balancing each in his fingers which had grown clumsy and unresponsive.

Beneath the flap inside the instrument case there lay a piece of parchment. Andrew pulled it out and stared at the lines of Latin script. The parchment said that Andrew Lochiel Cameron had in 1846 graduated "cum laude" from Edinburgh's Royal College of Surgeons.

Andrew gathered up the instruments and threw them pell-mell into the case with the parchment. He flung the case back into the cupboard and strode hatless out of the house into the vivid noon sunlight. His jerky steps took him up San Francisco Street, past the little adobe houses like his own, past the much larger town houses of the Delgados and the Candelarios whose smooth mud walls gave no hint of the graceful life of the flowering patios inside. He passed through the plaza without

seeing any of its colour and bustle. Only an hour before, a caravan had rumbled into the plaza at the end of the Santa Fe Trail,
over eight hundred plodding and dangerous miles from Independence, Missouri, so far back in the States. The bull-whackers
and the mule-drivers were celebrating already. The saloons
were teeming. A stream of whooping, excited men thronged in
and out of La Fonda, the hotel on the south-east corner of the
plaza, and clinging to most of the brawny, sweating arms were
Mexican girls in best chemises and rebozos, their black eyes
limpid with excited anticipation. Despite the fresh white picket
fence and prim rows of alfalfa newly planted by the Americans
in the centre of the plaza, the little square had given itself once
again to pagan riot. There was a cockfight in front of the military chapel, two games of monte beneath the portale of the
Governor's Palace, and the constant explosion of whip-crackers
and pistol shots. The latter from three drunken American soldiers who had willingly caught the infection, as did almost all
the Americans who wrote sanctimonious letters home about
Sante Fe's vicious lack of morals while they drank and lecher-
ized and gambled to an extent never dreamed of by the more
temperate Mexicans.

Andrew had neither eyes nor ears for this scene, which was
repeated at the arrival of each caravan, and of which he had
himself been a part two years ago. He picked his way around a
dying ox which had collapsed in the middle of the street,
avoided two braying burros loaded with vegetables, and a
Tesuque Pueblo Indian who stood motionless on the corner of
Palace Avenue surveying the bedlam with calm contempt. He
skirted the east side of the Governor's so-called "Palace," a long
one-storey mud building behind a colonnade, and continued his
way north near Fort Marcy Hill until he reached the beginning
of the road which led to Taos—and beyond—to Arroyo Hondo
in the high mountains—the road he had travelled in April a
year ago and which had taken him to the Valdez hacienda and
Conchita. This road, too, had finally ended in bitterness, as had
every other road down which he had briefly glimpsed happiness
during his twenty-six years of living.

Andrew's pace slowed. He climbed the first juniper-covered
hill and sat down on a piñon stump near the dusty trail. The
summer sun poured warmly stimulating from a turquoise sky,
a peon trotted by on his burro, his serape a vivid patch of
orange against the distant Jemez Mountains. The peon hailed
Andrew, "Holá! Buenos dias, amigo!" But Andrew was not
warmed by the sun, nor did he hear the friendly greeting. He

stared down at the dry sagebrush near his foot and saw it dissolve into the purple heather of the moors at home. He smelled the salt tang of the mist swirling in from Loch Fyne and the fragrance of peat smoke. He saw once more the piled grey stone of the house where he had been born and the face of his father, twisted with anger, etched clear against the great doorway. He could no longer remember the words his father had hurled at him because of a sharper memory—the stepmother's triumphant face peering over Sir James's shoulder, her thin lips curled, her eyes like a gloating ferret's.

There had been another witness to that scene on the steps of Cameron Hall. The Duke of Argyll, his father's powerful friend as the Argylls since the days of Lochiel and Culloden had been staunch patrons to all the Camerons. The Duke had stood to one side, his grizzled head held stiffly turned from Andrew in whom he had hitherto taken so much interest.

The Glasgow stepmother had done her work well. She had contrived through guile and clever lies not only to expel Andrew from his home, but to banish him from Scotland. Andrew had hated her from the moment old Sir James had brought her to the Hall scarcely a year after his wife's death. The sly, sneck-drawing face of the quean! thought Andrew, clenching his hands, the rawness of the hurt she had dealt him as fresh as it had been that day in Scotland. The lustful little eyes of her! She had cocked those eyes at Andrew himself until he made plain his disgust. And then one night he had caught her naked behind a haycock with the stable boy, and she had acted after that with incredible speed.

Andrew, fresh from medical college, had been called to the Castle to attend the Duke's own cousin. The Lady Margaret had a cancer and she died, but no sooner was she laid in the ducal vault than the stepmother raised somehow a miasma of suspicion. How queer that the Lady Margaret had seemed perfectly well the week before; how strange that as soon as Andrew appeared, she grew worse and that she should die so quickly. How queer—how strange—until the whole of Inveraray, the whole of Argyllshire, had heard and inflated the whispers to a roar. There must have been, they said, a dreadful mistake made in the medicines—there had been malpractice—it was as good as murder. The Duke was frantic, they said; only his long friendship for poor disgraced Sir James kept him from clapping the wicked young doctor into jail.

It was then that Andrew tried to tell his father some of the reason for the stepmother's persecution. And Sir James had disowned him, shouting and stamping. "Get ye out o' my sight for aye! I dinna care gin ye go straight to the de'il that must'a' spawned ye!"

So Andrew had left Cameron Hall, his instrument case in his hand, his cowhide trunk under his arm. He was the younger son, and Sir James had had no troublesome matter of inheritance to worry him. The stepmother was left alone in triumph at the Hall with her infatuated old husband.

Andrew went to Glasgow and there he bought passage to the States with three of the hundred gold sovereigns left him by his mother. He had tried to settle in New York, but not two months after he had hung out his shingle, the *Bonnie Clyde* put in from Glasgow. Andrew was down at the pier. He despised himself for it, but whenever a ship from home docked, he found himself on the wharf, his nostrils sniffing for a breath of heather and smoky kipper, his ears straining for the cadenced burr of the Highlands.

An Inveraray man, Jem MacGregor, had come down the gangplank that day and Andrew, recognizing him with a great leap in his heart, had rushed forward, unthinking, his hands outstretched. But Jem, whose own child Andrew had doctored through pneumonia, turned as purple as the tartan muffler around his neck. "So, young Cameron," sneered Jem, putting his hands in his pockets, "'tis the puir bodies o' New York ye're murr-r-dering the noo?" And, turning his back, he had shuffled rapidly down the pier.

After that, the bitterness and the restlessness had had full dominion over Andrew. He took down the shingle, which had brought him no patients anyway, and turned his face like many another toward the West. He locked his remaining gold into the cowhide trunk and worked his way on foot and on barges, taking morose satisfaction in physical labour that left over no strength for thought. It was easy enough to find work. He was big and powerful, with the rawboned ruggedness of the Highlands, and his taciturnity increased his value. The farther West he got, the more people there were who neither asked nor welcomed questions. Many times he passed through communities where the settlers would have been fervently grateful for a physician amongst them, but he concealed his knowledge. There had grown in him a carking doubt of his own skill, and the restlessness drove him on. He had reached Independence, Missouri, in the spring of 1848, when the frontier was beginning to seethe over the rumours of Sutter's gold strike back in January. Andrew was unaffected by the gold fever. It seemed

13

to him that he shared few emotions with the rest of mankind and that his brain and body had no urge but a ceaseless yearning for change.

On August the tenth, Alexander Major's first organized freight outfit set out over the Santa Fe Trail from Independence, and Andrew went with them as driver of one of the ox-teams for a dollar a day and keep. He was not popular with the other men, for he would not join in their songs or bawdy reminiscences around the campfire at night, nor would he use the rich profanity with which the bull-whackers belaboured their stupid animals. He was, however, an expert shot, and his trained surgeon's fingers could splice a rope or mend a broken spoke far faster than theirs could. By the time they reached Council Grove, a hundred and forty-five miles along the way, they had accepted him. And a month later, when the exhausted teams plodded into Pecos Village, only a day and a half from Santa Fe, he had earned a grudging admiration. Mosquitoes, mud, thirst, and Indian scares had not feazed the silent Scot. The other bull-whackers thought him a queer stick, and promptly forgot him after they reached Santa Fe, but they respected him.

Andrew, like many another, was disappointed by his first view of the ancient royal city. The huddle of adobe houses in a treeless valley reminded him only of a large brickyard with scattered kilns ready for the firing. Nor after he had goaded his team across the little Santa Fe River and entered the town was he attracted by a closer view. There was too much dust and dryness, too much monotony of smooth mud walls, and at the joyous cries, "La Entrada de la Caravana! Los Americanos! Los carros!" too much hysterical excitement. The Mexican populace mobbed the new arrivals; children begged for pennies; the old market women, shrilly quoting prices, brandished ristras of chilli or sizzling hot tortillas. And the dark-eyed girls clustered a dozen strong around each Americano, cooing, "Fandango to-night! You come wiz me, Señor, I Frasquita," or Dolores, or Josefa. "I your sweetheart, I fine sweetheart, por Dios!"

Andrew escaped from the barrage of languishing eyes into La Fonda's bar-room, where to his surprise he found whisky excellent even to his Scottish palate. After three drinks he was able to view Santa Fe with greater tolerance. He strolled quickly through the hotel's sala, a huge room filled with faro and monte players. He wandered out into the great patio and seeing that food was being served sat down at a small table. He intensely disliked this food when it came—unknown messes of

14

beans and chopped meat and corn meal all raised to the same blistering level of red chilli heat; still, as he sat on in the flower-filled patio, there came to him a certain relaxation and pleasure. Mocking-birds, in cages hung from the beams of the portale, trilled melodious imitation of lazy strumming from a guitar in the hotel corral. The air was exquisitely perfumed with the fragrance of burning cedar from a log fire in the sala, and this rare, clear air, seven thousand feet above sea level, exhilarated the blood.

Here, at last in this foreign place, thought Andrew, there was nothing to remind him of home, not even the language. The few Americans might easily be avoided. Here, he thought with a rare spurt of optimism and confidence, he might be able to establish himself and start life again. He went back to the bar, ordered another whisky, and decided to winter in Santa Fe.

But the winter passed by and he had made no niche for himself in the town. He had not the gift for making friends, and the unreasonable buried fear that the Argyllshire scandal would track him down constantly inhibited him. He was exceedingly lonely without quite knowing it, and by April the restlessness had come on him again. He bought a horse and set out through snowdrifts and spring mud on the road to the north. By the fifth of April, he had ridden through Taos and pushed on fifteen miles farther to the little Spanish village of Arroyo Hondo. Andrew hitched his exhausted horse to a post in the village's tiny plaza, and was heading for the only posada and a drink when he saw Conchita.

She was sitting on the back seat of a covered spring wagon waiting for her mother, who was shopping, and the girl was alone except for the coachman, who snored lustily from beneath a forward-tilted sombrero.

Andrew stopped short with an unconscious exclamation. Conchita was beautiful, and her huge dark eyes were staring at him in naïve astonishment, beneath the black lace of her mantilla which romantically shadowed her little face and glossy hair. But it was not her beauty, it was a mystical feeling of completion, as though he had been an empty vessel into which pure water had at last been allowed to flow. Between one second and the next, as he looked at Conchita, the vessel filled and the aching emptiness was gone.

She gave a faint, embarrassed smile and gently pulled her mantilla across her face. She had never seen a man anything like this one before, so big and ruddy, with his sunburned skin

15

and hair the colour of the red earth cliff behind the hacienda. Estranjero, she thought, Americano, perhaps, and this dismayed her, for her family and all the other Spaniards who lived up here in the Colorado country hated the Americans, who had conquered them three years ago after the shameful, inexplicable defeats in Old Mexico.

Then Conchita grew frightened, for the stranger kept on staring as though she were a miraculous vision, and if la madre came back and caught them like this, she would be very angry. But Conchita, too, found it impossible to look away, and her heart began to beat in slow, shaking thuds. For there at high noon in the sun-drenched plaza they began to say deep things to each other without sound, while the Gaelic and Spanish temperaments mingled in one trait, the capacity for swift, passionate love.

Suddenly he walked to the wagon and put his hand on the seat beside her with an imploring gesture. "Tell me your name and where you live."

He spoke in such queer rough Spanish that it was her heart and not her brain that understood him. She glanced nervously at the driver, who still snored, then at the house across the plaza where her mother was buying silk just arrived from Chihuahua.

She leaned toward him, and as her mantilla brushed across his hand, he trembled. "María de la Concepcion Valdez y Peña," she whispered, "Hacienda Alamosa, two miles down the arroyo."

She saw that he had not followed her quick Spanish and a look of straining disappointment came to his eyes so that she smiled and simplified it. "I am Conchita Valdez," she said, touching her breast with a white ringless hand. "I live at Hacienda Alamosa."

He nodded and started to tell her some of the crowding, impulsive things he must say to her, but she gave a little gasp, "Mi madre!" and turning her back on him shrank to the farthest part of the seat.

Andrew respected her fear because he loved her, though he had no interest in or respect for Spanish conventions, and he drew back into the shadow of the portale. Doña Eloisa Valdez had not noticed him. She was flushed with the heat of the battle over the purchase of the silk, and pleased because she had bullied the shopkeeper into adding a length of gerga which would do very well on the floor of the small sala. She climbed heavily into the wagon beside her daughter, poked the coachman into wakefulness, and the mules trotted off, not, however, before Conchita, blushing, but unable to stop herself, had managed to look back once.

That look settled things for both of them.

Andrew, with a subtlety he had not known he possessed, checked his blunt, impatient nature and descended to subterfuge. That night he knocked at the great door of the Hacienda Alamosa, representing himself as an exhausted traveller from the wild Ute country up north, and in need of shelter. The Valdez, courteous and hospitable as were all the Spaniards, took him in and treated him with great kindness, especially after Don Diego had by tactful questions discovered that his guest was not one of the detested Americanos, but instead some peculiar variety of Anglo from across the sea with which the Spaniards had no special quarrel. Moreover, their mild interest in his medical knowledge turned to gratitude when he treated three of the Valdez peons for minor ailments. Don Diego urged him to stay with them as long as he could. "My house and all I have is yours, amigo," said the fiery Don enthusiastically, and Andrew, unaccustomed to polite extravagances, was misled. He chafed because he was never alone with Conchita. Always her mother or a wizened old aunt materialized beside the girl when he tried to speak to her, but their love blazed in spite of the handicaps. After a week, Andrew could stand it no longer. He and Conchita had stolen one unchaperoned meeting in the shadow of a huge cottonwood beside the arroyo; he had held her at last in his arms and kissed her, and he saw no reason for waiting to ask her father for her. Conchita knew what the outcome would be, but she could not dissuade him.

Andrew was dumbfounded by the fury with which Don Diego received the proposal. "You have insulted my hospitality, gringo! Were you not in my house I would shoot you like a jacál!" shouted the Don, his face glistening.

"Why should it be insulting to have me love your daughter?" said Andrew, cursing his slow Spanish, and still too much bewildered by the courteous host's transformation to be angry.

"Jesús!" cried the Don, casting his eyes to heaven, "he asks me why! Because, gringo, we Valdez are of the Spanish sangre azul, and you are nothing but an Anglo adventurer, without money or land, and a heretic as well."

"My Scottish blood is as blue as yours," said Andrew sharply, "and I can earn money by my profession to support Conchita."

"Bah!" said Don Diego, "what is 'Scottish'! what is a 'profession'! I don't know and I don't wish to know. You will leave

17

my house in an hour, Señor, and Conchita will marry Don Enriquez Mora from Rio Colorado next month as I have arranged."

It never occurred to the old Don that his daughter was involved or indeed knew anything of the big red gringo's monstrous proposal. It never occurred to him that she or any aristocratic Spanish girl might defy a father, so after Andrew had ridden off toward the village of Arroyo Hondo, no special watch was kept over her now that there was no longer a strange man in the house.

The lovers had made their plan in a desperate second of whispers, and two nights later, Conchita slipped from her home with only a shawl and the little figure of Our Lady of Guadalupe for luggage. She ran along the dark road to the village, the tears flowing down her face for the wrong she was doing her parents and conscience, but she had no doubts of her destiny. Andrew met her behind the ruined chapel on the hill, pulled her up before him on the horse, and they started on the long, hard road back to Santa Fe, pausing only at dawn the next day to be married by a sleepy priest at Ranchos de Taos.

There was no pursuit. Doña Eloisa filled the days with tears and lamentations, but Don Diego announced that his daughter was henceforth dead to him, and that no one might ever again mention her name in the hacienda.

The servants placed the black strips of mourning cloth above all the doors and windows, the pictures and mirrors were turned to the wall, and the Valdez held a solemn velorio as for a funeral.

The news of this reached Santa Fe a month later.

"And so, ma bonnie lassie," said Andrew in his broadest Scots and with the gentle rueful humour he had never shown to another human being, "the twain of us're cut off from our pasts for aye, and we maunna greet about it, but gae staunchly forward into the future taegether-r."

She kissed him and smiled, understanding the sense, as she always understood him. They were living in the little house on San Francisco Street, and for eight months they were happy, an ecstatic unreasoning happiness granted to few lovers. Then, on that January night of Fey's birth, the vessel which Conchita had filled for him emptied and shattered. Nor would it ever again be whole.

Padre Miguel had been making a parish call at a house on the Marcy Road and had seen the young doctor pass on his

18

head-long rush to the Taos trail. The priest watched with troubled eyes. Now, he thought, comes a new stage, maybe good, maybe bad, but the sight of the baby has had some effect, and the man at least looks alive again. The padre was a simple man from the peon class; the type of priest common to New Mexico before the coming of Bishop Lamy and the reform; he had had no education beyond two years at the Seminary in Durango, but he was wise in the management of souls. While he chatted with his parishioners he watched through the open door to see Andrew come back; when after an hour he had not, the little padre got up sighing. He was hungry and thirsty; he thought of his own cool room where there awaited him a pot of chilli con carne and a tall bottle of El Paso wine. Outside, the afternoon sun was pitiless. But he sighed again, put on his cape, and going to the street mounted his plump grey burro, Pancha, and turned her to the north.

A mile out of town he found Andrew sitting on the piñon stump and staring at a clump of sagebrush.

"Well, my friend," called the padre cheerfully, pulling up his donkey, "it's good to see you out in the open. You've been shut up too long. Come home with me and we'll have a little talk over a bottle of good wine."

Andrew looked up slowly, his gaze unfocused.

The padre frowned, but he went on patiently, "Come, come, Señor—one must not go on for ever biting the edge of a grief; this is the behaviour of"—he deliberately raised his voice—"of a coward."

Andrew flushed; he got up from the piñon stump. "No Cameron was ever called a coward!"

"Well," answered the padre, smiling, "I have not called you one, my son. I but point out a possible basis for misunderstanding. Come home with me out of this dust and heat, and let's have a talk."

"So ye can have another whack at trying to conver-rt me, nae doot," said Andrew sourly in his own language, but the priest understood him.

He shrugged his shoulders under the black cape. "I cannot see that you've had much comfort from your own creed, but we'll not speak of that just now." Padre Miguel paused and dexterously flicked a fly from Pancha's ear. He was considering the best method of dealing with this big truculent Scot. It was true, of course, that he hoped eventually to usher Andrew into the welcoming arms of the Faith, but his concern with this embittered soul had always sprung from pity as much as duty. As

19

Conchita's confessor, he alone, in the whole of Santa Fe, had known the tragic romance, and his sympathies had been moved by its outcome and the fate of the baby. The padre had a sentimental streak through his practical Latin soul, and he was human enough to enjoy the game of solving a psychological problem. Too, he knew that Andrew had been some kind of Don in his own country, just as Conchita came from one of the best "rico" Spanish families in New Mexico, and to the son of illiterate peons this aristocratic tinge added lustre.

"You must get back into life, Señor," said the priest at last. "You have a good trade, you are a médico."

Andrew laughed. "A doctor nobody wants. A doctor whose patients die."

The priest's eyes widened at the tone of the laugh and answer. Aha! he thought, now I begin to see.

"Look, amigo," he said softly. "Not the best midwife in the whole of Mexico could have saved Doña Conchita. I know. I have seen those hæmorrhages happen before. It was the Will of God, and you must not torture yourself."

Andrew said nothing. He picked up his hat and, turning his back, began to walk down the road. The priest dug his heels into Pancha and trotted along beside his quarry. After a while he cleared his dry throat.

"You know," he said to the side of Andrew's head, "over by the Rosario Chapel, there lives an old woman, Maria Ruiz, who has the strangest lump on her neck that I have ever seen. This lump is big as your fist and red as a chilli—a most remarkable malady."

Andrew's pace slackened a trifle, but he gave no sign of hearing.

"Like all priests I have had to learn something of medicine," continued the padre; "still, I have never seen anything at all like this lump. The poor María suffers much pain."

"Get the army surgeon to look at it, then," said Andrew, without turning.

"An Amerian soldier!" snorted the priest in real astonishment. "Maybe he's a good hombre, but María would rather keep her pain and her remarkable lump."

In silence Andrew continued to stride, and the padre continued to bounce along on Pancha until they passed the first adobe house on the outskirts of town.

Then Andrew spoke. "Does the lump move beneath the skin when you touch it, or is it rigid?"

Padre Miguel permitted himself a small secret smile. "I don't remember, amigo; my fingers are not trained. But there is an easy way to find out—after we sit in the cool for a while and drink our wine," he added hastily.

So it was through the kind heart of a little New Mexican priest that Andrew was persuaded back into a semblance of normal living. Some weeks later he successfully cut the tumour out of María Ruiz's neck, and this feat gradually brought him a few patients. Not many, for Andrew's brusque manner repelled the courteous Mexicans. Anyway, they saw little need for doctors. When one is sick, one lights a candle to Our Lady, one brews perhaps a few herbs, one goes to bed, and after a while one gets well. Or if not—then it is the Will of God.

As for the Americans, what few families there were outside the garrison were all of military connection and they had Doctor Simpson, their army surgeon. They knew nothing of Andrew.

Still, in time, with the padre's help Andrew made his limping adjustment to reality, and a more complete adjustment to his baby—Fey. Not long after he had taken over the care of her, he yielded one night to an impulse. He wrote a brief, unemotional letter to his father, telling of his whereabouts, his marriage to Conchita, her death, and the birth of the baby. He did not refer to the circumstances of his exile; he made no mention of the stepmother; he kept to a dry recital of fact. But he hoped—and all through the following summer, while the wagon trains brought in regular mail, he haunted the little post-office on the plaza. There was never any answer.

CHAPTER

2

FEY was seven when her father first discovered the child's strange gift. They were still living in the little house on San Francisco Street, all alone together, except that Fey's former nurse Ramona came in sometimes to help clean and cook.

On this May afternoon, Andrew came back from seeing a patient, one of the Saldivars who had a large house near the plaza and were of the rico class which he was never invited to visit. He had been called as a last resort at the suggestion of one of the house servants whom he had cured of the fi·

lady of the house, Doña Dolores Saldívar, lay very ill of a persistent and unexplainable vomiting, and, besides this, there were other unpleasant gastric symptoms. Andrew had considered and rejected a dozen diagnoses which did not fit the picture, and he walked home with dragging steps, let himself heavily into the house, and sat down at his table to stare into the small fire.

Fey, who had been playing with a corn-husk doll she had made, ran to greet her father as usual, but she saw at once that he was troubled, and without speaking the child settled on the colchón near him—the rolled-up mattress which served as seat by day and as her bed by night.

"I dinna ken what ails the woman," said Andrew aloud. Failure again. She was going to die, this first influential patient. And the old fear and doubt of his own worth sprang at him. He pulled from his pocket a torn linen cloth and unfolded it carefully. It was caked with bloody vomitus from the poor woman's retchings. He had brought it for another examination which he knew would be futile. If he only had a microscope! There was no money for a microscope. Though living was fairly cheap in Santa Fe, and he had hoarded the remaining gold pieces with Scottish thriftiness, they had had to be spent for rent and clothes. There were none left now. His few patients mostly paid him in produce: an olla of goat's milk, a chicken, or firewood cut from the near-by forests. When they paid at all.

Andrew's friend, the little padre, had left Santa Fe four years ago in 1853 after the arrival of Bishop Lamy and his energetic vicar, Joseph Macheboeuf. These cultured French priests had taken over the neglected New Mexican see under direct orders from Rome, and they had been scandalized at the laxness of the native clergy. The Reverends Juan Ortiz in Santa Fe and Antonio Martínez in Taos constantly behaved in most unclerical fashion, fomenting revolts against the Americans, including the '47, which had resulted in the massacre of Governor Charles Bent, and Martínez at least kept a shameless harem of concubines. The new bishop and his vicar met violent hostility to their attempts at discipline, and it had been necessary to make a clean sweep. The good had necessarily gone with the bad, and Padre Miguel had found himself transferred to a distant mountain parish eighty miles away. He had philosophically accepted his orders like a true soldier of the Cross, but his grief at leaving home under an undeserved cloud had included disappointment at never having accomplished Andrew's conversion.

With the departure of Padre Miguel, Andrew's tenuous contact with Catholicism ceased. Nor was there at that time any Presbyterian Church for him to attend. He seldom thought of the Kirk at all, but he did send to Missouri for a Bible and from this he taught Fey to read. She had learned very quickly, for she was intelligent and wanted to please her father, who was sometimes harsh, though she knew that he loved her. When he was cross, it was just because he was unhappy. She had always known this, just as she had always known how to woo him out of his black moods until he gave her the reward of his rare difficult smile.

She watched him now from her colchón while he frowned at the soiled cloth on the table. She saw and intuitively understood the droop of his big shoulders, the bitter way his mouth curved in. Something was very wrong this time, and she ached to help him.

She watched his face and the ache grew until it was almost pain. Suddenly the pain quivered and stopped. There was an instant of suspension and then it seemed as though her mind were bathed in a soft golden light. This was a delicious feeling, but she could not wait to enjoy it. The light tunnelled, focusing into a scene. A vague picture without meaning which yet conveyed to her an essence of compulsion. There was something she must do.

Fey slid off the colchón and walked to the table. She reached out her hand and picked up a corner of the stained linen. At once the picture grew vivid.

"Don't!" cried Andrew sharply. "What ails ye, bairn?"

Fey shook her head, still holding the linen. "Dada," she said in a slow, clear voice, "I see a lady in bed, dreadful sick. She has long brown hair and a gold chain at her neck. There's four candles by the bed and an old woman praying. There's pink calico around the walls and a silver looking-glass. I see a brown-and-green colcha on the bed and a great picture of a bird stitched in the middle."

Andrew stared at the little figure beside him. "Ye're daft, Fey! What new game is this?" He spoke with sharpened authority, but his voice wavered. Had the bairn ever been in the Saldivar bedroom which she was describing so exactly? But he knew she had not.

"The lady was sick on this cloth," said the child, paying no attention to the interruption. "She threw up something bad." Fey hesitated, compelled now to find words for impression as

23

well as scene. "I think somebody gives the bad stuff to her—to make her die."

"What!" cried Andrew, starting up. Poison! Of course not, fantastic nonsense. He settled back. "Whisht, lassie. Stop this havering!"

"In a wee, white cup with water," continued Fey, unheeding. "A woman gives it to her, a young bonnie-looking woman with a red mouth that smiles and smiles."

"What's the woman's name?" said Andrew, in spite of himself.

Fey heard him for the first time. She drew her eyebrows together.

"It's going," she said uncertainly. "The light's going, Dada. I dinna ken the woman's name. It feels like M—" She thought a moment. "María—Marta—I canna get it. Nor see the fine room any more."

She sighed, and, staring at her hand in a puzzled way, she let the linen corner drop from her fingers.

Andrew swallowed. "Wash your hands," he commanded.

The child obediently went to the back room and poured water into a bowl, then she returned to her father, who was still sitting by the table.

"You're not fashed, are you?" she asked nervously, when he did not speak. "I wanted to help you, and of a sudden I felt a bonnie warm light, and I saw pictures"—she hesitated, searching through her meagre experience for a simile—"a bit like looking into that black box you showed me with the candle behind it and the coloured picture in the back. You're not vexed, are you, Dada?" she persisted piteously.

Andrew looked at his daughter. She was not a pretty child. She was small for her age and skinny, and her head seemed over-weighted by the quantities of long curly black hair. She had a wide mouth too big for her face, and the translucent Castilian skin she had inherited from her mother seemed startlingly pale for a healthy child. Her one beauty was her eyes, large and smoky-grey between the black lashes. Sometimes they sparkled with dancing lights; often they were grave and shadowed; but always they reminded Andrew of the mighty Northern waters half the world away.

"I'm not fashed, bairn," he said at last, "but I'm thinking you've a tre-e-mendous imagination."

"I dinna help you, after all, did I?" she said, her mouth drooping.

Andrew pulled her to him and kissed her on the forehead.

"I doot it, lassie, but the things you said are unco' strange. Mind you forget it all now. Put the pot on to boil for our supper, and do your page of writing 'till I come back. I'm going out for a bit."

While Andrew walked back to the Saldivars, one half of his brain chided him for being a credulous, superstitious coof. The child lived too much alone. She was getting fanciful—or worse —she was play-acting. It was folly she had talked, and if he acted on it he would make a fool of himself before the Saldivars, who already had no faith in him.

Still he continued to walk toward the plaza, for an impulse sprung from his Gaelic heritage vanquished reasoning.

"It canna be," murmured Andrew out loud as he approached the Saldivar portale. "I'm a man of science, and I weel know the bairn canna see through walls." But he knocked on the carved pine door, and when a sulky servant had admitted him, and while he walked hesitantly through the patio, he saw a face peer quickly at him through a half-shut door. The face of a handsome girl with a red, smiling mouth. "Who's that?" he cried to the servant in so sharp a tone that the startled woman answered him at once. "That is Doña Marcheta, doctór, our poor Señora's cousin."

Andrew went up to the sick-room, and on a table beside the bed he saw a small white cup with clear liquid in it. He sniffed and tasted it. Then he asked to see Don José Saldivar. The young man came immediately, his face drawn with worry, for he loved his wife. Andrew motioned him into an adjoining room and said, with grim courage, "I think at last, Señor, that I know what is wrong with Doña Dolores, and I think we can save her."

Andrew did save her. Marcheta, upon being questioned, broke into hysterical confession. Her motive in trying to poison her cousin was very simple. She had fallen in love with Don José, who ignored her and obstinately preferred his wife. There was, of course, no scandal. Doña Marcheta was packed back to El Paso from whence she had come four months ago, and in the course of some weeks Doña Dolores got well. Andrew received a hundred pesos for his services and formal expressions of gratitude. But that was the end of it, and after that the Saldivars politely ignored him, moved by the human desire to obliterate all connection with so unsavoury an event.

Andrew had one talk with Fey about her strange part in the Saldivar case and before doing so he had thought long and earnestly. It had startled him out of the unemotional world in

25

which he preferred to live and focused a new awareness on his child. He loved her; he had conscientiously tried to rear her as well as a lonely embittered man can raise a child, but he fought entanglement with anything, ever again. Now he was jarred from his absorption.

"Lassie," he said one evening after supper, "put your writing away, I want to talk to ye."

Fey looked up. She had, at his direction, been laboriously copying the sixty-ninth Psalm. "Save me, O God; for the waters are come in unto my soul. I sink in deep mire, where there is no standing; I am come into deep waters, where the floods overflow me. . . ." Its meaning did not touch her except for a vague distaste for so much muddiness. It was simply an exercise in which Andrew later would correct punctuation and each carelessly formed letter, as he did every evening. She wiped her pen on a scrap of goat leather, closed the little tin inkwell and waited.

Andrew nodded and said, "Did ye ever before that other night have visions of things ye canna really see?"

"No Dada," she was surprised by the question and the gentleness of its tone. Over a week had passed since that night and she had almost forgotten it. "I dream sometimes," she added, "strange, true-feeling dreams, but not like that."

Andrew leaned back on the hard chair and crossed his legs. "It may be that ye never will again; and there's few would believe it did they know. There isna doot, however, that ye saw the truth that time."

"Did I?" she asked, her eyes widening. "I dinna rightly remember what I said."

"Nor do I want ye to try," he said decidedly. "But your vision or whatever it was did good. Great good."

Andrew frowned, searching for words where words came hard. "I'm not a re-legious man, Fey. Since—" The two grooves between his sandy eyebrows deepened. He went on in a voice edged with anger that the child knew was not for her. "Some years back I ceased to believe in Deity, except perhaps a personification of evil—Auld Clootie, the deil, who lies in wait to snatch all comfort and joy and blast it with his stinking breath. Ay' the deil is easy enough to believe in—"

He clamped his mouth shut, seeing Fey's eyes soften to a curiously mature pity. "Forgive me, bairn. It wasna that I meant to say. I'm wrong to haver at ye like that, because, though there may not be God, there is goodness. I've not met it often, but I believe it. That's what I want ye to remember about your vision, if ye ever have the like again. 'Tis a rare gift and must be used for good. To help others, not yourself. As ye wanted to help me that night. Will ye remember, lassie?"

Fey got up and went to her father; she slipped her hand into his, impressed by his earnestness, wanting to comfort him. "I'll remember, Faither," she said. He patted her cheek and pulled her on to his knee. She curled up against him, and began to smooth very quietly one of the leather buttons on his buckskin vest. Enjoying the cool smoothness of the button, playing a little game with it in her mind.

"My mother had the sight," continued Andrew, half to himself. "And many others in the Highlands. 'Tis an uncanny thing —and science will na admit it exists." He paused, thinking. The pineal gland, perhaps, was the site of this extra sense, the rudimentary extra eye for which there seemed no purpose. He remembered a lesson on the anatomy of the brain, and the scornful voice of the old professor while he dissected out a tiny grey blob, saying, "And for this, gentlemen, we can find no function at all, unless indeed it be the gateway to the land of fairies and bogles as I've heard tell the heathen Hindu believes." The students had all laughed dutifully. But we didna know then the functions and site of the soul, and we don't know now, thought Andrew. He sighed, and Fey, who had been waiting for his attention to return to her, said eagerly, "Please, Dada, tell some more about Granny and when you were a little boy in Scotland. Tell about the time you and Granny took the boat to the Isle of Skye and you saw where Flora MacDonald hid Bonnie Prince Charlie."

These stories, on the rare occasions when she could persuade her father to tell them, were her greatest entertainment. She listened with parted lips and shining eyes to any tale of his Scottish boyhood. It was not until she was grown-up that she realized how abruptly these stories always stopped at his mother's death, when Andrew was eighteen. Of his later years, his trip to America, or Conchita, he seldom spoke at all.

"Have ye no heard enough about Prince Charlie, bairn?" said Andrew, smiling. "But 'tis in your blood as in mine, for our ancestor the Great Lochiel Cameron near got him back on his rightful throne, and would have except for the slaughter at Culloden."

"Tell about the battle," Fey pleaded.

Andrew looked at the excited little face and his conscience awoke further. The child should not have to beg for tales of long-past battles, or of a country she could not possibly imagine. She should have friends her own age; she should have games and running and playing like other children, and she should go to school. But where? The Sisters of Loretto had recently opened an academy for well-to-do Catholic children, but its religious auspices made that out of the question for Andrew. The only alternative was a tiny school run by Mrs. Howe, wife of a United States Army officer. There were objections to this too—its probable cost and his own strong disinclination to meeting new people or explaining himself in any way. Still, it would have to do.

"I think I must send ye to school in the fall, lass," he said abruptly.

Fey was used to his long silences and arbitrary changes of subject, but this one floored her. "School?" she repeated blankly. "What school, Dada?"

"The small American one over by Fort Marcy."

"American!" she cried. "Oh please not—with all those noisy rough soldiers!"

Andrew laughed. "Not with the soldiers, with their bairns. Come to that, Fey," he added soberly, "you're an American yourself."

The child stared up at him, trying to adjust to this new idea. "But you're Scottish, Dada, and"—she hesitated—"and my mother was Spanish."

Andrew winced; even from this child he could not bear mention of Conchita.

"Yes," he said briefly. "A Spanish doña. But ye were born under the American flag. Most Americans come from mixed parentage. It makes no difference. And I've decided that ye shall go to school in the fall."

Unless, he added to himself, we move from here altogether before that. For there was nothing but memories to keep him in Santa Fe, and his sense of duty to his little girl brought realization that they could go back East to a city where he might establish a flourishing practice at last and she have many advantages. In September, perhaps, he thought, I might have enough money to buy our way in an east-bound wagon to Independence, and then across to St. Louis. They needed doctors there nine years ago, very like they still do.

Fey never knew this plan. When September came, Andrew was buried four feet beneath the sage in the town of San Miguel where he had ridden to meet and consult with Doctor Kane from Mora.

On that August morning, when she saw her father for the

28

last time, Fey had no premonition. Nothing warned her that he would not be back in three days as he had promised. He had shown her how to bolt their door at night, and Ramona was to come in every day so that Fey would be quite safe and cared for. The child walked a little way along the Pecos road beside her father's horse, and though she felt a trifle disconsolate at the thought of the separation, the prospect was much lightened by the promise of a gift which Andrew meant to bring back to her. He leaned from his horse to kiss her good-bye and she trotted home quite happily. She was used to being alone, and both her nature and her upbringing had made her self-reliant. She cleaned the house with Ramona's help, played with her corn-husk doll, did the lessons Andrew had assigned to her, and told herself long stories, for like all solitary children she had an active imaginative life.

On the third evening, she prepared their simple supper and sat down on the doorstep to wait. The vanished sun sent a vivid afterglow from the hills by the Rio Grande, tinting in rose and purple shadows the adobe walls and the dusty road. In that altitude even the August air chilled quickly, and Fey shivered, while she strained her eyes for the first glimpse of a horseman coming down San Francisco Street. No horseman came, only two tired burros laden with wood and a small boy who stared at her inquisitively, but did not speak. Fey watched the burros until they turned left on the Agua Fria road. If I don't look back again until I've counted twenty-five, Dada will surely be here, she thought. And she played the little game with herself, counting very slowly. But when she had completed the count and turned, the street from the plaza was deserted. A moment later the Parroquia bell began to toll for vespers. It was answered by the lighter chime from Guadalupe Church across the river. The child was so accustomed to the sound of church bells that ordinarily she did not hear them. Tonight the first dong, dong, dong, from the Parroquia hammered against her ears like a warning. She sat up straight, listening in mounting unease to the measured dissonance as the other church answered. The churches were trying to tell her something and the something was fear. She knew it with a swift and terrifying certainty. "Alone. Alone. Alone." That was what the bells said. She jumped from the doorstep and running into the house slammed the door. She flung herself down on the colchón, her fingers rammed into her ears. After a while the bells stopped, but the fear did not pass. She was too young to reason, to convince herself that it was not late, and that on a fifty-mile ride there might be a dozen simple explanations for delay. She knew only the wild, unreasoning fear which had been produced by the message of the bells. She lay rigid on the colchón for a long time, and little by little the blackness of terror lightened. She had not been taught to pray, the words of the Bible which Andrew had used chiefly as textbook did not come to comfort her, but it was a desperate prayer which she sent forth, nevertheless. And the answer came. Not in words, nor in any outward happening within the still room. It was a sensation of comfort and strength. A feeling that no matter what happened to her there would always be strength enough to meet it, a strength from without and within herself inextricably mingled. She fell at last into a deep, undreaming sleep.

In the village of San Miguel, Andrew's body was hastily buried outside the churchyard wall. The black cholera, legacy from a west-bound caravan, had appeared in a brief fierce epidemic to strike down, as always, the least likely victims. On the night of Andrew's arrival, he had gone with Doctor Kane to examine a patient with a severe case of bladder stones. Kane, the first man in the territory to dare a lithotomy, had heard through an itinerant peon that there was a good gringo doctor in Santa Fe. Kane had been interested and dispatched a Jemez Indian with a note suggesting consultation. Andrew had been profoundly gratified to receive this note. He polished all his instruments, packed his saddlebag, rented a horse, and set off enthusiastically. It had been years since he had talked to one of his own profession. He had agreed with Doctor Kane and they had decided to operate together the next morning. But the patient, besides stones, had the cholera, that incredibly swift form which attacks and kills in a few hours. By the next morning he was dead, and by the next evening, when the anxious Kane went to the little posada to see what was detaining his young colleague, he found the Scot already unconscious. There was nothing to be done.

Kane fortified himself with whisky and later intimidated the priest and a terrified peon into performing the burial, then he hurried back to his home at Mora, breathing thanksgiving for his own immunity. Andrew, with characteristic reserve, had told nothing about himself, so that Kane naturally assumed him to be one of the myriad unattached wanderers who constantly turned up in the West. He did his duty by sending the same Jemez Indian back to Santa Fe with a message and determined to forget the whole unfortunate matter. Death in one or another of its violent forms was a constant companion on the plains and one did not sentimentalize it.

Alejo, the Jemez Indian, was bored by this second trip to Santa Fe; he was anxious to get back to his pueblo, which he had left only to make the annual pilgrimage to the ruined pueblo at Pecos—the home of his ancestors. But the white medicine man had paid him with three pieces of silver, and no Pueblo Indian ever failed to discharge a debt. So he rode down San Francisco Street on the second day after Andrew's death, and knocked at the house he had found before.

Ramona opened the door. "Ay de mi!" she said, staring stupidly at the tall Indian. "We thought it was the médico come home at last."

Behind the woman's fat shoulder, Alejo saw the white, anxious face of a child, and the expressionless eyes softened a trifle; the Pueblos were fond of children.

"Doctor Cameron is dead, very quick," said Alejo, carefully repeating the words Kane had made him memorize.

Ramona's jaw dropped. "Muerto . . ." she echoed. She made the sign of the cross.

Fey, who had learned, perforce, some Spanish from Ramona, made an inarticulate sound.

The Indian shifted his eyes to the little face. "You Cameron's child?" he asked.

She nodded, her strained eyes fixed on his.

"He died of bad sickness in San Miguel," said Alejo, finishing Kane's message.

He saw the child stiffen, and her pallor become white as the wall behind her, but she made no sound, and the Indian approved. It was thus that one should receive bad news; even a child must learn courage and strength.

He pushed past Ramona, and, looking down at Fey, said in his own Tewa tongue, "I feel sad, little one, to be a bearer of evil, but the sadness will pass as dry times pass when rain comes at last to nourish the parched earth. The sky spirits guard you."

Fey listened to the unknown musical words, feeling their intent. Her mouth quivered, but she did not move. Alejo turned and mounted his horse in one swift motion. "Adios," he said softly, and was gone.

Ramona immediately burst forth with a long wail. "Ay de mi —pobrecita que lástima!" she crossed herself again and sobbed noisily. The fate of the gringo doctor whom she had always feared interested her not at all, but she had affection for her nursling—and besides, a disquieting thought began to prick at her sluggish brain. What was to be done with the niña? She could not stay on here alone. Ramona mulled this over for a few minutes. There was a simple and obvious solution, but would Pedro beat her when he found there was yet another mouth to fill at home? She continued to weep perfunctorily while her gaze wandered around the little house. She knew that it was rented, but what furnishings there were belonged to the médico. Ramona stopped sobbing as a brilliant idea struck her. The médico was dead; therefore these fine things —the real table and chairs, the colchones, the little trunk and the cooking utensils, even the beautiful statue of Nuestra Señora de Guadalupe—belonged to Feyita. Instead of beating her, Pedro would be glad when he got all these luxuries with the child. They would have the best-furnished home in the Analco.

"Cease crying, pobrecita," said Ramona happily, though Fey was not crying and still stood by the door in the same rigid position. "You will come home with me now. I will make a good chile with the lamb Domingo so fortunately found up the cañon. A full stomach digests sorrow. Later Pedro can come on the burro and fetch these." She made a sweeping gesture with her thick begrimed hand.

Fey said nothing. Her mind had shrunk into a small white kernel which nothing dented. The bells were right, she thought, I'm all alone. But the night of the bells and the terror seemed far in the past. It didn't hurt now. Nothing did.

She obediently followed Ramona from the house. They walked to the Rio footbridge very slowly. Ramona was fat and five months pregnant besides. They crossed the creeks, ascended the path between two corn patches, and across the road from the seldom-used Chapel of San Miguel they entered the Torres dwelling. This leaky, two-roomed mud hovel was to be Fey's home for ten years.

CHAPTER

3

THE memory of Andrew and her first seven years sank to the lowest depths of Fey's consciousness. Urged by the self-protective instinct of childhood, she became as like her companions

32

as possible. These were Domingo, the oldest Torres, three months older than Fey, and her foster brother, since they had nursed from the same breast; María, Pepita, and Juanito, the new baby. By day she played with them, wandered the streets with them, or shared the few household tasks which Ramona's relaxed housekeeping system demanded. This meant that the copper pot in which all food was stewed would sometimes be carried down to the river, swished out, and filled with amole—the yucca root which the children dug from the hills—until it produced suds enough in conjunction with the stream to do the minimum of laundry. Once in a while, when the leaks in the house became too pronounced, Ramona, Fey, and the two little girls would mix a fresh batch of mud and plaster their walls. Sometimes the goatskins on which all the family slept were carried out to the Torres corn and bean patch, shaken and sunned. These were occasional tasks. There was only one which was constant and inescapable: the pounding of boiled corn into paste in a stone metate for the baking of the daily tortillas.

It was an uncomplicated life, and on the whole a healthy one. Ramona was placid and kind enough. Pedro was neither, especially when drunk, but though he beat his wife and children whenever he felt like it, he never touched Fey. The extraordinary fact of her being able to read and write English awed him, and he had, as Ramona expected, felt that the dowry she brought with her repaid him for the bother of feeding her.

He had been an important man in the Barrio Analco for months after Fey's arrival. People had come from as far as Agua Fria to stare at the pine table and chairs made just like those in the houses of the ricos. They had poked at the colchones and wool blankets, genuflected enviously before the elaborate figure of Guadalupe. El Pedro was a lucky hombre, por Dios! He sold the cowhide trunk in the plaza. An American soldier bought the Cameron dirk, and a captain's wife paid four pesos for the sporran, which she considered a truly elegant pocketbook and thereafter carried to market. For the moth-eaten kilt there was no sale, and Ramona used it to swaddle the baby whose earliest amusement was the chewing of new holes in the proud Cameron tartan.

For a long time Pedro was relieved from the tedious necessity of earning a living. Instead of trips to the mountains for wood, he could now spend his days in the saloons, or sprawled under the portales playing monte, or gambling on the cockfights like a caballero. And when the first cash had gone, the fine new furnishings went after it, one by one. In a year the Torres home had reverted to its original state of nudity. Only the Bible and the figure of Gaudalupe were spared, because for these he had a superstitious veneration. He had never before touched a book, much less a Protestant Bible, but it was an awesome thing full of little black marks which the gringa child could translate into words. So it went in the niche with the statue of the Virgin and a wooden bulto of San Francisco.

Fey was too young and too much bewildered to make any objection to the disappearance of her property. With the other small Torres she ate and slept and played like a healthy puppy. It was only at night, sometimes, that she would wake up suddenly to find herself crying for no reason, and María, next to her on the goatskin, would say crossly, "Stop making that noise, Feyita. It woke me."

When she was nine, she made her first communion with the other children, and by now so perfect was her Spanish that the busy priest never was aware that this child was any different from the rest of the little Mexicans. On the surface, Fey herself was not aware of any difference, but the knowledge was there, and when she was fourteen an episode awakened her.

She was still small for her age, but the first physical signs of womanhood were approaching. To her astonishment her breasts, under the chemise which she wore day and night, had suddenly grown large and firm as gourds. Strange new pains that were partly pleasant attacked her body, just as strange new thoughts assailed her mind. Her mouth, always wide, lost its childish innocence, and the lips revealed a passionate curve. Her skin grew moister and more glowing; beneath the dirt and tan shone the velvety whiteness of her Castilian inheritance.

She was still a thin, ugly child, her grey eyes were still too big for the small face and gave her a goblin look, but she now sometimes showed the first indications of the sex magnetism which was later to give her an illusion of beauty more seductive than actual symmetry.

It was on a June day that Fey experienced her first awakening.

Two American officers' wives, Mrs. Wilson and Mrs. Bray, having put on walking boots and their shortest hoopskirts, decided to cross the river on a slumming expedition to the Barrio Analco with a view to discovering some woman who might be hired as extra maid for the Fourth-of-July party they were planning.

Way back in the States the Civil War was raging, but its brief comic-opera contact with New Mexico had occurred two years ago in 1862. For Santa Fe and the majority of its population the excitement had been very mild indeed, and very hard to understand. On March the tenth, General Sibley and a great many grey uniforms marched into Santa Fe without the slightest opposition. It developed that this meant that New Mexico was now something called "Confederate." Nobody cared particularly, except that there were more soldiers around than usual, more fandangos, and bailes, more gaiety. On March twenty-seventh and twenty-eighth there were skirmishes in Apache Cañon and at Glorieta. The Confederates were defeated. On April eighth, the populace lined the streets, waving farewell, and watched all these soldiers march out of Santa Fe. There were three days of quiet, and American uniforms of any kind were scarcer than they had been for years. Then on April eleventh, there came once more the tramp of marching feet along the Pecos road. "Otra vez los soldados!" cried everybody, much interested in this new development. These soldiers were in blue uniforms, and many of their faces were familiar, for they had been stationed here before. The townspeople flocked to the plaza and watched the Stars and Stripes replace the Confederate flag on the central pole. The band played and there were polite huzzas. There was a speech, too, and now it seemed that New Mexico was something called "Union."

What did it matter as long as one must put up with gringo soldiers, anyway? There were virtually no Negro slaves in the territory, and the internal disagreement amongst these Americanos thousands of miles away concerned nobody. On the whole, though, it was probably better to be "Union" because the rumour got around that the soldiers in grey were friendly to the Texans. And no one liked the Texans. So there was a further week of merrymaking; then Santa Fe settled back to its normal pace, and for them the war was over.

For Mrs. Captain Bray and Mrs. Lieutenant Wilson, exiled so far from civilization, the war was over too. They talked of this desultorily while they picked their way over the wooden footbridge to the Analco. "How strange it seems," said Mrs. Wilson, influenced by the sun on the stream, the languid murmur of the cottonwood trees, and the sight of a peon fast asleep in his corn patch, "that there should be such dreadful fighting going on in the States. Don't you think so, love?"

Mrs. Bray, who was fatter, stepped carefully off the bridge before nodding. "Hard to imagine when one gets so little news through from home these days. My Ned quite chafes to be in it, but I tell him that someone has to guard these poor people." She waved her plump gloved hand in a vague circle. "And besides, there's always danger from those horrid Indians."

Mrs. Wilson gave a delicate shudder. "Very true, love."

Both ladies, who were unused to exercise and found that their hoopskirts continually caught on the bushes, breathed a bit heavily as they climbed up the path to the Cañon road.

"Squalor," said Mrs. Bray, with distaste eyeing the cluster of tumbledown 'dobes around the walls of San Miguel's Chapel. "I suppose the lazy things're taking a siesta as usual." For the road was deserted.

"There's a child over there," said Mrs. Wilson, pointing. "We might ask her if she knows of anyone—or perhaps her mother—"

The ladies moved majestically toward the end house. The child was Fey and she was kneeling beside the Torres door while she mixed earth and water in a pan. A sharp rain last night had developed a particularly violent leak in the roof. Ramona had yawned and said that it must surely be fixed mañana, but today the sun shone brightly, it probably would not rain again for days, so why bother? Domingo and his father were off wood-chopping, so Ramona and the small children had gone to the plaza in search of diversion. Fey was cut to a different pattern. If one didn't like water trickling on one in bed, one must do something. The bright sunlight was necessary to harden the mud, and by the time it rained again the roof would be tight. Besides, she enjoyed moistening dirt to just the right consistency, then smoothing and patting it into the wall with the square of sheepskin which was reserved for the purpose.

While she stirred and kneaded the mud, she hummed a little tune to herself.

> "Me gusta la leche,
> Me gusta el café,
> Pero más me gusta
> Bailar con usted."

This silly jingle, "I like milk and I like coffee, but better yet I like to dance with you," gave her a festive feeling because Juan Perez, who was a big man of twenty, had sung it to her last Sunday night at a fandango. She didn't particularly like Juan, who smelled bad, but it was the first time she had been singled out in a grown-up way. Old and young, and within certain limits rich and poor, all mingled at the dances. Of course, one did not go to the private bailes given by the ricos or the

36

elegant public ones at La Fonda. The Barrio Analco had its own fandangos, held in a loft over a store. Fey had always loved the dancing; it was just recently she discovered that she was even better at it than many of the older girls. Perhaps, she thought, stirring her dirt and humming, at the next fandango some young man would ask her again and she could startle him with her quickness at whirling through the "cura."

So busy was she with her pleasant thoughts that she didn't hear the approach of Mrs. Wilson and Mrs. Bray, who came to a stop behind the girl.

"Gracious!" said the latter, "but isn't the little thing dirty! And that hair! I don't suppose they even own a comb."

Fey stiffened. She had had no contact with the Americans during her years with the Torres and this woman's voice had an intonation quite different from her father's, but after a second she understood.

She put the pan down, wiped her muddy hands on her skirt, and stood up silently gazing at the two gringa ladies in hoop-skirts.

Mrs. Bray cleared her throat; what little Spanish she knew always deserted her when she needed it, but her friend knew none at all. "Buenos dias, muchacha," she began uncertainly; it always paid to be polite to them. "Es—I mean, esta tu madre—Mercy, how the child stares at us!" she cried, breaking down entirely.

"What queer light eyes she has for a Mexican," agreed Mrs. Wilson, inspecting Fey. "Somehow she doesn't look quite—"

"Ah, my love," said Mrs. Bray, pursing her lips. "Evidently another sad example—our American soldiers—you know what I mean—the father—"

Mrs. Wilson turned pink; really dear Maud was sometimes so coarse.

Fey also, after a bewildered moment, caught Mrs. Bray's meaning. She did not turn pink; she whitened until the dirt stood out like a fresco on her small face. Her eyes blazed, and she took one violent step toward the ladies.

"I'm as well-bor-rn as you or anybody in this land!" she said, with concentrated fury.

The appalled ladies retreated a step.

"Heavens!" whispered Mrs. Wilson, clutching her friend's arm, "she speaks English!"

Mrs. Bray recovered herself. "Well, that's fine," she said weakly. She decided to ignore the unfortunate allusion, went

37

on in a rush, "Then, little girl, perhaps you can tell us of some woman who might—"

"Váyase!" cried Fey in a tense, choked voice. "Get out!"

"But little girl—" said Mrs. Bray placatingly.

"Go!" shouted Fey, glaring at the smooth, smug faces. As they still didn't move, but stood staring at her like two billowing images, Fey reached down to the pan and grabbed a handful of mud.

The ladies, emitting a dual squeak of horror, were galvanized. They turned and fled, scuttling down the road, their hoops swaying and bumping as they ran. "These disgusting, dreadful greasers!" panted Mrs. Wilson, and her friend wheezily agreed. Both ladies were too much shattered to pursue their errand. They limped back across the river, and, upon reaching their snug quarters in the garrison, solaced themselves with cup after cup of strong, expensive tea.

Fey stood perfectly still, her arm upraised, and watched the flight. Then her muscles suddenly relaxed, and the mud ball fell from her hand to the ground. Her head drooped. She walked slowly into the house and sat down on a pile of goatskins. After a few minutes she touched her cheeks in a dazed way. They were wet. She mopped her eyes with a corner of the muddy skirt, then stared at the stains on the flannel skirt which had once been turkey red but was now a filthy pinkish-grey.

She got up and, going out to their corn patch, peered into the little irrigation ditch. This acequia was nearly dry and she could not catch her reflection in it.

The Brios had a looking-glass, the only one in the Analco. La Gertrudis, Manuel Brio's woman, had been a popular Burro Alley courtesan in her younger days and she still had her vanities.

Fey walked a little way along the road up towards the cañon. Past García Street she came to the Brios'. La Gertrudis stood in the doorway watching for her Manuel to come home. She was smoking a tiny black cigarette, her dark heavy-lidded eyes half-closed as she inhaled voluptuously. Her thick hair was well oiled and over one ear she wore a pink hollyhock blossom.

"God keep you in good health, Feyita," she greeted the girl with lazy politeness. "Are you going up the mountain to pick chamiza?"

"May Our Lady of Sorrows lighten all yours," responded Fey in the conventional courtesy. "I was coming to see you, Gertrudis."

"Bueno," said the woman, smiling. "My house is yours, niña.

I will make you a cup of chocolate." She smiled at the girl and moved to one side so that Fey might enter.

On the far wall in the place of honour hung the looking-glass. It had a frame of carved and gilded curlicues and, though its surface was fly-specked, it was a good mirror. It had come from New Orleans and then over the Trail, and one of Gertrudis's rico lovers had bought it for her.

Fey walked straight toward it and stood silently staring at her reflection.

She saw a small, peaked face with a smooch of mud across the chin. Her neck and frayed chemise were filmed with dust. The fine matted black hair straggled into two frowzy braids from a crooked centre parting. The Torres owned one coarse wooden comb amongst them, but it was usually mislaid, and anyway the rebozo was always worn over the head when one went out, so why bother about the hair?

Gertrudis saw the girl's face contract, and she laughed. "Come, little one, it's not as bad as that. There's some young man whom you wish for a sweetheart, I suppose? I'll tell you how to get him."

Fey did not hear. She turned from the mirror. "Those gringa señoras were right," she said, in a small voice. "I am dirty and I look like a bastard."

"Jesús María!" cried Gertrudis, still amused. "What a thing to say! I remember that at your age everything is a tragedy, but if your sweetheart is so fastidious we can soon clean you up."

Fey raised her chin, and her grey eyes, sombre now and quiet, rested on the woman's rouged face. "There's no young man, no sweetheart," she said. "It's for myself—for me—Santa Fe Cameron. Do you understand, Gertrudis?"

Gertrudis did not understand this surcharged intensity over such a trivial matter. In her extensive experience only one thing made a girl worry about her looks. But she suddenly remembered, Feyita was not a Torres, was even, if the old long-forgotten story were true, half gringa, and therefore totally unpredictable. Still, thought Gertrudis, who had a good heart, she is certainly very dirty like all the Torres, and it makes her unhappy, so I will help her.

"Here, drink this good chocolate," said Gertrudis, in a soothing voice, pouring a frothing brown stream from a pitcher, "and then we'll wash your hair, chiquita. It happens that I have a whole olla full of amole root soaking behind the house."

Fey accepted her hostess's ministrations with passionate gratitude. While she had never been mistreated at the Torres', she had never received active love or interest either. She had been allowed to grow as did the other children, unfettered and unguided. In the cluttered promiscuity in which they lived, there had been no impulse towards recognition of personality, and no caresses. There had been no one to love.

"You're good to me, Tula," she said softly, when the shampooing was finished, and she stood naked and clean before the fire while the woman patiently combed out the tangles of hair.

Gertrudis laughed her rich laugh. She was enjoying herself, beginning to take pride in her handiwork. Who would have thought that the little thing would have such fine white skin, and the hair—soft and black as a crow's breast. "You'll go far with this hair, Feyita," she said, with a touch of envy. "The men will like it. So long—to your knees almost, and curly. It must be," she added thoughtfully, "that you have no Indian blood." She herself and ninety per cent. of the inhabitants of New Mexico had an Indian strain, and on the whole they were proud of it. At any rate, it was better than gringo blood, thought Gertrudis pityingly. That made one restless and discontented, always wanting more and more of everything, money, women, whisky. She had had several American lovers.

"No," said Fey, "I have no Indian blood." And she felt forlorn and lost. All these years she had thought herself a Torres, but she wasn't. She knew now how different she was from them, and she no longer wished to be like them, but after this revelation had come a stab of the devastating loneliness which she had not suffered since the night her father died.

"Now," said Gertrudis affectionately, having braided Fey's hair and patted musk-scented pomatum into it. "I'll lend you a skirt, chemise, and rebozo until yours are dry." She brought the garments from a chest, and when Fey was dressed, Gertrudis backed off, hands on hips, and surveyed the girl, smiling.

Fey smiled back and was astonished to see the carmined mouth tremble and the heavy eyes fill with tears.

"Oh, what is it, Gertrudis?" she cried.

"Nothing," said the woman immediately, tossing her head. "Except that standing there in my clothes you make me feel as if you're my daughter. The child I never had." She gave a brittle laugh and patted the hollyhock blossom above her ear.

Fey, decked in Gertrudis's finery, stood in the middle of the floor and stared at her friend. A shaft of light seemed to strike through her mind, and beneath the other's flouncing, vulgarly coquettish gestures she saw an aching sorrow. The light expanded, reaching out until it touched Gertrudis.

"Feyita—you look so strange," said the woman, backing off.

Fey shut her eyes, and as in that episode so long ago with her father, the love, the pity, and the glowing clarity fused into compulsion.

"You will have a baby," said Fey. "Even now it is a tiny growing seed inside your womb. I can see it."

"Madre de Dios!" whispered Gertrudis, crossing herself. "What's the matter with you?"

"It's true," said Fey. "You will see." She opened her eyes and sighed, for the force flowed out of her leaving her empty and tired.

"You don't know what you're talking about, niña," said Gertrudis, recovered now from a momentary thrill of awe and wild hope. For here was nothing but the litle Torres girl whom she had just washed. "You meant well, I know, but I'm too old. Already the monthly signs of fertility are slackening, and I've always been barren."

"It makes no difference," said Fey. "It will happen," though she no longer felt the certainty and the exaltation, but only its memory.

"Well," said Gertrudis, laughing gustily, "if such a miracle should happen, then you must be a bruja—eh?" and she bent and kissed her, at the same time spanking her playfully.

For the Analco was as terrified of witches as the distant mountain dwellers at Abiquiu or Truchas, and to make a joke about them lessened their power. Therefore, too, though Gertrudis was duly delivered of a son nine months later, out of affection for the girl she never mentioned Fey's prophecy to anyone, not even to her Manuel. They would think in the Barrio Analco that the biggest Torres girl was somehow in league with the devil, and Gertrudis knew that, however Feyita had performed her witchcraft, it had not sprung from badness, but from gratitude and a wish to comfort.

Fey herself gave little attention to that moment of in-seeing. It had come and it had gone—nor, except for emotional intensity, did it feel less natural than the occasional flashes she thought of vaguely as "the other thing."

These flashes were moments when she glimpsed a thought in someone's mind. This was like gazing into a shadowed mountain trout pool, and seeing the clear silvery outline dart through a sun ray and disappear.

Once, when Domingo had tearfully reported the loss of three pesos to his father, Fey had seen beneath her foster-brother's frightened excuses, and knew that the loss was not three pesos, but six, and that they had not somehow fallen through a hole in his pants, but had been gambled away in a surreptitious game of monte. She had, of course, said nothing; Pedro was angry enough already, and she had learned to keep these certainties to herself. One or two earlier experiences had taught her that mention of them brought only disbelief and annoyance. And the moments came seldom. In all other ways she had been as much like the Torres as possible until the afternoon with La Gertrudis. And she returned to them because there was no other place to go, but now she was dully unhappy.

According to their separate natures the Torres resented her fierce attempts to keep herself clean. The younger children thought all this washing and combing very tiresome, because Feyita wouldn't play with them any more. Ramona shrugged her shoulders, said, "Hoy por ti, mañana por mi— You'll make yourself skinnier than you are already with all this useless work."

As for Pedro, he openly jeered at the girl. "So La Gertrudis has been teaching you some of her lewd tricks. You think to set up business in Burro Alley, no doubt, little fool!" His attitude did not stem from moral principle, but from resentment toward Gertrudis and her angry refusal to lie with him after she had first moved to the Analco. Actually he thought that it might be a good thing if Fey went out to earn her living in the only way which really paid. But she was still too childish, and who would have her? thought Pedro, eyeing her with distaste. Little bag of bones and those ugly light eyes that stared straight at one. A man wanted warm brown curves to hold, and black eyes that narrowed and beckoned in bold promise. Even Ramona, old and fat as she had become, was better. He turned his sullen, lowering gaze on his wife, who stood by the fireplace as usual, stirring chilli with a stick.

He lumbered over to her and, giving her a slap on her backside grunted to the children, "Andale cochinitos! Pronto!"

Without interest they all obeyed this command as they had a hundred times before, and scrambled out of the back room, while Pedro yanked down the goatskin which served imperfectly as curtain over the doorway. María and Pepita immediately continued an interrupted squabble in the other room over a ribbon they had found on the Pecos road. Little Juanito pelted away toward the plaza to see a scheduled cockfight. Only Fey knew what was going on in the back room, and a shamed curiosity battled disgust so violent that she ran out to

42

the corn patch and, lying flat amongst the tender green stalks, fought off nausea.

After a while the dizziness passed. The sun was warm on her back, and the air was fragrant with juniper and the lighter, fruitful smell of the ripening corn. She sat up and carefully dusted her skirt. I've got to get away, she thought. But how and to what? There was no answer.

She turned her head to the east and her eyes fell on Atalaya, the sharp high peak, nearest foothill of the Sangre de Cristo Mountains. It guarded the town, and in the days before the Spaniards came, the Indians had thought it a sacred mountain; then the Spaniards themselves had used it for a watch-tower. Fey loved the peak; she had often climbed it and found peace and exhilaration on its summit. There from the topmost rock one could look miles across the Rio Grande Valley, and houses in the Barrio Analco, even the whole town of Santa Fe far below, dwindled to the size of massed pebbles.

I'll go to Atalaya, thought Fey; perhaps it will tell me what to do. She rose to her knees and this familiar position of worship released a different impulse. Against the neighbouring adobe house there grew a carefully cherished hollyhock. Flowers were scarce in Santa Fe, the precious water could not be wasted on ornaments. But the hollyhock had religious sanction, for was it not Saint Joseph's staff? When the blessed saints were gathered together to see upon which would fall the honour of being spouse to Our Lady, Joseph's old wooden staff had turned green and burst into flower as a heavenly sign. This staff was the hollyhock, and Fey, looking at the pink blossoms, was reminded of her duty.

Perhaps Saint Joseph would help her. And it was wicked to think of asking Atalaya—a heathen notion worthy only of the unconverted Indians. It was to a padre that she must go.

She wrapped her rebozo around her head and started off across the footbridge for the Parroquia. This chief church of Santa Fe stood a little to the east of the plaza; it was built like a mud fortress surmounted by two pierced towers, and it was Bishop Lamy's as yet unrealized dream to erect in its place a Cathedral worthy of the New Mexican capital. Fey, however, who had never known anything else, admired the Parroquia. She experienced a mystical devoutness in the cool, dark interior. Above the flickering points of light in ruby glass, the faces of the saints seemed to smile and welcome her, and the subdued chants mingled with incense to give her a hazy sensual pleasure.

This afternoon a priest whom she did not know was in the confessional, a French padre with a queer name, Etienne. She saw that the ladies who preceded her in line were for the most part ricas. They wore silk which rustled and gave forth waves of perfume; their heads were covered, not by rebozos, but by black lace mantillas, and around their necks gleamed the dull gold of carved crucifixes. Fey shrank nervously, twisting her bare feet under the bench. *They* didn't have bare feet; they had kid slippers and fine cotton stockings, and their small plump hands were white as goat's milk.

The pain and rebellion grew stronger in Fey's heart. She clasped her hands, fixing beseeching eyes on the image of the Virgin in the far transept. "Dear Mother of God," she prayed, "please let me be like them. Let me have a silk dress and shoes. I want to *be* somebody."

The lady ahead of Fey stood up and rustled into the confessional. Fey watched her from the depths of envy and hopelessness. Suddenly she straightened. My own mother was like that, she thought, in a flooding excitement.

She had always vaguely known this, of course, but now for a moment it was real.

The courage it gave her swept her into the confessional, determined to make the padre understand that she must get away from the Barrio Analco.

But Father Etienne's Spanish was still imperfect; he had spent a weary afternoon straining to understand the venal trivialities murmured at him by the pampered doñas this and that. He was tired, and, though he was a conscientious priest, Fey's incoherent and passionate whispers conveyed nothing to him except that here was a rebellious child, feeling herself misunderstood and wickedly thinking of running away.

He interrupted her sharply to remind her of the fifth commandment.

"They're *not* my father and mother," said Fey, desperately pressing her face against the grill in her frenzy to make him understand. "I'm an orphan."

"But these good people have befriended you and brought you up as their own?"

"Yes, padre, but—"

"All the more reason for you to show filial gratitude and obedience."

"But they don't want me!" cried Fey.

"Have they said so, my child?"

"No," said Fey hopelessly. "I just know it. I'm different from them."

Father Etienne sighed. How often had he heard this cry from adolescents. "I'm different. They don't understand." The age-old tussle between the generations.

"How old are you, my daughter?" he asked. "Fourteen! Exactly. Now I wish you to keep still and listen to me." He lectured her for five minutes and then dismissed her.

Fey walked slowly out of the church. The brilliant sunlight in the plaza hurt her eyes after the dimness inside and her throat was tight with despair. The padre had not understood; Saint Joseph, and even Our Blessed Lady, had not been interested. She thought again of her mother, piecing together the meagre facts which she remembered. She did not even know the site of Conchita's grave, since Andrew would never visit it. But somewhere, way up north past Taos, my mother's people lived, thought Fey. She hesitated a minute, then, moved by much the same impulse as that which had moved her father fourteen years ago, she turned to the north and the road which led toward the memory of Conchita.

I'll find them somehow, the Valdez, she thought; and even though they were so angry long ago, perhaps they'll have got over it now, and they'll be glad to see me. And she trudged along the road.

She had no idea of the distance which separated her from Arroyo Hondo, a difficult three-day trip on horseback; and even had she been able to get there, it would have been useless, for after the death of old Don Diego ten years back, the two Valdez women had ceased to struggle with this new terrifying country. They had made one last act of courage, endured the rigours of the Chihuahua Trail, and returned to Mexico City.

The Hacienda Alamoso was deserted, its pink adobe walls cracked and crumbling.

At seven, the swift September twilight fell over the Taos road, and at once the clear air grew cold and an evening star shone near and brilliant above Truchas Peak. A Navajo Indian, mounted on a superb black stallion, topped one of the hills near Tesuque village. His hand tightened on the bridle as he saw a small figure plodding up the next rise. The shawled head was bent, and as the Navajo pulled up his horse, he caught the sound of sharp breathing.

"Holá, chiquita!" said the Indian quietly. "Is it not late for you to be out here alone? It may be I can help you to wherever you are going."

Fey looked up. She saw by the silver conch shells at his belt, the two braids of hair and the black hat, that he was a Navajo, and she shrank to the side of the road. The Navajos were bad Indians; even in the Barrio Analco one heard about the horrible things they did and the hard time Colonel Kit Carson was having to subdue them.

"You needn't be afraid of a Navajo, child," said the Indian, in a calm and bitter voice. "My people have become weak as rabbits and our warriors no longer fight for what is their own."

The bitter sadness of the voice startled Fey, and she looked up at the Indian again. She saw now that he had a good face. He was not young, and in the dark, regular features there were power and wisdom. Suddenly she was no longer afraid of him; there was about him a little of her father and a little of the kindly asceticism of the image of San Francisco which stood in the niche at home.

"I am Natanay, shaman to the Navajos," said the Indian, "and I go to Tesuque pueblo for the night. Where are you going?"

"I don't know," whispered Fey. Cold, hunger, and the futility of her trip swept over her at once in a black flood. She was still part child, and she could no longer hold back the tears which she had tried to check.

Silently Natanay leaned over and picked her up. He held her slight figure against him and wrapped his blanket around her while he flicked the bridle. The stallion leaped forward, then settled to a swift, easy pace. Warmth and comfort stole over Fey. While the two of them rode through the night to the pueblo, she did not think. Her cheek rested against Natanay's wool shirt beside the silver and turquoise necklace and he smelt good, of tobacco and clean, sweet earth.

She was half asleep and wholly dazed when they reached the pueblo. Natanay set her gently down on the little sandy plaza, and she had a momentary confused impression of many brown faces peering at her, of soft Indian voices, and flickering rectangles of ruddy firelight from countless open doorways. She clung to Natanay, who stood beside her, tall and stern, his hand on the stallion's mane.

"Go with Sahn Pové, little one," said Natanay, and a handsome young squaw took Fey's hand and led the girl toward the largest of the piled dwellings which surrounded the plaza. They mounted a ladder to the second floor and entered a whitewashed room, bright with fire.

This apartment belonged to the governor of the pueblo, and Sahn Pové was the governor's wife. She was far too courteous to show any curiosity as she brought Fey hot water to wash in, then fed the girl steaming atóle gruel and meat. Colour came back into Fey's cheeks. "Thank you," she said, smiling timidly at the pretty brown face. "I don't know why you're so good to me."

All the Indians knew some Spanish; it was their chief language for intertribal communication. So Sahn Pové smiled back and answered, "Natanay is our honoured guest. You come with him, so you are honoured guest too."

"Who *is* Natanay?" cried Fey. The tone of her voice expressed part of the feeling the Navajo had aroused in her; trust—and a wondering reverence. Sahn Pové nodded, as though she understood.

"He is great medicine man," she said, sweeping her immaculate hearth with a corn-husk broom, "but his heart is torn by sorrow because the Americanos have killed so many of his people in the far sacred cañon across the desert, and now they drive those that are left from their homeland. They force them to go many days' journey to a new country. They will die."

Sahn Pové shook her head and rose from her knees. She walked across the low room to the corner by the inner door, where there hung from the ceiling a wicker basket. She lifted a tiny baby from the basket and put it to her breast. She looked down at the nursing baby and her gentle face was darkened by a fierce protectiveness. "If they should take me and my baby from this pueblo, which has been the home of our fathers since long before the white man came, we would die," she said.

Fey stared at them and looked away, thrust for an instant outside the wall of self to realization of a bigger problem than hers. Then self inevitably swept back, and the personal application. *I* have no home, she thought. I belong nowhere and to no one. And she envied Sahn Pové the sense of place, of a continuance worth fighting for.

There was a stir at the door, and Natanay stepped over the high threshold, followed by the governor and the cacique of the pueblo. Sahn Pové shrank into the background as a woman should, but Fey stood uncertainly by the fireplace. Natanay paused, then walked straight to her. They stood looking at one another, the Navajo shaman and the bewildered, unhappy girl. His wise eyes gravely searched her face and her heart.

The two pueblo leaders waited quietly. The room grew tensely silent.

47

Then Natanay put his hand on Fey's forehead. "Shut your eyes, little one."

Fey obeyed. The touch on her forehead had vibrancy and goodness. Her desolation vanished and was replaced by a tremulous sense of waiting. Her mind stilled.

"What do you see?" asked Natanay.

At first she saw nothing but a rushing blackness. Gradually this faded into grey mist, until through the clearing mist she saw a green, happy valley bright between encircling cliffs. While she watched, the valley darkened and became blood-red, and it seemed that the red heaved and bubbled around small anguished figures whose faces were upturned in supplication.

She described this in a halting voice and the pressure of Natanay's hand deepened as he answered, "That is the desecrated cañon of my people. Do you see more?"

She waited, and against the back of her eyelids the scene changed to a far-off place on a plain where were gathered a hushed, beaten race. In the fraction of a second in which she saw them time telescoped. She saw four winter snows drifting down on their bowed shoulders, and then the sun burst out while they raised their hands toward it and shouted thanksgiving. And they began to march again towards the west.

She opened her eyes and Natanay removed his hand. "It is so," he said. "It is what the sacred voice of the cañon tells me, too. After four winters my people will be freed. You have power, little white girl."

The two Tesuque Indians murmured and nodded. From the back of the room, Sahn Pové gazed at Fey in awe.

"Our council will wait," said Natanay to the Tesuques. "First I must talk with this child and help her."

He pulled a deerhide pouch from his belt, taking from it three curiously shaped earthen figures and several small bags of coloured sand. Crouching on the spotless floor, he poured the sands, blue, black, yellow, and red, to form a geometric picture. This was not one of the traditional Navajo sand paintings; neither the place nor the occasion was appropriate for that. It was a symbolic ceremony to heighten perception, sand divination such as desert peoples have used since the beginning.

The firelight glowed on Natanay's calm face, on the lean, brown hands skilfully and swiftly directing the little streams of sand. When he had finished, he spoke low, chanting words in his own tongue.

Fey, watching, felt the rhythm of the chant. It lulled her like

48

the wind singing through the pines on Atalaya, and like the beat of rain on sunbaked earth.

The chant ended, and Natanay stood up. He looked down at Fey and spoke to her in Spanish, slowly, while his voice retained the deep, singing tone.

"You are born to great vision, little one. For you they have made thin the curtain which hides the real. But there is danger. You must listen to the voice of the spirit, or your body and its passions will betray you."

He stopped, gazing at her intensely, as though that were all. And Fey, obscurely disappointed, repeated the words to herself.

"Why, that's the sort of thing the padres say," she murmured, surprised.

Natanay's grave mouth moved in a smile.

"Ay, pobrecita," he said. "Do you think Truth is different on different lips? It is the same. There are many trails up the mountain, but in time they all reach the top."

He sighed, seeing that she did not understand him. He took another pinch of blue sand and encircled the little painting on the floor. "You must go back to the life you are living. You are not yet ready. When the time comes for change, be certain that you go through the right door."

He paused and looked at her again.

"Will I really get away?" cried Fey, her face shining. "Will I have a silk dress and a fine house like the Delgados? Will I be somebody?"

Natanay passed his hand slowly over the sand picture, destroying it.

"You will make of your life what you will," he said quietly. "And it may be that some day you will long for the simple beauties of the sunlight and the winds and the high mountains again. Crave them as the desert wanderer craves water. And you will not be able to find them."

Fey said nothing. Reverence for Natanay kept her quiet, but he read her face. He shook his head and his eyes grew weary, full of a pitying gentleness.

He reached inside his woollen shirt and pulled out a turquoise pendant, roughly triangular, big as a sparrow's egg. It was strung on a red wool thread. He broke the thread and held the turquoise out to Fey. "This is our sky-stone," he said, "sacred to my people because it is made of the colour of the Great Spirit's dwelling. I, Natanay, the shaman, give it to you, white child, that you may remember that your power comes from the Spirit."

Fey flushed with joy. The blue stone was lovelier than any she had ever seen on the Indians; not the greenish matrix turquoise from the Cerillos mines, but a burning azure without flaw.

Natanay cut across her delighted thanks. "Now go with Sahn Pové. She will show you where to sleep. In the morning a Tesuque boy can take you back to Santa Fe." He looked for confirmation to the governor of the pueblo, who nodded.

"Won't I see you again?" cried Fey piteously. She had been deaf to his warning; it had held too much flavour of the exhortations delivered by the padres on fiesta days, but for the man she felt hero-worship.

Natanay shook his head. "I go to Taos to plead with Cristóbal Carson for my people." He raised his hand and uttered a Navajo blessing. He paused a moment and repeated it in Spanish. "Que Dios te bendiga muchacha." Then he pulled his fine-woven blanket around his shoulders, and the three men gathered together around the hearth.

The next morning Fey returned to the Barrio Analco, having jogged back the fifteen miles on an Indian burro. Ramona was exceedingly glad to see her, and Fey was touched by the children's greeting. They had imagined dreadful things; she had been eaten by bears or wildcats in the mountains, a rattlesnake had bitten her, or, worse yet, a band of wicked Indians had kidnapped and ravished her. To all this Fey gave no answer except to smile and tell them she had been lost. She never mentioned Natanay or the night in Tesuque pueblo, knowing that Ramona would be horrified at such heathen doings. And she explained the turquoise only by saying that she had found it. She strung it on a gilt thread filched from the altar cloth La Gertrudis was penitently embroidering, and she wore it constantly, not for the symbolic meaning which Natanay had tried to give her, but because it was beautiful and the first thing of value she had owned.

4

In August of 1867, when Fey was seventeen, Natanay's prophecy came true, and the first plase of her life ended. Escape offered itself through two doors, but so eager was she to rush through the first that it was not for years that she discovered the other one had been there.

From time to time, during these past years, Fey had gone to rico homes near the plaza to help in the kitchens or diningroom when the Delgados or the Señas or the Garciás were entertaining. In the beginning she had been rebellious and accompanied Ramona with ill grace, but gradually she became used to it, and she learned many things which she stored away for the future. Not only the material secrets of fine living—such as the proper preparation of rich foaming chocolate and the frying of the delicious sopai-pillas which accompanied it, or the perfuming and pressing of the lace mantillas from Spain—but really helpful knowledge. She went silently and efficiently about her duties. None of the families who employed her ever noticed her particularly, but she watched and learned. It is so, with downcast eyes and a half-smile, that a young lady encourages a lover, even under her mother's disapproving nose. It is so, with a barely visible twist of the fan, that a doña warns an admirer that the husband is coming. It is thus, with tears and blandishments and little counter-accusations, that one raises such a cloying fog that a husband cannot penetrate it when one has lost unconscionable sums at monte and baccarat. Fey went back each time to the Barrio Analco and pondered these things. She neither approved nor disapproved, but she was intensely interested, and always there was the sensation of marking time.

In July, she had her first association with an American. The same Mrs. Wilson who, together with Mrs. Bray, now transferred back East, had been the unwitting causes of Fey's rebellion.

This time Mrs. Wilson crossed the river alone in search of a maid, and this time she was successful. Mrs. Wilson, too, had learned much in three years, and in this encounter with Fey she was tactful and courteous. Neither remembered the other

51

and Fey went back to the garrison out of simple curiosity. It was a good thing, perhaps, that she should discover something about the Americanos, because, incredible as it was, it appeared that the greater part of the country outside was composed of women exactly like Mrs. Wilson.

From the first Minnie Wilson was delighted with her, and Fey was forced by excited questions into telling her fascinated employer something of her history.

"My dear," boasted Mrs. Wilson to the other officers' wives, "the girl tells the most extraordinary story. I know one can't ever believe anything they say, but really it rings true. It seems she isn't related to those peons at all; her father was a Scotch doctor here and her mother positively from a good Spanish family. I do feel we should do something for her. She isn't the servant type at all, and she does speak quite a Scotchy kind of English with a little Spanish accent, it's too romantic for words."

Mrs. Wilson talked so much and so long about her find that her husband was moved to come home early one day and view this treasure. Mrs. Wilson flutteringly ushered him out to the kitchen where Fey sat on the floor expertly shucking blue corn into a brown earthenware dish.

"Here's Captain Wilson come to see you, Fey," said the lady importantly.

Fey raised her lids; the grey eyes looked up at the captain, her full red lips parted in a faint smile. "How do you do," she said carefully.

"Howdy do, I'm sure," said the captain in a startled voice; his hand flew to glossy side whiskers and patted them. He straightened his shoulders.

Fey lowered her lashes and went on shucking corn. She wasn't interested in the captain; she was thinking not very happily about the baile tonight. She loved the dancing, but it was getting harder and harder to parry the assaults of the men. Lately they had taken to pinching her breasts or buttocks, to pressing thick wet lips on her neck. There wasn't one of them that she liked and she had not the faintest intention of acceding to Ramona's pleadings or Pedro's commands that a great girl of seventeen had better get herself a man while she could. But the bailes were getting impossible.

"Come, love," said Mrs. Wilson to her husband, faintly astonished that he continued to stand in the middle of the kitchen staring at Fey.

"Well, what do you think of her?" said the lady eagerly as

soon as the door closed. "Don't you think she looks quite aristocratic and the story might be true?"

The captain cleared his throat, pulled a cigar from a china jar, and clipped the end. "She's a devilish attractive little piece, at any rate."

Mrs. Wilson's jaw dropped, then she swallowed. "I shouldn't think so at all—so small and pale and thin, scarcely more than a child."

"True. True," said the captain, hastily redeeming himself. "Certainly not my type. I like an armful." He winked coarsely at his wife, who had grown plump as a quail on years of Mexican cooking.

Minnie Wilson was mollified, but she decided not to go to Governor Mitchell with Fey's story just yet; there was plenty of time. Some days later, when the young lawyer from Scotland appeared, she regretted this decision, for by then it was too late and Fey had gone.

It was on the following afternoon that Fey, returning from the Wilson's at about five, passed through the plaza. It seemed unnaturally quiet—deserted except for two nuns nervously scurrying past La Fonda on the way to the Parroquia for vespers. Even the sidewalks beneath the portales were bare of their usual groups of monte players and sprawling beggars.

Fey stopped and looked around, and the reason became clear. All the usual loungers and passers-by were huddled in a group at the west end of the Governor's Palace. Fey, craning to see what held their attention, caught a glimpse of a tall, bearded figure in a long red coat and a black stovepipe hat. The figure was standing in a wagon and brandishing its arms. Fey walked over and pushed through the edges of the crowd. She still could not see, so she edged to one of the palace's wide window-sills and mounted on that. This brought her up on a level with the bearded face and only about twenty feet away from him. He was waving a brown bottle.

"Now folks," said a deep voice issuing from the beard, "before I give you the wonderful chance of a lifetime to buy Doctor Xavier T. Dillon's Extra Special Elixir, positively guaranteed to cure any cough or cold, night sweats, kidney stone, backache, rheumatism, and female complaint, I'll put on a little show for you."

This speech was delivered in a mixture of English and very bad Spanish, and the faces of the crowd showed interested incomprehension. Travelling medicine shows did not usually hit Santa Fe.

"I myself, yo mismo, am Doctor Xavier T. Dillon," shouted the figure, with a touch of desperation, thumping its red-coated breast. "I invented this marvellous elixir to help suffering humanity. I am a great doctor. I make medicines but I can also" —here the voice sank to a bloodcurdling eerie note—"read your minds! Because the spirits in the other world—assist me!"

The crowd continued to stare at him blankly, on the fringe a few began to drift away.

"Damn these greaser yokels!" said Doctor Xavier T. Dillon.

Fey heard him distinctly and was puzzled. Why was the doctor angry? What did he want them to do? She understood no better than the rest of the crowd, but she felt sorry for him. He was a doctor like her father, and she knew what a hard time Andrew had often had. Besides, she liked this strange bearded man's voice, it was deep and magnetic—in English, that is; in Spanish, it was all barbarous Americano accent.

"Look!" cried the doctor, waving a pack of greasy cards, "any one of you can pick out a card without-my-seeing-it! And I'll tell you what it is."

Cards! That was different. Everybody understood those. The crowd pressed closer again. After much urging and signals from the doctor, a sheepish youth stepped up, selected a card, and showed it to those around him.

"The trey of hearts," announced the doctor, and there were murmurs of wonder. This performance he repeated three times, then he quickly shoved the pack into a black satchel.

That was marvellous, thought Fey, glowing. That faculty, then, that she sometimes had of seeing things without actually using her eyes, it wasn't a peculiarity of which she need be faintly ashamed. Others had it, too. And she felt for the doctor a grateful sympathy.

"Now," said Doctor Dillon, taking a dramatic step to the edge of his wagon, "one of you come up here, and I will show you that with the spirits' help I can actually see into your pockets! You cannot see into mine, oh, no!—not one of you in all this crowd could tell what, for instance, I have in here—" He pointed at the breast pocket of his red coat, and paused, hand uplifted.

Fey leaned forward, obediently staring like everyone else at the pocket, then she raised her eyes to the bearded profile, and a vivid impression came to her.

"Yes," she called clearly in English, "I know what you have in the pocket. You have a small yellow pencil, a photograph of a lady, and one peso, but the peso is not real, it is made of lata"

—she thought for a second and found the word—"of tin."

The doctor swung violently around on his heel and stared at Fey. He saw a small figure perched on a window-sill and a pair of inquiring grey eyes under a faded pink rebozo. The crowd also turned its collective head, then looked back at the wagon. Some of them knew the little Torres girl, but nobody knew what she had said. Interest was waning again.

"I'll be damned," murmured the doctor in a fierce and shaken voice. He dived through the wagon curtains and reappeared with a banjo. "We'll have some music!" he cried, and broke immediately into a galloping rendition of "Oh, Susannah." Coincidental with the last bar, he seized the brown bottle again and waved it. "Now, folks, step up while they last, only one peso, Doctor Dillon's famous Elixir. The chance of a lifetime!"

The crowd evaporated. One old woman sidled up, examined the bottle, handed it back with a contemptuous sniff. "Only Americanos rot their bellies with strange medicines," she said and hobbled off.

Fey got down off the window-sill. She felt very sorry for the doctor, who stood all alone on the wagon.

"Hey, you, come here!" he called suddenly.

Fey turned and walked over to him, stood looking up quietly.

"How the devil did you know what was in my pocket, and what do you mean by queering my show?"

Fey was puzzled and distressed. Strange that he seemed to be angry with her now, and how odd he looked seen near to. The black beard and the black stovepipe hat hid most of his face, and they didn't match his eyes, which were greenish-hazel under heavy auburn eyebrows.

She didn't answer him because she did not know what to say. The doctor made an impatient exclamation and, reaching down a muscular hand covered by fine golden hairs, said, "Come up into the wagon. Don't stand gawking there!"

She stepped nimbly up on to the wheel and followed him through the canvas curtains. The wagon was furnished with a cot, a stool, a large trunk, and neat boxed piles of the Extra Special Elixir. A rifle, a frying-pan, and a coffee-pot stood in the corner on the floor.

The doctor was over six feet, and his head grazed the canvas ceiling, even though he at once flung the stovepipe hat on the floor beside the frying-pan. This disclosed a great deal of curly dark auburn hair, very much the colour of the maple dresser of which Mrs. Wilson was so proud, and which she had transported from her New England home. Fey was amazed, and still more so when the doctor unhooked the luxuriant black beard from around his ears and flung that after the hat.

Fey stood by the curtains, staring. Terry Dillon was unlike any man she had ever seen, and from that moment he captured her imagination. He was twenty-three and of that dashing Irish type which rouses many a woman's imagination. He had, in fact, done very well along that line. The chin was pugnacious, the mouth, warmly sensual, also showed humour, while the greenish eyes, ill-tempered now, as they often were, seldom produced that impression on women because of their romantic setting of thick dark lashes.

He was vivid and very male. Fey, unaccustomed to height and breadth of shoulder, gazed at the ripple of muscles beneath his white silk shirt, and thought him miraculous.

Xavier Terence Dillon had been born in Baltimore to roving actor parents whose dramatic talents he had not inherited, though not for want of trying, since he had been playing small parts with them from the cradle. The Dillons had wandered to California in the wake of the gold rush, and Terry had grown up in San Francisco. A year ago his parents had died in an epidemic of yellow jack and Terry had decided to head East.

There were many ways of accomplishing this, but few congenial ones. The one-man medicine show had been a happy solution. He had procured a sturdy spring wagon, a pair of mules, and a great many empty bottles, then set forth eastward on the Overland Trail. The costumes and the banjo he already had.

He had done fairly well in the small mining camps, and had had a spectacular success in Salt Lake City where he wintered. The decision to see something of New Mexico before picking up the Santa Fe Trail he now regretted. Business had been exceedingly bad, but never as bad as today in the capital itself, and this little Mexican chit, standing with her mouth open and staring at him as though she wanted to eat him, had been part of the trouble. "Sit down, child," he said irritably, flinging himself on the cot, "and take that pink rag off your head. Why in hell do all women tie their heads up in this blasted place!"

Fey's American was still rusty, but she understood him after a moment. She sat down on the stool and lowered the rebozo.

Terry surveyed the result in a mild astonishment. "You're older than I thought," he said accusingly.

"Seventeen," returned Fey with composure. She was relaxed and perfectly happy, experiencing new delightful sensations. All the gropings and rebellions and desires of her life were in the process of merging into one passionate channel.

56

Terry sat up, his original purpose in inviting her into the wagon momentarily forgotten. The little creature was a bit scrawny, but she was not unattractive as he had first thought. Her bare feet were well-shaped. She had beautiful skin and eyes, and those long braids of black hair might be seductive if loosened.

She didn't twitter like most of the Mexican girls either, though on the other hand she lacked their lusciousness. By a natural sequence of thought, he mentally undressed Fey. The result was quite appealing, and he considered it briefly, but he had been given the name of a famous beauty in Burro Alley, the echo of whose superlative charms had reached as far as Salt Lake, and his plans for the evening were made. Besides, tomorrow he'd be on his way, since this town was obviously a financial dud. This reminded him of the afternoon's failure.

"How in the world did you know what was in my pocket?" he said, leaning forward.

A warm pink stained Fey's cheeks; she gave him a faint, shy smile. "I can sometimes, you know. You can too. I saw you."

"Can what?" said Terry.

"Why—know things without really seeing them," she answered, astonished. "Like you did with the cards."

"Holy Saint Bridget!" cried Terry, laughing.

Fey continued to look at him in wide-eyed candour.

"That's probably the hoariest card trick known to the profession, my dear," he said. "I learned it from a monte dealer in Cañon City, and I'm not very good at it." He added, scowling, "Are you by any chance making fun of me?"

The girl's eyes widened still further, and Terry was astonished to see a hurt bewilderment cloud them.

"How could I be? I don't understand," she said.

Terry was discomfited; a rare feeling for him. The girl seemed completely sincere, and the whole thing didn't make sense; moreover, the obvious admiration for himself which he saw in her face was beginning to have an effect.

"Look," he said, smiling, "I can see you're a nice girl and I like you. I won't give you away, I promise, but I sure am curious. So far as I know, I never laid eyes on you before this afternoon, so will you kindly tell me how you knew exactly what was in my pocket?"

"I just did. I told you I can sometimes. I thought you wanted someone to tell you, and I thought"—she added wistfully—"you'd understand."

Terry sat and looked at her. Then he stood up and, walking

57

to the corner of the wagon, he reached into a box and brought up one of the brown bottles flamboyantly labelled "Doctor Xavier T. Dillon's Extra Special Elixir." Under the list of symptoms for which it guaranteed cure, the label asserted in larger type, "This miraculous elixir is composed of the most expensive secret remedies discovered by Doctor Dillon after years of research."

"Can you tell me what's in this bottle?" said Terry, putting it in Fey's hand.

She looked down at the brown bottle, then up at Terry's quizzical face. Uncertainty and an obscure reluctance seized her. She had never deliberately tried to use the gift; it had always come spontaneously and usually when she least expected it. But she wanted very much to please him and to remove his obvious scepticism. This hurt her, not that he should disbelieve her faculty, but that he should doubt her for any reason.

"Well," said Terry, sitting down on the cot again, "if you could see what was in my pocket, you certainly ought to be able to see what the Elixir is made of—maybe."

"I can, I think," she said. She looked steadily at Terry, then again at the bottle for an instant of quivering, receptive blankness. I mustn't try too hard, she thought, and she waited. There came the sensation of light and a swift impression which she translated into words.

"In this bottle, there is river water—" She paused, then amplified, "Water from the Rio Grande where you filled it."

Terry made an exclamation and uncrossed his legs.

Fey continued calmly, "There is also whisky, a little sugar and—chilli powder. No more." She put the bottle on the floor beside her stool, and raised her eyes.

Terry said nothing. He stared at the bottle as though he expected to see it ringed with unholy incandescence, and for an instant he felt a shiver of awe. She really did it, he thought, in amazement. Might be different if she had tasted the stuff, but she hadn't even touched the cork. And then that item about Rio Grande water! There was certainly no way for the girl to know that he made up a fresh batch of Elixir before entering each town.

He thought of the little he had heard about mesmerism and spiritualism. The latter movement had begun nearly twenty years ago when the Fox sisters started their spirit rappings in New York State, and every now and then someone had held a séance in San Francisco. But I don't believe in that rubbish, thought Terry, and this girl certainly isn't controlled by any Laughing Water or Little Bright-Eyes.

Still there was the incontrovertible fact. She had known what was in his pocket and she had known what was in the Elixir.

"Could you do it once more?" he said suddenly. "Please," he added, on a soft, coaxing note, for Fey shrank back and looked distressed. She didn't want to go on doing tricks for him, she wanted him to look at her and talk to her as a girl—as a woman.

Terry rummaged in his trouser pocket and brought out a notebook and pencil. He scribbled quickly, shielding the page with his hand so that she could not possibly see. "What number did I write here?" he asked.

Fey drew her brows together; she gave an unconscious tired little sigh. But after a second she answered, "Seven, one, nine, I think—no, two."

Terry nodded, his eyes were elated. "Seven, one, two is right, but I thought nine first. You read my mind—that's what it is. Heavenly saints, that's a useful talent you've got there! Have you any idea how you do it?" He spoke with excitement. His quick but unanalytical brain had already accepted the fact and now he had the glimmering of a brilliant idea.

"I don't know," answered Fey unhappily. "I guess it's just that sometimes I see the truth in people's minds or hearts. I guess it's just a special thing like being able to play the guitar right off or smelling when there's snow in the air on a sunny morning."

"Maybe," agreed Terry. He was not interested in the mechanics of her gift, but he was very much interested in its possibilities.

"Please don't talk of it any more," said Fey, with a mixture of pleading and dignity, and she gave him an uncertain little smile.

"All right," said Terry pomptly, though he intended to talk about it a great deal more in the future. "Come over here beside me and tell me about yourself. How come you speak English?" He took her hand, noting the flicker of delight in her eyes when he touched her, and pulled her down beside him on the cot.

Under his adroit questioning, Fey willingly told her life story —all but the episode at Tesuque pueblo with Natanay, of which she had never spoken to anyone.

Terry, child of the stage and accustomed to spinning some

pretty tall stories himself when it suited his purpose, discounted most of what she told him. If the girl wanted to represent herself as the forsaken daughter of Scotch and Spanish nobility forced into lowly life by cruel fate, it was all right with him. He'd walked on in a dozen melodramas that had the same plot. The important and gratifying fact was that she apparently had no family, no strong ties in Santa Fe, and a further bit of luck—she had no wish to stay in Santa Fe either.

"Though I don't see why not," said Terry, still cautious. "After all, you were born here, you're even named for the place. And you don't know what the country's like outside."

"But I want to find out," said Fey. The expression of docility, of childlike admiration, left her. Her eyes grew dark and intense. She threw her head back and her arms wide in a passionate gesture. "I'm not *me*, yet. I want to come through—to be somebody. To be *me!*" She spoke in a quick, vehement voice. "I want much—many things. I want a silk dress and to give orders instead of taking them. I want poder—power—and—" Her eyes focused again on Terry, their look, though half-unconscious, was unmistakable, "Most I want—love."

"Well!" ejaculated Terry, and he gave a startled laugh. Women before this had thrown themselves at him, and his vanity filed her neatly into a familiar category. And yet she did not quite fit. She had been almost beautiful when she blazed like that. Something else, too—disquieting. This subtle, unfamiliar element he did not like.

So he said coldly: "That all boils down to one thing. You want money. And so, my pet, do I. That's why I'm heading East. San Francisco's not the boom town it was, and mining's not my line. I think New York's the place for my talents." He was not very sure what these were, except that they did not include a taste for hard physical labour.

"New York," repeated Fey, shining. Again she was a child, her hands clasped on her lap, leaning forward, listening to him avidly.

Terry opened his mouth and shut it, annoyed by a feeling of embarrassment. It was ludicrously easy. The girl was a ripe plum yearning to be plucked, and what was she, after all, but a foundling? He was going to be a big help to her, help give her the things she wanted. No reason for scruples.

He turned his back on her, drew the tattered cards from the bag, and began to shuffle them absently. His sleight-of-hand needed constant practice. He scowled at the eight of spades which persistently eluded his efforts to palm it and said, in an abrupt, off-hand voice, "I'm pulling out of here in the morning." He heard Fey catch her breath, and went on faster. "I'm heading East up the Trail, expect to give shows after I hit civilization again, play through Kansas until I get to the railroad, maybe further. I aim to keep going until I make enough to reach New York. Want to come along?"

The silence after this speech lasted so long that he turned around. The girl was staring at him with a strange expression. There were both joy and fear in the luminous grey eyes, and stronger than either was a question.

"Business arrangement only, of course," said Terry, who had meant no such thing, but felt acutely uncomfortable under that steady gaze. "I need a smart partner. We can work up quite an act. I've got costumes for you. We'll rake in a lot of cash with that mind-reading stunt of yours."

Fey stiffened and her lids drooped. "I couldn't do that for money."

Terry brushed that aside; he had half-expected it, and he had no doubts of being able to handle her later, in that matter and others too. "Oh, well, there's lots of things you can do. Can you dance Spanish?"

She nodded.

"Capital!" cried Terry. "Want to come?" and he smiled at her. Terry's grin was heart-warming and very young. It redeemed a face which for all its attraction could be sullen, and both men and women usually responded to it.

"Yes. I'll come," said Fey quietly.

Terry stetched out his arms to pull her to him. The occasion naturally called for a kiss. He felt Fey tremble and saw her mouth quiver. She melted toward him for so brief an instant that he wasn't sure, then she gave a soft little laugh and slid out from his arms. Terry knew all about this sort of game and jumped up to catch her.

To his surprise his arms dropped. Fey had drawn herself together with an incisive dignity. She was barely as high as his shoulder and yet she contrived to look regal, to look, thought Terry, amused and impressed, rather like his mother in her favourite rôle of Lady Macbeth.

"What time do you go in the morning?" said Fey steadily.

"Ten o'clock," answered Terry, equally matter-of-fact. "After I buy supplies."

"I'll be here." Fey wrapped the rebozo about her head and vanished through the canvas curtains.

Terry sat down on the cot again. Now, what have I let myself in for? he thought gloomily. That's a very odd girl. Impulsive actions and misgivings later were both familiar to Terry. Still, she would undoubtedly be a great help to the act. She had personality and that extraordinary mind-reading stunt. And I can get rid of her all right after we reach the railroad in Kansas, he thought, give her some money and shoo her off. She's plenty old enough to know what she's getting into, and she was wild to come. It's not as though she was anybody special. Just one of these little greaser half-breeds. His face darkened at an unpleasant memory. A year ago he had been mixed up with a girl in San Francisco who was somebody special. There had been an exceedingly disagreeable episode with her family. That was one of the reasons for leaving San Francisco.

He thought about Fey for another minute or two, then he got up and dressed himself in his best buckskin pants, fresh white silk shirt, and grey sombrero. He did not, however, go to the house of the famous beauty in Burro Alley. He found that he was not in that mood. He went to the bar at La Fonda, where he unfortunately encountered a jealous Mexican who decided that the big red-haired gringo was making eyes at his young wife. Terry, for once, was guiltless, the flirtation had been entirely on the lady's side, but the ensuing fight dissipated all the pleasant effects of La Fonda's drinks. Terry went back to the wagon and went to bed.

Terry might have misgivings about his impulsive invitation to join the medicine show, but Fey had none about her acceptance. She had always known that some day the way would open, and that some day she would find love. And now here they were, these two things most gloriously combined.

True, there were certain aspects which did not entirely please her, but she put them resolutely from her consciousness, and she ran back to the Barrio Analco with light, dancing steps. She went first, not to the Torres—she knew that there would be only conventional sorrow at her departure there—but to see her only friend, La Gertrudis.

Gertrudis had changed in the last three years; after the birth of the baby, her Manuel had married her, and Gertrudis had become gentle and very devout. She no longer flaunted a pink hollyhock blossom over her ear, but dressed in black, and a black rebozo as a respectable matron should. This evening, when Fey stuck her head in at the open door, Gertrudis sat on the colchón holding her little Toñico in her lap, and crooning a song to him.

"Bien venida, Feyita!" she called softly over the child's

round head. "Aren't you home late from work?—Jesús María!"
she added in astonishment as Fey stepped into the firelight,
"what's happened? You look as bright as if you'd swallowed a
candle."

Fey gave a low, excited laugh. She knelt on the floor beside
her friend, turning dazzled eyes up to her. "I've found my man,
Gertrudis, at last! He is big and handsome as the statue of
San Antonio in the Parroquia and his hair flames like the sun
on the Sangre de Cristos."

"Dios!" cried Gertrudis, in troubled disbelief. "A gringo,
then!"

Fey nodded. "It wouldn't matter what he was. I'm going with
him in the morning, going to the States."

Gertrudis gazed down at the girl's transfigured face, and her
brows drew together. She put the drowsy child on the colchón
behind her and reached out her hands to touch Fey's shoulders.
The girl had been dear to her ever since that day when she had
foretold the coming of the baby.

"Feyita," said Gertrudis earnestly, "will he marry you?"

Fey's clear gaze wavered, she was silent, and Gertrudis went
on passionately. "You're different from me, different from the
rest of us in the Barrio Analco. We are clay pots, we women
here, useful, even sometimes pretty—but you are like that shining crystal vase in the window of Esteban's shop. Rough handling will shatter you. You must not run off with the first gringo
who wants to sleep with you. When did you meet this man?"

"A few hours ago," said Fey.

"You see!" cried Gertrudis. "Oh, believe me, child, this is
nothing that you feel but the surgings of hot blood, the desire
for mating. Do you think I do not know? You must wait, Feyita.
Have still a little more patience. I feel that you are meant for a
great destiny. I have always thought so. You must not fill your
crystal vase with muddy water."

Fey gave her friend a smile in which affection and impatience mingled. She stood up, smoothing her short skirt,
tilting her head back. 'I don't hold myself cheaply," she said,
and Gertrudis was silenced.

"I love him," said Fey. "I must go with him, and I think,
though it has not yet occurred to him, that we will be married."

Gertrudis smiled wryly. Ah, there, little one, she thought,
you are not the first woman to delude herself with that hope,
and you won't be the last. Her heart was heavy. She saw that
the girl was blinded by passion and her desire for change.
There had always been a headstrong, impulsive streak in

Feyita. One had always felt a powerful will beneath the delicacy, the fastidiousness, the gentleness.

"It is a mistake, Feyita, this thing you want to do," said Gertrudis sadly. "I feel it, and for each of our mistakes we must pay bitterly—cruelly. I know—" she added, sighing.

"Then," said Fey, "I will pay."

"At least," cried the other, seizing the girl's arm, "ask Our Lady about it. Please, I implore you. Ask her now—" And she pointed to her own statue of the Virgin of Guadalupe which stood by the fireplace.

Fey hesitated. She did not want guidance, she felt no need for prayer. Her will and her desires were centred to a burning point on the man she had left in the wagon. The thought of journeying with him outward, eastward, brought an almost unbearable excitement. She wanted nothing to disturb it. But Gertrudis's distress touched her.

She fell slowly to her knees before the Virgin and her lips moved hurriedly in the Ave María. She did not raise her eyes above the crescent moon at the Lady's feet. As she finished the prayer, she closed her heart to a faint impulse, a tremor of doubt and apprehension. For one second it seemed to her that the crudely painted crescent wavered and glowed and that a tiny voice in her mind echoed the word Gertrudis had uttered —"Wait." Then the echo was gone, and she heard instead Terry's wooing voice.

Fey got up, and smiled again at Gertrudis's anxious face. "I shall go in the morning, amiga," she said. "I'll miss you and little Toñico, but I must go. Adios, Gertrudis." And she threw her arms around the woman's neck.

That was Fey's true farewell to the life of her girlhood. Except for Ramona, the Torres were scarcely interested. Surely it was high time the muchacha got herself off with a man, and of course all gringos were rich. Ramona shed a few tears over her nursling, but they dried at Fey's promise to send back a real pair of button shoes like the ricas wore. That would be something to show the Analco indeed!

The next morning, the tenth of August, 1867, Fey wrapped her other chemise, a comb, and some yucca root for soap in a large cotton handkerchief; these, with her skirt, rebozo, and the turquoise pendant, were her only possessions. She left her Guadalupe and the Bible with the Torres, since they greatly desired them. At ten o'clock she entered the plaza, and saw at once that the wagon had moved and now stood outside Jones's General Store, where Terry had bought supplies for the trip.

The wagon was easily identified, since the canvas top on both sides had "Doctor Xavier T. Dillon" painted on it in splashing orange letters.

Fey found Terry sitting on the driver's seat and flicking flies off his two mules.

"Oh, so you really are coming," he said ungraciously, barely looking at her. This morning he had a headache, and was even less certain that he wanted to take the girl with him. Had she been a second late, he would have started without her.

"Yes, I'm here," said Fey. Her heart beat thickly in her chest as she obeyed Terry's brusque gesture to climb up. There was a large bruise on his cheek, result of last night's fight, and she saw at once that he had been drinking. She sat primly on the seat beside him. He flicked his whip and the mules started. The wagon rattled along the dusty road past La Fonda, and the Convent of Loretto across the tiny river, past the Chapel of San Miguel, and branched east on the beginning of the Santa Fe Trail.

On the evening of the eleventh of August, young Ewen MacDonald from Inveraray arrived at Santa Fe with an incoming wagon train. He put up at La Fonda and decided that, as it was so late, he would postpone until next day inquiries which he knew would be involved and difficult. He had left Scotland four months ago, and had enjoyed every moment of his travels through the strange new country. Particularly did he appreciate the West, for he was both adventurous and sensitive to beauty. Ewen was a dark Highlander, of medium height, lean and vigorous. And the latter quality also applied to his mind. At twenty-five he was already a successful young barrister, whose opinions were respected, all the more because he tempered them by an unusual amount of tolerance. He was kin to the Camerons and popular even with old Sir James, who liked few people. It was Sir James who had begged the young man to set out on the long quest.

In nineteen years the picture had changed at Cameron Hall. Ten years back, the Glasgow stepmother had hidden herself behind a haycock with a stable boy once too often, and this time it had been her husband himself who had discovered her. He had half-strangled her with his powerful hands, and then he had divorced her. Even this justification for Andrew's conduct so long ago had not softened the old man toward his youngest son. "Once a Cameron maks up his mind," said the Inveraray folk, "the de'il himsel' canna change it." But the old laird had found Andrew's never-answered letter and re-read it thoughtfully. Still he had done nothing. Then this past year complete tragedy struck the Camerons. The oldest son, his lady, and their child were wiped out by fire in one terrible night, and Sir James had had to remember Andrew, who was now the heir. He had written a letter to Santa Fe, which was returned marked "Unknown." It was then that he summoned Ewen MacDonald and sent him forth on the long journey. "Find Andy and his little lass," commanded Sir James, "and bring them back to me. Tell him I need him, and I regret the past. Tell him I'll dearly love to hae the lassie here, for I never had one of my ane. And if by bad mischance Andy is nae mair, for 'tis a wild and thawking country I hear, bring me the lass at least, and I'll do my best by her."

Sir James was seventy-nine now and he had mellowed. He prepared a suite of rooms for his granddaughter, invited a widowed cousin, the Lady Ann Hamilton, to the Hall for Fey's guidance and companionship, and settled to impatient waiting. Oblivious as always to possibilities which did not please him, he refused to admit that the lass might not be found. Instead, he concentrated all his desires and hopes on Fey, the last of this branch of the Camerons. Her Spanish side did not displease him. There had been Spanish blood before this in the best Scottish families. Ewen himself had a Spanish ancestor. In fact, thought the old man, nothing would please him better than a match between these two, Ewen and the little lass, after she'd been home a bit and the rough edges rubbed off. "I dinna doot they might fit each other verra weel," he told the Lady Ann Hamilton, who listened patiently, and privately thought the old laird was maundering a bit. But in this instance he was right.

Fey and Ewen MacDonald would have suited each other very well; each would have found in the other understanding and spiritual strength and love.

So Sir James yearned for his granddaughter and waited, while Ewen made inquiries in Santa Fe. These led him to the governor and eventually to Mrs. Wilson, who was overcome by the young lawyer's revelations.

"I knew it! The minute I saw the girl I knew she had blue blood," she cried, somewhat inaccurately. "To think that her grandfather's a Scotch lord and she sat right on my floor shucking corn!"

Ewen waited impatiently until the lady's excitement abated enough for her to guide him to the Torres. And here the trail ended in a high, impervious wall. The Torres family, certain that an eager-eyed Anglo and a flustered Americana could only mean trouble, received all questions in sullen silence. No, they did not know where the girl had gone. She had simply gone two, three, maybe four days ago.

"We brought the poor orphan up as our own. We were good to her," reiterated Pedro angrily, and MacDonald's assurances that that was not the point in question produced no effect. Even the presentation of gold pieces produced no effect, though they were accepted. All the more reason to protect Feyita if knowledge of her whereabouts was so valuable. No doubt, the foolish girl had got herself into trouble, had run off perhaps with an outlaw. Well, that was no longer any concern of the Torres. She had found a man she wanted and gone with him, as all women did sooner or later. This fact was all they knew, but even that little they did not tell the insistent and annoying gringos.

MacDonald had at last to retire defeated; he lingered another week in Santa Fe, but he found out nothing more. Mrs. Wilson was provided with an anecdote to garnish her table chat for years, during which Fey gradually became the daughter of a royal duke and a Spanish princess endowed with supernatural beauty and virtue.

And Fey herself, through the days in which Ewen MacDonald was in Santa Fe making futile efforts to find the girl and restore her to her heritage, was jogging along in the gaudily painted spring wagon beside Terry.

CHAPTER

5

TERRY and Fey covered the first miles along the Trail from Santa Fe in complete silence. As they topped the rise near Sun Mountain, Fey turned and, craning around the side of the canvas top, looked back. Already the cluster of adobe houses had merged into the sandy valley, and only the twin towers of the Parroquia stood out distinctly. To the east Atalaya, the watch-peak, seemed to have turned its back on her as it brooded over the little town below. Pain shot through Fey, pain quickly denied. That was never really my home, she thought; I never belonged to it. And still she looked back and still it seemed that Atalaya and Santa Fe had drawn into themselves, quiet and secure, into an understanding from which she was excluded; that all these years they had held for her a message which she had never tried hard enough to receive. She lengthened her gaze to the horizon, the calm, magnificent range of the Sangre de Cristo Mountains—their snowy tops hazy against the summer sky.

The wagon bumped into a deep rut. Terry swore and cracked his whip. Fey turned her head and looked up at him. At once she forgot the town she was leaving and the mountains.

"Can't you say something?" snapped Terry, as the mules pulled the wagon out of the rut and trotted forward again. "Never knew a woman keep so quiet in my life."

"I was waiting for you to speak," answered Fey demurely. She had a low, clear voice, and the Scottish lilt, emphasized by a trace of Spanish accent, gave a startling quality to everything she said. Particularly as she still spoke English slowly and used the mature vocabulary she had learned from her father.

Terry rested the reins on his knees and examined his companion. Her small bare feet scarcely reached to the planks, the braids of black hair thick as her own wrists hung down each shoulder, rising and falling over the swell of her surprisingly well-developed breasts outlined under the thin white chemise. Excitement had brought a faint pink to the smooth cream skin that reminded Terry of a yucca petal. She certainly was not pretty, he thought; nose too short, mouth too big, chin too pointed, and the angles of the jaw too pronounced. Then suddenly she lifted her lashes and gave him a sly, caressing smile.

Instantly Terry's bad temper evaporated. She wasn't exactly pretty, but when she smiled like that, she made you want to touch her, explore the texture of that thick petal skin, taste the warmth of that flexible mouth.

He shifted the reins to one hand and, putting the other arm around her waist, pulled her toward him along the bench.

Fey gently disengaged herself. "I think I'll go in back and fix up the wagon," she said. In one quick motion she whirled on the seat and slipped through the curtains behind.

Terry shrugged, and went on driving. On the whole, he was amused. There was plenty of time, weeks and weeks of this, before they reached civilization. He pulled a map out of his pocket and studied it. Tonight they'd likely camp in Apache Cañon. He thought of the night with pleasure and anticipation.

He was to be disillusioned. They entered the dark high-

68

walled cañon at five. It had been the haunt of Apaches and a dangerous place in the early days, though it had seen no bloodshed since the brief battle between Union and Confederate forces in 1862. Tonight it was peaceful, and after Terry had made a camp-fire, positively cheerful. The encircling walls of piñon-tufted rock gave the two at the bottom beside the wagon a feeling of isolation and security.

Fey boiled coffee and fried bacon and eggs in half the time it had always taken Terry, and he was pleased. He laughed at her dismay upon finding that there was no chilli. "You've got to eat American now, my pet," he said, stretching himself beside the fire and deftly rolling a long black cigarette.

Fey nodded. "I know, but there's no taste to it. Like eating water." She whisked around washing the frying-pan and coffeepot in the stream. Terry watched her, and his amiability increased. "Now, come over here to me," he said lazily, as she walked back to the camp-fire. Fey did not obey; instead, she stopped by the two mules, who had returned from a foraging expedition and were now standing side by side staring at the fire and wearing twin expressions of mournful patience. "They look sad," said Fey, stroking the mouse-grey noses. "Maybe they're cold."

"Calvin and Harriet are never sad or cold," said Terry, willing to spar a bit longer if she wished. "They're healthy, good-tempered brutes."

"Calvin and Harriet?" repeated Fey, smoothing the long ears.

"Named, of course," said Terry, "after the remarkable author of *Uncle Tom's Cabin*—and her husband."

Fey had never heard of *Uncle Tom's Cabin*, but she pondered the explanation a moment, then she moved two steps nearer to Terry, who looked up at her invitingly. His red hair gleamed in the firelight, and his long muscular body rested on the ground with easy grace. He reached his hand out to Fey, who did not respond.

"*Mules*," she said, giving faint emphasis to the word, "don't have husbands."

Terry sat up. He stared at the small, composed figure which stood just out of reach. Good God, he thought, what does she mean by that? Surely this little Mex girl can't be getting fancy ideas.

"I'm a bit tired," said Fey. "There's a buffalo-hide in the wagon. I'll take that, if you don't mind, and sleep over there." She indicated a natural hollow beneath two arching rocks and a juniper bush.

Terry swallowed. "You can't sleep outside; it's ridiculous."

"I have done it often in the summer, when we would go to gather chamiza or yucca, and you are used to sleeping in the wagon; you will be more comfortable."

Terry, still uncertain, stood up, towering over her, scowling. He put his hand on her thinly covered shoulder, and he felt her quick response, the flesh seemed to quiver and yield itself to his fingers. And yet she retreated from him. She looked at him steadily, her eyes pleading, frightened but determined. "No," she whispered.

Terry's hand dropped. He put it in his pocket. His lips thinned. "Enter the pure village maiden. Act One. Scene two." His voice rose to a vicious falsetto. "Oh, sir, I am poor, but I am so very virtuous. No lily so unstained as I!"

He climbed into the wagon and flung the buffalo-hide down on the ground beside her. "Here, go and crawl into your hole, then."

Fey's breath caught in her throat. Heat stung her eyes. She took a step toward the wagon, but Terry had disappeared between the flaps. She heard the clink of the whisky bottle. She picked up the buffalo-hide and dragged it over to the rocks.

The next morning Terry was slightly ashamed. When he came out of the wagon, Fey had already made a fire and started the coffee. She threw him a quick look of welcome and pleading. Terry grinned at her, sluiced his head and shoulders in the stream, then went in search of the hobbled mules. Calvin and Harriet had not strayed far this morning and in all ways the day began auspiciously. Soon after they had started and were entering Glorieta Pass, a wild turkey settled on a cliff beside the trail and obligingly furnished an easy shot for Terry's rifle. Fresh meat for several days, and the side of bacon might be kept for emergency. Youth, sunlight, mountain air, and the eternal pleasure of being on the march outdoors affected both of them, and Terry reacted in spite of resentment to Fey's eager interest in everything he said. She was charmingly responsive, her eyes caressed him, and her mouth seemed continually to invite him. Yet she would not let him touch her. They camped outside of the ruins of Pecos pueblo and they camped near Las Vegas, and still each night Fey took the buffalo-hide and slept by herself outside the wagon. Terry allowed the situation to remain as it was for the present. It was new to his experience and he found that it intrigued him. He might have taken her by force, of course, and indeed the impulse had occurred to him very powerfully in the evening at Las Vegas when he had caught her bathing in the Gallinas River. The long unbound curly hair hid most of her body, but what he had seen shone pearl white and smooth as velvet against the background of willows on the river's edge.

Fey had looked up and seen him watching. Instead of giggling or screaming, as most girls would have done, she had lifted her chin, and smiling faintly had looked at him with that little air of dignified poise which always baffled him. She gazed at him quietly until, against all desire and reason, he made her a mock-heroic bow and walked away.

Neither of them referred to this episode, but Terry discovered that he was giving a disproportionate amount of his nights on the cot to thinking about her.

On the fourth afternoon out, they reached Fort Union. This important post stood in the foothills of the Turkey Mountains, south-west of the strangely shaped landmark called Wagon Mound. Here the desert and plains began, and near here the Santa Fe Trail forked. One branch went straight east and eventually crossed the terrifying Jornada, a fifty-mile pull without tree, hill, or water. The other way went north through Raton Pass and Colorado, a longer but of recent years safer and far more popular route. Terry had already made up his mind to go through Raton and Trinidad; he was in no particular hurry, and unless they could attach themselves to an outgoing wagon train, the braving of the Jornada would be folly.

Fort Union at this time had the appearance—as nearly as the army wives could make it—of a prim Yankee village. The cottages were of white-painted boards and clapboard, encircled by the cherished picket fences; the windows were neatly curtained; the parade ground in the centre was kept tidily swept between arrivals of the wagon trains or the Barlow-Sanderson stages, and in its centre the bandstand had been tastefully surrounded by white stones and a few spindly geraniums. Between the Fort and the Arsenal, half a mile to the north, there were a great many shops, a church, school, and even Masonic buildings. Besides the personnel of the Ninth Military Department and the purveyors of supplies, over a thousand carpenters, smiths, harness-makers, and wheelwrights worked at the post.

For both Terry and Fey it was the first sight of a typically American town; Terry scarcely remembered his early travels in the East, and neither San Francisco nor Santa Fe gave any such impression of glistening order and New England purity.

"Regular little city," remarked Terry, astonished, driving toward the parade ground. "I think it'd pay us to hold a show,"

As they passed one of the picket fences, a woman, who had been watering a two-foot square of brownish grass, straightened, staring at Doctor Xavier T. Dillon's wagon and its occupants. She was tall and spare in a striped cotton dress and her knob of grey hair was so neat that it looked sculptured. Her eyes hardened into disapproval. Red-headed gambler type, if she ever saw one, too handsome for his own good, and a barefoot Mexican girl. Worthless trash always turning up at the post— She turned her back and went on watering the strip of unresponsive grass.

Terry and Fey both correctly interpreted the woman's action. Fey drew her feet under her and sat very still struggling against a puzzled dismay.

"Guess, when we hold the show, we better say you're my sister," remarked Terry, pulling up before the headquarters store.

"Sister!" repeated Fey, in a faint voice.

Terry threw her a quick look. "Come on, Fey," he said. "Likely this'll be a fine place for a show. I'm sure that sour old hag has female troubles. I bet I can sell her a couple of bottles. You promised to help, you know."

"Yes, I know."

"Well—" Terry wound the reins around the whip-handle and used a tone of airy nonchalance. He was no longer so sure of being able to manage her as he had been in Santa Fe. "We'll work up that mind-reading thing of yours as a climax; that'll bring 'em." He felt her recoil, and went on quickly, "If we make enough, I'll buy you some clothes over there at the store. Shoes and stockings, too; you'd like that, wouldn't you."

Fey looked down at her chemise and skirt. She had washed them in the Gallinas River, but they were both wrinkled and darned. She thrust out her feet; they were dusty, and across the high right instep ran a deep scratch from a cactus.

"Yes—but I couldn't—"

"Listen, Fey." He swung her around by the shoulders, oblivious to the gratified hoots from two passing soldiers who had stopped to read the wagon sign. "I've put up with a lot," said Terry vehemently. "You know what I mean. But I won't put up with this, too. You came along as a partner." His hands tightened on her shoulders, his voice dropped to its wooing note. "You *like* me, don't you, darling?" he added softly.

Her expression was answer enough, and he bent his head and kissed her—for the first time. The soldiers, who had been watching the wagon seat, burst into a delighted cheer.

A violent red flamed up in Fey's face, but Terry laughed and released her. "We'll put on a much better show than that for you," he said amiably to the soldiers. " 'Bout seven o'clock, here in the plaza. A little music—this young lady will dance, real genuine Spanish dances like they do 'em in Chihuahua, and then we'll show you some magic that'll take your breath away. The young lady has gypsy blood, she's the seventh daughter of a seventh daughter—you know what that means. She can tell the past or the future, she can tell if your sweetheart loves you, or if your old granny's going to die and leave you a million. Don't miss it, boys!"

"We sure won't, mister," answered the tallest soldier. "Things've been mighty dull around here lately; no wagons in for three days, and not even a stinking Ute around to take a shot at."

The soldiers drifted off and spread the news through the barracks. Terry was exultant; he knew the show would be a success, and Fey's kiss had been even more agreeable than he had expected. He had had a moment of real emotion while her lips parted under his. She was a good kid, after all. And from now on it would be easy.

"Come on, honey," he cried, jumping off the wagon. "We'll buy a few things in the store, then I guess we better pull out of town a ways and rehearse."

"Terry," said Fey, looking down at him as he stood beside the wagon. She was still limp, and her heart beat in painful thuds. "Terry—I can't really do all those things you said—tell the past and the future—"

"Of course not. That's just patter. But if you can work that trick you do do, it'll be plenty good enough." He reached up and scooped her off the seat. Involuntarily she held her breath, but the instant her feet touched the ground, she ran ahead of him into the store. Terry was content to wait. Business came first.

And so it was that, out of desire for Terry, Fey conquered her reluctance and forced from herself a demonstration of the inseeing gift that evening on the parade ground.

The demonstration was imperfect; nervousness at first prevented any response at all. It took her several minutes to realize that the only sure method was for Terry to send her from his own mind the knowledge she must discover. She got it easily from him, but except in one instance the impression received from strangers was vague and uncertain.

They had drawn a satisfactory crowd: soldiers, workmen,

and most of the housewives, all eager for diversion. When the wagon pulled up beside the empty bandstand and Terry, now disguised in the black beard, stovepipe hat, and long red coat, struck up a song on the banjo, people came running from all quarters of the post. The wagon and the entertainers were sufficiently exotic to provoke excited interest. Calvin and Harriet, troupers at heart, were decorated with bells and pink cockades, and they stood like lambs, long furry ears tilted forward, apparently enjoying Terry's interpretation of the "Camptown Races." He got most of the crowd to singing with "Oh, Susannah"—prime favourite on the plains; then he set the gentler sex to sniffling with "Ben Bolt" and "Nellie was a Lady."

He had a pleasing baritone, which, even though slightly muffled by the beard, carried to and affected the farthest bystander. When he judged them to be sufficiently mellowed, he put down his banjo and went into the first or ground-laying spiel about the Extra Special Elixir. Before they tired of this, it had always been his habit to give them the card tricks. Tonight, instead, he produced Fey.

"My sister, Carmencita Dillon," shouted Terry, waving his arm, "will now dance for you a vo-lup-tuous, a highly sensational Spanish dance, the very identical dance which she performed before the Emperor and Empress of Mexico!"

Here there were some murmurs of awe, and when Fey appeared, her knees shaking as hard as the tambourine she held in her cold hand, there was a round of applause. Terry hastily handed her down to the ground and seized his banjo. He played scraps of the only Spanish music he knew, heavily accented, and Fey, after a paralysed moment, caught the rhythm on her tambourine and danced. She had never seen a tambourine before. It had come from the costume trunk, as had the red cotton rose in her flowing hair and the tarnished gilt sash around her waist, nor had she ever danced solo.

But she was a born dancer, and all the fandangos back home had taught her. She improvised a mixture of bolero and cura, and the crowd, pressing closer, paid her the compliment of quiet. When she finished with a whirl, arms gracefully arched above her head and the tambourine quivering, there was hearty hand-clapping and whistles from the soldiers.

This was all very well, and Terry was delighted, but it didn't necessarily sell Elixir. He had rapidly rearranged his usual patter to strike the right note and include Fey's mind-reading. This patter he had worked out a couple of hours ago while he filled dozens of the Elixir bottles from the Coyote River behind the fort.

"Now, folks," called Terry, holding up his hands for quiet, "I'm a doctor, as you all know. I can diagnose any ailment; besides that, I have studied extensively and I am thoroughly conversant with magnetism, mesmerism, hypnotism. That, friends, is how I was able to discover this marvellous remedy, my Extra Special Elixir, positively guaranteed to cure bodily disfunction—any cough or backache, kidney trouble, night sweats, female complaint, or loss of manhood. Because I KNOW," said Terry in a tremendous voice, "just what ailments that the Elixir can cure are hidden inside your bodies, just as my sister"—here he pushed Fey forward—"can TELL THE HIDDEN SECRETS OF YOUR MINDS!"

Now there were more murmurs. A masculine voice shouted, "She better not read my mind; it might make her blush!"

"Ah, you don't believe it!" cried Terry, quickly quelling the laughter. "Just wait!" The light was dimming, about right for atmosphere. He put his arm around Fey and gave her a quick squeeze. "Come on," he whispered, "you can do it!"

She remained alone on the back of the wagon, and Terry strode into the crowd. Fortunately for his first victim, he picked a frightened little drummer boy, who, at Terry's question about the contents of the lad's pockets, answered wildly, "That's right," when Fey murmured uncertainly that she thought it was a handkerchief and some money. But the next was a woman, wife of one of the carpenters, and she stood in shadow at the very back of the crowd. Terry examined the woman's hand and called over the other heads to the wagon, "What kind of a ring is this lady wearing?"

And Fey called back, promptly and clearly, "A silver ring on her little finger, made like a heart, and she has a broad gold wedding ring as well."

The carpenter's wife gave a cry of surprise, and everyone near her crowded around to look. They were impressed, and even the few sophisticated ones, who thought of signals or collusion, could find no evidence of it.

Before Terry could select the next candidate, there was a disturbance in front of the wagon; a girl scarcely older than Fey flounced into the cleared space. She wore a shoddy green silk dress and her elaborately bleached hair towered under a creation of green velvet and ostrich feathers. "Say, I've seen this trick before and better done," she cried, addressing the crowd in a nasal voice; "seen it in Buffalo, seen it in Noo

Orleans. Come on, girlie"—she turned to Fey—"think you're so smart, tell me something your pal over there in the phoney beard don't know."

"Atta girl, Belle!" cried some of the soldiers. Belle had been on her way to the new mining camps in Colorado, and had reached Fort Lyon when her protector disappeared. Since then she had drifted down to the various Western army posts.

"What do you want me to tell you?" said Fey.

"Tell me my reel name, the one I was born with, for there ain't no one in the world knows it now, and it's God's truth I've near forgot it myself," said Belle, tossing her ringlets and delighted to have captured everyone's attention.

Fey stared at the girl steadily. "Your name," she said, so low that only those nearest heard, "was Minnie Hawkins."

The girl gave a frightened gasp and backed away. "How in hell did you know that?" she whispered, staring at the small figure on the wagon.

Fey did not answer; she looked into the shallow blue eyes upturned to hers and felt a sharp pity. "Your lungs are sick," she said gently. "You know it, don't you? You've been spitting blood. You must see a doctor."

Belle put her hand slowly to her mouth; under the purple rouge her skin grew clay-coloured. Terry arrived up front in time to hear Fey's last speech. "Exactly," he cried heartily. "And Doctor Dillon's Elixir is just the thing for you." He whisked a bottle off the wagon and held it out to the terrified girl.

"No!" cried Fey, involuntarily, "that won't do any—"

Terry gave her a furious look. "Only one dollar, my beauty," he said to Belle. "Positively fix you up."

Belle shook her head in a dazed way. She gathered her gaudy shawl tight about her thin shoulders and walked slowly off alone toward her tent behind the arsenal.

"Get inside!" snapped Terry to Fey, anxious that she should not ruin any more sales, and when the girl obeyed him, he mounted the wagon and began to sell Elixir.

A few people had heard the conversation between Belle and Fey, and these murmured to others near them. At first, only one or two came up, embarrassed, and hastily plunked down a silver dollar; then, under the influence of Terry's voice and by the usual process of mass suggestion, they came more quickly. Soon all the fifty bottles which Terry had optimistically prepared were sold. He announced this sad fact and sang "Home,

Sweet Home" for them by way of finale. The crowd gradually drifted away and Terry went into the wagon.

"We're in the money!" he cried, flinging his hat and beard into the corner. "Fifty elegant shiny cartwheels, never did as well before!" He poured them into a silver pile on the cot beside Fey. "Nearly clear profit, for I used mighty little whisky in this batch. Have to get hold of some more bottles pretty soon, though. Still, you'd be surprised what the junk piles'll yield, once we get back to civilized towns."

It occurred to him that the girl was very quiet. She had not looked at the heap of dollars. She had taken off her cotton roses and sash, rebraided her hair, and sat on the extreme edge of the cot's foot.

"You did mighty well," said Terry amiably. "I'll get you some decent duds in the morning. When we get the act polished up a bit, there's no telling what bonanzas we might hit back East. One thing, though; you mustn't go telling the customers the Elixir won't help 'em, my dear."

"But it won't," said Fey tonelessly. "And when they're really sick, like that girl Belle, it's terrible to pretend it will."

"Suffering Saints!" cried Terry. "It won't hurt them either. Do a lot of 'em good if they believe in it. It's human nature to believe in something you've paid a whole dollar for. My God, Fey, I wish you'd quit balking all the time; you're worse than the mules. You wanted money, and now we're getting it. If you do what I tell you, we'll get rich. Plenty of fortunes started from smaller beginnings than this. Look at old Astor, he began by peddling furs and cheating the Indians; look at Vanderbilt, hired himself out in a sailboat, or Jim Fisk. There's a buccaneer for you!" Terry had forgotten Fey, whom he knew very well would recognize none of these names. Exhilaration produced by the show's success and several swigs of "Taos lightning" had released one of Terry's dominant interests. With vague but steadily strengthening ambition he had followed every newspaper mention of Eastern financiers. They had all begun in the humblest of ways, but amongst them now they controlled pretty nearly all the big money in the country. And they had done it by a mixture of opportunism, shrewdness, and guts. That's all you need, thought Terry, exultantly, and I'll bet I'm on my way.

He took another drink and reverted to speech. Solitary musings soon bored him. "There's Simeon Tower, too. I read a piece about him in the Salt Lake paper. He isn't forty yet, but they say he holds the New York Stock Exchange in the palm of his

77

hand. Every time he winks it goes up, and every time he spits it goes down. And what was he doing twenty years ago?"

Fey knew this to be a rhetorical question. She had no means of knowing that Simeon Tower would ever be more to her than an obtrusive name, repugnant because by means of it Terry was blithely escaping from the subject which profoundly disturbed her—the rightness of selling Elixir to the sick—into interests which she did not share.

After a moment Terry answered himself. "Why, this Simeon Tower was nothing but a hotel waiter, and they say he made his first extra dollars by fixing the clients up with fancy women on the side. So you see," said Terry, returning to the point after all and giving her the surprisingly warm coaxing smile that was his greatest charm, "you can't be too squeamish, my pet, if you want to be a millionaire. One way's as good as another, and I promise you, when the time comes for us to part, you'll get a fair slice of the take."

"When the time comes for us to part," thought Fey. And she thought, too, of her confident speeches to La Gertrudis. She turned slowly and looked at Terry. By the light of their one candle, his red head flamed against the canvas wall of the wagon. His legs were crossed and he sprawled beside her with his usual effect of long-limbed ease. From his body came the odour of tobacco and leather; stronger than these was the indefinable flavour of young virility.

"It's about time we repeated that kiss," murmured Terry, his eyelids drooping. "I enjoyed the sample this afternoon and so did you."

As she did not move or speak, his muscles tautened. He grabbed her roughly and, forcing her head back, began to kiss her mouth and her throat.

In the midst of his mounting passion, Terry had room for annoyance. She was as inert and limp under his kisses as a dead kitten. None of the swift response she had shown before.

And suddenly, though she made no sound, tears welled down her cheeks and into his mouth, and she began to cry with the hopeless abandon of a hurt child.

He straightened, releasing her, so that her head fell to the cot.

"For heaven's sake!" he shouted at her. "What's the matter with you? I thought you liked me."

She made a great effort and controlled her sobs. "I do," she whispered. "I love you, but you don't love me."

Terry straightened and looked down at her. Huddled on the

78

cot, her cheeks wet and her mouth quivering, she looked about twelve. All her coolly poised little manner, her self-contained dignity, had vanished. She seemed completely defenceless.

"Oh, my God!" cried Terry, moved by exasperation and something else which he didn't want to feel. He picked up his sombrero and the bottle of Taos lightning. "Here, you can have the cot tonight. I'll find some place for myself. Some place more amusing." He stalked through the canvas flaps and jumped lightly over the wheel. She heard the diminishing sound of his footsteps on the gravel of the parade ground.

After a while Fey straightened full length on the cot, pulled her shawl over her, and tried to think. It was neither virtue nor morality which made her deny herself to Terry, for whom her body yearned. That type of morality was seldom considered in the Barrio Analco. There you naturally slept with a man if both you and he wanted it. If there was enough money to pay the priest and get the sanction of the Church, why, that was all the better, but by no means essential. Many of the happiest couples had never dreamed of bothering the padre about their union, and until the coming of Bishop Lamy and the reform, the attitude had been reciprocal. But Fey knew that the Americanos felt differently. La Gertrudis, who had had so much experience, felt differently. She had been bathed in grateful tears for days when her Manuel at last decided to marry her.

But these considerations would not have deterred Fey if she had felt that Terry loved her. As it was, she knew that she would soon lose him if she yielded. But they could not go on indefinitely like this either. She lay on her back, staring through the darkness at the grimy canvas roof. As often, when she was alone, her fingers closed around the turquoise pendant. It had much of the same texture and smoothness as her own flesh, but it was colder than her skin. Contact with the stone gave her a tingling awareness in her fingertips. The awareness reached her conscious mind in the form of a question. "Sometimes I see hidden things for others—why can't I do it for myself?" And she calmed her mind to the listening stillness and waited for the golden light—the feeling of certainty. It did not come.

Instead, confused, vaguely menacing images drifted through her mind, and her heart grew heavy with apprehension. After a while her fingers relaxed, dropping the turquoise. She gave a painful sigh and fell asleep.

She dreamed that she was alone in the desert, lost and unhappy, wandering without purpose. And as she stumbled along, she heard herself crying; a thin, monotonous sound. Suddenly she was no longer alone. A man walked beside her, and there was great comfort in his presence. She could not see his face, but she heard his voice. "Turn back," he said. "Turn back with me. You and I must go up there." And he pointed behind them to a mountain which she knew to be Atalaya, though it looked different from Atalaya. Much sharper and steeper, and its sides jagged with rocks.

"It's too steep," she said, but she hesitated beside the stranger, feeling closeness to him and a poignant sympathy. Then the scene changed. On the horizon she saw a single high cottonwood tree. "There's a spring there by that tree," she cried. "I'm very thirsty." And she rushed over the desert, leaving her companion behind. Beneath the tree beside the spring, Terry was waiting for her. He laughed, holding out his arms as she ran toward him. Panting and desirous, she threw herself against him.

Fey stirred and awoke. In the first semi-waking moment she knew fear. Then a cock crowed lustily from a near-by back yard, and one of the mules gave an answering bray. The fear vanished and was replaced by a vivid sensual bliss. And her body reproduced for her the dream sensation of her rush into Terry's arms.

CHAPTER

6

WHEN Terry reappeared the next morning, he brought a man with him, a gnarled, bearded specimen of a rapidly vanishing type—the frontier scout.

"This is Sam Bridges," announced Terry brusquely; "going to ride with us up through Raton Pass." And he added, in a malicious aside to Fey, "He can be our chaperon, my dear."

"Pleased to meetcha, ma'am," said Sam, lifting his coonskin cap one inch. "Glad of the lift. Want to get back home to the Colorady Springs before them Goddam Utes goes on the warpath again." He shifted his tobacco quid, shot a brown stream at the mules' hoofs, and laid his rifle on the wagon seat.

"Utes going on the warpath?" inquired Terry. He knew that it was reckless to start up through Raton alone, even though it was a much safer route than the Cimarron crossing. Prudence would suggest waiting a day or two in Fort Union until they could attach themselves to one of the regular wagon trains. But Terry did not consider it; he could not have endured plodding along behind the oxen for a daily trek of twelve or fifteen miles when the mules could often do fifty. And though the extra gun might turn out to be useful, Terry had not included the filthy old scout from any prudent motives; he had invited him into the wagon with the idea of punishing Fey.

"Been some trouble in Trinidad at the horse-races 'twixt the Injuns and the Mex greasers—beggin' your pardon, ma'am," said Sam delicately—his rheumy eyes had shown him a little Mexican wench and the Mexes didn't like being called greasers —"but the fuss'll likely smooth down. Uncle Dick Wootton'll handle them Utes, like he's done before."

"That the man who built the tollroad over Raton?" Terry asked.

Sam nodded. "With luck, we'll spend tomorrow night at his hotel to the top o' the pass."

"We better get going, then," said Terry. He hitched up Calvin and Harriet, drove around the parade ground to Cunner's Emporium. He reached in his pocket. "Here," he said roughly to Fey, "get yourself something decent to wear."

Fey looked at the fifteen silver dollars in Terry's big hand. Her first instinct was to refuse them; she liked neither the way they had been earned nor the method of presentation. On the other hand, she knew that, as they left Spanish country behind, her tattered clothes would become increasingly outlandish, and Sam's contemptuous "greaser" had stung.

She cupped her two hands and silently received the heavy load of silver. Then she slowly entered the emporium. Merchandise was scarce and high-priced on the Trail, and there were, of course, no ready-made dresses. She would have failed of any purchase except a needle and spool of thread if Mrs. Cunner, the storekeeper's wife, had not been touched by Fey's obvious disappointment. "You poor little thing," she said. "You sure do need some good Christian duds. Nice girl like you don't want to be going around half nekkid." And she found for Fey some black strapped slippers, cotton stockings, and solved the dress problem with a second-hand but serviceable calico, a soft blue, sprigged in yellow, made with a tight high bodice and long skirts. " 'Twas meant for a bigger woman, dearie," said Mrs. Cunner, "but it's all I can give you and you can take it in a mite."

Fey thanked her, added at her guide's suggestion a packet of hairpins, and returned to the wagon with her bundles.

All that day Fey stayed inside the wagon, altering the sprigged cotton dress as best she could. Her task was hard because she had only the barest knowledge of sewing and the wagon bumped and joggled continually in the deep but—at present—mercifully dry ruts of the Santa Fe Trail.

The two men sat in front and talked across a bottle of whisky which stood on the seat between them. The whisky had little effect on Terry, but old Sam gradually became garrulous and maudlin.

In the afternoon, after they had forded the Cimarron Creek and were rattling along the level sagebrush plain, Sam began to see Utes hiding behind every mound and hillock. Much time was lost while he took shots at distant objects which later turned out to be stones or sagebrush, or even in one case an inquisitive prairie dog.

Thus they did not reach Maxwell's hospitable ranch that night, as they had hoped, but camped again in the open. At suppertime Fey quietly appeared in her new dress, and her braids were no longer hanging but pinned neatly around her head. Both men were startled at the change.

"Tasty little piece," mumbled Sam. "Don't look like a greaser no more." And he sidled up to Fey and gave her a tentative pinch on the arm. She turned her head and sent him a long cool stare. The old mountaineer's hand dropped and he spat nervously at a mesquite stump.

Terry's reaction was scarcely more complicated. He, too, wanted to touch her, but she now seemed to him really unattainable. With shoes and stockings and a long-skirted calico and her hair up, she looked like any respectable American and this effect automatically released the ingrained chivalry with which all Western men were early taught to view those valuable, because rare, specimens on the frontier. Moreover, he noticed for the first time the proud carriage of her head, the fineness not only of her ankles but of her wrists. It occurred to him that her wild tale of aristocratic blood might have some foundation. In common with the rest of the country, Terry shared a grudging awe of lineage and established ancestry. They didn't mean anything, of course, in a democracy, but all the same they added value. This disconcerted him, and during the rest of the two days before they reached the top of Raton Pass he was unusually quiet. All the last afternoon the tired mules plodded up the long steep grades. Not nearly as long

nor as steep as they had been before Richens Wootton gave up
freighting and Indian fighting to start a highly successful business enterprise. Two years ago he had obtained charters from
Colorado and New Mexico and proceeded to build his famous
tollroad over Raton Pass—the roughest and hardest part of
the entire trail. Greatly improved though it was, it remained a
difficult pull, and the men and Fey walked most of the time to
spare the animals. Her feet swelled and ached in the confinement of shoes. Often she was tempted to take them off, but she
had seen the effect on Terry of her new type of clothes and she
was unwilling to lose any advantage.

At dusk they finally reached the crest and "Uncle Dick"
Wootton's hotel, an overgrown log and adobe cabin beside a
stream. Along the rooftree ran a large sign, "Wootton &
McBride, Lodging, Supplies," an incongruous commercial note
which usually delighted travellers surfeited by wilderness
scenery and mountain grandeur.

Even more businesslike was the tollgate which barred the
road. The mules stopped of their own accord, and Harriet, resting her head over the top bar, gave a mournful weary bray. At
once Uncle Dick himself strode out of his house. "Howdy,
folks," he called, his shrewd good-natured face beaming. "One-
fifty'll get you through. You aiming to stop here tonight, or go
on and camp out? Don't advise it, though. Injuns on the
Colorady side're kinda restless just now. Got a big party of 'em
here for a pow-wow."

He pointed a stumpy finger down the gulch, where the light
of campfires silhouetted shadowy figures on horseback, and
there was the sound of stamping feet and rhythmic shouting.

"Utes?" asked Terry, handing over a silver dollar and a
fifty-cent piece.

"Mostly," answered Wootton; "a few Navajos and Apaches
too, seeing as them tribes ain't squabbling with each other
right at this moment, for a wonder. I let 'em all go through the
gate free. Makes 'em friendly, and when they figger they've
got some grievance they'll come and tell me before they go on
the warpath stravaging after scalps."

"We'll stay with you tonight," said Terry, grinning. "We
need supplies, anyhow. This is my sister." He indicated Fey by
a careless wave. At this, old Sam, who had been mumbling
alcoholically to himself, gave a derisive snort.

Uncle Dick peered at the mountaineer, then he turned his
head and thoughtfully inspected Terry, Fey, and the wagon.
Wootton was a philosopher and within certain limits a moral-

ist. He had experienced a great deal of raw living in his fifty years and now he had reached a more contemplative stage. Isolated as he was at the top of a mountain pass, he took a keen interest in every aspect of the pageantry which flowed along his tollroad. Some of it was routine, empty freight trains returning East, and the bull-whackers who drove them as stupid as their oxen, but there were also any number of strange travellers, not counting the Indians.

The Barlow-Sanderson stages always yielded interesting passengers, and contact with these was his great pleasure. He savoured situations, and his own Jove-like position, which sometimes afforded him the opportunity of resolving them. The money he took in was not important, and he tossed it all into an old whisky keg which he kept behind the bar. While he led the way into his hotel and flung the silver received from Terry into the keg, he was examining Fey. Women were rarities on the Santa Fe Trail. Those who did come through were almost always army wives or enterprising harlots. This girl was neither, and she puzzled him.

"Have a seat by the fire, ma'am," he said to her hospitably. "I'll make you up my Ladies' Special to warm your stomach while you're waiting for vittles." Fey gave him a small polite smile and sat down on a bench by the great fireplace. She was tired, and the evening air was chilly.

Terry leaned over the bar while Uncle Dick busied himself among the bottles. Old Sam had managed to lurch inside the door and then collapsed in a heap in the corner, where no one paid any attention to him. There were three other men at a table, and a couple more playing checkers on the far side of the room. They were all prospectors hurrying South to investigate a rumour of pay dirt in the Moreno Valley.

After a few minutes, a half-breed woman waddled in from the kitchen bearing a plate of thick meat sandwiches which she offered to Fey and Terry. These and Wootton's "Ladies' Special"—which turned out to be whisky and milk—revived Fey. She leaned back in her rustic chair by the fireplace and a hazy glow of well-being stole over her. Her eyes turned inevitably to Terry. He was lounging at the bar in the immemorial masculine attitude, one foot on the rail and a supporting elbow near the open whisky bottle. This revealed the lithe lines of his body in the open blue shirt and buckskin trousers, and his bright crisp curls vivid against the stone wall behind. She heard his easy laugh and Wootton's answering chuckle. Terry was recounting an incident of the trip, making a good joke out of it now, and yet, at the time, when dealing with one of the inevitable frictions or annoyances of travel, he did not respond with humour, but with a quick irritability. Fey knew this discrepancy, and many others in his nature. Knew them intellectually, and immediately discounted them. What mattered was the occasional piercing charm of his smile, the set of his brown neck on the heavily muscled shoulders, the careless grace of his movements.

She continued to watch him, and the unaccustomed whisky relaxed her defences so that her unguarded eyes were easily read by Uncle Dick. He observed her shrewdly, then brought his gaze back to Terry, who was pouring himself another drink.

"Whyn't you marry that gel, Dillon?" said Wootton, cutting across Terry's flow of anecdote.

Terry was startled. He threw Wootton a quick look. "I told you she was my sister," he said resentfully.

"Rot!" said the older man.

"Well, she might as well be," snapped Terry, and he stuck his jaw out. The whisky was beginning to take effect.

"You don't say," said Wootton. "So that's the way it is." He examined Fey again, but this time the girl had seen him, and she turned her head and gazed at the fire. Her motion held both pride and pathos. Wootton frowned.

"How's she happen to be travelling with you if you ain't sleeping together?" he inquired in a lower tone.

Terry's eyes glinted. "I'm damned if I know. I thought when we started out, she was crazy for me."

Wootton's mouth twitched. She must have been a right smart little girl to hold off.

"I reckon she *is* crazy for you, boy," he said. "But did the idee ever occur to you she might be a decent woman? Whyn't you marry her?"

"Hell!" cried Terry, angrily grabbing the bottle. "You keep harping on that like an old biddy. I'm not a marrying man, and certainly not a little piece of fluff I picked out of Santa Fe."

"She don't look like a little piece of fluff," said Wootton patiently, moving the bottle out of Terry's reach. "She's quiet and she's got breeding. I ain't knocked around for fifty years without knowing breeding when I see it."

Terry scowled, and his anger rose. Nosy old duffer, yammering away, none of his business. Anger at Fey, too, surging hot above the current of puzzled resentment.

Wootton perfectly understood Terry's reaction. He'd seen dozens like Dillon here on the frontier; uncomplicated males, always ready for a fight or a woman, always craving adventure and change—avid for easy money, but lacking the calm drive necessary to obtain it. Sometimes marriage to a good woman was the making of them, and, anyway, it was high time the West settled down into respectability like the rest of the country.

Too much lawlessness still, too much of this sort of thing, free, easy morals—giving the West a bad name.

"I could hitch you two up good and legal right now," he said, in his quiet drawl. "I'm the law up hereabouts."

Terry lifted his empty glass in a violent gesture, but his arm paused in mid-air as Wootton's words penetrated his mind. "You a J.P.?" he asked slowly.

The other man nodded, threw back his buckskin coat and pointed with some pride to a shiny badge. "I'm all the law there is, boy, between Cimarron and Trinidad."

Terry put the glass down thoughtfully. A few words mumbled here in a mountain shack by this old duffer would hardly be a marriage at all, not to count. But it would doubtless satisfy Fey. Then for the rest of their trip back East, there'd be no more nonsense about sleeping arrangements, nor would she be able to balk over her part of the medicine show act. She'd be grateful to him and a wife does as she's told.

He swung around and looked at Fey. "Come here, honey," he called.

She turned, and her white skin, already flushed by the fire, deepened in tone, for his voice was wooing and tender. The checker-players in the corner looked up and winked at each other. Terry saw the lascivious looks they gave Fey as she moved slowly to him across the bare boards. He put his arm around her waist, savouring its firm flesh and the pressure of her breast against his side.

He leaned down and kissed the top of her head on the glossy black braids.

Uncle Dick Wootton nodded to himself and disappeared behind the red cotton curtain at the side of the bar.

Fey stood quiet, leaning against him a little, and waiting for the explanation of this new mood. Since the night at Fort Union, he had not even been civil to her. Her stillness and drooped lids betrayed nothing of the wild turmoil inside her. His physical nearness was like drowning, drowning in waves of suffocating gold. Her body ached with swift desire.

"What do you say we get married, Fey?" said Terry, grinning

down at her, the grin of a small boy presenting a bird's egg to his first sweetheart.

He waited a minute, and as she did not answer, he added in some irritation, "What's the matter with you? That's what you've been after right along."

She moistened her lips, and moved. "Yes," she said. The first blankness was passing. Of course, that was what she had wanted, from almost the first moment of seeing him. "When we get to Trinidad there must be a padre—"

"Can't wait that long, my girl, now I've made up my mind. Old Wootton here's a J.P. We'll do it right now, tonight. Find a padre later some place, of course," he added quickly.

"Tonight," she repeated. She looked at the bar beside her; its stained pine surface exuded a stench of spilled whisky and tobacco juice. The mirror behind it, Wootton's great pride, had one corner starred by a spent bullet from a long-forgotten fight, but its good surface faithfully reflected the huge room: the stuffed heads of Rocky Mountain sheep and an elk, the rough boulder walls, the smoky oil lamp swaying on a chain from the roof, the five frowzy, malodorous prospectors grouped around the far table and the checker game, the tin spittoons on the floor edging the buffalo-hide rug, and in one corner old Sam, crumpled into a heap and snoring acridly.

Terry was not unintuitive, and he sensed some of the girl's dismay. He knew that to her marriage must have always meant church and priest, new clothes and ceremony, as it did to most women; and since he was now passionately eager for her, he controlled his annoyance at her hesitation, and drew her away from the bar to a recess by the fireplace.

"Look, Fey," he said, holding her shoulders in his big hands, "I'm crazy for you." His voice deepened and throbbed. "I'm proving it, aren't I? I've treated you mighty fine, haven't I, leaving you alone, respecting you? Why, we belong together. We were made for each other, sweetheart, ever since the world began."

He had forgotten that this last speech was a direct quotation from a part he had once played. She listened only to his words and his voice, determinedly deaf to an undertone which reverberated far below the surface of her rushing joy. For now it seemed that her heart would burst in the clamour of its excitement, and she raised her arms with a kind of violence and threw them around her neck.

"Plenty of time for that later," said Uncle Dick's dryly humorous voice behind them. "Get slicked up, you two. I'm fixing as much of a jamboree as we can manage up here. Got the squaw to making flapjacks out in the kitchen shed, and I've sent word to the Injuns there's going to be a party. They like that; takes their minds off the warpath."

"Got the bridal chamber ready, too?" shouted Terry, and he showed his white teeth in a triumphant laugh while his arm tightened around Fey. The prospectors chuckled, and abandoning the checker game crowded around the bar demanding drinks on the house.

Colour flowed up Fey's neck and she turned her head, but her body pulsed and tingled, and her right side pressed against Terry's seemed seared by heat.

"I'll change my shirt," said Terry. "We haven't any fancy duds for the great event, but I guess the Injuns won't mind."

"You look good to me just the way you are," he added ardently to Fey, "but pull out that blue gewgaw you wear; it'll liven up your dress." He reached a possessive hand inside the neck of her bodice and drew out the turquoise pendant.

She made a quick, reflective gesture, but after all, why not? In the bar mirror she could see the radiant blue of the jewel against the darker blue and yellow of her calico dress. It did look pretty, and she had no other ornament.

"One little drink for the groom to get up his courage!" cried Terry, winking at the delighted audience, and he drew Fey with him over to the bar.

"To you, my love and my bride!" he cried. He kissed her on the mouth, then raising his glass began to drink.

Her nostrils dilated and she gave him a slow, answering smile.

There was a stir in the back of the room. The door opened and shut. Fey was hardly aware that people had entered, and with them a wave of cold resinous air from the mountains. But in another moment she experienced a sharp unease. It pounded like a black wedge through the sensuous warmth. She stiffened, hating the intrusion, aware that her heart had begun to beat not with the expectant passion of a moment ago, but in the mounting rhythm of that separating wedge.

It seemed to her that this went on for a long time while she resentfully searched for the meaning. Yet it was not a long time, for as Terry placed his glass on the bar and murmured, "I'm going to spruce up now, honey—be right back," she saw the cause.

The Indians had come in, old Conmach, the Ute chief, some

of his council, and one other, who stood apart, silent in the corner of the room.

"Natanay," Fey whispered; she took a quick step away from Terry, and across the room she received the full impact of the Navajo shaman's calm gaze. His eyes moved slowly down to the turquoise on her breast, they rested on Terry, who was entirely oblivious, then returned to Fey's face with added intensity, an edge of anger.

Terry went out through the kitchen shed to find the wagon and a change of clothes; the prospectors clustered around one end of the bar, tactfully leaving the bride alone; the Ute chief and his warriors drew apart beside the fireplace and conferred in low tones; but Fey saw nothing except the tall figure by the door.

At last she walked reluctantly over to him. His unshifting gaze did not lighten. When she stood in front of him, he inclined his head. "Que Dios te bendiga, muchacha," he said, and went on in his measured Spanish. "Is it to this your vision has brought you, my child?" There was contempt and reproof in his tone.

Fey lifted her chin. "Tonight I will be married to the man I love. To what better place could my vision have brought me?"

The lines deepened around Natanay's eyes. "Lust, muchacha," he said. "Not love."

Fey's face blazed. "That's not true!"

Natanay shook his head. "It is true. You are not the first to mistake lust for love, but for those others—most of them—it does not matter. For you it is different. Your soul was awakening. The Great Spirit meant you for a better destiny."

Fey's lips set. She looked down at the floor. "What do you know about me or my destiny?" she said sullenly. "You're an Indian and a heathen. I'm a white girl and a good Catholic."

Natanay made a faint sound, but when he spoke it was in a tone of pitying sadness. "Come outside where the air is pure. One cannot discuss truth in the stench of drunkenness and passion."

She did not wish to obey him, but she went to the chair by the fire and, picking up her shawl, silently followed the Navajo outside. He led her across the tollroad and up a little rise of ground on the other side. Here the air was fragrant with the fresh smell of the forest, and the stars—each a shimmering silver lamp—seemed as near as the treetops on Raton Mountain.

Natanay turned his back on the cabin below them and lifted

89

his arms toward the west. He stood for several minutes in silent invocation and Fey waited impatiently. Her awe of him kept her quiet. He was a magnificent figure silhouetted against the sky, his head thrown back as though he listened, his dark face raised to the starlight.

At last he began to speak, and between each word there was a pause as he translated from his own language in Spanish.

"Three summers ago, while my people were banished from their own land into degradation, you had a vision of their return. It gave me—their shaman—courage and hope. Now they are beginning to go back to their own place, and the weight of sorrow is rolling from me. In payment for this vision of yours, I try to help you now."

He lowered his arms and folded them. She saw the dark bronze of his face in the dimness and it seemed that his eyes caught the eternal light of the stars.

"You have taken the wrong trail," he said. "Your body has deafened you to the song of the Spirit. Go back!"

"Never!" she whispered. "Natanay, you're old, you're a Navajo. How could you understand? I've found my man, and there was nothing for me in Santa Fe. Nothing," she repeated vehemently. The word echoed and died away, while Natanay waited motionless.

When there was peace again, he spoke. "This man down there"—he gestured toward Wooton's cabin—"is not your true mate. He is weak."

"He isn't," she cried. "I love him."

The Navajo continued imperturbably, "He is weak and you will make him weaker. You will be bad for him as he for you."

"You can't know that," she said. "You're wrong. You don't understand."

He raised his hand and the passionate denials were silenced on her lips. "You will not listen." He spoke in sadness, and added in a low, meditative voice: "Poor little one. A few are born for true greatness, and when these stubbornly deny the voice of the Spirit, it is their punishment that later they must look back and see the wrong turnings when they can no longer go back."

A cold wind blew along the valley. Fey shivered and pulled her shawl tighter around her shoulders. From the cabin below she heard the thrumming of the banjo and Terry's voice singing "The Arkansas Traveller."

"I must go down," she said. "He's waiting."

Natanay folded his arms again beneath the Navajo blanket.

He lowered his head once in assent. "Adios, chiquita." His eyes rested on the turquoise which gleamed blue between the folds of her shawl. "You still wear the sky-stone," he said quietly. "May you never lose it."

He walked away from her, his moccasined feet noiseless on the rough ground. He vanished into the darkness of the pines.

"Natanay," she whispered, and for an instant the near, protecting stars seemed to withdraw into frozen distance. Sharply in her memory she heard the church bells as they had clanged ten years ago in Santa Fe for a frightened, lonely child. She shut her eyes and stood swaying against the ever-freshening night wind. Then she walked down the hillside.

Terry met her outside the cabin. "Where in thunder've you been?" he cried, catching her to him. "I thought you were fixing up, but they told me in there you went out strolling with an Injun."

"He was an old friend, Terry," she said. "I met him long ago".

Terry roared. His teeth gleamed. His silk shirt clung to his slim, powerful body. He gave out a strong aroma of bay rum and whisky. "Can't make me jealous tonight. If he's an old friend, ask the Injun to the wedding."

She shook her head. "He wouldn't come."

Terry was not interested. He swept her in through the door, calling, "Found my bride, boys!" and they were received with boozy cheers from the prospectors.

Twenty minutes later, Fey and Terry were married. During the ceremony they stood before a table which Wootton had pulled out from behind the bar and hastily wiped off. He had also placed a tattered Bible upon it, with a hazy idea of lending some proper solemnity to the occasion. He produced Fey's ring from a box of trinkets which he kept on hand for bartering with the Indians—it was made of two gold-washed wires clumsily entwined into a lover's knot.

"And so—by the power invested in me by the territories of Colorady and New Mexico I now pronounce you man and wife," finished Uncle Dick, and went on at once uncertainly, "Don't know but it seems like we ought to do something more—kind of round it off." He looked at the young couple in front of him. They both looked frightened. Dillon's eyes were easy enough to read, startled misgiving. The look of a brusquely sobered man who awakens to find himself in a predicament. The girl's face was harder. Her grey eyes were wide and staring at some point past his head. She was unnaturally still except for her

91

hands. Her right index finger and thumb twisted the shiny wedding ring round and round in a slow mechanical way which Wootton found disquieting.

"Let's sing a hymn, boys!" cried Uncle Dick to the five prospectors. "Come on, you Injuns," he called to the silent gathering at the back of the room. "You sing, too—got to have music at a wedding." He cleared his throat and struck up the first tune which occurred to him.

"From Greenland's icy mountains, from India's coral strand—"

The prospectors joined in hoarsely. The Indians politely shuffled in rhythm and made low, chanting noises.

Fey lowered her gaze in a bewildered way, and stopped twisting the ring, but Terry's eyes cleared. "By God," he cried, "we can do better than that—sounds like a funeral." He grabbed his banjo. "Give me a drink," he said to Wootton, and he burst into a rollicking version of "Jingle Bells." "Jingle bells, jingle bells, jingle all the way—"

He sang at the top of his voice, purposely falsetto, and he stamped his foot on each beat. The Indians fell silent again, but one of the prospectors seized the half-breed squaw and cavorted around the room with her. Wootton beat time on the bar and sang too.

Fey continued to stand by the table.

"Liven up and dance, sweetheart," called Terry. "Dance with the minister." He gave her a little push toward Wootton.

She shook her head. Her hands were clasped tight together. The thin twang of the banjo rattled in her ears, jingle, jingle, like tin, like pellets of ice.

Terry had been watching her. He finished in a spatter of chords, flung the banjo on a chair. "G'night, all!" he cried. "And don't you dass to give us a chivari."

He reached down and picked Fey up in his arms, stood holding her a moment like that high in the air.

The prospectors snickered and nudged each other, looking at them enviously.

"This way, folks," said Wootton, frowning. "We've fixed up the downstairs bedroom for you tonight." He was displeased. There wasn't much decency about the way the young fellow was acting. Bed, of course, was the proper place for a new-married couple, but there was something animal-like, uncouth, about the way things were going. And the girl, with her eyes shut, looking half-drowned. He averted his gaze from the sight of Terry laying the girl down on the big double bed. The squaw had put on the best goose-feather pillows and a fancy quilt from the East. The girl was so light she hardly made a dent on it, but her bosom was fluttering—like she was in pain.

Well, they are married, anyhow, and all legal, thought Uncle Dick, trying to recapture his early feeling of triumph. He shut the bedroom door.

CHAPTER

7

TERRY and Fey spent three weeks travelling eastward on the remainder of the Santa Fe Trail. For them both the discomforts of the journey—stifling dust and pitiless beating sun, drenching thunderstorms, swollen fords, mosquitoes, and broken axles—all were hazed and diminished by their preoccupation with each other. Even for Terry, the companionship of this responsive passionate girl was enough, and her presence beside him attuned him to beauty he would never otherwise have noticed. He shared in her delighted interest when they first heard the whip-poor-will and the delicate song of the lark. He stopped the wagon to gaze with her at a distant herd of antelope, floating like fairy beasts into the violet dusk. And earlier, after they had left Old Fort Bent on the Arkansas and had their last glimpse of the mountains, he had felt as she did the poignancy of this farewell.

"It's so flat," whispered Fey, staring at the unbroken plains ahead of them. "I didn't know it would be so flat." And she strained back to see the Spanish Peaks; two lone, snow-topped sentinels on the western horizon, last outposts of the Rockies behind them. "Terry, are there no more mountains?"

He shook his head. "Not for over a thousand miles." He bent and kissed her, and they clung together, both awed by the vast indifferent prairie stretching limitlessly to meet the vast and indifferent sky.

"We'll get used to it, darling," he said. "We'll get along."

Her heart swelled that he should understand and comfort her. Mountains had been part of her life, the Sangre de Cristos, the Sandias, and on the Trail there had still been the Ratons— all guardians, protecting one from this feeling of pressed-down, terrifying insignificance.

93

Terry picked up the reins and flicked the mules. The wagon creaked, the wheels resumed their rhythmical dry swish through the buffalo grass. Fey leaned against Terry's shoulder. "Yes—we have each other," she whispered, closing her eyes, and resting softly against him.

See, she said to Natanay and La Gertrudis, see how wrong you were. His *is* my man, and he loves me. And she felt for them a scornful pity.

But she seldom thought of the past and never of the future. At night in the wagon or under the buffalo robe beneath the stars, she gave herself to Terry with an eager pagan joyousness. And he was deeply moved. For those weeks he did not regret the marriage nor look ahead to anything but a continuation of this vivid physical bliss. When he sometimes remembered that this girl, who was so delightful a mistress, was also his wife, he felt astonishment and complacency. They had not, however, found a padre to perform the religious ceremony. "In Leavenworth, perhaps," he told Fey, "or maybe in New York." And she had acquiesced, as she did in everything.

Below the unfolding excitement of their passion the material incidents of the journey rolled on inexorably. One day they reached Fort Dodge—a collection of mud hovels at the edge of the arid country—and here they had two glimpses of buffalo. At Fort Larned they picked up the perennial rumour that the vicious Kiowas were on the warpath, and though neither of them wished for company, they were persuaded by excited warnings to join forces for a few days with an empty homebound wagon train. But once the scare was over, they shot ahead of the slow oxen. Neither of them had the knowledge or experience to fear the plains Indians. Terry was constitutionally incapable of worry, and Fey naturally thought of all Indians in terms of the Pueblos—and Natanay.

In any case the Trail was no longer the dangerous adventure that it had been; during this summer of 1867 over six thousand wagons had deepened the ruts and mud-holes between Leavenworth and Santa Fe, and from Bent's Fort eastward Terry and Fey were often in sight of other travellers.

These they punctiliously greeted as the courtesy of the Trail demanded, but except for the days of the Kiowa scare, they were alone and content.

Each morning was an adventure, and each meal a delight to their sharp appetites. Sometimes there was buffalo steak and home-made bread bought from one of the sod shanties which were beginning to dot the plains. More often there was a rabbit or plover which Terry himself had shot and which Fey had become expert at cooking in their frying-pan.

They drank quarts of scalding-hot coffee or sweet water from an unexpected spring, and Terry did not miss whisky, which was unprocurable except at the forts and too expensive for them there.

They discovered, as lovers always have, the joy of childish games—teasing, coaxing games rewarded by kisses; of a private language and silly jokes. Often in the evening, while they sat by their little fire, Terry amused her by reciting extracts from romantic rôles he had played. He had a good memory, and her adoring interest stimulated him to better acting than he had ever done on the stage. She responded by singing him Spanish love-songs while he lay with his head on her lap listening drowsily. Her low voice throbbed in its new maturity, and she sang the plaintive melodies so that each soft note was a caress.

One afternoon, near Pawnee Rock, they rejoiced to find a deep spot in the Arkansas—disappointing river, all too often thinned by a yellow trickle oozing over the mud flats. But this pool was deep enough for bathing, and the flat alkaline water, sheltered by a fringe of scrubby willows, was unexpectedly cool.

They had splashed and ducked each other until their bodies glowed, then, refreshed and clean, they had clambered back up the bank to lie in the shade of cottonwoods. The Kansas prairie did not seem intimidating then. Outside the shelter of their grove it lay like a warm brown ocean lapped in content. A small breeze came with the sunset and the gentle insect noises increased; the plop of grasshoppers in the gamma grass and the prolonged clickings like a thousand tiny stemwinder watches. Near the wagon the mules munched and swished their tails.

"Peaceful," murmured Terry. He yawned and turned to watch Fey.

She was languidly drying her hair, shaking it, combing it out over her naked shoulders and breasts. It rippled over them like live black silk, iridescent in the deep waves, catching the light as she combed. She was frowning a little, mysterious and entirely unself-conscious, absorbed in the feminine rite.

His heartbeats slowed and thickened. He reached out and touched a strand of the long gleaming hair.

"Don't braid it," he whispered. "You're beautiful like that."

At once she loosed the part she had gathered in her hand and put the comb on the ground. She leaned back on her elbow, smiling down at him. "As you wish—Terry. Always—"

They looked deep into each other's eyes.

"Don't!" He made a violent motion with his hand, bringing it down sharply between them.

"Don't what?" she breathed. She drew back. The tender smile faded from her mouth. She crossed her arms hard over her breasts.

Don't what? He did not know. She had brought him pain, dim—unnamed.

He jumped up, shaking back his curls. His eyes were hostile. "It's getting cold. Better get some clothes on."

She bowed her head, pulling her hair around her. She walked silently to the wagon.

Later, after they had eaten, he was still brusque, and he would not look at her. They talked of practical things. How many miles tomorrow? The mules' feed was getting low again.

Fey, now dressed in the sprigged calico, her braids pinned tight around her head, busied herself in washing and putting away the cooking utensils.

Terry rambled around their camp-site, picking up sticks for the morning fire, shying pebbles at a green butterfly, examining for the third time a small stone bruise on Calvin's hoof.

Suddenly he went into the wagon, came out carrying his banjo. He flung himself down on a fallen log and played "Turkey in the Straw" very fast and loud, banging time on the ground with his foot. He finished in a discordant jangle.

"That was a most strangely angry turkey," said Fey. She had moved over beside him, and stood looking down at him. There was a faint smile on her mouth, but her eyes were serious and questioning.

Terry stared at her. Then his sullen face cleared. He threw back his head and laughed, and, catching up a handful of her skirt, he pulled her down on to his lap. "You sing, then. Sing 'Chula la Mañana'."

Fey hesitated, pushing back the sombre cloud—denying it.

He put his hands around her waist, giving her an impatient squeeze.

"Sing, 'Chula'!"

So she sang that blithest of all Mexican love-songs, and Terry, to whom she had taught it, harmonized the melody in his clear baritone. They sang together until the fire fell into embers, and light from the orange prairie moon sifted through the cotton-wood leaves on to their upturned faces. After that, in laughter and music and love-making, the gilded days slipped past them and vanished.

One afternoon toward dusk they arrived at Leavenworth City and the end of the Trail.

Leavenworth, with its population of over twenty thousand, was the metropolis of Kansas. During these latter years, as the railroad oozed slow tentacles westward, it had been the eastern terminus of the Trail, the joining-point of the wilds and civilization. Here it was that Fey saw her first train, slept in her first hotel, and it was here, too, that she was jarred out of the timeless idyll which she had shared with Terry.

They drove into the bustling little city, and each of them was at once affected by the new atmosphere of briskness and efficiency. The weary mules broke into a startled trot as the wagon rattled down Kickapoo Street toward Main and they encountered a crush of traffic—buggies, stages, and even an elegant brougham. The wooden sidewalks teemed with ladies in stylish crinolines, bewhiskered gentlemen in top hats. No one paid any attention to the travel-worn wagon, and Fey, accustomed to friendly greetings, was dismayed by a sudden feeling of anonymity. It was her first experience of the impersonality of civilization.

Terry had no misgivings and no dismay. He sat very erect on the seat, negligently guiding the nervous mules, his eyes darting from side to side and taking pleased inventory of the city's attractions. Three whole blocks of stores, good ones, too, with show windows; plenty of prosperous-looking saloons, and actually four hotels which did not compare too unfavourably with those in San Francisco.

"Of course, this can't be a patch on the real Eastern towns," he observed. "But, God, it sure seems good to see something going on. I'm sick of prairies and Injuns and greasers."

Fey gave him a quick look, and her throat tightened. She saw that he was no longer conscious of her. The honeymoon was over, and Terry, as was his wont, immediately grew bored by the past while he strained to capture the new experience.

It happened that they were near the depot when the five-fifteen snorted and clanged in from Wyandotte. Calvin and Harriet at once became totally unmanageable, and Terry, swearing richly, was forced to yield to their terror. He hitched them around the corner out of sight of the train. "Come on," he said to Fey. "Let's look it over."

She got down from the wagon and followed him to the platform. They stood silently side by side, staring. Smoke and cinders still belched from the locomotive's funnel-shaped stack, and begrimed passengers were still clambering down the high steps from the three wooden cars. "Fine trip, George," called a stout man with a gold watch-chain to another man who emerged from the depot. "Made it in two hours; remember when it took two days, and not so long ago neither."

"Did you clear up that deal, Joe?" asked the Leavenworth man.

"Like taking candy from a bebby," answered he of the gold watch-chain, flourishing his wallet. "Money's flowing like a river back East. All you got to do is get out your little pail and scoop it up."

Terry watched and listened. He cast one more eager look at the train.

"Sell the wagon and the mules," he said, under his breath— "hold a couple of shows—" For the first time since they had reached the city, he returned his attention to Fey.

"Think you can do your stunt by tomorrow, if we rehearse it again and freshen it up? I got to have time, anyway, to make the Elixir."

"What are you planning, Terry?" said Fey slowly.

"Make enough money to get East on the cars, of course," he answered, astonished. "Like I said from the very beginning."

Yes, she thought, that was always his plan, and I guess it was mine, too, back there in Santa Fe. Why, then, during the last weeks had she forgotten it so completely? Why, in passing the little sod shanties on the prairies, had she unconsciously pictured herself and Terry in one like them, still alone together, loving and striving and building toward a dream as did those other young couples.

"What's the matter with you?" he said negligently as they walked back to the wagon. "You ought to be excited over your first sight of the cars. Thing is to scrape together enough to ride on 'em."

"I wish we didn't have to hold a show," she said, very low.

They were back on the wagon seat and Terry turned on her a quick anger. "You're my wife now, and you'll do what I say."

She answered his look by one of such sadness and yearning that his anger melted. He pulled her against him and began to kiss her.

The medicine show was very nearly a fiasco. They held it on an open lot just north of town and they attracted a fair crowd, since Terry had repainted the sign on the wagon and had driven all day through the streets, pausing on the corners to make speeches.

The music and the Spanish dances were received with mild interest, but this urban audience was used to more sophisticated amusement. They even had an opera house where travelling companies had given them *East Lynne* and *Uncle Tom's Cabin.* Those who had come had been chiefly attracted by Terry's promise of "miracles of clairvoyance and communication with the spirits who will positively, through the mediumship of my wife, a Spanish gypsy from across the seas, diagnose your every ailment!"

Fey stood at the back of the wagon as she had stood before at Fort Union, and when Terry mingling amongst the people paused by a woman and demanded to know what name was written on her gold bangle, Fey tried to still her mind and wait for that moment of calm receptivity which presaged the certainty of the name in Terry's mind. And none of this happened. She could not still her mind, which kept darting and doubling like a small animal down panicky cul-de-sacs. She heard the audience begin to murmur, and she made a small, helpless gesture.

Terry, quickly dropping the woman's bracelet, said, "The spirits take a little time to come through, folks." He turned to an oafish-looking teamster, who stood breathing heavily through his mouth. "You don't look like you felt good, brother," he said. "You been sick?"

The teamster nodded. "Yeah," he said solemnly, "I got the flux. Sure I'm sick."

"What you need is my Extra Special Elixir," interrupted Terry, as those nearest guffawed. He rushed back to the wagon for a bottle.

"What's the matter?" he hissed to Fey.

"I can't do it," she whispered back. "It's gone." There was a finality about her that even Terry accepted. He made an exasperated noise, vaulted from the wagon, and strode back to the teamster, who docilely bought the Elixir.

Terry did what he could to placate the disappointed audience. He made the routine Elixir speech, he told jokes, he played for them again on the banjo, and sold a few more bottles. But the people drifted off. There were a few jeers and insults, but on the whole they were good-natured. After all, they had had some entertainment which had cost nothing.

Fey continued to stand under the shadow of the wagon curtain in her tawdry Spanish costume. She was unconscious of the dispersing crowd. Her eyes were listed to the western horizon where a pink afterglow turned the distant plains to mauve.

It's really gone, she thought, and a bleak emptiness ran over her like wind. She was no longer attuned to Terry's mind, now that she had become so closely attuned to his body. And it was worse than the loss of that extra faculty which had always seemed so normal that it was hard to understand that others did not have it. Something else was gone, too. An awareness of deeper currents, a warmth and sense of inner sustenance; this had always been there, but she had not known it until now that it had left her.

Her hand went uncertainly to her bodice. She pulled out the turquoise pendant and stared down at it.

"It's a pretty good stone," said Terry, who had finished with the last reluctant customer. "But there's no market for that Injun stuff here. Wouldn't be worth trying to sell."

Fey's eyes turned to him in such blank astonishment that he was disconcerted. "You sure let me down tonight," he went on, but without rancour. His angers were always short, and besides, she had that faraway queer listening look in her big eyes. It made him uncomfortable, but it was attractive, too, mysterious and untouchable.

"It's gone, Terry," she said. "Gone."

Terry looked down at the eleven paper dollars in his hand. Greenbacks instead of good reliable silver, but money, anyway. Enough to go down to one of the saloons and have a real binge. And high time, too, after weeks of desert dryness. "Well, if 'it's' gone, we'll have to fake it for the next show. Work out some signals," he answered cheerfully. "Never did take much stock in 'it,' anyway, whatever it was; maybe you just made a lot of lucky guesses."

He knows that isn't true, she thought, or has he really forgotten. But what difference did it make?

"I'm tired," she said vaguely. "Very tired."

Terry picked her up and carried her into the wagon, put her down on the cot. "You tuck in, honey, and get a nice rest. I'm going out for awhile—see the town."

Her arms fell into their accustomed place around his neck. He stayed with her awhile on the cot. Before he left the wagon, he said, "Now, don't worry about a thing. I've a hunch our luck's about to turn."

Fey did not answer. She lay flattened on the bed and watched his bright head disappear through the slit in the curtain.

100

It was noon of the next day before Terry came back. Fey's hurt bewilderment at his desertion changed to amazement as she recognized him striding along the dusty road from town. When he had left her, he had been wearing buckskin pants, a wrinkled cream-coloured shirt, and the old dusty sombrero. He was now transformed, by a tight pepper-and-salt suit, flowing four-in-hand tie, and pearl-grey hat, into an approximation of the travelled gentleman whom they had seen getting off the train. Terry also carried a large pink bandbox which he deposited on the ground at her feet.

"Did I not tell thee, gentle maiden, that Lady Fortune would yield to my stalwart wooing?" he cried thickly, striking an attitude. "Cast, oh, cast those luminous optics upon this." He waved a thick roll of bills.

Fey stared at them blankly, then back at Terry. He was handsomer than ever in the new clothes, but she did not like them. She did not put into words the first instinctive recoil, but it was the realization that he now looked theatrical—glossy. And he's still pretty drunk, she thought. There was no censure in this thought. All men drank when they felt like it, particularly Americanos. Women accepted that without question. Still, it made a difference. When one's man had been drinking, one had to adjust and temporize for awhile. Her eyes returned to the bank roll, and now at last its significance penetrated. Greenbacks did not look like money.

"How?" she said.

Terry scowled.

"Faro," he answered sulkily. "I broke the bank. There's near four hundred here. The outfit'll fetch another couple of hundred. Enough to get—us to New York."

There was a hesitation before the "us" which stuck fear into Fey, and awakened her to his annoyance.

"That's wonderful, Terry!" she cried. "Wonderful! Such a great lot of money. I couldn't believe it."

He was mollified. "Put on the dress I got you."

"Do you think it will fit?" she asked, as she untied the tapes.

"Oh, yes—I took along a girl about—" He stopped, gave her a quick look, and walking over to the mules began to whistle and tighten their bridles.

Fey's fingers clenched on the pasteboard-box top. The rim tore off with a sharp crack. She said nothing. After a moment she shook the dress free from paper and held it against her. It was a garish red-and-blue plaid trimmed in cherry velvet, and it had a small crinoline. There was also a cheap wool shawl and a red plush bonnet.

"Thank you," she said, in a choked voice. "They're beautiful."

"No one will ever guess we came from the West," nodded Terry. "Hold our own anywhere." He resumed his whistling.

Fey went into the wagon and put on the clothes. There was, of course, no mirror, but she knew the dress fitted fairly well, even as she knew that it did not suit her. All her delicacy and air of breeding were eclipsed, the raw colours made her tanned skin sallow. The bonnet was too large and submerged her small piquant face.

Terry, however, was pleased. She now looked right smart, something like the gay young lady who had helped him choose the dress. That Fey also looked like a fancy woman rather than a wife did not occur to him.

They stayed at Leavenworth for three more days at the Planters' House—the city's best hotel. Fey was left much alone and her initial interest in the elaborate walnut furniture, thick carpets, and washbowls that gushed running water quickly evaporated.

Harriet and Calvin were sold to a newly married couple who were soon to set out along the Trail for Colorado.

Terry had conferences with this young couple, and gave them much helpful advice. He was astonished that Fey did not wish to go with him on these visits. She gave no reason. Even to herself she did not admit the envy and the pain caused by thought of the young Boltons' projected journey. She suppressed the memory of those starlit, passionate nights, the exhilarating days when they had been close together and alone. She was now as eager to board the train and get East as Terry was. In New York it would be different. They would be at journey's end. They could settle into real marriage.

On the afternoon before their departure, Fey slipped out of the hotel alone and went to the barn where the mules were temporarily stabled. They recognized her by warm nuzzlings, and she kissed them both on their soft fur noses. Adios, amigos, she said to them silently. And then she spoke to them out loud in Spanish; it was easier for her to say foolish childish things in that language. "When you feel the buffalo wind again blowing across the prairie, think of me," she told them, "and when you hear the song of the lark, and when you see the mountains again—the first mountains, the Spanish Peaks guarding the high country beyond—ah, think of me."

The mules whickered softly when at last she left them,

hurrying along the crowded Main Street in her gaudy dress. Terry was in their room waiting for her. He had bought their railroad tickets and was in a very good humour. "We're on our way, honey," he cried, pulling her down on the bed beside him. He yawned and stretched, easing his long body into the thick feather matress of the walnut bed.

"This is sure a lot better for love-making than the ground and an old buffalo robe," he said languidly.

CHAPTER

8

FEY and Terry arrived in New York City in the middle of October. They crossed on the ferry from Jersey City to Chambers Street, and both of them were too hungry, dirty, exhausted by travel and sated with new sights to be much interested in Manhattan's famous sky-line, still dominated as it had been for nearly a hundred years by the steeple of Trinity Church.

On the journey across the continent from Kansas, they had ridden on eleven different railroads, and had stopped perforce at many different towns while awaiting connections. Jefferson City, St. Louis, Vincennes, Cincinnati, Buffalo—each lost its individual characteristic for Fey, each was represented by a sooty station and increasingly drab accommodations. Neither of them had realized how many expenses the trip would necessitate besides the cost of tickets.

In the beginning there had been nights in the new sleepers invented by Mr. Pullman; these were the pleasantest nights despite the cars' soot-grimed ornateness, the lack of privacy, the constant use of brass spittoons along the aisle, and the stench from the flickering oil lamps. But as far back as Missouri it had become evident that they could not afford sleepers, and since then they had either sat up in the uncomfortable coaches or hunted for cheap lodgings in the various towns.

Terry had been possessed of a desire to push on, no matter what—on to the sure haven of New York. Once there, he had convinced himself and Fey that, by some miraculous alchemy, all financial problems would be solved.

The actual arrival was a dismal anticlimax. They got off the ferry, Terry holding his carpet-bag, Fey the bandbox in which

103

were packed her few possessions. They stood uncertainly on the wharf, shoved and jostled by a hurrying throng who were in no doubt as to their own destinations. They stood expectant—and nothing happened.

"We ought to go to the best hotel," said Terry at last. "The Fifth Avenue, or the Hoffman House, start off right."

Fey put her bandbox on the dusty planks, straightened her tired back. "We can't do that," she answered quietly. "We have no money."

This unpalatable truth focused Terry's frustration and disappointment on her.

"And you've no imagination!" he shouted. "It's no wonder we get here dead-beat. All you do is balk and make trouble. Man can't get up in the world with a millstone around his neck."

Hatred. He was looking at her with the flint eyes of hatred. The corners of her mouth trembled, and she turned away.

"What would you do if I weren't here?" she asked, in the carefully controlled tone which always daunted him.

Spanish temperament, he thought, supposed to be hot and explosive. Give a man some satisfaction to fight with something that fought back. Cold as a cucumber she was, except in bed, and lately that hadn't been so good either. And look at her, white and droopy, like a nincompoop in that bright plaid dress. I'd make my way all right without her.

He continued to glare at her, while his mind caressed many vague seductive plans. Go to the best hotel; they didn't make you pay in advance if you had the brass to impress them. Get into the proper setting and something was bound to turn up. This was New York, at last.

The other ferry passengers had all vanished. A guard looked at them curiously and Terry reddened. He saw tears in Fey's eyes, and his rage lessened, though not the underlying resentment.

He picked up his carpet-bag. "Can't stay here all day. People will take us for hicks."

Fey gave a fleeting bitter smile. They walked along Chambers Street to Broadway, where they turned north and wandered up the crowded, noisy thoroughfare. The fashionably dressed people, the great shop windows, the clanging stages and private carriages had for Fey the unreality of a rushing dream. Her attention was given to two sentences which repeated themselves like a litany in her head.

He didn't mean it. I'm his wife.

Terry, excited as always by the lure of novelty, had already forgotten his tirade by the time they reached the Saint Nicholas Hotel. He left Fey in a far corner of the lobby while he tried to engage a room. The hotel, however, was full, it seemed, and the Metropolitan was, too. New York room clerks were not nearly as gullible or willing to take a chance as those in San Francisco. They had no difficulty in appraising Terry, and Celtic charm was a drug on the market in this immigrant haven.

So they continued to trudge up Broadway, and Terry was now as silent as Fey. They came at last to Bleecker Street. It had a raffish and Bohemian air. Twenty-five years ago its brownstone mansions had been fashionable residences of the élite, all of whom had now moved far uptown. The houses had suffered the incredibly rapid degeneration peculiar to New York. They were now a trifle better than the tenements around the Five-Points, but they were nearly as crowded and dingy. Almost every fly-specked parlour window exhibited a tattered sign, "Roomers," and those which did not were middle-class brothels, patronized by counting-house clerks and petty city officials.

"Maybe one of these places might take us," said Fey, wearily indicating the signs, and speaking for the first time since they had left the ferry house.

Terry shrugged, but he did not object. He was chastened and also very tired.

In the middle of the block between Lafayette Street and the Bowery, they finally found Mrs. Flynn and a vacancy. Mrs. Flynn had watery serpentine eyes and a mordant tongue. A wizened infant suckled from one pendulous breast while its mother shoved open a creaking door on a dark passageway. "Take it or leave it, folks," she said, hunching her shoulder toward the room inside. "Two-fifty per and breakfasts if ye get up before nine. The w.c.'s on the lower landing."

Fey looked at the room. It had once been papered in a sulphurous yellow, as shown by rectangles on the wall left by long-removed pictures. There was a rickety three-quarter bed covered by a grey cotton blanket. The original Axminster carpet, never moved since the day it was placed on the floor thirty years ago, showed a threadbare path from the door to the bed. There was a straight broom chair, a cracked washbowl on a deal table, and a row of nails for clothing on the back of the walnut door. The high window had once looked out upon a garden which had now shrunk to an alley six feet wide, flanked

105

by a four-story warehouse. The resultant perpetual gloom could be mitigated by a kerosene lamp which hung from a bracket.

"We'll take it," said Fey slowly.

The landlady gave her an appraising glance, detached the baby and buttoned her bodice. "Foreigner, ain't you, dearie?" She cocked her head at Fey and emitted a faint smell of gin. She turned and examined Terry, the serpentine eyes disillusioned and knowing.

"I'm an American," said Fey, but Mrs. Flynn was no longer interested in the girl.

"Handsome gossoon ye are, my lad," she said, nudging Terry and chuckling. "Sure, and I think there's a bit of Ould Erin some place abouts."

Terry's rigidity melted. "Sure, and ye're a foine figger of a woman yourself, macushla," he said, smiling his brilliant smile, and pinching the skinny arm, "and I'd be stealing a kiss were it not my wife'd be jealous."

Mrs. Flynn bridled, making a satirical but gratified sound.

"That'll hold the rent off awhile," remarked Terry when they were alone. "Maybe even good for a meal and a bottle of gin. She's got that around somewhere, for certain."

Fey took off her red plush bonnet. She dragged herself over to the bed and lay down. She lay flattened, rocking on long black surges of exhaustion, a tiny boat alone on the oily black waves.

Terry kicked the carpet-bag into the corner, came over to the bed, and stood looking down at her. He leaned over the bed, and she opened her eyes.

"No, Terry, please. Not now," she whispered, and she tried to smile at him.

"Very well, my pet." He spoke after a moment's silence. He kissed her once, quite gently. "I'll wheedle that old harridan into bringing you up some food. Myself I'm going out to see the city."

For a few minutes she heard him moving about the room and humming. He sluiced his face and neck in the washbowl. She heard the tiny crackling sound of the comb through his thick hair, the pause in his wordless song as he concentrated on the exact arrangement of his tie, finally the creak of the door shutting behind him.

Madre de Dios, she thought, help me. She stared up at the stained yellowish ceiling. The stain directly above the bed was sharp and irregular like a little mountain. She followed this outline slowly until it shimmered and grew green against a bright mauve distance. "Atalaya," she whispered. But the little peak vanished. There was nothing but a stain on the ceiling, and outside the muffled sounds of New York; street cries, the rattle of drays on cobblestones. Near-by from the next room, somebody hiccupped, somebody else giggled.

She turned and hid her head under the lumpy pillow, pressing it around her ears.

They lived together for a week in the back room on Bleecker Street. By the second day, Terry had money. When no longer encumbered by Fey, he had found little difficulty in following his established and so far successful pattern. After leaving Fey in Bleecker Street, he had spent an agreeable hour strolling up Fifth Avenue until he reached Delmonico's at Fourteenth Street. Here he entered the café side, ordered a beer, and awaited developments. They came quickly. Three portly middle-aged men and four actresses sat down at a table near Terry. They ordered champagne and brandy.

Terry edged over and listened. The men were celebrating the successful outcome of the Erie Railroad's stockholders' meeting that day. Flushed and excited, they bandied names. Terry, avidly listening, heard mention of Drew—"smart as a whip, he's pulled it off again"; Vanderbilt—"his goose is cooked this time." The men ordered more brandy and, temporarily ignoring the girls, branched into speculation on the reaction of the stock market as a whole, making intimate use of other great financial names, Jay Gould and Jim Fisk.

Terry was quite shrewd enough to realize that these men were small fry—hangers-on, each trying to outshine the other by the possession of doubtful knowledge. But they were obviously prosperous and they were New Yorkers.

Terry spent his last quarter for another beer, and examined the extra girl, the one who had no partner. She was a pretty blonde in violet satin and ruffles. She had a bored, restless eye which Terry caught without difficulty. Terry, me lad, he thought, your luck is back again. This'll be easy.

It was. He swiftly considered the best approach. Boldness, of course, and flattery, no need for subtlety at this point since the men were well liquored-up.

"Excuse me," he said, smiling and addressing the oldest of the men, "I couldn't help but hear a bit you said. I'm a Westerner just got to town today, and to stand near men who actually know Vanderbilt and Drew and Fisk fair throws me off my balance. Please pardon me for butting in."

107

The men stared at him, while the lady in violet rustled appreciatively. Terry turned his warm smile from one to the other; there was in it just the proper touch of ingenuousness.

"Well," said the oldest man at length, frowning a little, "I'd no motion we were talking so loud." He wiped his moustache methodically, easing himself on the gilt chair. "So you're a stranger, are you? Well—" he hesitated again, but it was the era of treating and extravagant hospitality, and one lived up to the code. "Will you join us for a drink, sir?"

Terry would. They plied him with questions about the West, and gradually, as drink succeeded drink and Terry obliged the untravelled with ever more highly coloured tales of his adventures, the men lost their patronizing amiability and became interested. As for the girls, they thought him romantic, a handsome, heroic Westerner, and they vied with each other for his attention. He confined this, however, to Maude, the blonde. She was better dressed than the others; she had rings and a diamond brooch; she was sophisticated and knowing. No flies on her, thought Terry, and he felt for her a kinship.

By the time they left Delmonico's, Terry was accepted as one of the party for the evening. They went to Fortuna's. This was one of the most ornate and discreet of the city's twenty-five hundred gambling houses. It was hidden on the upper floor of a marble mansion on Nineteenth Street.

It was Maude who arranged this move. She spoke quickly to Terry at the café entrance, her white kid glove exerting a subtle pressure on his arm. "Flat broke, aren't you?" she whispered. He nodded. "Ever tried faro or roulette?"

He nodded again, looking down at her appreciatively.

"I'll stake you," she said, and she slipped a twenty-dollar gold piece into his hand.

The others crowded around them, while Terry's mouth sent her the outline of a kiss. They understood each other.

Terry won. Not spectacularly, but the twenty dollars grew to two hundred.

Then Maude stopped him. "That's enough," she said. "It's going to turn."

Terry glanced at the suave banker, imperturbably dealing.

"Crooked?" he asked, raising his eyebrows.

She shrugged her violet shoulders, gave him a half-smile. Terry accurately deduced that she had a connection with the salon. Smart girl who lived by her wits, and pretty, too. It occurred to him that she would have been an immense help with the medicine show. A girl like this, talk back to and amuse the crowd, work out a real act, one that depended on partnership instead of a crazy hit-or-miss guessing, or whatever Fey had done.

He and Maude were strolling through the brilliantly lighted rooms looking for the rest of their party when Terry thought of Fey and his resolution about her crystallized. With the decision came an unexpected thrust of pain and guilt. It was so strong and so unexpected that he stopped walking.

"Whatever's wrong?" said Maude, looking up at him and laughing. "You look very black all of a sudden."

"Nothing wrong, my beauty," he smiled at her. "This is the happiest night of my life."

"I'm going to Chicago next week," said Maude, glancing at him through lowered lids. "Got a job there at the Variety Theatre."

Terry's face showed real dismay.

Maude took a paper of rice powder from her reticule, patted her nose and cheeks delicately; the powder released a wave of heliotrope.

"There's lots of easy money in Chicago," she said. "Heaps more ways of laying hands on it than in New York, if a person's smart. Real estate's the thing there, like it used to be here. Somebody with a few hundreds could run it up in no time, if he knew where to buy and when to sell."

Terry said nothing.

"A person can have a lot of fun in Chicago," continued Maude, without special emphasis. "Free and easy, not stiff like New York."

"You don't say," said Terry.

She tilted her blonde head and, looking up into his face, gave him her knowing little smile.

When Terry returned to the house on Bleecker Street at four that morning, he found Fey fast asleep. He did not waken her. He stared for a long time at the shadowy outline of her little face in the faint grey dawn light before he turned on his back on the lumpy bed and presently slept, too.

For the next six days he was exceedingly kind to her. He left her only for a few hours each evening, and the rest of the time he devoted himself to her. She told herself that all was well at last, and she clung to him with a frantic love, studying to please him in all things, forbearing to question him, since that always annoyed him.

On the Monday morning he awoke early and got up. Her

dazed eyes watched him from the bed while he packed the carpet-bag. He clicked it shut and, fully dressed, came over to her.

She sat up slowly, pulling the ruffled nightgown around her. She pushed back her long loose hair. "Where are you going, Terry?" She exhaled her breath, waiting without motion, her eyes lambent and fixed.

"I'm pulling out, for good." He did not look at her. His voice was high and offhand. "We never meant it to last, you know." He went on faster. "Way back in Santa Fe, it was just a business arrangement. We never meant it to go on and on. I got you East where you wanted to be, didn't I? You'll be all right. Here's some money for you."

He shoved a roll of bills at her and, as she did not move to take them, he put them carefully on the table. "You can find work easy enough. You dance and sing, real well. Or you might set up for a fortune-teller, especially if that mind-reading trick of yours'll work. Lots of fortune-tellers in the city and I hear they do fine. There's one on Broadway—Madame Astra—they say makes a mint out of the business; old Commodore Vanderbilt himself goes to her."

He paused and looked at Fey for the first time directly. "Don't take it like that, honey," he said. "We've had a grand time together and I'm fonder of you than anybody else, but—"

"We're married," said Fey.

Terry's lips thinned; he glanced at the twisted gold-plated ring on her finger. "Oh," he said, in a reasonable tone, "that wasn't a real marriage, not for two Catholics or anybody else. More of a joke that was. Dozen words in a mountain shack spoke by an old Injun scout. That wasn't any marriage and you know it."

"It was to me," said Fey. She reached her hands out, clenching them on a fold in the blanket.

"It was marriage for me!" she cried, in a strangled voice. "I love you."

"Oh, sure, so do I you. You're a wonderful sweetheart, and a good kid, but you see—" Sweat suddenly beaded his forehead. This was worse than he had anticipated. He hadn't actually previsioned this scene at all. He had during the last days managed to persuade himself that Fey felt as he did. That they were simply enjoying together a graceful rounding-off of a romantic episode.

Fey shut her eyes once, opened them, and looked straight at him; at the ruddy brightness of his hair where it sprang from

110

the tanned skin on his forehead, the gold hairs on the lean plane of his cheeks, the cleft in his chin, and his mouth whose hungry warmth she knew so intimately. Last of all, she looked into his eyes. They were shuttered to her, and showed only the rueful resentment of the escaping male delayed against his will.

She got out of bed and stood leaning against the footboard; her night gown fell to her bare feet.

"Go, then," she said. Her voice was a shaft of cold light that struck across his startled face.

He pulled himself up, relief submerged by the usual baffled annoyance. One minute she claimed she loved him and the next this unwomanly coolness. If she had sobbed and thrown her arms around him, if she had begged him, perhaps—

"Go," repeated Fey. "Vaya con Dios!"

The contempt, the bitterness she put into the Spanish fare-well exploded the anger he had hoped for earlier.

"You needn't put on airs with me!" he shouted. "You've done yourself well for a little greaser wench."

He picked up the carpet-bag and his hat. He hesitated one more moment at the door. Fey said nothing; she continued to stand holding on to the footboard. He stamped out of the room. His steps dwindled to silence on the bare stairs.

Fey's hand dropped. She shut the creaking door. She walked slowly to the window and stared out at the warehouse wall. She stood at the window for a long time looking at the wall.

Toward noon Mrs. Flynn tapped perfunctorily on the door and, receiving no answer, pushed it open. She had noted Terry's early departure with the bag, and curiosity had been nagging at her for some time. Curiosity and finally anxiety as no sound came from the back bedroom. Wouldn't do to have any trouble. Never could tell what them girls mightn't do, specially foreigners. Never would do to have anything happen that would bring the perlice, she thought, with rising appre-hension, and she knew a moment of real fear as she saw Fey lying on the bed in her nightgown.

But the girl was all right, leastways right enough, for her eyes were open, and she turned her head and looked at the landlady.

"Come, there, dearie," said Mrs. Flynn, her gaze darting about the room and verifying her suspicions. "Your fancy man walk out on you? Well, don't take on. There's plenty more for a gel like you. You're young and you've got style; you ain't exactly purty, but sometimes your kind goes further with the

111

men. I don't say you'll get yourself another as good-lookin', they don't grow on every bush."

"He is my husband," said Fey.

Mrs. Flynn looked at her sharply. The girl sounded queer, desperate like, unpleasantly like a woman who'd been here last year and done a daft thing with scissors.

"Sure, he was your husband," said Mrs. Flynn soothingly. "Get up, dearie, do, and get dressed. You'll feel better."

Fey gave a peculiar little laugh. "I'm alone, you see, all alone again. Just as the bells said."

"Here, now, none of that!" cried Mrs. Flynn. "No hy-sterics, if you please." She thrust the corner of her apron into the water jug and forcibly washed Fey's face. Fey lay inert under the rough handling.

"Holy Saint Bridget," said Mrs. Flynn. "You're in the family way, ain't you?"

"Yes."

The same queer voice, like her mouth was muffled by a blanket.

Mrs. Flynn nodded. "I c'n always tell by the look around the eyes. You got to do something quick. Did you tell *him*?"

"No," said Fey, "I didn't tell him."

Mrs. Flynn was exasperated, all the more so as she felt an unwilling pity. She had seen the roll of bills on the table, and she was itching to count them. The girl didn't seem to be noticing anything, so it was possible to inch over to the money. A hundred and twenty dollars!

She abstracted a ten-dollar bill and put it in her bodice. This increased her pity for Fey and reduced the exasperation.

She turned around again. "No decent place'll take you in and I can't keep you after you begin to show; you'll never get no place anyways with a brat around." She lowered her voice to a sibilant whisper. "You've got to get rid of it—like many another's done."

Fey raised her lids and looked at the woman. "Get rid of it?"

"Sure," said Mrs. Flynn, still whispering. "Plenty of places'd do it, but they're kind of risky, it don't turn out so good. You got money enough to go to the best. Wait a bit, I'll show you."

She went out, and Fey heard her dragging steps descend the stairs.

After awhile she came back and forced a newspaper clipping into the girl's limp hand. "Read it, dearie," she urged. "Madame Restell's! That's the place for you. The great house on Fifth

Avenue she's got, and the foine ladies what go to her when they've had a bit of a slip, you might say. Thousands a day she makes, and perlice can't touch her no more, though they've had many a whack at it. I'll warrant she'd do you for fifty dollars, it being so early, and you looking almost like a lady and all."

Fey's eyes travelled vaguely down the cleverly written advertisement. It mentioned "medicine for distressed young wives" and "procedures for curing unhealthful delay," and its meaning was plain enough.

There had been a woman like this in the Barrio Analco. Juana La Vieja, she was called. She knew a great many curious herbs and other things, too. Sometimes women went to her stealthily, padding at night along the dusty footpath, their faces completely hidden by the rebozo.

The clipping fluttered from her fingers and, caught by the draught, fell on the dirty carpet.

Mrs. Flynn was annoyed. Trying to help the fool girl out of her trouble, and not a word of gratitude or interest. Laying there like a dummy, gawking out the winder like she was alone in the room.

Mrs. Flynn thought of leaving, but she sat down on the bed instead. Anything was better than the heap of dirty dishes and sour diapers which awaited her attention in the basement kitchen, and the baby, praise be, was quiet in his cradle downstairs for the moment.

"Wished I'd had someone'd give me a bit of smart advice twelve year back when I was first caught with Timmy," she said. "I was a right purty gel then myself, could've gone places mebbe in the concert saloons. You gotta pull yourself together, dearie," she went on. "He's left you alone like you said, and you gotta *make* your way alone. You don't want no handicaps."

"You gotta make your way alone." The thin, sharp voice, spiralling through the room like a spring coil. And what is my way? There was love and Terry like a thicket of white mountain aspens with murmuring golden leaves, the trunks so close you couldn't get out of the thicket. The leaves were gold, but not from the sun. The trees were too close together for the sun to shine through, or the turquoise sky.

Fey sat up; she glared at the startled Mrs. Flynn. "Let me be!" she said violently. "He's my husband, I tell you, and he'll be back."

"Oh, no, he wont!" Mrs. Flynn tossed her head, nettled by Fey's tone, but gratified to have elicited some response. "I know his kind like I know the back of me hand. He's gone off with another gel. I seen him with her oncet last week coming out the Hoffman House."

Fey made a sound.

"Oh, yes, me dear," said Mrs. Flynn, with a blend of malice and contemptuous pity. "Big blonde, she was, and a su-perb bosom, though mebbe 'twas padded—they was a-holding hands all lovey-dovey. She'd a hot brassy look. She's not the one to get herself into your fix, not her!"

Mrs. Flynn stood up, smoothed out her stained apron, and unbuttoned the top of her straining bodice. "Me milk's coming in," she said, "and there's that brat beginning to yell punctual like he knew. 'Tis the woman who pays, dearie, like they say in the theeayter, and I'm sorry for you. That's why I'm a-telling you how to get out of your trouble."

"Go away! Leave me alone!"

The landlady bridled again, her slack mouth set. Of all the thankless— and then she encountered Fey's eyes. They were brilliant and fixed on the woman's face; strength was behind them and command so powerful that Mrs. Flynn gasped. The little thing on the bed, a gel in trouble, speaking and looking like a countess. Mrs. Flynn had never seen a countess, but she accurately judged Fey's expression.

It was the product of two ancestral lines equally accustomed to obedience, equally resentful of indignity, and though Mrs. Flynn's own ancestry had never encountered either Spanish grandee or Highland chieftain, she responded quickly. She muttered, "Yes, mum," which later annoyed her very much, and scuttled from the room.

Fey got off the bed, washed, carefully brushed and coiled her hair, then she put on the red plaid dress Terry had given her. She had no other. While she performed these mechanical tasks, a voice spoke in her head. It used neither the new English she had learned, nor the Spanish. It spoke in the language of her early childhood. Ah, there, Fey, it said, dinna fash yoursel' because your man has left you. It has happened to many, my lass; did you think you were different? You were different, maybe, you had "the sight," but 'tis gone too. There's naught to help you in the whole wide world but yoursel'. 'Tis strong you must be, lassie, no longer soft and whimpering. Strong. Hard and strong as rock.

Wi' strength you can get the things you want, the dear bonnie things you've never had. The soft clean linen, the bright gowns, and the horse and carriage of your own. 'Tis maybe a man'll get them for you, lassie. A man you dinna love, so you

114

may rule. For love is a craven, hapless thing that makes one servant. For you no more love, and no fruit of love to hamper. The woman was right—the base meddling woman was right.

The voice spoke like this in Fey's head. When her hat was on, she put the money, still uncounted, in her purse, then she leaned over and picked Madame Restell's advertisement off the rug. She put that also in her purse. Outside in the street, she pulled off the twisted brass wedding ring and dropped it in the gutter.

She walked from the lodging-house in Bleecker Street, up Broadway to Madison Square, and then up Fifth Avenue. She walked very fast, but with a jerky movement. Passers-by stared at her. Her mouth was indrawn, her face so white and tense as to be shocking against the garish red of her bonnet. Above Forty-Second Street the monotonous line of brownstone stoops thinned out; there were many vacant lots. Fey walked steadily on. The house on Fifth Avenue she sought was at Fiftieth Street. She raised her eyes only to glance at the street signs.

It was late afternoon when she reached Fiftieth Street. Ahead on the right there was a solitary brownstone house looming five stories high above vacant lots, for no one would build near Madame Restell's infamous mansion. It stood alone. Fey walked faster. At each window were crimson brocaded shades like red eyelids; through the corner window there was a glimpse of Parian marble and a shimmering cut-glass gasolier.

At the foot of the brownstone steps, Fey stopped. She looked up at the glass front door, and behind the Brussels lace curtain a face peered and went away. Fey put her foot on the bottom step, and in so doing she turned a little. She saw an unfinished building in the next block. She had passed it without noticing it, but now there was a familiarity in its outline. She stared at the rough grey stone, and the scaffolding which hid part of it, at the low towers not yet topped by spires. Her heart gave a slow, sideways lurch. There was a thickening and pressure in her chest as though she were afraid. The fear was not in her head, just in her chest. A workman came by, on the sidewalk, whistling and swinging his lunch-pail.

"What is that building?" said Fey, pointing. She spoke in a whisper, and for a moment the man did not understand her.

"That'll be Saint Patrick's Cathedral, miss," he said. "And when it's finished, it'll be the finest church in all the States." He glanced sharply at Fey, up at the brownstone house behind her, spat explosively on the step by her skirt, and walked on.

"The Parroquia," said Fey. The thickness and pressure in her

115

chest turned to cold pain. She began to move toward the cathedral. She walked now as one who walks through water, each step dragged forward in struggle.

She saw that a small side door was open. "Only for a moment," she said to the protesting voice. She slid through the door into a vast dimness. From behind the chancel came the faint tap of hammering. She stood looking, and the darkness cleared. There seemed no limits to the great empty cathedral, its magnificent forest of marble piers glimmered endlessly into shadowy space. She moved between them and her hushed feet made no noise on the marble floor.

The distant hammering stopped, and silence like the silence of the Sangre de Christos at dawn filled the cathedral.

She fell to her knees on the lowest step which would lead up to the High Altar. There was nothing there now, but her straining eyes saw it as it would be. She saw the golden cross and the white figures of priests. She heard their voices and the answering hum of the worshipping multitude behind. She smelled the delicate odour of wax and incense. She felt the vibrations of music, rolling like a many-coloured river, resounding from the vaulted grey stone high above.

"It will be beautiful," she whispered.

She knelt there, and the unfinished cathedral spoke in her heart. Unfinished. Only begun. But *it* would go on building, until, completed and glorious, it fulfilled the purpose for which it had been conceived. No vandal would destroy *it*, no gigantic ruthless hand stay its courageous growth.

The warm pool crept from her heart to her eyes. She turned her head and gazed fearfully into the left transept where La Conquistadora, Our Lady of Victory, had stood in the Parroquia. She did not see the Blessed Lady in any of her forms. She saw instead the remembered image of the Santo Niño, the little Christ Child of Chimayo. She saw him as she had seen him represented a hundred times in the Analco—holding his cotton gown up from his bare feet, his small face puckered in tenderness and concern as he wandered the muddy roads on his errands of mercy.

"Perdoneme!" she cried to Him. She rested her forehead on the cold step.

After a while she rose. She went out through the small door and on to Fifth Avenue. She began to walk back toward Bleecker Street.

9

FEY returned to the back room at Mrs. Flynn's and existed for two days in a hazy trance-like state. She was neither happy nor unhappy. No emotion coloured the numbness, and she slept almost continuously.

She awoke on the third morning to find that she was achingly hungry, and that her mind presented her with a cool practical diagram of her problem. She must have food and she must have work.

Of Terry she did not think at all. Sometime during those two days an iron door had clanged shut upon the past. She felt the hardness and the coldness of metal in her mind like actual iron. She welcomed it and turned her back on it, trusting in its strength.

She went down to the basement to Mrs. Flynn, who received her frigidly, knowing that her advice had not been taken. "And what would you be wanting, *Mrs.* Dillon?" said the landlady, twitching her shoulder and rattling pots.

Fey put a dollar bill on the table. "I need food—will you buy some? I'll cook it myself."

The woman took the dollar. "You look bad," she said, more amiably. "Ten year older, I do believe, and you'll be worse afore you're through. If you hadn't been so pig-headed—"

"We won't talk about it, I think," said Fey, her eyes glinting. There she goes again—the countess—thought Mrs. Flynn, but she felt a grudging respect. She put on her bonnet and shawl and went out to buy food while Fey sat in the kitchen and watched the sour, puny baby in his cradle. Mine won't be like that, she thought. Mine will have the best there is from the beginning, and I shall get it for him.

"What will you be doing now with yourself?" questioned the landlady after Fey had eaten. Curiosity had again conquered her resentment.

"Look for work," said Fey. "I can work for maybe six months."

Mrs. Flynn cocked her sardonic eye. "What kind of work; are you skilled?"

"You mentioned the concert saloons. I've seen them on the Bowery. I can sing a bit, wait on table."

"They're not for the likes of you!" cried Mrs. Flynn, genuinely horrified. "Them's mostly fancy gels; their job's to get the men to buy drinks."

"I could do that," said Fey.

"But in your condition!" protested the woman. " 'Twouldn't do!"

"No one will know my condition, and I can take care of myself."

Mrs. Flynn stared at the small pale face. The full mouth was set, the grey eyes were steady and calm. Bedad, but mebbe she can at that, thought the woman. She's a deep one, and yet I'm still sorry for her. You can't get around it that she's a gel in trouble whose man's walked out on her.

"You'd best go in to service, dearie. 'Twould be easier in some good place—though why I'm bothering to give you advice again I wouldn't be knowing."

"I know you mean to help," said Fey. "I might go into service, but I think I can earn more in a concert saloon until I find something better. I want money."

Mrs. Flynn gave a raucous snort. "And what will you be doing when your time comes, money or no money? I'll have no brats birthed here in my house."

"No," said Fey. "I think I shall go to a hospital."

"Horspital!" screamed Mrs. Flynn. "Now I know you're out of your head. They kill you in them places; you never come out but feet first. Whoever heard of birthing a baby in the horspital!"

Who, indeed? thought Fey; no one in New Mexico, no one whom she had ever known, and for a moment her new composure was shaken. Last week in that different life which was gone for ever, she and Terry had been walking down Second Avenue. She had noticed a small building near the corner of Seventh Street. There had been a sign, "New York Infirmary for Women and Children," and underneath, "Doctor Elizabeth Blackwell and Doctor Emily Blackwell, Directors."

Terry had been humorous at the expense of women doctors, and for Fey the small brown building had had little interest then. It was just now in talking to Mrs. Flynn that the idea had come to her with the force of inner command. She did not know whether a baby might be born there, she knew nothing about it, but the thought of the building brought comfort and

118

certainty. She said no more about it to Mrs. Flynn. She listened quietly to the landlady's spate of words.

After a while she went out to Broadway with her purse in her hand. She found a small cheap shop not far from A. T. Stewart's magnificent dry goods store on Eighth Street. Here she bought a black skirt, a white lace shawl, high comb, and coral lip salve. She also bought a red silk rose imported from Paris and this cost more than all the rest put together. She took these home and laying them on the bed stared at them. Then she packed them all in a small box, and holding it under her arm she went downstairs.

As she passed the areaway, Mrs. Flynn hung out of the basement window. "If you're looking for work," she called, "the Louvre and Oriental on Broadway and the Arcadia on the Bowery's the most respectable."

"Thank you," said Fey, turning and nodding gravely.

They'll never take her, thought Mrs. Flynn; she ain't got the looks or the come-hither for that work.

Mrs. Flynn opinion was shared by the doormen at the Louvre and the Oriental. Neither would let her get near the manager. Fey trudged on doggedly back to the Bowery and down to Grand Street. Here at the dingy gilt entrance to the Arcadia, she stood a moment and collected herself.

She lifted her chin and walked into the nearly deserted hall. It was afternoon, and the Arcadia did not open for business until six. She pushed her way amongst the beer-stained tables. A bored bartender in shirt-sleeves, called, "Whatcher want, girlie?"

"The manager," said Fey.

The bartender hunched a shoulder toward a fat man on the stage.

"That's him."

Fey mounted the two steps to the stage and moved with her peculiarly graceful gliding walk toward the fat man. He watched her morosely, drumming his fingers on the piano top.

"I want to work here as a waiter-girl," said Fey, without preliminary.

"Not the type," said the manager, equally brief. He went on drumming at the piano.

"Wait," said Fey. She threw her cloak on to the piano, flung off her bonnet, and opened her box. The manager watched in mild astonishment. She thrust the high comb into her hair and threw over that the white lace shawl and tucked the red rose low on her neck. She drew a deep breath and resting her hands

119

on her hips, she drooped her eyelids and smiled up into the startled face. "I'm Spanish," she said. "Frasquita Gomez is my name. I can sing Spanish songs and"—she hesitated—"dance a little."

A gleam came into the fat man's lack-lustre eye. Like a conjuring trick that was. Nothing at all when she come in, nondescript; then all of a sudden she wraps a white scarf around her head and smiles and you've got as fetching a little piece as you could find anywhere. Fine eyes and hair. Big mouth, but passionate-like. Good ankles.

"Let's hear you sing," he said.

"Is there a guitar?"

"Sure—we got a full dancing or-chestra. Hey, Joe—bring out a guitar from the back!"

Fey accompanied herself with a few simple chords she knew. She sang a gay New Mexican "Indita" and she sang "La Golondrina." While she sang, she was nearly overpowered by a sudden lacerating homesickness. This gave her husky voice a poignancy and appeal which decided the manager. The customers wouldn't understand a word she sang, but she would be a novelty.

Nobody'd ever had a Spanish waiter-girl; mostly they were harps or kicks off the farms. The Louvre had a girl was supposed to come from Paris, and now the Arcadia would have a Spaniard.

"Can you start tonight?" he said.

Fey nodded.

"Ten dollars a week and your commissions from the drinks you can talk 'em into. We pay good here. You can go home with the customers if you want to make a little extra, that's your business. But keep it clean and respectable on the premises. We're a high-class place.'"

"Yes," said Fey. "I understand."

Fey worked through the winter at the Arcadia Concert Saloon. She was not popular with the other girls, nor very successful with the customers, whom she continually disappointed. While she sang, wandering from table to table strumming her guitar and smiling, she diffused sex magnetism, and she titillated the goggling out-of-towners who comprised three-quarters of the Arcadias patronage. But later, in her other job of waitress, she was less alluring. She took orders, and transported steins of beer and glasses of raw whisky from the bar to the tables, and she dutifully sat down with those who in-

120

vited her. But she was subtly, very tactfully unapproachable. This was easier because she pretended to speak no English, and met all invitations and proposals with a faintly smiling silence. Usually it took no longer than the first drink for the customer to begin to wonder why he had even thought her pretty, and by the second he would have summoned another waiter-girl. Her commissions were, therefore, small, but the manager kept her on. She gave class to the place, she was different, and she was a modest attraction. Sometimes a party of swells from uptown would come slumming at the Arcadia and they applauded Frasquita Gomez far more vigorously than did the regular patrons.

The Arcadia was thus patronized one cold February night two weeks after Fey's eighteenth birthday. The day itself had passed as uneventfully as did all her days. She slept until nine, then went down to Mrs. Flynn's kitchen and made her own breakfast. She seldom saw her landlady now, as Mrs. Flynn had discovered a crony in a dilapidated ballet girl on the top floor and had lost interest in Fey.

Fey spent the greater part of her days in reading. She haunted a small bookstore on Broadway where Mr. Tibbins, the proprietor, took an interest in her and often lent her books to take home. He soon understood that it was a programme of self-education which she wished, and, flattered by her eager attention to anything he recommended, he guided her through those classics which appealed to him personally. In this way she consumed some of Shakespeare, in an abridged and expurgated edition, Pope's translation of the *Iliad*, and Longfellow's newly published *Dante*.

She read *Snowbound* and *The Vision of Sir Launfal* and *The House of the Seven Gables*—Mr. Tibbins did not approve of *The Scarlet Letter*; she read several works by Mrs. Sedgwick and Fanny Fern; she read *David Copperfield* and *The Bride's Tragic Secret*, each with the same devouring speed. Mr. Tibbins soon realized that there was quest beneath all these feverish gulping of pages, interest stronger than desire for knowledge. Her imagination seemed to be captured by what one might call "success stories," in any character who achieved success despite material handicaps. Too, she soon depleted his scanty stock of books about New York. "I want to understand this city," she told Mr. Tibbins in one of her rare explanations. "I want to know what those people who live in the big houses think about, what they wear and what they do." To this end she also bought newspapers and magazines and read them with equal concentration, her purpose no less intense for being un-formulated. This was preparation, and when the time came she would be ready.

On the whole, poetry bored her, and most of the novels did, too. She enjoyed the story in them, but each time as she achieved the last page there was disappointment. The people were not real; at no point did they talk or behave in any way familiar to her, and for most of Mr. Tibbins's preferred heroes and heroines she felt contempt. They got themselves into trouble and they lay down under it, whining noble sentiments and suffering, until a hazy thing called "Heaven" or "the state of grace" or even just "Providence" pitied and extricated them.

However, for weeks, humbled by her own ignorance, she docilely followed Mr. Tibbins's guidance. It was in the back of the store on a corner shelf that she unearthed a book which did not whine or bore her. Its words, rhythm, and thought seemed to strike lightning into her heart and find there an answering flash.

She opened first at a short stanza—"Quicksand years that whirl me I know not whither," and she read on,

> *"One's-self must never give way—that is the final substance*
> *—that out of all is sure,*
> *Out of politics, triumphs, battles, life, what at last finally*
> *remains?*
> *When shows break up what but One's-Self is sure?"*

Fey breathed sharply. *That's* what I mean, she thought. She pulled the high stool back from the shelves, so that the dusty sunlight from the window might fall on it. She crouched over the book, her heart beating fast.

Mr. Tibbins, at length noting her absorption, finished a sale and walked back to inquire what she had found. She looked up and showed him the title, *Leaves of Grass*.

"This is for me," she said, her eyes shining. "This man understands."

Mr. Tibbins had flushed a dull red. "That's not a proper book for a young woman to read!"

"Oh, but it is!" said Fey, hardly conscious of him. "It's true and good. It makes me strong." And her rapt eyes re-read a page.

> *"Be not ashamed, women, your privilege encloses the rest,*
> *and is the exit of the rest,*

*You are the gates of the body, and you are the gates of the
        soul.
The female contains all qualities and tempers them . . .
She is to conceive daughters as well as sons, and sons as well
        as daughters."*

Fey read this, and deep within her she felt the stirring and
fluttering of the new life which was forming. It had no reality
yet. She could not imagine it as a separate being. But this book
seemed to give it meaning and dignity.

Mr. Tibbins, scowling, peered over Fey's shoulder, then retreated sharply. "I Sing the Body Electric," the girl was reading, one of the very worst in the book. The flush ran up into
his sparse grizzled hair. Could it be that this young woman was
not a proper female at all, and he had been most indiscreet to
give her so much attention? After all, he knew nothing about
her. And somehow he had never mentioned her to Mrs. Tibbins. This sudden remembrance gave him new discomfort.

He cleared his throat harshly. "That's an immoral book—
it's disgusting—and not poetry either!"

Fey looked up astonished. The little man was purple and
quivering, above his mutton-chop whiskers his lips were indrawn to a pallid line.

"I think it's beautiful," she said, oblivious to his horrified
glare, and, turning the page to "One Hour to Madness and
Joy," she added, "I want to buy it. I hope I have enough
money."

He bent over and snatched the book from her hands. "It's
not for sale. I'm sending it back!" And he hid it behind him.

Fey was puzzled and hurt. All through these months Mr.
Tibbins had been her one friend. He had helped her and she
needed him. The blurred smoke-hazed evenings in the Arcadia
Concert Saloon, the drab hours in her room at Mrs. Flynn's,
would not have been endurable without Mr. Tibbins and his
books. There had been nothing personal between them—she
had not thought of him as a man. She saw now that she must
do so if she were not to lose all the books.

She got off the stool and gave him a sideways, pleading, and
immensely flattering smile. "Perhaps you're right," she said.
"I don't know anything—except what you've taught me, and
I'm grateful."

Mr. Tibbins, caught by her magnetism as men always were
when she chose to use it, took an involuntary step toward her.
He checked his hand before it touched her, and said coldly,

"It's my business to know books—" He sent her home that day with a volume of Mead's *Sermons*, and *Nosegays from the Garden of Piety*, both of which presentations of the Christian life as a timorous morality Fey dutifully ploughed through in a vague bewilderment.

Mr. Tibbins had no idea that his protégée was married, since she told him nothing whatsoever about herself. He assumed that she was a governess; this fitted her air of quiet refinement and the faintly foreign intonation in her speech. After the *Leaves of Grass* episode and that flash of provocative awareness which he had seen, he had been disturbed. He began to dream about her, and awaken to stare resentfully at the mountainous form of Mrs. Tibbins beside him in the walnut bed.

To this Fey was oblivious. Like all pregnant women, she was caught up by a different life rhythm. No day had separate meaning in itself, but only as it marked inexorable progress toward the month of June. Her health was perfect. Her eighteen-year-old body, early trained to hardship and endurance, silently adjusted itself to its natural burden. Her mind had not the knowledge to initiate fears which might trouble that body's own exquisite adjustment. In the Barrio Analco, pregnancy had been as usual as any other of Life's stages, childhood or senility, and one accepted it as matter-of-factly.

She never returned to the unfinished cathedral, but on Sundays she went around the corner to Mass, and sometimes to confession. She felt no sympathy with the Irish priest; in the new and garish little church she experienced no mystical joy nor guidance; but the observance of her faith gave her a mild comfort.

And then on that February night in the Arcadia her uniformed purpose and preparation found a goal.

All day a soft snow had been falling and melting on the streets, the lazy flakes drifting down like feathers. By evening the flakes no longer melted; they merged to form a thin glassy sheet over the sidewalks and cobblestones. Though it was Saturday night the Arcadia was only half-filled. The musicians played "You Naughty, Naughty Men" from the *Black Crook* in a dragging and dispirited manner. No one applauded. Most of the waiter-girls, including Fey, sat in a doleful row beneath the stage, their services unsummoned. The manager bit his fingernails and wondered gloomily whether it was wise to renew the contract with the Alabama Minstrel Show which was preparing to go on. They were class, a real high-toned act, but it would be cheaper to get a couple of girls in tights. Let 'em wiggle around and kick their legs; that was good enough for this kind of crowd.

The Bowery entrance door opened and a large party came in, bringing with them a surge of perfume, the swish of taffetas and trills of self-conscious laughter. A short, stocky blond man in a black opera cape preceded the rest down the aisle between the tables.

The manager jumped and lumbered down off the stage, his face beaming. "Mr. Tower," he cried, his voice loud enough to inform all the other apathetic patrons of their good fortune. "Mr. Simeon Tower," he repeated, "this is indeed an honour."

A thrill ran through the line of waiter-girls. They straightened and pulled up their skirts to the professionally seductive level. They arched their bosoms and curved their lips. "Gawd," said the girl next to Fey, "look wot the wind blew in. He must've got sick of his champagne and his gold plates and his pattee de foy grass uptown. Gawd, he don't look so much," she added after avid inspection. "They say he's most as rich as Vanderbilt, but he don't look different from any other swell. He's not married, though—chance for us, maybe," said the waiter-girl, heavily sarcastic and digging a sharp little elbow into Fey's ribs.

Fey did not respond. She had drawn into a listening stillness; her grey eyes were fixed on Simeon Tower's unconscious face.

The other girl gave a disgusted shrug and subsided. Nasty stuck-up piece the Spanish girl was, hardly give you the time of day.

Simeon Tower, said Fey silently. I wonder— She inspected him very carefully. There was no hurry. She saw a well-fed man in the late thirties, whose blond hair was thinning a trifle, and whose pale moustache was clipped and disciplined above a smiling mouth. He radiated a surface geniality; there were laughter lines around his small shrewd eyes, an expansiveness in the gestures he made with his well-kept hands. The nails, she saw, were shiny and pink, there was a large diamond ring on his middle finger. His shirt studs were huge black pearls, and his stickpin was of diamonds and pearls. Everything about his dress was discreetly ornate, and this rich sparkle was reflected in his manner.

But I don't believe he's like that at all inside, thought Fey. She looked at his hands again, no longer seeing the pink shiny nails and the diamond. The hands were square and powerful, blunt workman's hands, and yet the fingers were sensitive and unquiet. When he laid his right hand on the table beside his plate, the fingers seemed to shrink a little from the rough table-cloth. Fey raised her intent gaze to his face. He was smiling at the eager befrilled young woman beside him, a suggestive smile gay and pursuing, but his eyes did not smile. They were cynically remote, and behind the blue irises she saw power and something else—a curious frustration.

Why does he pretend? thought Fey, and yet she was not really puzzled. From that first moment when he walked through the door, she had felt an interior assurance. Here was a man whose surface was transparent for her. In dispassionate calmness she might understand him, there would be few surprises, no matter how cleverly he concealed the secret springs.

She withdrew her gaze and considered now what she knew of him. The mention by Terry in the wagon at Fort Union, and mention in the newspapers and magazines she had read. "Simeon Tower acquires the Transic Steamship Line." "A visit to Mr. Simeon Tower's Historical Gem Collection."

The name had meant no more to her than any other, but now she remembered everything she had read of him. She watched him again, seeing that he devoted himself rather jerkily first to one young lady then another, and that they—vying with each other for his attention and resorting to rather frantic coquetry—displeased him, though he patted their plump hands, sipped from their wineglasses, and once rested his own hand on a satin-clad knee.

"Hey, Spanish," hissed the manager, coming over to her, "get up and sing—what d'ye think I'm paying you for?"

Fey hesitated. She did not dare jeopardize her job, but far more important would be the danger of Tower's recognizing her later as an Arcadia waiter-girl. She had no idea how or when the "later" was to be arranged, but it would be. For I shall make it happen, she thought, when the time comes.

She threw the end of the white lace shawl across her face and pinned it to the red rose. Now only her eyes showed.

"Tell them it is a Spanish custom, they won't know," she said indifferently in answer to the manager's protest.

She borrowed the guitar and followed the manager.

"Special attraction, Mr. Tower," the man whispered. "Spanish girl, very high-born, covers her face like a Turk so she won't feel ashamed singing before men."

"Indeed," said Tower. "How extremely quaint! I never heard that S-Spaniards were famous for their modesty with men." He crossed his legs and showed his strong blunt teeth.

The ladies tittered appreciatively.

Fey was standing close to him, waiting. In this first remark which she had heard him make she noted several things. His voice was harsher than she had expected and there was a suggestion of a stammer. She saw also that he was already bored with the impulse which had led him to take his party to such a place as the Arcadia. He would gather them all up soon and move on, and she did not wish to keep him. She sang her Spanish songs without much conviction, and her voice lacked its usual appeal. When she finished, there was only a feeble spatter of applause.

"Can't you sing something in English?" said Simeon, without interest while he motioned for the check.

Fey looked directly at him and shook her head. "No ahora," she said. "Un día cantaré por te solamente."

For an instant Tower was startled, not by her words which he took to be a conventional murmur of regret, but by the expression of her eyes. They were clear as grey water touched by sparkles of light and they rested on his face in greeting and intimacy. She lowered her lids at once and walked back to the stools by the stage.

Simeon Tower frowned. He was annoyed by happenings which he did not understand. Usually he focused all his power of concentration on such happenings until he did understand them and had reduced them to the commonplace. This incident of a look from a Bowery waiter-girl was too trivial.

He laughed a hearty, booming laugh, said, "This place is dull, let's try the Oriental next," and paid the check liberally.

Fey glided over to the front windows and watched the party get into the waiting carriage. She watched the square bulky figure hand the ladies politely inside; his motions were quick and a trifle awkward, like a machine run by imperfectly controlled power. She heard again his booming, unmirthful laugh. She saw his carriage start. It was a maroon brougham with yellow wheels; there was both a coachman and footman on the box, and before them two cream-coloured horses slipping and straining on the ice. She watched the brougham until it disappeared.

10

In April, Fey left the Arcadia Concert Saloon. She could no longer hide her condition, but she had managed to support herself all winter and save twenty-eight dollars for the baby. She had barely touched the sum Terry had left her. She had rolled it up in a muslin bag and hidden it in a crevice beneath the washstand, and for that little muslin bag she felt a sharp hostility. In all other ways the dingy room had become hers without reminder of the past.

There were no more visits to Mr. Tibbins's Book Store, because there had been a dreadful scene when that gentleman saw her one day with her cloak thrown open and her distorted figure unmistakable. He had turned on his *protégée* all the venom of outraged virtue and unsatisfied desire.

So Fey read the newspapers, and was several times rewarded by items mentioning Simeon Tower. She tried without much success to understand the stock market, gold speculation, and the Erie War, because his name was associated with these. Once he was denounced in an editorial and once given fulsome praise because he had endowed an orphanage on Staten Island.

One afternoon she walked uptown to look at the outside of his house at Twenty-Ninth Street and Fifth Avenue. From Washington Square to Alexander Stewart's marble palace at Thirty-Fourth Street, there were many huge mansions on the avenue, and Fey was for a moment disappointed that the massive Tower brownstone was not bigger than any of them, nor did she think it attractive. She was not yet accustomed to the inevitable brownstone facing lavishly ornamented with Italian iron grille work and Greek cornices, nor to windows particoloured by lozenge-shaped stained glass in sulphurous yellows and magenta. It was, however, an impressive mansion surrounded by wide strips of grass, and it occupied nearly half the block.

She continued to stare at it from the sidewalk, noting every detail; the high stoop on which stood a pink alabaster urn filled with hydrangeas, the gold-fringed draperies at a first-floor window, the cast-iron stag coyly peering from behind a rhododendron in the south-west corner of the lawn.

As Fey was turning to leave, she saw a plump young woman approach from Fifth Avenue. She had fair ringlets and a high colour, and she was well but not fashionably dressed in a striped taffeta edged with sealskin. There was something bouncing and good-natured and common about her. There was also an indecision, almost a furtiveness.

Fey drew back behind one of the ailanthus trees which shaded the sidewalk and watched the woman pause before the Tower mansion. She looked up at it, then down at an envelope which she twisted nervously in her hands. Then, having apparently renewed her courage, she walked very fast up the path and rang the doorbell. The door was opened by a butler, who received the note and shut the door. The woman returned down the path, her steps dragging. Fey had a full view of her face. There were tears in the big vapid eyes, and as she reached the sidewalk she looked back toward two large windows on the second floor and her face twisted in yearning. "I hope he don't mind, this once," she whispered. Fey heard her distinctly. So—she thought, and with a painful interest she watched the woman walk down the street.

After a moment Fey went, too. She was not disturbed. There would be a woman like that in his life, of course. In Santa Fe all the ricos, the caballeros, had women like this. Poor thing, thought Fey, and dismissed her. It made no difference.

She strolled down the avenue, adjusting her steps to their added burden, unconscious of the outraged stares from fashionable ladies. Women in that condition did not appear in public.

Fey breathed in the spring sunshine, and the pungent smell of geraniums from the window-boxes. She was content to wait, as she must wait.

On an afternoon in May, Fey went to 126 Second Avenue, the "New York Infirmary for Women and Children," to make inquiry. The three-story house was old and dingy outside, but the partitioned rooms and scrubbed halls inside reflected the far-seeing progressiveness of the two intrepid sisters who had braved public censure and masculine scorn, not only to found this little hospital and training school, but by harrying a reluctant faculty into letting them become physicians at all. Doctor Elizabeth Blackwell had been the pioneer twenty years ago, and since then a hundred other women had followed the trail she had blazed. Three of these were attached as residents to the New York Infirmary, besides Doctor Emily Blackwell, who had taken over the administrative burden since her sister was crusading in England.

Doctor Rachel Moreton was in temporary charge of the dispensary on the May day when Fey dragged her increasingly heavy body up the stone steps and into the first cubicle beside the door. There were no other patients waiting, and Fey suffered a spasm of nervousness as she walked to the cheap pine desk behind which a woman sat and wrote upon a pad.

"Yes?" said Doctor Rachel Moreton encouragingly, putting down her pen and looking up at the silent girl.

"I—" began Fey. She moved a step toward the desk, staring "Are you a doctor?" she said.

Rachel Moreton smiled; she was used to this. "Yes, indeed I am. Many women are now, you know." Her serene eyes examined the girl; they softened to quick sympathy as she saw what the trouble was. "Do sit down," she said gently. "Please don't be frightened."

"No," said Fey, on a soft breath, "I'm not. But the sun is shining on your face. You're beautiful. I think it's you that I came here to find."

"My dear child—what a lovely thing to say!" The doctor laughed, examining again the small square face, drawn and pale beneath an ugly red-plush shawl, but lit by brilliantly grey eyes.

"I'm anything but beautiful, I fear," the doctor added, "but I'd like to help you. I'm so glad you came to us."

It was the keynote of Rachel Moreton's character—the wish to help, and besides that there was an all-embracing tolerance not incompatible with occasional sharp irritation which she struggled to control, and she lived by a practical mysticism which belonged to her faith, for she was a Quaker.

She was forty-three, a big rawboned woman; silver-rimmed spectacles aided her far-sighted eyes and made a ridge across the top of the aquiline nose, and her wiry brown hair was already streaked with grey. She was indeed anything but beautiful by ordinary standards, but Fey had seen deeper to a true loveliness of spirit, and to her Rachel was always beautiful, imbued by the calm grandeur of mountains and rocks.

"*Do* sit down," said Rachel, again laughing, for like all wise people she was often amused, and the whole-souled admiration she saw in the unknown girl's face touched her.

"My dear, I'm a very ordinary doctor; don't stare at me like that, but tell me all about yourself."

"Yes, I think to you I could," said Fey, earnestly leaning forward. "Would you listen?"

Rachel saw that there was appeal in this, a call that went deeper than the need for physical advice. She saw now, too, that this was not one of the little immigrant girls from over by the river as she had first thought. There was something unusual about this young woman, something compelling. Surely hers would not be just the ordinary story of seduction. And yet, thought Rachel sadly, is it ever ordinary? Is it not always for a little while a glory and a brightness, no matter how tawdry it seems to us who try to mend the broken pieces

"Wait until the dispensary hour is over then," she said to Fey. "I'll make you some tea, and we can talk."

Rachel Moreton's little sitting-room next to the six-bedded ward was more plainly furnished and cleaner than any room Fey had seen since leaving Santa Fe. It was not austere, for there were blue chintz curtains at the windows and two good landscapes on the walls. But it was a simple and serene room like its owner. She made the tea on a gas-ring and poured it into two thin white porcelain cups.

"They're plain," she said, seeing Fey look at the cups, "but good china. You see I'm a Quaker and the Friends like good things, but we don't believe in much ornament." She spoke entirely from tact to allow the girl to orient herself, but to her surprise Fey considered this carefully.

"Yes, plain usually, but good is the way it was in the fine homes—back where I come from," said Fey. She looked at Rachel's neat brown bombazine edged at neck and wrist by immaculate white ruching. "You do not, I think, like *my* dress," added Fey ruefully. "It is neither plain nor good," and suddenly she smiled, making a little gesture of disgust at the red plaid dress with the cherry trim.

Rachel smiled too. "Then why do you wear it?"

"Because," said Fey, "I must save every penny for the baby. But it fits no more. See I have had to let out and patch."

"Ah," said Rachel soberly. "Forgive me—but are you married, my dear?"

Fey turned her head a little. Her mobile face became older and harder, the animation and the touch of humour left it. Rachel watching felt pity. She was drawn to the girl, and she had seen this reaction many times before to that question. But the answer surprised her as Fey was often to surprise her.

"My baby is not a bastard," Fey said.

Rachel, accustomed as she was to the East Side slums, flushed at the word so calmly spoken, so incongruous in that low voice.

131

"You mean that you are married?"

"I mean that I was married to him, but not he to me, it seems," said Fey.

Rachel's thick eyebrows contracted. She leaned forward and put her large capable hand on the girl's arm. "You're too young to be so wise and so bitter. Tell me about it—"

Fey stayed with her new friend throughout that soft May afternoon. There were interruptions; several times the doctor went downstairs to see patients, twice she visited an old German woman who was recovering from pneumonia in the nearby ward.

These absences did not disconcert Fey, nor break the mood of peace and security. She could and did talk to Rachel as she had never talked to anyone, for the doctor had the gift of listening calmly, sympathetically, and without astonishment.

Rachel Moreton had had an unusually broad experience. She had been born in Philadelphia to cultured, wealthy Quakers who had given her a far more advanced education than was customary. She had travelled in Europe, and been happily married for ten years until her husband died. After the first shock of this loss she had faced life with courage and altruism and, making use of a natural talent for healing and superior intelligence, had at the age of thirty-five entered the Philadelphia Medical College for Women. After graduation she had been attracted by the opportunities for services offered by the struggling little New York Infirmary founded by Quaker women like herself. Now at forty-three she was a great physician, for she combined technical skill and intuition; had she been a man, her name would have been known from the Atlantic to the Mississippi, but she had no personal ambition. She was content to do her best in the only field so far opened to her sex—the treatment of women and small children from districts so destitute that they never dared aspire to the services of a "real" male doctor. To this work she brought spiritual insight. The stilling of her mind to Silence, and then the effortless waiting for communion with the Light and the message of the Inner Voice were observances of her faith as natural to her as eating. The Friends taught a religion which must justify itself in results; they believed in Guidance, and they accepted Vision. Fey's few wavering references to her lost clairvoyant faculty did not astonish Rachel. She accepted them at once. Everyone had, at times, more or less perception of events usually veiled. Everyone in dreams or waking flashes occasionally transcended time. And that the gift of intuition

132

shared by all might extend through the physical world and bring back an accurate register of impression without using the physical eye seemed to her in no way surprising.

But the outward events of Fey's brief life she did find amazing and she felt increasing admiration and pity.

"You must not go back to that dreadful rooming house, Fey," she said at the end of the afternoon. "Come here to us; there's a little room on the top floor near the nursery that you may have. You can help us a bit in the wards, and when your time comes I will deliver you."

Fey got up heavily and walked over to the older woman. She threw her arms around Rachel's neck and kissed her with a passionate gratitude.

"My mother and my friend," she said. "I have never had either before. I will help you and thank you as long as I live."

Rachel, though embarrassed by demonstration and physical caresses, was deeply touched. She felt the girl's sincerity, and an empty place in her heart, too, was filled. But she was too wise not to realize that she did not completely understand Fey. How should I, she thought reasonably, when every experience of her life so far has been so utterly different from mine? She tried to imagine the life of the little orphan in a mud hovel in Santa Fe, to imagine the Indians of whom Fey spoke with affection and respect. The Friends, too, had respected the Indians, but that was long ago in Penn's time, and Indians were to Rachel only exotic words. She tried to reconstruct from Fey's few sentences that extraordinary meeting with the red-haired scamp of a quack doctor, and to understand the instantaneous, unthinking passion which had bound Fey to him, or that pathetic mockery of a marriage six days later.

She thought, too, about Fey's abandonment in New York. But there was nothing strange in that old story, given the type of man which Dillon apparently was; the sequel was stranger. That Fey had considered going to the infamous Madame Restell —and yet that a visit to the unfinished cathedral had somehow saved her. And then these last months in a Bowery concert saloon, a degrading experience from which she had apparently emerged quite untouched. A baffling mixture she is, thought Rachel, for even in that first afternoon she had divined that Fey had a large share of contradictory qualities. There was a soft dependence and gentleness, but there had been glimpses of a steely obstinacy, too, and the strength of shrewd purpose. And combined with spiritual enlightenment and acutely sensitive perception there was also bitterness and egotism. But I

133

believe that she can develop into a remarkable woman, said Rachel to herself. Two other people had felt in Fey that intangible aura of potential greatness, the Mexican harlot, La Gertrudis, and the Navajo shaman, Natanay. The Quaker doctor, Rachel Moreton—halfway across the country from them—shared the feeling and another element in their response to Fey—a foreboding. If she will not be guided by the Spirit, she may have the strength to do great harm, thought Rachel.

Perhaps, she thought humbly, God will use me to help her find her highest realization.

The next day Fey thankfully left Mrs. Flynn's and moved to a tiny bare attic room in the Infirmary. For that last month of her pregnancy she was placidly contented. Her body, for all its burden, gave her no trouble, and except for one emotion—loving gratitude toward Rachel Moreton—she thought and felt very little. She ceased to read, or to look either backward or forward; all life was in abeyance until she should be delivered and alone again.

She did, however, make herself extremely useful around the hospital. She displayed from the beginning a swift competence in caring for the sick, and she seemed able to follow Rachel's directions intuitively and almost before they were formulated.

"Now will you admit my experiment is a success?" said Rachel one day to her colleague, Doctor Annie Daniel, who was in charge of the Out-Patient Department. "Why, that girl, despite her handicap, is already as good as any of our trained nurses after three months' training. She has a talent for it, a vocation." She spoke with a natural triumph, since she had been criticized for her impulsiveness in taking in an unknown derelict.

"She has, at any rate, a talent for trying to please you, Rachel," said Doctor Daniel tolerantly, "and that's not surprising considering what you've done for her. But I don't think she has much interest in the patients for themselves."

Rachel smiled and let the matter drop. She knew that the rest of the staff did not think Fey as remarkable as she did, nor did they guess the ambition which Rachel was beginning to cherish. On two occasions Fey had shown extraordinary powers of diagnosis. If Fey could do this without training, what wonders might she not perform as a physician, thought Rachel, and she loved the girl even more because of the hope she had for her. She began to plan for Fey as she would have for her own daughter, and every morning, when she closed herself into her room and stilled her mind into the silent receptivity whose fruits would later sustain her through the harried day, she prayed for Fey.

The baby was born in the early morning hours of June twenty-fifth. Rachel had little need of her skill in midwifery; the labour and birth were normal. For the last terrible pains, Fey refused the chloroform which Rachel wished to administer, crying, "No, please! I must know it all. I want to be here while my baby is born." And though her small body strained and writhed, she endured all in panting silence. The baby was a girl.

Rachel laid the swaddled bundle in Fey's arms and said gently, "She's a beautiful mite, my dear, and I hope she'll be as brave as her mother."

The baby had a wealth of fluffy red-gold curls, and the tiny features bore no resemblance to Fey's.

Rachel, drawing back to look down at them both, shook her head. It would be even harder for the girl to make her way alone with this little replica of the man who had deserted them both.

Fey raised herself weakly on her elbow and looked into the small crumpled face. Her head fell back on the pillow and the tears which had not come earlier began to run down her white cheeks.

"Don't, dear," said Rachel, stroking back the damp matted hair. "I'll help you. I've a plan for you, when you're stronger. A wonderful plan."

Fey's eyes opened; they wandered to the kind face above her, but they did not rest there. They hardened a little and grew intent.

"I shall help myself," she said. "I can manage alone for both of us."

That was pride, the fastidious independence of spirit which she had admired from the first, thought Rachel, but she was nevertheless chilled.

"Will you send for a priest?" said Fey. "I want her baptized."

"Of course," answered Rachel, turning from the bed. She believed neither in baptism nor priests, but she was perfectly tolerant of other faiths. It was not that which dismayed her; it was the flavour of command in Fey's voice. She saw that the girl was following some separate preoccupation and unconscious of Rachel as a person or anything except an instrument to carry out her wishes.

But later, when the Irish priest had come, Fey was again the gentle affectionate girl she had been before. She smiled up at them both, explaining that she wished the baby to be called "Luz. María de la Luz." Both doctor and priest were uncomprehending until Fey explained that "Luz" meant "the Light" in Spanish. Rachel thought it charming, seeing a mystical application dear to the Quakers. And the priest, too, was satisfied when he had translated the peculiar word into Lucia, a proper saint's name. So the baby became Lucia Mary Dillon, anglicized into Lucy by Rachel. But Fey always called her child Lucita, as they would have in Santa Fe.

All during the hot summer months Fey lived at the Infirmary and tended her baby in a passionate concentration. She found both an emotional and physical pleasure in suckling her and showed this pleasure with a lack of self-consciousness which sometimes embarrassed Rachel. It was Fey's strange upbringing amongst those New Mexican peasants, she thought, in extenuation. Always she was ready with excuses for any of Fey's conduct which disturbed her. Those months were happy ones for the doctor. Her interest in Fey and little Lucy filled her heart, which had since her husband's death had no stronger nourishment than the fleeting gratitude of patients.

Then, too, as soon as she was strong enough, Fey had insisted on resuming her duties in the wards. She became expert at making poultices, at dressing wounds, and at keeping Rachel's instruments cleaned and in order. She made beds, washed sick bodies, and emptied bedpans, all with the same quiet efficiency. The other two nurses were jealous of her, partly because some of the patients frankly expressed a preference for "little Mrs. Dillon's" care, and partly because of her privileged position as friend and protégée of the resident doctor. Rachel, indeed, careful as she was of other people's feelings, did show preference. It was only natural that she should try to spare the girl the heaviest tasks, since much of her strength must go to the baby, and she taught Fey techniques and procedures not permitted to the other nurses, who were clumsy ignorant Irish girls. Besides, she had no intention of allowing Fey to remain a simple nurse; the new profession required as yet no more general knowledge than did domestic service.

So for those summer months Rachel had a companion and disciple, and she dreamed sometimes of the great work she and Fey might do together in alleviating the misery of the slums. For, she thought, the girl is a born physician, she has stamina and intelligence, and she has the most precious of all talents for a doctor, a brilliant intuition.

This was true, but Rachel would not recognize the further factor referred to by Doctor Annie Daniel. Fey tended the sick at the Infirmary and applied her innate skill to learning what Rachel wished her to learn, not from sympathy for human misery nor any ideal of service. She worked entirely for Rachel Moreton because she loved her and because a debt of gratitude must be repaid. This trait was bequeathed twofold through the Spanish and the Highland blood; and just as no personal insult might stand unavenged, so no personal kindness might go unrequited.

Fey loathed the smell of poverty in the wards, she despised the filth and the lice which dropped from the patients' emaciated bodies. When, before they were bedded in the coarse hospital shifts, she had to handle their own clothes—patched and sleazy, reeking with body odours—she felt no pity, but only a fierce disgust. It did not occur to her that most of this was the result of the abominable tenement system where two hundred souls existed without air or light in one rickety frame building. She thought neither of causes nor the possibility of improvement. She thought only of escape.

After her hours in the wards she would rush upstairs to her baby. And while she rocked and gave her breast to the avid little lips, she talked. "Never fear, chiquita, we'll get out of this. You shall wear white clothes embroidered in silk, you shall have a gold dish and spoon to eat with. You shall never know ugliness and sickness and want. For I won't let you. We're going to the top together, you and I."

She sat this way many times with her baby. And she thought with lucidity and purpose of Simeon Tower.

One noontime in October, Rachel tapped at the door, opened it and found them like that. Bright sunlight slanted through the attic window and illumined the two. Fey had taken off her striped nurse's uniform as she always did before touching the baby. She sat in white petticoat and bodice. This was unbuttoned and her breasts, blue-veined and nearly as white as the bodice, jutted out proudly in a pagan abandon. Above them on its golden thread hung the turquoise pendant. The girl's head was bent; the great coil of black hair had slipped down one naked shoulder. Her profile against the black wave had the pure æsthetic line of a Leonardo da Vinci madonna. She was smiling down at the baby, who gurgled and struck at her mother's breast with a rosy wandering hand.

Fey's eyes half-closed in purely sensuous enjoyment. "Little bad one," she said, kissing the baby's red-gold curls. "She is so greedy." She smiled lazy greeting at Rachel, but the doctor did not respond.

She stood looking, and for the first time she doubted the possibility of the ambition she had formed for Fey. The girl was beautiful; she had never realized it before. Or if not exactly beautiful, something far more disturbing. She was alluring; every line of her body, partly unclothed as it now was, pointed to seductive allure. She had never seen this before. Fey's body had been previously handicapped by pregnancy and the recovery.

Rachel turned her eyes away at last. There was a pain in her heart. "Put the baby down, and fasten up your bodice, do," she said sharply. "I want to talk to you."

Fey nodded with the instant docility she always showed to Rachel; she laid the baby in the cradle, reached for her blue-and-white overall. "I'd better put some more ice on Mrs. Petroni's belly, before she starts bleeding again?" she suggested.

"I told Nellie Molloy what to do," answered Rachel. "Your ward's quiet for the moment. Sit down, Fey, I want to talk to you."

Fey hooked herself into the coverall, and tied the enveloping white apron over that. She coiled her hair neatly on her neck, where it made an enormous bun. Then she sat down on the bed, Rachel having taken the rocker, and waited quietly. Fey saw that withdrawn, listening look in her friend's eyes, and knew that Rachel was waiting in silence for the moment of communication. No stranger would have noticed, the serene big-boned face showed no outward change, but Fey, who loved her, knew how often and how naturally Rachel subdued the clamour of mind and emotion to ask the Indwelling Spirit for guidance. Fey respected and understood this, though she could not share its simplicity. She, too, had had moments of mystic exaltation, but they had been violently emotional and shattering. They had always come unsummoned and resolved themselves into concrete symbols and episodes, highly coloured in memory. There was the warning of the bells, the constant inspiration of Atalaya, the first meeting with Natanay, and the vision of the Santo Niño in the cathedral. These had all had that quality of illumination and awe, these had all for a little while brought peace. But she could not control these moments, and they had nothing to do with her faith, as Rachel's did. Of late, Fey had not thought about God at all, even at Mass. Her waking thoughts, her dreams, and her prayers had all been focused on one idea, but she had given Rachel no inkling of it.

"I want to talk to you about your future, yours and little Lucy's," said the doctor at last. "You know I'm fond of you both. You are like my daughter, Fey." She spoke matter-of-factly and to the point. The Friends did not waste words.

"Oh, I know!" cried Fey, and her eyes stung with rare tears. "And I love you better than anyone in the world except Lucita and—" She stopped, and fear slipped across her face. What cruel trick had her tongue nearly played on her? She hated Terry, she had forgotten Terry. She had dissolved him from her life as the sun evaporated a rain puddle on the Cañon Road. "I love you better than anybody but my baby," she said evenly.

Rachel, intent on her plan, had not noticed. She smiled and went on. "You have great aptitude for medicine, I think. Have you thought that you might become a physician?"

She misread the girl's astonished silence, which was one of pure dismay.

"Oh, yes, you could do it," said Rachel. "Doctor Blackwell and Doctor Daniel think it a splendid idea; you can join our classes right here, and I can coach you."

Fey moistened her lips and looked away from Rachel's enthusiastic face. She did not want to hurt her friend nor to disappoint her. She would not say: "I loathe sick people and poor people. I loathe the Infirmary sights and smells and drabness. Human suffering disgusts me. It's only because of you and your great kindness that I've endured it. I want nothing now of life but luxury and refinement for myself and the baby." She could not say these things, but she saw that she must check Rachel and disclose at least some part of her plan.

"Doctor Rachel," she said gently, "I'm not unselfish like you. I am ambitious. I want money, a great deal of money. I want Lucita to have all the things I didn't. She must never be hungry or dirty. She must have the best the world can give."

This hankering after material riches was so alien to Rachel's nature that she misunderstood again. "Why, child, you can live on here with Lucy for your three years of training. I'll take care of you as I would the daughter I never had. You'd let me do that, wouldn't you, Fey?"

"Ah, you are so good, always!" cried the girl, her voice thickened. "But I must make you understand." She laced her fingers and her hands trembled. "I want power," she said passionately, "and I want money! I've had nothing yet, nothing. I had no home, no people of my own. I thought I had love, but I didn't. Oh, don't you see!—I don't want to live here at the Infirmary as you do, working from morning till night, drudging, sacrificing, and no pay but the few dollars salary they can afford to give!"

Rachel stared at the transformed face. Fey's cheeks glowed. Her pupils, so often hidden by the demure lids, dilated so that the clear grey merged into lambent black, sultry, vehement as a Goya gypsy.

"I see that you are not happy here, and I was stupid to think you were," said Rachel.

She got up and walked to the window, turning her back on the girl while she strove to conquer bitter disappointment. There was silence in the small room, except for the baby, who gurgled cheerfully to herself in the cradle.

Gradually Rachel's rigid back relaxed. How long, she said to herself, does it take to learn that no one may control another's life?—and her hurt vanished.

She came back to Fey and sat beside her on the bed. "I had forgotten how young thee is, dear," she said. "Forgive me." And she went on in the plain speech which she never used to non-Quakers, but had lately slipped into with Fey. "Thee doesn't know the world yet; power and money aren't to be had for the asking. There's nothing open to women which will bring those."

"Ah, but there is," said Fey. "For there are men who have them."

"I see," said Rachel. How stupid she had been and a little ridiculous too! Why should she have assumed that because Fey had had one bitter disillusionment, and because she had always seemed so self-contained, dedicated to her work and baby; how had she dared assume that Fey had no interest in men? This talk of power and money was self-delusion, thought Rachel, pitying. It was the imperious urge of that ripened, seductive body speaking, and a natural desire for love. Rachel was too fine a woman to feel a lessening of affection because its object did not fit into the mould she had made, and she touched Fey's arm in one of her rare caresses. "I do understand now. But thee must be practical, my poor child. Thee is married already. I think in this case thee might rightly get free by divorce, but where in the world will a divorced woman with a child find a good husband?"

"I think I shall manage," said Fey. She smiled into the kind

140

eyes beside her, but she could not tell more. She was not ashamed of her intention, but she knew that to Rachel it would be shocking and preposterous. She knew, too, unhappily, that it might some day lead to a breach between them, but nothing caused her to falter, no fear of pain or doubts of success. "I think, Doctor Rachel," she said, "that if one wills a thing to happen with all one's strength, if one wants it hard enough and long enough, and is willing to pay the price, one is sure to get it."

"Perhaps," said Rachel soberly; "but thee has left God out, Fey, in all this willing and wishing."

Fey drew a long, unsteady breath. She looked at Rachel and she saw beside her the face of Natanay, and that the gaze of both of them mingled into sadness. They shared a quietness and a selflessness which shut her out; behind the doctor's eyes as behind Natanay's there was a secret wisdom.

"I don't know where or what God is," she said, half-angrily, "but I have faith in myself."

Rachel shook her head. "Some day thee'll learn that's not enough," she said, and changed the subject. "Thee is welcome to stay here as long as thee wishes, Fey. I want thee to." And perhaps, after all, she may enter the medical classes, she added to herself, for she saw little hope of any other future for the girl.

Fey thanked her by a warm kiss, but when the doctor had gone out and shut the door, she pulled the morning *Tribune* from the table and re-read an item. It said, "Mr. Simeon Tower, the financier, has recently closed his villa at Long Branch and returned to his New York residence." Fey put down the paper and opened the small pine cupboard which served as closet. She took out a new suit. It was of grosgrain, a shade called "feuille morte," a vivid yellow-brown trimmed with darker bands of velvet. It was a colour few could wear, but it made Fey's white skin whiter, her hair blacker, and her grey eyes more luminous.

Rachel had during the past months insisted upon Fey's going out each afternoon for air and exercise. It was during these expeditions that she had bought the dress, also bronze kid shoes and a tiny velvet bonnet to match. She had spent for these the money left her by Terry, and its use to buy this particular outfit gave her a savage satisfaction.

She picked up Lucita, who responded by a gratified crow.

"I'll not be gone too long, mi corazón," she whispered into the little fat neck. The baby gurgled and opened her eyes wide. They were blue and would stay blue. Like my father's, thought Fey, and the hair, too, may be like his was once. She has nothing of Terry, nothing. "Be good and patient until I come back," she said to the baby. "It is for us, you know."

She carried Lucita into the adjacent nursery, where she put her in a crib amongst the other babies. She hated to do this, for the others were sickly and wizened, and they kept up an incessant whimper, but the little nurse would keep an eye on Lucita until Fey returned. Fey glanced at the wall clock and its swaying brass pendulum. Two-thirty. Plenty of time.

She returned to her room, washed, and dressed very carefully in the feuille morte suit. It gave precisely the impression she wished. The lines of the tight bodice accented her bosom and small waist, but discreetly so that one thought it accidental. Just as feuille morte was striking and exotic on her, yet, after all, it was brown. No one could consider brown flashy. The bonnet left most of her magnificent hair uncovered, and instead of her usual prim knot, she had gathered it loosely into a net, where it made a tremendous "waterfall" to her shoulders; a fashionable effect seldom achieved by other women without the lavish use of false hair. When she was ready, she leaned close to the mirror and applied coral salve to her lips, and she made no attempt to reduce their full outline to the rosebud pout which beauty demanded.

Last of all, she put a paper in her pocketbook. On it she had written an address in her unpractised but small incisive script: "57 Wall Street."

CHAPTER

11

SIMEON TOWER was born in 1830 in the back room of a small hardware shop on the outskirts of Danbury, Connecticut. He was born Simon Turmstein. His father was an enterprising Jewish peddler who had chafed at life in the Frankfort ghetto, saved his pfennigs, and bought steerage passage for the new world, decades before this method of escape had occurred to others of his patient race. Isaac Turmstein had not liked the confinement of New York, and he had wandered on foot through most of New England—his peddler's pack slung over his shoulder—until one day he happened upon Danbury and

Annie Mason. She was plump and blonde and placid, the daughter of a mill hand employed by the newly established Mallory Hat Company. She fell in love with the dark romantic-looking peddler, and he, being attracted by her pink blondeness and being also tired of roaming, soon married her.

There was opposition from Annie's family, not particularly because Isaac was a Jew, which meant very little to the provincial Yankees, but because he was a foreigner and spoke with a heavy guttural accent. However, he soon proved himself an adaptable family man, amiably joined the Masons at worship in the Congregational Church, and improved his English as much as possible. The Turmsteins set up a store on South Street, where they sold tin pots and pans, iron skillets, nails, screws, and simple tools. Isaac's father-in-law soon became reconciled to the marriage and sent them customers. They prospered in a modest way. Isaac gave good value and was respected, but he was never quite one of them. His fellow citizens had trouble pronouncing his name. By an analogy of sound it gradually became "Tombstone." "Run down to Old Jew Tombstone's and get me a pennyworth of nails," fathers would tell their children, and the children always giggled at the incongruous name. Isaac did not mind. One who had spent thirty years amongst the niggling restrictions, the indignities, and sometimes bloody terror of the Frankfort "Judengasse," would scarcely mind a sobriquet, which was patronizing certainly, but on the whole affectionate. Simon, however, minded intensely from the moment that he was old enough to understand.

When at fourteen he took his first job as bar-boy in the Taylor Tavern, he anglicized Turmstein by translating the first syllable, and by adding an "e" to Simon he transformed it into unequivocal Yankee. Much later, when his shrewdness, luck, and financial dexterity had brought him to New York, he was glad of this. An easy, English-sounding name was a distinct asset, and August Belmont, born Schoenberg, had already set a precedent.

Of the Turmsteins' five children, Simeon was the only one who resembled his mother, and the only one who caused her constant heartache and worry. As a child he was exceptionally self-willed and moody, and he was delicate. This gave him a frequent means of avoiding school, which he hated. When he was seven, he developed a marked stammer, and this, of course, made him the butt of the other children. Recitations were a nightmare. He would stand on one foot, scarlet with misery even to his scalp under the tow hair, his small blunt fingers clenched in anguish, and recite, "'S' s-s-s-t-t-ands f-for the s-s-s-erpent lowly and m-m-mean," and the whole class, giggling and squirming joyfully, would accompany him in a chorus of "s-s-s-s," and "t-t-t-t"s. They called him "Little T-t-t-Tombstone," and without special malice, but simply because he was different, left him out of all their play and projects.

Isaac was sorry for his son, but he much preferred the rest of his brood, a merry, uncomplicated lot with soft dark eyes and slightly aquiline noses who took life as it came.

Simeon endured school spasmodically until he was fourteen, when he reached adolescence and his full height of five feet seven. He broadened into a wide, stocky build and became powerful. He discovered in himself at the same time an independence and contempt for the society of the other boys, though before this he had passionately yearned for their approval. He announced that he had had enough schooling and was going to work.

Isaac was saddened; he had the Jewish reverence for education; but he was forced to admit that the boy knew enough to get on in the world. He read and wrote perfectly and he had a genius for figures. Since he was ten, Simeon had handled the hardware store's bookkeeping in half the time that it took Isaac to do it.

From then on Simeon ran his own life. He changed his name and took the job at Taylor's Tavern. This did not please him for long. There were too many people in Danbury who knew him as "Little T-t-t-Tombstone." One day he packed his belongings in a carpet-bag, bade his mother an affectionate but inarticulate farewell, and, having already arranged a lift in a farm wagon, went to Bridgeport and got a job at the Stanley House as a waiter. When he left the Stanley five years later, he was assistant manager and he had learned a great many things. His stammer was nearly gone—it had improved the moment he left home—and he had developed a talent for telling stories, mostly smutty, since these had the greatest success with the Stanley's commercial patrons. He had also acquired a hearty, booming laugh. He was known as a smart, jolly fellow, mighty helpful, too. Sim Tower'd always know the name of a complacent girl if you wanted one, and no matter how late in the day you asked him, he could fix you up with a couple of seats to the travelling shows. You gave him a thumping commission, of course, but it was worth it.

Nobody suspected that the jolly good fellow never himself

patronized the complacent girls or took time to visit the theatre. He had, however, an absorbing secret life. Every spare hour and all his evenings he spent locked in his room with a ledger full of figures. He devoured the financial pages of the New York newspapers, he watched the stock-market quotations as anxiously as any bookie ever watched the Saratoga race entries, and he juggled many mythical hundreds of thousands in his ledger. At first he made many mistakes and lost paper fortunes. But gradually he developed a feel for it, and he took five hundred dollars of the twenty-five hundred he had saved and put them with a New York brokerage firm, Slate and Hatch.

He pestered these brokers unmercifully for information, he kept charts, and, aided by the country's expansion and a rising market, he had soon doubled his money. This, however, was practice; he was too shrewd to plunge, and geographically too far away from the financial centre. The time for New York would come, but in the meantime he demanded and got a rise from the Stanley House, unobtrusively studied business methods in Bridgeport, and awaited opportunity. It came when he was twenty-two.

One night in the Stanley bar he overheard a disgruntled mill-owner complaining bitterly over a glass of beer. The man, it seemed, had a small wool mill on the Saugatuck River and he was sick of the whole business. "Headaches all the time," he grumbled. "If it ain't the price of raw wool, or the looms breaking down, it's the hands wanting more pay or a ten-hour day. Could I find anyone fool enough to take the blasted mill, I'd be off to Californy in a trice."

Simeon said nothing, but the next morning at dawn he hired a horse, rode to the Saugatuck, and inspected the mill. He also went through the company's books, by the simple method of telling the unsuspicious old bookkeeper that he had been authorized. He saw that, even with the present muddle-headed management, the mill was worth about five thousand. He walked again through the mill, and he saw where new machinery might be put in and inefficiency banished. He rode thoughtfully back to Bridgeport and decided to take a chance.

He found the owner in the Stanley bar and commiserated with him. "Too bad Tyson's cancelling that felt order," he said sympathetically. The owner had heard nothing of cancellation, but as he also knew nothing of Simeon's visit to the mill, he thought the Stanley's manager must have picked up an authentic rumour. Anyway, he was sick of the place and wished to head West. After Simeon had spent three hours feeding him liquor and talking, the man was frightened, too. By evening he had sold the mill to Simeon for eighteen hundred dollars cash.

That was the beginning. Simeon promptly moved to a shack beside his mill and stayed there. He kept the books himself and he supervised every detail. His five years' experience at hotel management proved invaluable. He picked the right foremen and he was tactful in smoothing over contentions. He introduced new machinery and refurbished the old, and he put every cent back into the business.

After three years the Tower Woollen Mill was filling orders from as far away as Springfield and Worcester. And Simeon was tired of it. He looked around for a buyer, and soon found one. He sold the mill for fifteen thousand dollars, but out of a trace of superstition and sentimentality he retained a small interest in it. He moved at last to New York, as he had always meant to do. He went to Slate and Hatch, the brokers who handled his modest investments, and bought himself an interest in the firm.

Then he applied himself single-heartedly and successfully to speculation, and gradually, like many another enterprising young man in those expansive years, he accumulated a fortune, and he followed very much the same pattern as the others. Cheap railroad stock scooped up for a song in the panic of 1857, and later sold at great profit. Shares in industries which during the Civil War years provided dazzling army contracts, fatly padded. City politicians cunningly placated with the object of mutual and pleasing exploitation. Simeon, like Drew, Gould, Fisk, Vanderbilt, and a dozen other successful men, believed in expediency. Business ethics were founded on expediency and nobody expected them to conform to the vague moralities one learned at Sunday School.

It was necessary for the financial titans to throw plums to Big Bill Tweed as he rose to power by means of the most corrupt politics ever known in New York. Simeon deplored the politics, but he saw the wisdom of friendship with the Tammany Boss as soon as any of them. He accompanied Tweed on the latter's gaudy yacht to Americus Club outings in Greenwich, Connecticut, just as matter-of-factly as he accompanied Jim Fisk to the "bower of love" on Twenty-Fourth Street where Fisk kept his luscious Josie Mansfield.

So Simeon made a great deal of money, and he anxiously forced himself through the various motions which he believed the public expected from its millionaires. He acquired horses, though he did not much like them, and a villa at Long Branch.

He gave supper parties for prominent actresses and endowed worthy charities. He also acquired a hobby—all rich men had them. He collected strange or historical jewels, particularly those which were reputed to have belonged to famous people. It gave him comfort and a curious security to hold crushed in his hand a carnelian amulet said to have been carried by Napoleon, or a rock-crystal cross which had belonged to Catherine the Great. The Napoleons, the Catherines, the George Washingtons—reduced to a keepsake which Simeon Tower could own. He had built cases in the library for his gem collection, and he spent much time with it, more pleasurable hours than the social ones which dissatisfied him, since he was increasingly aware that the company he was able to command was distinctly second-rate. Society ignored Simeon Tower.

In the February of 1868, when Fey saw him at the Arcadia, he was beginning to realize that he was lonely and discontented. The making of money no longer required so much attention. The fortune snowballed along by itself. There was nothing to stop it, no taxes, no government restrictions, not even as yet much public indignation or censure.

Simeon began to think, not for the first time, of marriage. Two things had so far held him back. The strongest of these was an unconscious fear.

When he had been nineteen in Bridgeport and working at the Stanley House, he had fallen in love with an older girl, Mellie Reynolds. Her father was a banker and she moved in the city's highest social circles. He had been delirious with excitement to find her receptive. Even he, diffident and inexperienced as he was, had presently realized that she was more than receptive to his love-making. She was eager. Then one summer night on the sand by the edge of the Sound, there had been an episode of unbearable humiliation. He had utterly failed to accomplish that which they had both ardently desired, and she had turned on him in a fury, jeering at his looks and his stammer, pitilessly mimicking certain little mannerisms which he hadn't known he had. He had been too young and horribly mortified to realize that her savagery sprang from her own disappointment. He knew only that she was jeering at his failure as a man; that she had seen that, after all, he was nothing but "Little T-t-t-Tombstone"—a hopeless outsider.

His conscious mind soon buried this episode, but its ghost writhed upward whenever he thought of marriage. He did not know it, but he was afraid, and he had never felt real passion.

The other factor which kept him from marriage was his

mistress, Pansy Miggs. With her there was no fear of inferiority or failure, because whatever he did or did not do was all right with Pansy. She adored him to the limits of her stupid loving nature. She had been a fifteen-year-old shuttle girl in his mill on the Saugatuck when he first noticed her fresh blonde comeliness.

They had drifted into an easy relationship, and soon after he had moved to New York, he had sent for Pansy and set her up in three rooms on Eleventh Street. Here she was perfectly happy. When his wealth increased, he tried to move her to more pretentious surroundings, but she had cried so much, big tears spilling from her prominent eyes, that he let her be. Her rooms were cluttered with heavy red-upholstered walnut furniture decorated whenever possible with satin bows. There was hardly room to walk between her whatnots loaded with souvenirs, china figures, wax-flower pieces and shells, and the tabourets, footstools, and rockers. She had a canary and a fat taffy-coloured spaniel which resembled her. The Eleventh Street flat was her home and she wanted no other. She was always good-tempered and anxious to please. Sometimes Simeon did not visit her for weeks, but she seldom questioned. When he did come, she was acquiescent to his infrequent sexual needs if that were what he wanted, but if he did not, she fixed him a nice little meal instead.

Simeon was fond of her and always shrank from the thought of disturbing such a comfortable arrangement. He was, in fact, thinking of visiting Pansy that evening at the precise moment of the October afternoon that Fey entered the granite building at 57 Wall Street.

It is seldom in life that one knows that a coming event is to be of crucial importance. This foreknowledge gives advantage, it allows time for previsioning and meeting difficulties, for studying the best approach, and for acquiring inner poise. These factors all helped Fey, but her greatest advantage was her complete ignorance. She knew nothing of social or business conventions. Except for Bleecker Street, a Bowery concert hall, and the Infirmary, she knew nothing about New York.

She quite naturally saw her visit to Simeon Tower in terms of Santa Fe, and the patriarchal system. Here the richest men in town were entirely approachable. The humblest peon might request an interview with Don Diego Seña and get it. Wealth and position which have been assured for generations do not need protection nor the trappings of superiority.

Fey, therefore, was not nervous as she entered the rather dingy granite building in Wall Street.

The brokerage firm of Slate and Hatch had once occupied the top floor, but now, Tower, Slate, and Hatch had taken over the whole building. In those thirteen years, Slate had died, Hatch retired, and Simeon had thrown their second-floor offices together to make an elaborate one for himself.

There were three rings of fortifications around Simeon, and Fey swept through two of them because she did not know that they existed.

"Where is Mr. Tower's office?" she asked calmly of the grizzled old doorman. His jaw dropped as she rustled past him. Young stylish ladies never rustled through the front doors of Tower, Slate, and Hatch. He'd hardly ever seen a lady on Wall Street at all.

"Upstairs, but ye can't—" he began uncertainly.

"Thank you," said Fey, and glided over to the stairs.

She had mounted one step when a startled junior clerk reached her. "Where are you going, madam?" he asked.

"To meet Mr. Tower," murmured Fey sweetly.

"You have an appointment?" said the clerk, falling back on the time-honoured defence.

Even Fey recognized that a negative answer was unwise. "If he's busy, I'll wait," she said, and giving the young clerk a brilliant melting smile, she ascended the stairs. He was dazzled by the smile and he was completely at sea. He was used to the dozens of importunates who daily tried to see Mr. Tower. Most of them he could classify at a glance. There were the deadbeats and the panhandlers. There were ward bosses and job-seekers. Occasionally there were furious competitors, and once in a while a frightened man whose small business had been incontinently devoured by the Tower interests. There were all these, but they were not women. The only women he had ever seen here had been two strong-jawed matrons, who demanded a contribution to the Temperance Union. They had been dealt with downstairs. The few others who had been sifted out and allowed upstairs had then encountered Mr. Lemming. Noah Lemming was Tower's confidential secretary. Very few people got past him.

Well, thought the clerk uneasily, old fox Noah'll deal with that girl, whoever she is. He was uneasy because Lemming did not like mistakes.

But even Noah Lemming was baffled by Fey. From the door of his small office which flanked Simeon's, he saw her standing uncertainly in the hall. She actually had her hand raised to knock upon the mahogany door which she correctly assumed to be Simeon's, when Lemming rushed at her. "Madam!" he cried, his voice shrilled in outrage. "What are you doing here!"

Fey lowered her hand, she turned, and they looked at each other.

"I'm sorry," she said. "I did not know there was anyone else up here. I want to talk to Mr. Tower."

Lemming's sharp face darkened. What's going on here? he thought. Brazen effrontery.

"What's your name, madam—and your business with Mr. Tower?" He tried by a gesture to get her out of the hall and into his own office. Fey did not move. Her brilliant eyes rested coldly on his tight, angry face. She did not like him, and she knew that he did not like her.

"I am Mrs. Dillon. Santa Fe Cameron Dillon. And my business with Mr. Tower, I will not tell you."

Lemming gasped. "Preposterous! I'll have you know, madam, that I'm Mr. Tower's confidential secretary. No one can see him unless I choose!"

"That I cannot believe," said Fey. "Lobo does not permit that coyotes should command him."

She's mad, thought Lemming, to whom this Mexican proverb was gibberish. He grabbed her silk-covered arm and at his touch her face blazed. She shook him off with a violent motion and knocked sharply on the mahogany door.

"Madam!" cried Lemming. He lunged again for her arm. Fey spat several words at him in Spanish and, eluding him in one sinuous twist, turned the knob and threw open the door.

Simeon, behind his enormous rosewood desk, looked up in amazement.

He saw his cool, efficient secretary turned purple in the face and sputtering, and he saw a girl in brown whose bosom was heaving and whose grey eyes were snapping with anger. She did not wait for him to speak, but ran straight to his desk. "He says no one may see you unless he chooses. Is it true he is so important?" She pointed over her shoulder at Lemming.

Fey had anticipated no difficulty in getting in to see Tower, but she had been realist enough to know that the first sentences of the interview were important. She had lain sleepless for many hours on her Infirmary bed and rehearsed opening gambits. They ranged from the politely dignified to the pleadingly frank in tone. Not one of them would have riveted Simeon's attention or pierced his guard as did this indignant question. Simeon had lately, and without giving the matter his complete attention, been resenting his secretary. The man was becoming arrogant and he knew too much.

Simeon said nothing for a full minute. He had long ago learned the value of impassive silence when confronted by emotion in others, and it was by this trick, too, that he had conquered the stammer. The tableau before him began to dissolve. Fey lowered her arm and took a quick breath. Lemming gave himself a mental shake, his sharp face resumed its usual mask of cold watchfulness.

"Now, what is all this?" said Simeon pleasantly.

"This young woman forced her way in, sir," said Lemming. "She has no business here."

"How do you know that?" said Simeon. "Did you ask me?"

Lemming flushed. "No, but I—" He clamped his mouth shut.

"No, but you've made it your business to find out everything that concerns me, haven't you?" Simeon leaned back in his mahogany swivelled chair, crossed his legs, and laughed easily. He had not decided how to treat the man's officiousness, and this was no moment to raise an issue with an employee. "Run along, Lemming," he said, with a quick smile. "I'll deal with the young lady."

Lemming shot Fey a venomous look and went. Neither the easy laugh nor the smile had deceived him, as they would have a casual observer. But he won't give me the sack, thought Lemming, as he strode back to his own office. Gould would pay plenty for the figures on that Transic deal. Besides, he'd never get another man'd do his dirty work for him as well as I do. So Lemming soothed himself. He had little feeling for his employer, but he passionately liked his job. Easy pickings, reflected glory. "You got to grease Lemming if you want to get at Tower"—that's what they said on the Street, only Tower hadn't known it because there'd never been a mistake before. It was all smooth and subtle, outward deference. Only that damn girl— He glared at the great closed door across the hall.

He picked up his pen and tried to continue the letter he had been writing to James E. King's Sons on a matter of foreign exchange. I'll find out who she is and what she wanted, he thought. I can always find out, like I found out about that wench he keeps on Eleventh Street.

Inside Tower's magnificent office, Simeon also was wondering who the girl was and what she wanted. But he did not hurry her.

"Will you sit down, Miss—Mrs.—?" he said, genially indicating a yellow plush armchair in front of his desk.

"Mrs. Dillon," said Fey, and complied slowly. She was still shaken, and all her speeches had deserted her. She gave him a nervous, apologetic little smile and instinctively waited for him to speak while she collected herself. As this was Simeon's own technique, the result was silence.

They sat and looked at each other, the small, vivid girl in brown, and the heavy, nearly middle-aged man.

Simeon was seldom genuinely amused, and lately little had interested him, but now he bit his blond moustache and raised his eyebrows quizzically.

"Well, Mrs. Dillon? To what exactly do I owe this honour?" Some kind of adventuress, he thought; no, guess not. She's awfully young. Actress wanting a job? No. Advice on investments? But she wouldn't have the nerve to force her way in here to me.

"Well, Mrs. Dillon," he repeated a trifle impatiently, "why did you want so badly to see me?"

Fey looked down at her lap, her eyes followed a thread of the feuille morte grosgrain until it disappeared under her tightly clasped hand. She raised her head and looked again full at Simeon.

"Because you are a great rich man, and I wanted to meet you."

So, this is something new in approaches, thought Simeon. He spoke even more slowly than usual.

"There are many rich men in the city. I assume you want something, my dear young lady. Will you tell me why you picked on me?"

"Because I saw you once, and I have learned a good deal about you, and I think we would like each other," answered Fey. She told the truth because it was natural for her to do so. But she was not so naïve that she could not see that she had made a mistake. His face tightened. His eyes, which had been amused, became guarded.

"That is a trifle crude," he said coldly. "Will you kindly state your business?" His blunt, well-manicured hand made a slight gesture, the prelude to dismissal. His glance wandered to the small lever under his desk. It pulled a wire which rang a bell in Lemming's office.

Fey correctly interpreted his glance and felt a sinking dismay. She had for so long built her hopes on this interview. Ever since February so many of her thoughts had been concentrated on the man who sat across the desk that it seemed incredible that he shouldn't feel it.

"I—I do want help!" she said. There was a faltering simplicity about this, and Simeon looked at her quickly and frowned.

"I've been asked for money in a lot of different ways," he said, "but most of them thought up a good story first." He was disappointed and bored again. There had seemed to be something different about the little thing, a fire and refinement, too. He by now had noted the slight foreign intonation in her voice. French probably, maybe Creole. Plenty of them drifted up from New Orleans to work the big city. War widows, they usually called themselves. Lemming was quite right, he thought wearily.

"Well, Mrs. Dillon," he said, "I like nerve, and you've got plenty of it." He slid open an upper desk drawer where he kept some cash. "I'll give you a hundred and we'll skip the hard-luck tale— with thanks."

"No!" cried Fey. "You don't understand!" In her panic she jumped up and put her hand out across the desk to stop him. Her mind worked frantically, and she could not hear herself speak. "You have—you have a collection of jewels!" she cried breathlessly. "I read about it in the newspaper. Would you be interested in this?"

Simeon, amazed, watched her unbutton the top of her bodice and jerk out a blue lump of stone on a gold string. She took it off over her head and held it out to him across the desk. Her hand trembled, and she looked into his astonished face with a sort of anguish.

"My dear young lady—" said Simeon. He stared at the sky-blue stone in her hand, and then at the white triangle of skin which showed at her unbuttoned collar. The skin looked soft and smooth. She was leaning so near him that a faint perfume came to him from her body.

He took the stone slowly from her and his fingers touched her hand. This tiny contact gave him a shock of pleasure and sudden warmth. He was not a voluptuary and this type of unexpected sensation was new to him.

He looked at the full high outline of her breasts under the leaf-brown silk, at the wide coral-tinted mouth.

"You want me to buy this rough lump of t-turquoise?" His tongue stumbled a little, as it seldom did nowadays.

Fey felt the change in him. She knew that at that instant of contact he had begun to see her as a desirable woman. If I let him buy it, she thought, I can get it back later. I know I can get it back. With this darting shield she held off a fierce thrust of shame, the echo of Natanay's words, "You still wear the skystone, may you never lose it." What has an old savage in that faraway country to do with me? she thought. This is what I want and if the stone can help me get it— she thought of her baby waiting for her in the Infirmary ward amongst all the sickly wailing ones.

"Yes, Mr. Tower," she said, "I want you to buy it."

He understood from her tone that there was something portentous about this proffering of the turquoise, and this kept him from telling her at once that it was worthless to him. He was not interested in crude unset stones, and certainly not in one so common as the turquoise. But he felt that he had perhaps misjudged her.

"I might be interested in buying it, but I'd like to have it appraised first," he said. "Suppose you tell me something about yourself."

Fey deftly, and without embarrassment, buttoned up her collar. Her poise had returned, and her faith in her star.

"Yes," she said. "I want you to know about me, and I want you to like me." She sat down again and gave him her slow, seductive smile.

Simeon swallowed. Their positions were abruptly reversed. It was he now who felt nervous and uncertain. She troubled him. He had become very much aware of her body, all the more so as she seemed unconscious of it. She sat in a voluptuous attitude, turned a bit sideways so that her slender hip line showed, and she looked at him through her lashes, the strange grey eyes caressing and intimate. And yet it didn't seem deliberate: nothing so simple as blatant sexual invitation. That had never appealed to him.

"Where shall I begin?" asked Fey softly. "My story is a little long, you will not understand much, but I will tell the truth, and then you will advise me, please?"

Simeon laughed. Suddenly he felt relaxed and young. At his elbow were that day's market quotations to which he had been giving his usual single-minded attention before the interruption. He could, however, return to them later instead of going to see Pansy.

"How about tea with me, Mrs. Dillon?" he said jovially. "Much better than an office for this long story and advice."

"I would be very pleased," said Fey, rising, "but I must be home at six."

154

"Why?" asked Simeon, also rising. Husband, he thought, with a faint repulsion.

Fey gave him a long, considering look. "I will tell you why later," she said.

Simeon shrugged, opened his closet door, put on his ulster, grey derby hat, and lemon-coloured gloves. He ushered Fey out of the office and noticed that he could look right over the top of her head, a rare experience for him. It gave him an agreeable sensation of masculine dominance.

In the outer office Lemming sprang to attention. Caution this time enabled him to hide the shock he felt at the two of them going out together. He stood, breathing hard through flaring nostrils, but otherwise deferential while Simeon gave him instructions.

Fey did not glance at Lemming. She loathed him and knew that it was mutual. It was not in her to use subterfuge. The coyote, she thought negligently, let him yap. It is his nature. And she stood calmly waiting by the stairs until Simeon finished. This composure disconcerted Lemming more than anything else had. It was as though something had been settled in there, her attitude appeared to him proprietorial. He watched the welcoming smile she gave Tower as he joined her, saw the chief smile back. Not the quick, rather nervous grimace with which he usually expressed goodwill, but a true light-hearted response.

Lemming went back to his desk muttering his frustrated and angry curiosity.

Simeon considered taking Fey to Delmonico's and immediately thought better of it. Too many people he knew would be there. His life had been extremely circumspect. He never took Pansy out in public, and he was unused to têtes-à-têtes with a woman. When he entertained, either those on the fringes of society who accepted him, or the smart actresses who built up the man-of-the-world picture, he always did the expected thing, and he moved always in a group.

This little excursion with an unknown, mysterious woman was unprecedented. They went out on Wall Street and the electric sunlight of the October afternoon added to his agreeable feeling of excitement.

"My carriage is around the corner," he said. "Shall we drive up to the Park and have an ice at the Refectory?"

"I'd like that," answered Fey simply. "I have never ridden in a private carriage."

Simeon gave her a quick, puzzled look. Such naïveté did not belong to her expensive clothes, her composure, nor the forceful way she had manœuvred their interview.

"You're a strange little lady. I'm getting very curious about you."

She did not answer, but she looked up at him and smiled. In the smile there was promise.

The victoria was waiting around the corner on Broadway. Briggs, the coachman, jumped down off the box when he saw his master's bulky figure approach. He was astonished at the earliness of the hour. Mr. Tower wouldn't usually leave the office until six. He was more astonished at the sight of a lady and orders to drive up Broadway to the Mall. 'Ere's somethink new, he thought, as he touched his cockaded hat and tucked the mink rug around Fey; master, 'e do look different, younger like, might be 'e's going courtin' at last. He returned to the box and clucked to the horses, and, while he drove expertly through the heavy Broadway traffic, he speculated in some gloom upon the effects of having a mistress over the easygoing Tower household.

No such idea entered Simeon's head, but by six o'clock, when at Fey's insistence, he drove her back to the Infirmary door, he was bewildered and flattered, and he was beginning to be romantically interested.

She had made him feel young and physically attractive. With her he had forgotten that he was thirty-eight, that his blond hair was thinning on top, that his stocky framework carried too many well-fed pounds. She was so small and lightly boned that in walking beside her he had forgotten the stretching for height which plagued him when he was with women. He had even for once forgotten all the extraneous paraphernalia of personality with which he built up the figure of Simeon Tower, Baron of Finance and Prince of Good Fellows. She had made him feel that she thought him truly a great man. She had led him on to boast a bit about his financial astuteness, about the rapidity of his rise. He knew in his soul that this quick acquiring of a fortune was not unique. Vanderbilt, Morgan, Stewart, Gould, Drew, Fisk, had all done it in the same period, and a dozen more were coming up—it took knack and concentration, one must be unencumbered by scruples and ready to grab every chance to exploit the new resources of the expanding country before someone else got there first. Given these traits and a bit of luck at the beginning, it wasn't so difficult. But Fey and her wide-eyed admiration had made him feel that it had been. She reflected back to him the image of a dashing, invincible conqueror. She had been the perfect Desdemona, and he had found it so pleasant to talk to her during their two hours' drive to Central Park and back that it wasn't until he delivered her to the dingy brownstone building on Second Avenue that he realized how little he had learned about her. She had come from the Spanish country out West somewhere, she had been married and had a baby. His impression was that she was a widow. She lived for the moment in a hospital, because one of those unsexed women medicos was her friend. This much he knew, and it had not seemed important while he was caught by the magic she had conjured up between them.

Briggs was already standing at attention on the littered sidewalk before the Infirmary when Simeon came to himself and threw a disgusted look at their surroundings. "See here," he said, "you can't really live in a place like this."

"I hate it," said Fey.

"You're hard up?" asked Simeon, frowning. He had forgotten his first suspicions of her. The scene in the office had become overlaid by this new enchantment.

"I have no money at all," she answered. "That's why I brought you the turquoise."

Oh, that turquoise, he thought impatiently. Can she really think it's of any value! But he no longer cared if it were a pretext.

"Let's drive out again Sunday!" he cried boyishly. "It's been great!" He knew that he sounded young and exuberant. The real thing, not the counterfeit he often used. "I'll be here about four. Bring you the price of your stone."

"Yes," said Fey. "Thank you." She turned and put her hand in his for farewell. He was electrified by her touch. On impulse he bent his head and pressed his lips to the small gloved hand. The coachman and two dirty urchins who were hanging around the carriage were transfixed. Fey had never had her hand kissed any more than Simeon had ever yielded to such an extravagant European impulse. But she received the salute with the quiet grace of her Spanish forbears, and therefore saved Simeon from the immediate backwash of feeling that he was ridiculous. He was grateful and all the more fascinated. It was her special gift that, while she evoked in him a sensual passion, she also gilded and bejewelled it with romance. *She* was not a romantic, she was a mystic and a realist. She knew what she wanted, and she knew instinctively what Simeon wanted.

She smiled good-bye to him, and ran lightly up the Infirmary steps.

Rachel had been drawn to her window by the sound of the carriage and the clop, clop, of pedigreed hoofs. She also witnessed the little farewell scene, and she rushed from her room and stopped Fey on the second-floor landing.

"My dear child," she cried, blocking the way, for Fey was in a fever to go up to Lucita, "who was that man, and what has thee been doing?"

Fey caught her lip and looked ruefully up at her friend like a naughty child who knows that its mother will be indulgent. The wind had loosened her sleek hair and soft tendrils curled around her face. She looked very young and she shone with triumph.

"That was Simeon Tower, Doctor Rachel, dear. He likes me, I knew he would."

"Simeon Tower—" repeated Rachel. "Thee means that rich man in the papers— But how—and why—? Fey, I don't understand. And that dress!"

The light was dim in the hallway outside Ward A and Rachel had just discovered what made Fey look so completely different.

Fey gave an excited laugh. "Oh, he didn't pay for it!" she said, with the outrageous frankness that even Rachel often found disconcerting.

"I did not assume that he had," she said stiffly. "But it would be no more incredible than that he should take thee home in his carriage, and kiss thy hand."

"I know," Fey said quickly, almost materially. The quivering elation melted into her usual mature calm. "It is strange, but I made it happen, and the rest, too, will come. I must go to my baby, she'll be crying for me."

Rachel followed upstairs to the third floor. She sat beside Fey while she nursed the hungry baby. She watched them in troubled silence. She was not worldly, but she was wise, and when, after the baby had once more gone to sleep, she drew the story of the afternoon bit by bit from Fey, she saw the true inwardness of the situation. The girl, always reticent, told very little, but Rachel understood. Fey had twice been mortally humiliated and abandoned by life. At her father's death and her husband's desertion she had been forced into a degradation of the spirit and body.

Small wonder, then, that now she was fighting life for herself and the baby, that she was determined to wrest from it the prizes which her strong and completely feminine nature now suggested to her as the only ones of value: money, with its attendant power, and a subtle form of revenge. She may succeed, thought Rachel sadly, and it will be sickeningly wrong.

She tried to reason with the girl; she showed her bitter doubts, and it was useless. Fey was remote and dutiful. She insisted on taking the night shift in her ward to even up time lost that afternoon. At midnight she relieved Nellie Molloy and efficiently solved several problems which that sleepy young woman had neglected. The screened corner bed hid a scabrous immigrant mother in protracted labour, and at dawn Fey expertly assisted Rachel in the delivery of a feeble scaly infant, misshapen and livid. The baby would not breathe properly, and it was Fey who grimly doused it in the cold and hot basins of water and blew her own breath into its lungs while Rachel worked on the mother. Between them they saved both, and when the chill dawn light sifted through the ward, the mother and child slept normally.

The doctor remained a few minutes beside the cot, then she followed Fey into the utensil room, where she found the girl violently scrubbing her hands under the cold trickle of the single tap.

"Ah, my dear," said Rachel, the relief in her voice roughened by exhaustion, "can thee not see what a fine work thee does here! What a future thee might have—honest, clean, unselfish. We saved life tonight, Fey—does thee not feel triumph?"

Fey slowly placed the bar of yellow soap on the zinc drain and turned toward the doctor. The naked gas jet hissed and sputtered and its glare pitilessly exposed Rachel. Her greying hair was dishevelled, tired furrows pulled her mouth, the tiny muscle which exhaustion had lately set to jumping, beat in her cheek. And the course linen apron that protected her dress was stained brownish with drying blood.

This tarnishing of Rachel exploded the disgust Fey had been controlling. She threw back her head.

"Look at you!" she cried, her voice breaking. "Dirt, blood, misery. You're killing yourself trying to stop it. And it's no use. It'll go on, no matter what you do. That mother and baby, they'd have died in the cellar they came from. But what good did it do to save them? They'll go back next week. They'll go on just the same—dirt, misery, drink, stupidity. What's the use of helping their bodies a little? You don't change their souls!"

Rachel's tired eyes brightened to sudden anger. "How does thee know!" she cried sharply. "We're put in this world to help each other. The bodies first, because those we can better understand."

The girl's mouth twisted; she shook her head, and turning back to the sink she began to fill the ward's water-jug. "I've been the 'poor' myself, Doctor Rachel," she said. "Only the strong get out. And they do it alone."

Rachel sighed, her anger gone. A swimming weariness ran along her bones and she sank on an iron stool beside the medicine cabinet. "I would not bother with thee, Fey," she said sadly, "did I not know thee has glimpses of the Light within, despite thee hardens thy heart. Dear child—we do nothing alone."

Fey was silent, her bowed head bent over the sink.

Rachel closed her eyes and began to speak, half to herself, quoting the words of the Quaker founder. "Every man—" she paused, and repeated, "*Every* man is enlightened by the divine light of Christ. I saw it shine through all, and that they that believed in it came out of condemnation to the light of life— and became the children of it—"

A tremor passed through Fey. Unwillingly she felt the shock of a different vibration. It was as though a crystal wind blew through the dingy utensil room. She resisted, struggling, resentful, but it caught her up inexorably. For an instant she apprehended meaning. She saw with Rachel. She was Rachel. She was one with that unclean new mother in the ward, with all the other patients and beyond—extended in identity through a million channels which sprayed eternally from the infinite fountainhead. And the water's essence was pain.

No! she cried desperately.

The brown cupboards and walls of the utensil room sped back encircling and compressing. The tap resumed its metallic drip. Through the wall came the sleepy whimper of a patient.

Rachel, strengthened by the words she had quoted, stood up and untied her apron. "Never mind the water-jug," she said. "Annie will be here to relieve thee." She smiled at Fey. "Get some sleep, child, this is no time for deep discussion. I should know better."

Fey kissed Rachel silently and went to her room. For a long time she lay awake, holding the baby tight against her. As the sweeps and the milk-boys started crying through the streets she fell asleep at last. When she awoke four hours later, her first thought was of Simeon Tower and that she would see him on Sunday.

12

RACHEL also had made plans for Fey on that October Sunday of 1868. Rachel had been invited to an "At Home" given by the Misses Phoebe and Alice Cary. Their Sunday parties, frequented by the literary, the cultured, and the semi-Bohemian, were New York's nearest approach to a salon, since it could no longer boast gauzy gatherings of "the starry sisterhood" in Charlotte Lynch Botta's or Mrs. Osgood's drawing-rooms.

Like them, the Cary sisters were authors, of course. Had not Phoebe writen *One Sweetly Solemn Thought*, Alice written *Married but Not Mated*, and both a great many affecting songs and lyrics? And had not Whittier himself dedicated a most flattering poem to them after they had visited him in Amesbury? They were, therefore, well-equipped to run a salon and they succeeded where so many had failed. The Steady Junoesque Alice understood the proper mixing of human ingredients: solid thinkers for body, a celebrity or two for flavour, and an eccentric for spice.

Phoebe, the domestic one, translated her sister's mixtures into their literal culinary terms and thereby produced excellent claret lemonade and fruitcake. One enjoyed one's self at the Carys'. Their house on Twentieth Street near Fourth Avenue had been furnished with conscious charm, and its motif was a forest glade. The thick carpets were patterned in oak leaves; the gasoliers, artfully shaded by yellow glass, gave the feeling of sunlight upon foliage touched by frost; and the vases, satin throws, and bound books were all of autumnal reds and oranges, or lemon yellows.

Horace Greeley, who never missed a Sunday unless he was at his Chappaqua farm, had said in print that the Carys had "the sunniest drawing-room (even by gaslight) to be found between Kingsbridge and the Battery."

Greeley would be there this Sunday evening, and perhaps Whittier, too, thought Rachel pleasurably. She had only recently met the Carys, and though she refused most social events, she found that she was anticipating this one with eager curiosity, and she determined to take Fey with her. It was what the girl needed; diversion, new people, change. Rachel reproached herself for not having thought of it sooner. Fey led too monotonous a life, no wonder she precipitated herself into foolish situations like the meeting with Simeon Tower. Fey had not mentioned him again and Rachel had persuaded herself that the incident was over.

After breakfast she called Fey into the little sitting-room, broached the subject of the Misses Carys' party, and was soon disillusioned.

"But Doctor Rachel," cried Fey, distressed but inflexible, "I can't go with you. I'm driving out with Mr. Tower this afternoon."

"Fey—thee mustn't! If he's coming, tell him thee can't go. I want thee with me. Thee'll meet real people, young ones, too, worth while. I beg thee, child—don't be so stubborn!"

It was hopeless. Fey had promised to go with Tower, and go she would. Rachel was too proud to implore, and too just to command. She had no authority over Fey, and the girl liberally repaid in work the food and shelter which she received from the Infirmary. So Rachel said nothing more. At four o'clock she watched from her window when the Tower brougham clattered up to the kerb. The matched bays sparkled with silver trimmings, their coats glowed like polished walnut, their blackened hoofs were as glossy as the maroon trim on the carriage. The two men on the box were resplendent in green livery and leather boots. Rachel saw the footman hold the door for Fey, and Fey, radiant in her feuille-morte dress, give him a gracious nod of thanks as she stepped into the brougham. She acts as though she were born to all that, thought Rachel, startled. And as the carriage turned on Second Avenue to drive north, she had a fleeting glimpse of the two inside. She saw the angle of Tower's back in the heavy furred greatcoat and his blunt profile inclined near Fey. There was unmistakable pursuit in his attitude, his hand, conspicuous in a mauve glove, hovered near the girl's knee, and Fey, though she sat demurely in the extreme right corner of the carriage, had her head tilted receptively and she was laughing. Rachel saw the flash of even white teeth, and realized, with new dismay, how seldom she had seen Fey laugh.

Rachel turned sadly from the window and began to dress herself for the Cary party. She arrived at five to find the little house already full. The Irish maid ushered her upstairs to the drawing-room and that forest glade was appropriately murmurous with birdlike voices. Phoebe and Alice received her

162

most graciously. They liked entertaining "strong-minded women" of accomplishment, knowing that for all their show of disdain it put the men on their mettle, and bred stimulating talk. There were several feminists present today and Alice Cary suavely drew Rachel over to a red settee where Susan B. Anthony and Elizabeth Cady Stanton were discussing—not woman's rights, but the deplorable advent of the bustle. Rachel had no interest in fashion, and quietly smiling and seating herself she examined the other guests. Whittier had not come, after all, and Rachel, who had just read *Snowbound* and had looked forward to expressing her admiration, was disappointed. Bayard Taylor was there, however, holding forth on his recent trip to Russia and at the same time paying court to the redoubtable Fanny Fern who made more money from her writings than any other authoress. Fanny was accompanied by her husband, James Parton, who gravitated persistently, notebook in hand, around Horace Greeley, a tall, shambling figure with a ludicrous old baby's face behind steel spectacles. Mr. Parton was industriously gathering material for a biography. Rachel was not much impressed by Mr. Greeley, whose squeaky voice and incessant flow of nervous opinions irritated her, nor did she read Mr. Greeley's *Tribune*. The two strong-minded ladies on the settee beside her had progressed from bustles to an enthusiastic condemnation of a Mrs. Victoria Claflin Woodhull's theories about free love, a subject as foreign to Rachel's interest as bustles. She began to feel out of place and a trifle forlorn. Her mind wandered back to the Infirmary and the management of a difficult case in Ward B; from there it moved with the familiar stab of worry to Fey.

The Cary sisters well merited their reputation as hostesses. They had instantly noticed Rachel's isolation and Alice now advanced across the room with a dark-haired young man in tow.

"Doctor Moreton, may I present Mr. Ewen MacDonald?" said Alice, smiling. "A stranger to our shores. Mr. Greeley brought him. He is much interested in your Infirmary and indeed in all our social conditions."

The young man smiled and bowed, clasping Rachel's hand in a quick, warm grip. "May I, Doctor?" he asked, pulling up a chair beside her. "I'd like very much to talk to you, but you're my first woman physician and I'm dreadful awed."

His grey eyes twinkled as he smiled at her and Rachel laughed. She liked him at once. He had simplicity and humour. He seemed so much interested in the Infirmary that Rachel found herself talking enthusiastically, and she was woman enough to be flattered that he showed no signs of restlessness. He brought her claret lemonade and cake, then reseated himself by her side in spite of the inviting glances sent him by Fanny Fern and a lovely languishing Miss Elkins.

Rachel was woman enough, too, to find Mr. MacDonald's own story quite romantic. Though he gave few details, she gathered that he had been sent from Scotland to find a lost heiress in the West, a distant cousin of his.

"And did you never find her?" asked Rachel.

"Never," he answered. "She'd vanished like an elf-wife and my quest is a failure." He spoke in a light tone, but he frowned a little and Rachel saw the subject disturbed him.

"It's quite like one of Fanny Fern's own romances, I believe," she said, smiling and nodding toward that lady across the room, "and no doubt it will yet have a happy ending."

"I fear not," he answered, drawing his thick brows together. "Old Sir James, the laird who sent me, is dying, and I sail for Scotland in the morning."

"Oh, I'm sorry," said Rachel, with warm sympathy.

At once MacDonald smiled. "You're a very nice woman, Doctor Moreton, and I don't mean to sound dejected. I've had a rare good time in your land. I've seen it all from Boston to the Pacific, from Chicago to New Orleans, and I like it. Sometime I'll be back, but now I must off to my ain bit country and settle down again."

He reminded her of someone, Rachel thought suddenly. Was it his voice, or was it the slow, warm smile? The impression was vague and yet pleasurable. She searched desultorily for the reason while they went on chatting. As usually happens, the feeling of recognition lessened as she tried to pin it down. By the time new arrivals surged into the little drawing-room and the hostess tactfully rearranged groupings, Rachel had lost the impression entirely. All during their conversation she had been charmed and stimulated, and she never once thought of Fey.

At nine o'clock, Doctor Moreton's hackney cab was announced, and Rachel was sorry that she had ordered it so early, for the talk had become general. The opening of the New West was the topic, and Greeley and Bayard Taylor engaged in a sparkling duet of enthusiasm, supported now and then by a quietly witty interpolation from MacDonald. He was the youngest man there and yet he held his own with grace and distinction. They listened to him.

Rachel left regretfully, feeling a real disappointment that Mr. MacDonald was sailing so soon.

She arrived home at the Infirmary full of the evening's pleasure and anxious to share it. She went up to Fey's room and found the girl already changed back into her uniform and the baby sleeping quietly in her cradle.

"You've had a good time!" cried Fey, her half-guilty, half-triumphant flush fading as she saw Rachel's face. She had been braced for a scolding.

"Thee *should* have been there, child!" Rachel sat down on the cot. "Such good talk, and interesting people with ideas. And a charming young Scotsman. Thee would have liked him, thee couldn't help it."

"Perhaps I might have," said Fey sweetly, and without the faintest interest. She would not hurt Rachel, but she longed to be left alone again to relive those hours with Simeon to evaluate each incident and decide on a course. Matters were moving very fast. They had driven up the Bloomingdale Road to Claremont. There they had had champagne punch and cakes and attracted a good deal of attention from a party of Sunday excursionists who recognized Simeon. So deeply had he been concentrating on her that he had scarcely noticed this attention, and Fey, remembering the nervous glances he had cast about during their other outing to the Mall, was delighted by this evidence of his increasing absorption. He had given her a thousand dollars for the turquoise, presented the roll of bills with an embarrassment which she did not share in the acceptance. It was far more than she had expected, but she was completely ignorant of its market value, and she was, moreover, well aware that the transaction had unexpressed overtones.

On the long drive back, she had let him kiss her. It had been almost a boy's kiss—fumbling, over-eager, and while she responded to him with instinctive tact, she had felt a sudden maternal pity.

"Thee's not listening, Fey," said Rachel. She had been telling Fey more about young MacDonald. Fey, examining and savouring the ripening relation with Simeon, had not heard one word.

"I'm sorry, Doctor Rachel," she said, starting and smiling apology.

Rachel sighed: "Well, out with it. Thee's thinking of thy afternoon's jaunt. There's little use my trying to interest thee in anyone else."

"Not in any handsome young man unless he could give me

riches and position," said Fey, laughing. She stood up and put her hands on her friend's shoulders. "I know I worry you, dear Doctor Rachel, and I'm sorry, but I must follow my fate."

"Fiddlesticks, child," snapped Rachel, suddenly impatient. "We make our own fortunes and we call it Fate. Does thee know what Plato said? 'All things are in Fate, yet all things are not decreed by Fate.' We have free will, and need not even listen to the Guide who would lead us to heaven."

Fey smiled and kissed Rachel's furrowed forehead. "You look so handsome in that lovely gown. I wish you'd dress up all the time."

Rachel looked down at the rich satin folds, and laughed. "Thee's incorrigible, but thee reminds me that I must put off this lovely gown and get to work. Please to start changing the dressing on Mrs. Samuelson's leg and wait with her until I get there."

The following Wednesday a case of scarlet fever appeared in the children's ward and Fey was terrified. She no longer dared leave Lucita at all, and she hung over the baby constantly watching for the first signs of fever, or the dreaded "strawberry" tongue.

Rachel's reassurances that nursing infants usually seemed immune did little to comfort Fey. Her fear provided the final spur to the decision she had been forming since Simeon gave her the thousand dollars. She rented a furnished apartment on West Eighteenth Street, near Sixth Avenue.

The parting scene between Rachel and Fey was keyed low. Neither woman said much and each allowed the tissue of affection to conceal her separate misgiving. Fey hid a pricking of guilt, as Rachel hid her profound disapproval of a move which she knew to be partially connected with Simeon Tower.

"You'll come to see me, won't you?" begged Fey, holding her friend's hand. "And as soon as I'm settled, I'll come and help you any time you need me."

Rachel nodded and smiled without speaking. They stood in the little hall outside the clinic door where they had first met. How different had been that other girl, frightened, bedraggled in her cheap dress, distorted by pregnancy! And yet, it seemed to Rachel that there had been also a delicacy, a sensitivity of spirit, which were now lost. Fey had been blurred then, and groping, while now she radiated assurance and vitality. I am wrong, perhaps, not to rejoice at the change, thought Rachel. Fey was a vivid figure in the leaf-brown silk which high-lighted her creamy skin, her red mouth like a geranium, the hair glossy black against the bonnet's tawny plume; and the baby was as vivid, her golden-red curls spraying like tiny feathers around the edges of the muslin cap. Both of them so brilliantly young and eager for life.

Rachel saw them into the hackney and kissed them. She waved good-bye from the brownstone stoop and turned back into the Infirmary feeling bleak, old and empty. Had it, after all, been selfishness which had fooled her into thinking she might keep them always? A clutching at vicarious maternity, or—worse offence against the Spirit—had she tried to dominate those two whom she loved?

If she had not been somehow at fault, why should she be punished now by this bitterness of failure? Why should the hospital work seem suddenly futile, a monotony of uphill ploddings never reaching a permanent summit?

She applied to these painful questionings her invariable remedy. Islanded by quiet in her locked room, she tried to free her heart and send it upward to the Light. She waited in the midst of silence for the secret word, and the peace. Not in years had the answer failed her as it did today. She could find no inner stillness, she could not even control her usually disciplined body which harried her by a dozen small discomforts. The muscle throbbed in her cheek, her right knee ached, and through her ears there was a rushing of blood. Age, drabness, and defeat circled around her bowed head like vultures, and blacker even than their shadows was the anguish of a stirring memory. She thought of her husband, not with the usual gentle tenderness, but with a sharp physical desire. A long-forgotten frenzy seized upon her; she felt again the ecstatic pressure of a man's hard body, heard the thick-voiced, broken words of passion and fulfilment. So long ago and never to come again. Why should this body shamefully betray her by a violent yearning of its own?

She looked down at the heavy middle-aged outline beneath the grey percale coverall. A shudder of disgust shook her, for with the pain of nostalgia came the recognition of envy. It was not then only thoughts of vicarious maternity with which Fey inspired her. There was the other too. And this further substitution was unbearably humiliating.

She slipped to her knees beside the bed and bent her head on her clasped hands. Slow tears oozed through her fingers and fell on the white counterpane.

She knelt, crouching by the bed, until outside on Second

Avenue the lamplighter shuffled by. The pale glow of gaslight struck through her uncurtained window. And there was a timid knock on the door.

"Doctor Moreton," called Nellie Molloy's anxious voice, "we do be a-needing of you, doctor—little Minnie's coughing fit to bust, and that slut in Ward A's bleeding again like a stuck pig."

Rachel got up slowly. She walked to the washbowl and, dipping a towel in the pitcher, she rubbed the wet end over her ravaged face.

"Be right with you, Nellie," she answered. "Get more ice up from the basement."

She tidied up her hair before the tiny mirror, picked up her stethoscope and instrument case. She unlocked the door and hurried down the hall to the ward. At her appearance the restless, fretful patients quieted and turned their faces to her, their different expressions of suffering fused into one collective look of hopeful relief. " 'Tis the doctor, God bless her, she'll ease ye now, Violet," whispered a voice to the little prostitute who was miscarrying.

Rachel gave them all her friendly smile, and walking to Violet's cot she laid her cool hand on the frightened girl's forehead, at the same time gently pulling down the sheet.

Fey was not happy during her first days on Eighteenth Street. She missed Rachel and even the Infirmary far more than she had expected to, and she was for a time bewildered by this new way of living. She had at last achieved elegance, but her crowded rooms oppressed her, and she had to grope her way into knowledge of each detail. Her apartment was on the second floor of a converted residence. She had a parlour, dining-room, back bedroom, and kitchen, all furnished by a welter of the owner's discarded pieces in overstuffed walnut, bird's-eye maple, and brass. The flat was expensive, fifty dollars a month, and there was even a bathroom with a boxed-in toilet and enormous tin tub rimmed in varnished pine. No hot water, of course, and the hastily installed cold-water pipe never yielded more than a discouraged trickle, so that Fey continued to bathe herself and the baby from the bedroom washbowl. Also the bathroom was freezing cold. It was now November, and all the rooms were cold because she had not yet made proper contact with a coal merchant, and since she had no servant she had to carry what coals were delivered up and down from the basement herself. It was necessary, too, to find a milkman, a baker

168

boy, and an ashman besides getting herself and Lucita and a basket down to the Jefferson Market at Tenth Street to buy food. The food once bought provided a further problem. Fey understood the management of an open fire, she could make tortillas and chilli, but for all her natural efficiency she was balked by the griffin-footed curlicued stove in her dark kitchen. The draughts were faulty and it went out—repeatedly.

All these troubles would have been avoided had she moved into a boarding-house. It was Simeon who had vetoed that and suggested that she try for an apartment. In a boarding-house there was no privacy, and no respectable lady might receive male callers except in the parlour. Fey had agreed with him that the apartment would be better. She knew that he intended to visit her, and she was as anxious for freedom of movement as he.

He called on the fourth evening after she had moved in. Fey had not expected him so soon, but he had not been able to wait. His nights were disturbed by dreams of her, and her image had begun to invade his office and interfere with plans for floating a new bond issue.

In April, Simeon had obtained a charter for the Gulf and San Diego Railroad. Only nine miles of track had actually been constructed and these were rapidly turning into the usual "streaks of rust," but nobody knew that or cared. An accommodating Congress had donated some twenty million acres of land, and if there were no tracks, at least there was an abundance of elegantly named town sites where depots might some day appear. Also it was obvious to anybody that rail connection between the Gulf of Mexico and Southern California would soon be a necessity. How convenient, too, that Simeon's newly acquired Transic Steamship Line should ply between New York and Galveston! Only Vanderbilt had as yet developed the technique of monopoly, and Simeon found the project alluring.

The arousing of congressional enthusiasm had not been difficult since the Union Pacific through the Crédit Mobilier had already worked out a delicately graduated and extremely successful scale. Five to ten thousand took care of a representative; floor leaders and senators came higher. With this precedent established, Simeon had found that three trips to Washington were sufficient, three trips, filled, of course, by stately inter-changes on patriotism, the Winning of the West, and the Expansion of Our Great Nation for the Benefit of the People.

The further negotiations for floating the bond issue through Jay Cooke's banking house provided exactly the type of problem which Simeon enjoyed. He was, therefore, astonished to find himself remembering Fey's smile, or the tone of her low, accented voice in the midst of interviews with Mr. Fahnestock, Cooke's New York partner.

On that Tuesday evening, Simeon, having discreetly walked down Sixth Avenue from his home on Twenty-Ninth, climbed the high stoop and pressed Fey's bell, had no thoughts for the Gulf and San Diego. His mouth was dry, and he was both apprehensive and exhilarated as he had not been since the unfortunate Bridgeport love-affair.

Fey was startled by the twanging of her bell. She had been having trouble with the baby, who objected to the substitution of cow's milk for the food she preferred. The strain of moving had affected Fey, who had finally realized that Lucita's fretful wailings came from hunger.

"O chiquita, who can that be?" she said wearily to the baby as the bell clamoured again. "Do be good and go to sleep, naughty one!"

She put the baby in the cradle, hastily rearranged the front of her long ruffled woollen wrapper, stuffed loosened strands of hair into her net, and ran downstairs.

Dios! Mr. Tower! she thought, peering through the stained-glass side-light. She hesitated, thinking of the wailing baby, the cold cluttered rooms upstairs—and herself in dishevelment—face shiny and tired, the rumpled wrapper and her feet! Not bare fortunately, though that was still the only way they were entirely comfortable, but stockingless and covered only by shapeless little kid slippers.

On the other side of the door she saw Simeon's outline raise the walking-stick and push her bell again.

Fey took a deep breath, shrugged her shoulders, and opened the door.

"Come in, Mr. Tower," she said. "It is nice that you come to see me. I'm sorry that I am not dressed for visitors."

For a moment Simeon was shocked. His image of Fey was a brilliant and sophisticated one, always exquisitely groomed. "If my call is not convenient, I can come another time," he said stiffly, fingering his mauve gloves and trying not to stare.

"I am happy to have you come up, if you will take me as I am—me and Lucita," said Fey, smiling, and there was emphasis in her tone. It intimated, "You had better know all about me, since we are going to know each other so well."

Simeon felt a quick masculine recoil; he had not thought about the future of their scarcely achieved relationship, nor had he admitted to himself that it would have a future. But her voice awakened the usual tremor of excitement. He bowed and followed her upstairs, thinking with astonishment that she was much younger than he had realized. He had assumed her to be in the twenties. This little figure, smaller than ever without heels, was almost that of a child.

And it was almost as to a child that he cried out, "My dear girl, this is a terrible way to live, you must get a servant and enough heat!"

"I don't know how to get a servant, yet," answered Fey, laughing at his appalled face. "And this is more luxury, though maybe not comfort, than I have ever had. It's warmer in the bedroom, shall we sit in there?"

He gave her a quick glance, and saw that she spoke as usual without self-consciousness.

The bedroom was much warmer, for Fey had finally learned how to manage its coal fire, but it was not cosy. The ceiling was too high, a draught blew from the window and under the door, and the draperies and rug, once respectively gold and figured ivory, had long merged into a faded drab.

Simeon looked around for a place to put his hat, stick, and coat.

"On the bed, I guess," said Fey calmly, and Simeon cleared his throat and complied. Ladies did not receive men in bed-rooms—unless— But he wasn't sure. From the beginning he hadn't been sure about Fey. Now she was composedly tidying her hair and powdering her face in front of the walnut mirror. Even Pansy had never let him see her do that.

He crossed the room and sat down in a mohair armchair before the fire. The chair creaked, and as if in answer there came a tiny bubbling sound from behind the big brass bed. He looked around startled.

"That's my baby," explained Fey, smiling. "For you she has stopped yelling. Don't you want to see her?"

Simeon did not. It annoyed him that Fey should have a baby, and before this he had been able to ignore it.

"Yes, I know," said Fey, watching him. "But I want you to see her, please."

Jove, she does understand, thought Simeon. He would have resented this perception from anyone else; half his financial success resulted from his ability to hide his thoughts, but Fey's intuition was deeply flattering.

171

They stood together and looked down into the cradle. "So —my Lucita," said Fey, "here is Mr. Tower, do you like him?"

The baby's solemn blue eyes travelled from her mother's face to the other strange rectangle near it. She examined the pinkish blur, the glint from the firelight on the blond moustache and light pomaded hair, then her wandering gaze was caught by Simeon's blue eyes, amused and admiring.

Lucita gave a delighted gurgle and reaching up a plump hand broke into an enchanting smile.

"So she likes you," laughed Fey.

"It's an extremely pretty baby," said Simeon, gratified in spite of himself. He put his arm quickly around Fey's shoulders. "Do you also like me, F-Fey?" He had never before used her Christian name.

She looked up at him under her lashes; her body, without moving, gave the impression of yielding against him. His hand closed on the soft bones of her shoulder. The warm scent of her body mingled with the odour of her perfume—frangipani, the red jasmine.

"I like you very much, Simeon." She escaped from him gently and sat down in the other chair by the fire. "More than any other man."

As always, her timing with Simeon was as perfect as it was instinctive. Always she saved him from self-consciousness and the deeply hidden fear of inadequacy, before his male pride made it necessary to put himself to the test. Each time his confidence increased, and Fey's attraction for him strengthened.

He sat down in the other fireside chair. "It's pleasant here," he said, looking across at her. She was curled up in the chair, her feet tucked under the edge of her robe for warmth, her head turned in delicate profile while she gazed thoughtfully at the ruddy coals. He had not considered the room pleasant before, he would physically have been far more comfortable in Pansy's snug domesticity, or even in his own great panelled library.

"I wonder if I'm falling in love with you, Fey," he added, astonished.

She turned her head. Her grey eyes contemplated him with indulgence and faint amusement. "Yes, I think you are," she said, her lips curving. "Didn't you know?" There was neither conceit nor coquetry in this. Strange that her utter lack of conventional pretences should lie in a nature and appearance so feminine.

172

"I haven't thought much about love," he said slowly. "Oh, there was a girl once, when I was very young—" His expression did not change, but Fey saw a nearly imperceptible tension flow over him. His eyes shifted from her to the grate.

She made a soft gesture. "And that experience was unpleasant, and it still distresses you."

His head snapped up. He had long ago managed to forget in consciousness the exact dénouement of that long-buried episode. "We were unsuited to each other," he said stiffly. "Her parents disapproved of me. I hadn't made money then."

"So"—said Fey—"you parted." She smiled into his defensive face. "And since then, many women have been after you, but you do not love?"

"No. I guess not. Of course—" He paused, considering. What was it about her that made it a voluptuous pleasure to have her know things he had always hidden? "Of course, there has been someone."

Fey nodded. "Of course. A mistress. I have seen her."

"The devil you have!" Simeon uncrossed his legs. He caught his moustache with his lower teeth. "I don't know how you know so much about me, and I don't know why I don't mind. I've kept Pansy pretty dark. I'm not a man like Fisk or Tweed. I like appearances kept decent."

Fey gave him her composed, considering look, seeing beneath his words, feeling the uncertainty, the thirst for approval which had driven him to achievement.

"So rich," she said softly, with an undertone of gentle raillery, "and yet you mind what people think. What more is it you want?"

I want to belong, he thought instantly, and as instantly rejected that childish answer. He gave an easy laugh. "Why, I suppose I want more money, and a wife and family, leave some permanent mark on the world. The usual things men want." Her question disconcerted him. He reached in his breast-pocket and pulled out a Havana cigar. "May I?"

"Oh, please do!" cried Fey. "I'm forgetting your comfort. You entertain me so beautifully with champagne and I give you nothing. Wait—we'll set a better mood."

Set a better mood, thought Simeon, amused. She used odd phrases, but they were never meaningless. He watched her lazily while she achieved just that. She darted from her chair and, disappearing into the kitchen, brought back a bottle of port and two glasses. She put a fresh shovelful of coals on the fire, and pulled the heavy window curtains which she had previously forgotten. She went to Lucita and, seeing that the baby was fast asleep, carried the cradle into the little dressing-room. Before settling back into her chair, she opened her bureau drawer and poured a dribble of tobacco from a silk pouch into her hand. This she transferred to a small square of white paper and rolled into a cigarette.

"This shocks you?" she asked, seeing Simeon's face. "In Santa Fe everybody smokes. I do it seldom. But it's friendly if we smoke together, don't you think?"

Simeon did. He found the experience as delightfully companionable as it was novel. The mingled fragrance of smoke and the warmth of the port—a very inferior port, but this he did not notice—evoked a sensuous haze. Fey leaned over to put her glass on the tray. Her wrapper parted a little and he saw the silhouette of her firm round breasts. He looked away and then back again, but Fey had resumed her former position. "Shall I sing to you?" she asked, and, without waiting for his assent, she leaned her head against the antimacassar, her eyes half-closed. She sang "El Venadito" in a throaty caressing voice. It was the same song she had sung for him in the Arcadia nearly a year ago. And she thought, almost awed, of how exactly the prophecy she had made him then had come true.

"Un día cantaré por te solamente." And now she was singing for him alone, and he was as moved by her song now as he had been bored then. She saw that he was not reminded of the Bowery waiter-girl, and she was glad. She suspected which of Simeon's conventions she must not shock.

Her voice prolonged the last note until it died away and she looked at him seductively but with gentleness too. She waited.

Simeon put his glass and cigar on the tray. His palms were coldly moist. "Beautiful," he said, too loud. He heard his voice, strange, out of key. He cleared his throat. "What is it a-b-bout?" The ludicrous thickening and stumbling of his tongue. Go to her, you fool, he thought, she's waiting for you. You won't be ridiculous; you are condescending to her, you're one of the richest men in the country. You are not too fat, too old for her—

"It's about love, of course—" She threw back her head and laughed softly, showing the long curve of her white throat. Her fingers uncurled and her right hand made an appealing gesture toward him, a gesture of friendship and intimacy.

A vibrant silence filled the little space between them. A glowing coal fell through the bars of the grate making a sharp thud on the hearthstone.

Simeon's indrawn breath sounded as loud. "Come here, Fey," he cried in a tone almost insulting. "I want you, I need you—"

Fey got up at once and came to him. "You need never pretend to me, Simeon," she whispered, "for I understand."

His arms closed around her convulsively.

On that November night in Fey's apartment, Simeon's tentative infatuation had been transformed into a compelling love. Not only had she given him pleasure which he had never before experienced or dared expect, but she had added profound release in creating for him the dear image of a conquering virility. With him her tact and emotional timing were as delicately unerring as her ardour. There was no hypocrisy in this. She was very fond of him and she wished to please him. Nor was she handicapped by her own blinded passion as she had been with Terry.

She never allowed herself to think of Terry, but sometimes, in the dark hour before waking, memory would jump at her like a cougar bringing a recoil of fear and hatred; completely awake, she would discover this panic limited to her mind while her body had grown heavy with a shameful longing.

As the weeks passed and her attachment to Simeon grew stronger, these moments ceased to assault her and she rejoiced in the victory.

Simeon, submerged though he was in love, did not at first think of marrying Fey. A part of him remained objective, and no desire for a woman's constant presence could offset the detriment which a marriage of that sort would be to his ambition. He longed for acceptance by the Astors, the Livingstons, the Gracies, and the Lorillards. He had not yet recovered from the humiliation of being blackballed by the Eastern and New York Yacht Clubs, as Jay Gould had been. He jealously watched August Belmont's social rise. But Belmont had married Caroline Slidell Perry of unimpeachable connections.

It was the discovery that Fey also was well-born, added to the increasing pressure of his need for her, which changed his mind.

175

He had avoided questioning her about her past. Though he had become fond of the baby, he loathed being forced to remember that Fey had had a husband, and too, he was afraid of finding out other things which he would prefer to ignore.

On Christmas Eve, however, after a shared bottle of champagne in her apartment, he suddenly felt both relaxed and curious. He had brought her a present, a gold and jewelled bracelet on the pattern of a "regard" ring. The gems, artfully separated by a pearl heart, stood for their combined initials. A sapphire and a topaz for Simeon Tower, another sapphire, carbuncle, and diamond for "Santa Fe Cameron Dillon."

"You've an odd name, darling," remarked Simeon, watching the bracelet sparkle on her wrist. "I never thought about it until I had the jeweller make this up. Where'd the Cameron come from?"

"From my father," answered Fey, laughing. "Where else? He was a Scottish doctor."

"Was he, indeed!" Simeon was startled. "But I thought you were Spanish."

"My mother only. My father was a Scot, and I myself, as he impressed on me long ago, am an American, for I was born under this flag."

"Why, I suppose you are," said Simeon doubtfully. Despite his ownership of the Gulf and San Diego Railroad, he had not yet been west of New Orleans and such necessary map-reading as he had done did not extend north of Texas. The rest of the South-west was a vaguely Spanish blur.

"There are a goodish many Camerons in this country," pursued Simeon. "D'you know if you're related to any?"

Fey shook her head. She began to see the drift of this.

"None in this country. My father came alone. He was the son of the Laird of Gleekbie, Sir James Cameron, near—I think—Inveraray."

Simeon sat up. "D'you mean to t-tell me that your grandfather was a baronet? Why didn't you tell me before?"

"You asked me nothing before. Is it so important?" But yes, I suppose to him it is, she thought. Stupid of me not to tell him sooner.

"My mother, too, came of very good Spanish blood," she said quietly. "Her father was a hidalgo."

He considered this a moment, but a hidalgo meant nothing, and the Spanish side did not interest him. He nodded, crossing his legs, resting his fingertips together and frowning as he did when concentrating on a problem. I'll cable to Glasgow, he thought, get confirmation.

"You do not believe me?" she said, smiling and shrugging. "Have you not yet learned, my Simeon, that I tell you the truth, always?"

Simeon got up restlessly and stood before the fire. "I suppose you do. You're a strange girl, Fey." He looked at her, at the brass bed, then down at the faded hearthrug. "What would you say if I suggested you get a divorce from that—from Dillon?"

At last! The certainty which had guided all her relationship with Simeon had not failed her.

"I would say—that I don't know how it can be done exactly, but I wish it very much."

He made an impatient gesture. "Oh, it's easy enough to fix. I'll get hold of Barnard."

Even Fey knew the name of this accommodating judge, who was Tweed's tool and who had lately with his patron changed sides in the Erie War, and now twirled the judicial machinery for the benefit of Fisk and Gould.

"Ah, yes—money . . . " murmured Fey. She glanced down at the jewelled bracelet on her wrist.

Simeon watched her and his effort at prudent reserve melted. The childish innocence of her bent head and the white hollows of her neck leading in startling contrast to the line of her seductive breasts, the scent of her hair now decorously netted but which he knew intimately as a wild luxuriance, the wide scarlet mouth which gave and inspired passion, but was now set in her faintly ironic smile—these things stirred him to sudden vehemence.

He reached down and pulled her up from her chair by the wrists. "Is it just my money you want, Fey? D'you really love me at all, my girl? Answer me—you boast you always tell the truth!" He took her chin in his hand, forcing her head back so that she must meet his question.

"I can't," she whispered, "not like this. Let me go a minute, Simeon."

His arms dropped. She saw in his eyes the quick wariness with which he protected himself. She was dismayed; she wanted neither to hurt him nor to lose him. But as she tried to answer, it seemed as though her mind grew empty, waiting in blankness and listening to a far-off din of murmuring confusion, from which she could not distinguish the sound of truth.

She spoke at last very softly. "But what is true, Simeon—or

what is love? There are, I think, so many kinds, aren't there?"

His mouth tightened. He sat down stiffly in the armchair. "I suppose so."

Fey knelt on the hearthrug beside his chair, leaning her head against his knee. She took his hand, and, ignoring his quick withdrawing pull, rested her cheek on it.

Her considering indrawn gaze wandered over the leaping flames in the grate, the brass scuttle, the pale indeterminate pattern of the hearthrug. "This is the truth, Simeon," she said at last. "I like you, more than any man I have known. I'm happy with you and I can make you happy. Also"—she twisted her head quickly and gave him a mischievous and affectionate look—"I like very much to sleep with you."

He made a shocked sound. Surely no woman of really good birth—one did not say such things—but underneath there rose the new sense of triumph.

Fey felt the hand relax beneath her cheek. She went on with a quiet assurance. "I am ambitious like you, Simeon. I want money, yes, and like you I want position in the world. The money you can give me. The position we can make together."

By God! I believe we can! he thought, suddenly and completely convinced. He looked down at the dark head by his knee. Wife. Mrs. Simeon Tower. A new delightful concept, but it brought the carking doubt which must be laid.

He withdrew his hand and pushed back his chair, leaving her unsupported. "Fey—have you ever, except, of course, with Dillon—" He rasped the name, and she waited, her head bowed —"Have you ever been like this—with any other man?"

She turned so as to face him. "No one," she said. "Nor will there be."

Simeon sighed deeply. He bent over and pulled her up on his lap, where she melted against him, so delicate and light a weight that he felt her a part of himself.

Later, when he had let himself cautiously from the house— and the need for caution was even greater now that he guarded her reputation as well as his own—Fey slipped from bed in response to the baby's whimper from the dressing-room. It was a cold dank night and Lucita, who had kicked off her covers, had become chilled. Fey wrapped her in a pink afghan and carried her to the still glowing fire. She curled up on the rug and rocked her baby.

"It's Christmas morning, Lucita," she whispered. "Next year we'll fill your little shoe with straw for the camels of the Three Wise Kings, and they'll bring you gifts, as they do at home."

The baby cooed, her eyelids drooped.

Why did I say "home"? thought Fey. That is finished. Everything now begins new as I wanted it. But she continued to stare into the fire, smelling, not the coal-gas acridity, but the aromatic perfume of the cedar bonfires that would be lit on every street corner tonight, wreathing the mountain air in fragrant blue smoke. The plaza would be mysterious and expectant in the glancing lights, filled by shawled figures moving silently toward the church. There would be candles—like tiny topazes—set in the upstairs windows of the houses to light the way for the little Santo Niño as He wandered the roads on Christmas Eve searching for those in need of His help. And soon the Christmas bells would ring out jubilantly from the Parroquia, and the people would pass through the streets—singing. The smell, the sight, the sound of Christmas—Pascua de Navidad; and back across the river in the hills—Atalaya, the watch-peak, guarding the festive town, indulgent to the happy, dancing celebrants, eternally serene in its ancient certainty.

The baby slept, but Fey sat on before the fire, and a bitter pain rose like water in her heart. Why must the past always mean pain? Why was there not release and comfort enough in the escape from it—and in the future? "The future"—she murmured the words as an incantation, arming herself with them. She thrust them into her heart and the pain receded, but there was no solace. Instead, before her brooding eyes the fire seemed to die away, and the grate become filled with shadows. As she watched, the shadows moved together and found substance. They became stones—grey stones, piled and forbidding, each one penetrated by anguish. Behind and through the sombre masonry she saw Simeon, not as he was now, but an old man's face, shrunken, defeated, and his bleared eyes gazed at her in an agonized reproach.

Her breath knotted in her throat, sweat broke out on her back. Simeon's face softened—and from it now came warning. The grey mass and his face fused back into shadow and vanished. The bright curtain of the firelit room shut them off.

Fey drew a long shaking breath. Mechanically she moved her legs, which were tense with cramp. She got up and carried Lucita back to the cradle. Then she washed her face and combed her hair and got into bed. She lay staring at the crack of dawn light as it ran down between the drawn curtains. The bed had become chilled while she sat so long outside, and she pulled the quilt tight around her shoulders. Gradually she became warmer and her mind began to work lucidly, logically. That wasn't "the sight," she thought. It was imagination, or the champagne, perhaps. The earthiness of this pleased her, and she restated it. I was a bit drunk, that was it. She felt herself become very reasonable and calm, repudiating superstition. She had learned that word from Simeon—"superstition." "That fool of a Vanderbilt," he had said, "superstitious as an old woman, trots around to fortune-tellers begging 'em to read the future—consulting the stars or the spirits—pure bosh!"

She had agreed without interest. "The sight," that tingle of awareness and reaching out of self into a different, clearer place, and the flood of golden light which sometimes had come with it—that was a personal inward happening. It had nothing to do with fortune-telling, stars, or spirits. Besides, the thing was gone—if she had ever really had it. The mind-reading she had done for Terry—he hadn't believed it finally. It had been an accident—a trick, as our love was a trick, she thought. That time long ago with Father—an accident, and I can't remember it. Natanay—a superstitious old Indian. "Superstitious," "pure bosh." There is nothing in me that can know more than my mind does. It was because I was a lonely child, because out there they are simple foolish people, the Indians and the Mexicans, it is easy to believe silly things as they do. Here in this big city it is different. Here they live by reality. Tomorrow at Mass, this will all be clearer. And I must go to confession again. The priest will tell me how foolish it is to be afraid of an imagined pile of shadows and a face.

The streak of dawn light grew bright. From around the corner on Sixth Avenue she heard the muffled sounds of the awakening city, the rattle of the milk wagons over the Belgian blocks. The shrill cry of an Italian vendor:

> *"Buy my sweeta oranges!*
> *Eat my sweeta oranges!*
> *Fine leetle oranges,*
> *For a Merry Christmas!"*

Warm and sleepy at last, Fey turned over on her side. Her hand went automatically to her breast, guided by an old habit when she had often used to go to sleep holding the turquoise.

Now she withdrew her hand impatiently, jarred into momentary wakefulness. She tucked her hand under the pillow, noticing before she again closed her eyes that the beautiful jewels in Simeon's "regard" bracelet gave out iridescent flashes even in the gloom.

Simeon cabled to a confidential agency in Glasgow and, as he directed that no expense be spared, got quick confirmation of Fey's Scottish ancestry. Three weeks later the *Caledonia* brought him a letter as well. It was from a Mr. Ewen Mac-Donald of Inveraray, and it said:

DEAR MR. TOWER:

Your cabled inquiry via Glasgow gave me great surprise and, I must confess, considerable mortification. You see, the lady about whom you asked is the very one for whom I spent a year of search through your magnificent United States. To think that she must have been in New York when I sailed for home! Alas, that I so badly bungled my mission. And now it is too late. Sir James Cameron, her grandfather, died three weeks after my return, and before doing so he altered his will. The title, of course, went to another branch of the family, but now his entire estate has gone there as well. There is no chance, I fear, of breaking the will, but if the lady is in any want please call upon me personally. Will you be good enough to give me her present name and address so that I may write to her, and forgive me—but I *am* her kinsman—will you tell me the reason why you have taken an interest in her? Several times in your country, and even now and then in the wilds of the Scottish Highlands, I have heard of Simeon Tower.

I cannot help but be curious.

I am, sir, your most obedient servant,

EWEN MACDONALD.

Simeon digested this letter with satisfaction, then tore it into shreds as he had the cable.

He wrote back to MacDonald an extremely brief note. "The lady is not in want, and as her kinsman I admit your right to know that I intend to marry her. It is unnecessary for you to know any other details, and I ask you never to mention to anyone any circumstances which you may have discovered about her early life."

He gave neither Fey's name nor address, and he never told her of this correspondence, unwilling to have her know that he had thought it necessary to confirm her story.

He had made up his mind, and the proceedings from now on were to me handled with a meticulous discretion, so that Fey after their marriage might be presented to public knowledge in precisely the best light.

First the divorce must be got out of the way, and then concealed for ever. This problem he took at once to Judge Barnard, who was astonished to have Simeon Tower appear in person at the ornate judicial offices.

"What brings me this honour, my friend?" asked Barnard amiably, rising and stroking his glossy black moustache. "Little misunderstanding with the Erie boys? or have you maybe got around to needing an injunction for your own Gulf and San Diego?"

"Neither, George," answered Simeon, equally amiable. "Personal matter, ticklish and needs absolute secrecy."

"Then let's go to the Hoffman bar," returned the judge. "Nobody'd overhear anything there if you bellowed, or believe it either."

They settled at a small corner table in the Hoffman and Simeon ordered two brandies, then went to the point. "Lady I know needs a quick divorce. Actual grounds—fifteen months' desertion."

"Won't do in this State," said Barnard slowly; he was feeling his way, wondering just how much this divorce was worth to Tower. "Could she go to Indiana for a bit?"

"No," said Simeon. "You can fix it up here. Any grounds that'll work. There's a block of Transic might interest you."

"Ah," said the judge, relaxing. His lustrous eyes glowed. He delicately flicked a wisp of lint from his immaculate cuff. "Anybody know where the husband is?" he inquired.

"No, but I think Chicago—I've made inquiries. I don't want him found or notified."

"That's all right," said Barnard. "Half the time one party or the other doesn't know they're being divorced. They'll change that law some day, but fortunately haven't yet."

"I don't care how you do it," said Simeon, "but I want it legal. Closed chambers, of course, and not a leak to the press or anyone, now or later. Just to make secrecy and speed more interesting for you, you can count on some useful information six months from today if everything's gone the way I want it."

"It shall be exactly as you want it," said the judge, smiling. He leaned back and sipped his brandy. "You're looking very fit," he observed playfully. "Thinner, aren't you? Could it be that the fair sex has at last really—"

Simeon got up, laying a five-dollar gold piece on the table for the waiter. "So we understand each other, I believe. Come to my house tomorrow night for a private interview with the lady—get the necessary information."

Barnard shrugged and bowed. Touchy! he thought. Whoever she is, she's fairly caught him. It smells like marriage. Then he thought of other things. He had not achieved the supreme court bench and the confidence of Tweed, Fisk, and Gould without learning discretion and detachment.

Fey was duly divorced from Xavier Terence Dillon on the first of March. She had one interview with Judge Barnard in Simeon's library, and one later in the judge's chambers, where she signed papers. Both times she was heavily veiled at Simeon's request and had neither time nor opportunity to examine her surroundings.

She now became, officially, a widow with a new name and a slightly different history. She became Mrs. Dawson, the widow of a Confederate officer who had finally died as the result of wounds sustained during the capture of New Orleans. Simeon picked New Orleans for this purpose because its distance from New York and the post-war confusion there would make it extremely difficult for anyone to check the story. He would have liked as well to suppress Fey's New Mexican birth, but her Spanish appearance and intonation must be explained. So he contented himself by cautioning her to leave the details of her childhood very vague.

Nobody knew much about Santa Fe, anyway, and the important mercifully true point which would impress New York society was her aristocratic Scotch descent. Everyone, even the Livingstons and the Astors, dearly loved the whiff of a title. And it could be proved, if necessary.

Fey acquiesced in all this. She was as eager as he for acceptance.

It was only in the matter of the actual marriage that he found her inflexible. This time she would be married by a priest. Her marriage to Terry had been no marriage at all in the eyes of the Church, or of Terry.

Simeon was angry and obdurate. He despised Catholicism, which was unfashionable, and like most New Englanders he thought of the Scarlet Woman of Rome in horrified capitals. Besides, he had a very different plan.

The wedding must be small, of necessity, but it must be public, and it should be celebrated at the fashionable First Presbyterian Church on Fifth Avenue at Eleventh Street, for it was a Presbyterian Church that a daughter of Calvinist Scotland would naturally choose. Also he hoped to persuade the social Mrs. Joseph Delatone to sponsor the wedding.

Fey listened sympathetically to his wishes and understood his reason, but she could not give in. Her faith had meant less

183

and less to her of late; influenced by Simeon's violent objections, and half-convinced by his exasperated arguments that Catholicism was for her an accident, anyway, because had her father lived she would have had no contact with it, she had begun to omit Mass. Nevertheless, on the matter of the marriage her emotion was stronger than argument. They had their first and only quarrel and Fey was frightened. Her desperation at length suggested a way out of the impasse.

She kissed the scowl from his face and said, "Hush, Simeon. There is a—what's the word?—a compromise. Oh, yes, there is —we will do both." And she silenced his scandalized protests, as she silenced her own misgivings. Surely it could not be a sin to gratify the wishes of two people who would have been miserable otherwise.

So it was that on the twentieth of March, Simeon and Fey, unobtrusively dressed in plain dark clothes, took the ferry to Jersey City and were married in an obscure waterfront chapel. They had no attendants except the priest's fat old housekeeper and an incurious parishioner hastily summoned from a near-by shop. Nor was the priest curious as he performed the ceremony proper to a mixed marriage. He had never heard of Simeon Tower, which ignorance for once profoundly gratified Simeon, who had no wish that the record of this marriage should ever be discovered.

He was still a trifle sulky on the ferry ride back. "I hope you're satisfied by that papist mumbo-jumbo we've just been through," he said to Fey.

She started, bringing her thoughts back to him with difficulty. She had not been thinking of Simeon or their marriage, but of the last time she had crossed toward New York on the ferry. Just here by the stern railing they had stood, his arm around her, his head thrown back, eager for the long-anticipated arrival in the city of promise where together they were to start a new glorious life.

That moment on the ferry had been the last that they were really close.

"I spoke to you, dear, where have you gone?" said Simeon, touching her arm. His voice had softened. Under cover of her mantle he drew her to him. She yielded gratefully. *This* one really loves me, she thought. What does it matter that he isn't big and tall? What does it matter that there are twenty years between us? He is kind and generous and we need each other.

"Thank you," she said gently, "for enduring that 'papist

mumbo-jumbo' for me. In all things from now on, Simeon, I shall do as you wish. I'm grateful to you from the bottom of my heart." Her voice trembled. She raised her head and he saw that her eyes were full of unshed tears.

He felt a great answering wave of emotion. He forgot appearances or the danger of recognition and, pressing his mouth to hers, whispered, "It is I who am grateful. I'll make you happy, Fey."

That same afternoon Fey and little Lucita left the Eighteenth Street apartment and moved to Miss Prendergast's select boarding-house on Madison Square, thus acquiring an utra-respectable aura which appalled Fey. The whole house, from the rubber plant in the front parlour to the blue glass skylight—blue glass was healthful for the nerves—smelt of mothballs and brass polish. The austere Miss Prendergast, whose niece was married to Emerson's cousin, received the young New Orleans widow graciously.

"I hope, dear Mrs. Dawson, that you and the little one will be quaite, quaite at home here. Our evening collation will be at six, and you will have the opportunity to meet my other charming guests. You will find them all ladies and gentlemen of breeding. I never receive anyone here who would not equally have graced dear Mama's hospitable board, I assure you."

Fey made a suitable murmur of appreciation, thinking, Santa María! I'm glad I don't have to stand this for long! And while she was here, she would not even be able to see Simeon except in the parlour, chaperoned by the highly-bred guests.

"You've just arrived in New York?" pursued Miss Prendergast, shedding a majestic smile. "And you met Mr. Tower in New Orleans?—I understand from Mr. Tower's letter that you are a friend of Mrs. Delatone's—" She pronounced both the Tower and Delatone names with unction. "Such an agreeable connection for you."

Fey made another murmur. All these lies—it was still doubtful whether Mrs. Delatone would consent to receive Fey.

"Forgive me—I'm afraid the baby—" Fey finally got rid of Miss Prendergast, shut and locked the bedroom door.

"Ah, Lucita," she said to the baby, who was hitching along the carpet on all fours, "this is a very funny way to be married. I'm really married now and it doesn't feel it. But we must do as Simeon says. He's been very good to us."

Lucita pulled herself up hand over hand on her mother's skirt, stood swaying and gurgling proudly.

"Oh, clever one!" cried Fey, snatching her up. "We'll pretend anything, won't we, for Simeon, because very soon you shall have a beautiful nursery all your own, and you'll have a real father, too, for he likes you very much."

It was true. Simeon was fond of the pretty baby, especially as Fey had always managed that Lucita should not annoy him. His passion for Fey had surmounted even that handicap and he knew that in his big house he need never be any more aware of the child than he wished to be.

The conquest of Mrs. Delatone proved easier than he had expected. Joseph Delatone was interested in handling part of the Gulf and San Diego deal through his banking house, and perfectly willing that in return his wife should call on a young Southern widow of, as Simeon represented it, unimpeachable background.

Mrs. Delatone duly left cards on "Mrs. Dawson," who reciprocated three days later and, finding Mrs. Delatone at home in her Fifth Avenue mansion, completed the conquest herself.

Clara Delatone was a woman of great sweetness and social grace, and she was charmed by Fey, who listened admirably, spoke little, and behaved with a touching wistful modesty.

"No wonder Mr. Tower interests himself in that attractive little widow," she told her husband later. "Such a tragic story and she comes of Scotch aristocracy too. I'm quite in love with her myself."

The next day, over shad roe at the downtown Delmonico's, Delatone passed this on to Simeon, who was delighted. The Delatones were not near the inner circle of society and he hoped to do much better eventually, but they were an excellent beginning.

It particularly pleased him to discover that he might safely leave the outcome of these social efforts to Fey. "Though how you knew exactly when to juggle the teacups, and behave yourself with the servants at the Delatones, is a mystery to me," he whispered during one of his formal calls in Miss Prendergast's parlour.

Fey gave him a naughty smile. "You forget that I have had opportunities to watch the rich in Santa Fe, where I myself was a servant," she whispered back.

"Hush!" cried Simeon violently, but as the other boarders turned startled heads toward their corner, he controlled himself, knitting his blond eyebrows into a frown.

"Ah, Simeon—laugh, my husband," she whispered. "All this is really very funny. Day after day I pretend to be exactly

186

what I'm not. Night after night I go to my narrow virgin's bed—"

Simeon did smile then reluctantly.

"Not for long, darling," he said. "I talked to the minister at the Presbyterian Church today. Will the twentieth of April suit you?"

A week before Fey's Presbyterian wedding day, she had a caller. By now the papers had carried the news of Simeon's intended marriage, brief mentions only, for the sanctities of life —birth, marriage, and death—were still handled with restraint.

Miss Prendergast, however, devoured every item, and, bleakly thrilled by the lustre reflected on her boarding-house, treated Fey to special attention. She herself knocked on Fey's door and announced the caller. "A rather peculiar person, Mrs. Dawson, not quaite to the manor born. A Miss Miggs. I said I would ascertain if you were at home in case you didn't wish—"

Miss Miggs, thought Fey blankly, I don't know any Miss Miggs. But she was excessively bored. Lucita was napping, and the refined confinement of her room stifled her.

"I'll come right down," she said.

She stopped on the threshold of the parlour which contained a plump, blowzy woman in a black plush hat. The woman sat on the extreme edge of her chair, mechanically opening and shutting her pocketbook. She saw Fey, started to rise, then sat down again, biting her lips.

Madre de Dios! thought Fey, it is Simeon's mistress. "Yes, Miss Miggs?" she said, advancing. "You wanted to see me?"

The glint of defiance in Pansy's prominent eyes dissolved into a swimming embarrassment. She nodded dumbly.

Fey became aware of the hovering landlady. "Well," she said, "come up to my room. I must watch the baby."

Pansy got up clumsily and followed Fey upstairs.

"Please take off your things and sit down," said Fey, smiling and indicating the curly-maple rocker.

"You dunno who I am," answered Pansy, in a strangled voice, stubbornly standing. Her natural high colour had flared to violet. Under the rakish hat her soft blonde hair straggled in wisps from slipping hairpins. She was thirty-three and in the chill light of Miss Prendergast's front room she looked more. Fey was reminded of an anxious Newfoundland lost from its master.

"I know who you are," she said, gently removing the camel's-hair shawl from Pansy's shoulders. "You've come to talk about Mr. Tower. Sit down, please."

Pansy gave her a dazed look and slumped into the rocker. "I never told nobody, all these years. I never made no fuss. I knew he might get married, but—" Her chin quivered, and she swallowed. "I didn't never really believe it," she whispered.

"Why did you come to see me?"

"I dunno—I had to see you," said Pansy. She clenched her hands on the rocker's arms. "He ain't been near me since last fall. I felt something, though plenty times before he wouldn't come often. But I'd know he was busy. I was happy waiting. I wouldn't make no fuss. But he's gone for good now." Again the flat voice stopped, added in that harsh whisper, "I can't stand it."

A sudden fear diverted Fey's pity. "You must be reasonable, Miss Miggs," she said sharply. "I know he's made a handsome provision for you."

Pansy's eyes turned to Fey's face. "Money don't do no good. I love him. There ain't never been nobody else since I was fifteen."

"But what can I do?" cried Fey. "I'm sorry, very sorry, but—"

"You can't do nothing now, I guess," said Pansy. "I knew I was a fool to come. But if you'd only let him alone in the beginning—I know him and it was *you* started it—you don't love him like I do—I feel it—you won't do him no good—" Her breath came in a wheezy gasp. She pulled herself out of the rocker. "You won't do him no good," she repeated.

"You've no right to say a thing like that!" Fey rose, too, her face white.

Pansy put out a groping hand and picked up her shawl. "Mebbe not," she said. "I've always been a fool. I guess it was good of you to let me see you." She dragged the shawl over her shoulders, and opened the door. "Good-bye," she said. "Don't tell Simmy I came. It'd upset him. I won't make no fuss." The door shut.

Two days later, the papers carried another item buried on the fourth page amongst the advertisements. A Miss Pansy Miggs had been found dead in her bed at her rooms on Eleventh Street as the result of an overdose of sleeping tablets. The chemist testified she had suffered for some time from insomnia and had been buying the tablets from him, and the death was doubtless accidental.

Neither Simeon nor Fey ever mentioned Pansy's name. After

the first bitter shock, Simeon managed to shut his mind to both remorse and pity. It was an accident, of course, stupid, docile Pansy was not capable of an action so deliberately shocking. And he'd done the right thing by her. She'd been fixed with a tidy income for life. There was no cause for reproach. It was an accident.

Fey was denied this consoling belief. Again and again memory thrust on her that last image of Pansy at the door, the vague, anxious eyes staring past Fey in a hopeless resignation. "But what could I have done?" Fey cried to this image as she had in reality. "Be reasonable, what could I have done?" And in reason there was never any answer.

On Tuesday, April 20, 1869, Fey thankfully returned "Mrs. Dawson" to oblivion and became Mrs. Simeon Tower to the world. In all details her Presbyterian wedding struck the right note of restrained elegance. Fey's instinctive taste supplemented Simeon's hazy and sometimes flamboyant ideas of social fitness. By tactful suggestion she subdued the colour and cut of his frock coat and prevented him from having the church decorated by a whole conservatory-full of crimson roses. She herself wore dove-grey silk, the high neck modestly filled by blonde lace, as befitted a widow.

Simeon had spent anxious moments over the invitations. The Tweeds, Goulds, and Jim Fisk were obviously unsuitable, since society ostracized them. On the other hand, it would be fatal to offend them. The only way around that was to keep the guest list exceedingly brief. A few innocuous nobodies and the Delatones. To this list Fey added only one name, Doctor Rachel Moreton. Simeon agreed very reluctantly.

"I know she's been good to you and all that, but are you sure she won't talk, Fey; I mean, she knows all about you and it's dangerous."

Fey sighed. "Yes, I know. But she won't talk. I'm going to see her first."

Back once more in Rachel's austere little room at the Infirmary, Fey found explanations harder than she had expected. The doctor received her affectionately and without reproach for the long silence, but as she listened to Fey her mouth tightened, and her eyes grew coldly patient as Fey had never seen them.

"So, my dear—you are building your new life on a tissue of lies, and you wish me to be careful not to give you away?"

She no longer says "thee" to me, thought Fey. "Oh, Doctor

Rachel, please, please try to understand. It's not for me, it's for Simeon. After all, my past isn't anybody's business, and I'll be such a good wife to him, help him get the things he wants."

"I wish you both success," said Rachel, after a minute.

Fey was stunned. She had never expected a tone like that from her one real friend. Her eyes stung with hot tears.

Rachel saw them, and she went to Fey, putting her arm around the girl.

"I'll come to your wedding, child, since you want me."

"Of course I want you," cried Fey, and she buried her face against Rachel's bosom. Rachel stood quiet, holding the small figure close to her.

Before she left, Fey pressed a hundred dollars on the doctor for the Infirmary. "I'll be rich now," she said, with a touch of defiance. "I can help you this way better than working in the wards."

Rachel accepted the money, voicing composed thanks and none of the objections which she felt. She attended the wedding, but not the small supper later for which Mrs. Delatone had very generously offered the use of her back parlour.

CHAPTER

14

THE Simeon Towers prospered. Simeon, in the privacy of their magnificent bedroom, sometimes congratulated Fey on this. "You've brought me luck, darling. Our marriage was the best thing that ever happened to me."

In public he naturally did not attribute to luck the way in which he managed to weather all financial storms. He had dropped the bluff, hearty manner; he no longer laboured to appear as a prince of good fellows. He had become nearly as silent and reserved as Gould, and his reputation for shrewdness grew.

On May 10, 1869, the Union Pacific tracks met near Ogden, and two months later the first through train joined the two oceans in six and a half days. Simeon's Gulf and San Diego stock leaped upward.

In September of that year a premonition of trouble made Simeon withdraw in time to sit calmly in a corner of the Stock

Exchange's "Gold Room" on that Black Friday, September twenty-fourth, when President Grant, at last realizing his brother-in-law's infamous conspiracy with Gould and Fisk, started selling gold from the United States Treasury, thereby ruining half the financial houses in New York.

Simeon increasingly played a lone hand, and had so far, by a judicious mixture of bribery, nerve, and hunches, managed to avoid the active enmity of Gould's clique on the one side or Vanderbilt's on the other. There were still pickings for everyone with power and capital enough to grab them.

Noah Lemming alone knew some of Simeon's projects, far more of them than his employer realized. He underrated his secretary, whose extreme usefulness had vanquished the resentment Simeon had felt the previous year when Fey had visited the Wall Street office. Since that visit, Lemming had been suave and discreet. There was still more advantage to be got from his position with Tower than from any of the other avenues which his self-interest had led him to explore.

He had been startled by Tower's marriage. Surely Mrs. "Dawson" was not the name that girl had given when she forced her way into the office that day? But he was not quite sure. And there seemed no way of finding out. He disliked Fey, and felt there was something fishy about her past, but think as he might he could see no particular gain to be got from investigation at the moment. So Lemming said nothing, worked hard for Simeon, and ran a highly profitable bureaucracy on the side.

Fey knew nothing of her husband's financial life, nor did he wish her to. Her duties were traditional and decreed by the best society which they had not yet achieved. She was to run his home, advance his position, and help him to found a dynasty.

The first two duties she performed with increasing and charming efficiency; at the third for some unaccountable reason she failed. That this might not be her fault in view of Lucita, Simeon usually managed to forget. And Fey allowed him to forget it. In all the ways that she could she gave him emotional security.

On the whole, Simeon was content. His days were agreeably filled by the business of making yet more money, and his nights with Fey in the enormous inlaid walnut bed continued to give him a wondering and romantic release.

Soon after their marriage, while Fey was still awed by her new possessions—the yacht (which Simeon rechristened *The*

Inveraray in her honour and as a subtle reminder to the public), the villa at Long Branch, and this grandiose town house—Simeon conducted her through his jewel collection. He had lost interest in it since his marriage and no longer spent evenings fondling the mute relics of the great or famous, but he delighted in Fey's wonder at all his possessions.

They stood side by side in the library while he unlocked the velvet-lined wall cases and explained each item. She exclaimed dutifully, but she was puzzled that he admired Frederick of Prussia's curlicued snuffbox, tortured into the shape of an obese silver mermaid, far more than an exquisitely simple jade tree which had once belonged to the Emperor Chu'ien-Lung. Aware of her ignorance, she distrusted her own taste, but as she watched his indiscriminating pride in the hodge-podge of mementoes, and heard the unconscious veneration with which he spoke royal names, she felt a twinge of maternal pity.

They had finished the inspection and Simeon was locking the last case, when Fey put her hand on his arm. "And where," she asked, "is my turquoise?"

He stared at her, startled to see that she was serious.

"My dear girl, you didn't really think that thing was valuable, or belonged in this collection?"

"I did. Yes." She spoke with a peculiar quiet. There was a suddenly strained look in her grey eyes.

"Why, you little minx—you couldn't have!" Simeon laughed a trifle uneasily. "That was just your excuse for getting to see me."

"Perhaps," she said. "But where is it?"

"I'll be damned if I know. I think I threw it in a drawer in my dressing-room. Thing isn't worth twenty-five dollars. Oh, it's pretty enough," he added kindly.

"I would like you to find it," she said. "Will you look, please?"

"Silly child, I'll buy you a whole bushel of turquoises—" His eyes sharpened. "Who gave you this thing, anyway, that you prize it so?"

Strange that he was still jealous of Terry.

"An Indian gave it to me long ago."

Simeon made an impatient sound. He disliked reminders of her outlandish girlhood almost as much as he disliked her first marriage.

"All right, I'll look for the blasted thing, since you're in such a taking about it."

They found the turquoise in the corner of a bureau drawer

under a pile of Simeon's coloured silk handkerchiefs. The gilt cord had tarnished, and the stone itself.

"It looks green!" cried Fey, taking it into her hand and staring down at it in dismay. She felt a shrinking of the spirit, almost a repulsion.

"Some of them do that in time. Oxidization, I think," said Simeon carelessly. "Well, are you satisfied now?" He put his arm around her.

Her fingers closed on the turquoise. She slipped away from Simeon into her own dressing-room.

How simple I was ever to have thought this crude lump beautiful! she thought. After a moment she unlocked her new jewel case and put the turquoise into the lowest tray next to some seldom-worn jet earrings. Simeon had given her so many pieces of jewellery that she had difficulty in remembering to wear them in rotation so that he should not be hurt.

In the spring of 1872, Simeon decided not to open the Long Branch villa that June, but to assault instead society's still tightly guarded fortress at Newport. Long Branch was all very well, but it was political rather than fashionable. To be sure, President Grant made it his summer home, but he was not fashionable, and for Simeon "The Branch" was tainted by Tweed and a rowdy theatrical crowd and haunted by the fat, disreputable ghost of Jim Fisk.

On January sixth, Jim Fisk had been shot and killed by Josie Mansfield's paramour, Edward Stokes. This sordid killing, culmination of even more sordid litigation between Fisk and his former mistress, had shocked all New York. Simeon's shock had in it also a vein of horrified repudiation. He had once patterned himself on Fisk, imitated the boisterous joviality, the free-and-easy ethics, had admired the buccaneer's outrageous tactics in the Erie War.

And now—Jim Fisk back where he started from in Brattleboro, Vermont, six feet underground, murdered, and nearly bankrupt as well.

Tweed, too, was in trouble, accused of filching the public moneys. Jay Gould's million-dollar bail alone had temporarily saved him.

Thank God, thought Simeon, I had sense enough to taper off connection with that crowd.

The shock of Fisk's murder and Tweed's arrest forced him to realize that, though he and Fey had climbed, they had not begun to reach that safe summit where murder and violence were literally unspeakable; that peaceful enclosed meadow where it seemed to him that everyone dwelt in stately security, smiling gentle contempt toward the clamorous ones outside.

The Towers had friends—what man of wealth had not?— Mrs. Delatone was kind, and they were accepted in her husband's flamboyant horsey set. But Simeon rode badly, and betting and gambling bored him. Besides, he wanted to be at the top.

He announced his intention to Fey one May morning at breakfast in the town house. He made a sign to the butler, who vanished, leaving them alone: Fey in a ruffled white morning robe seated at one end of the twelve-foot mahogany table behind the coffee urn, and Simeon in his Prince Albert coat distastefully eating a single boiled egg. Lately his stomach had been troubling him.

"My dear," he said abruptly, "I've rented the Grandisons' villa on Ocean Avenue at Newport for this summer. We will go there."

"Oh?" said Fey. She put down her coffee-cup and examined her husband. He had grown thinner in the last three years, and he did not look very well. The fair hair had receded a bit, and on either side of his clipped blond moustache there were deep lines. He is not yet satisfied, she thought, with an inward sigh. Her own social ambition had ebbed. They were exceedingly comfortable, they knew some congenial people, and what if they were not asked to the Patriarch Balls or Cotillion Dinners at Delmonico's? They could still give their own parties.

"Well," said Simeon, frowning, "do you think it'll work?"

He knew that she would understand him. He was so used to her instant comprehension that he no longer wondered at it.

"So we must start a new campaign—" she said, a trifle wearily. "What is it exactly that you want so much, Simeon?"

He flung down his napkin and stood up. "You know perfectly well! There are a hundred people in this town who don't speak to us, and who, if we bowed to them, would look vague and pass on. I want to belong to them."

"Why?" she asked. "If you ever do, I believe you'd be disappointed."

Simeon scowled. "If you've lost ambition for yourself, I should think you might remember little Lucy. Do you want her to grow up a second-rater? As things are now, we'd never get her into Miss Perrine's School, nor when she is older into the

Family Circle Dancing Class. She'll have no chance of a decent marriage."

Fey smiled. "You know that you've brought out a strong argument. I *am* ambitious for Lucita, and I bless you for being always so good to her."

"I'm fond of her," said Simeon. "Nice pretty child."

Fey looked down, feeling a quick rush of gratitude and regret. *Why* couldn't they have a baby together? She had prayed for it, though not in church. Once in a great while she stole out to Mass, but she was no longer a communicant. The Irish priest had made it very clear that, even if she might be forgiven the Protestant marriage, her subsequent conduct left no alternative to excommunication. For in fulfilment of her promise to Simeon, she accompanied him to the Presbyterian Church, where he had become a pewholder and usher. She had for a time felt guilt and a dull sense of loss, then it passed. Religion, like the Spanish part of her—like those flashes of true-sight—seemed to have no place in the new life.

Simeon, pursuing his thoughts, walked to the silver-laden buffet and selected a cigar from the humidor. He clipped the end, frowning. "If only we could make Ward McAllister notice us."

Fey instantly recalled her attention and considered his remark. Ward McAllister, the pompous little man who was rapidly becoming New York's social arbiter. He had made a career of it, and lately, backed by the powerful Mrs. William B. Astor, he had succeeded in imposing his own restrictions on a hitherto unguided and indolent society. It was he who had founded the Patriarch Balls with twenty-five patrons who were "crème de la crème"—his own phrase. It was he, too, who had initiated the ultra-exclusive Cotillion Dinners at Delmonico's.

"Can't put financial pressure on him," continued Simeon, pacing up and down beside the table. "It's been tried, and anyway everything he's got is gilt-edged. Don't see any way of getting at him."

"Oh, yes, there is," said Fey calmly. "I shall go and see him."

"But you can't!" cried Simeon. Her simple approach to problems always staggered him. She seemed never to see the uses of indirection or the necessity for preserving appearances. Yet this trait of hers provoked a reluctant admiration; he dimly recognized it as the product of generations of breeding. Whereas I—he thought—the son of a mill hand's daughter and an oppressed Jew—fear and confusion—the train of thought he never permitted himself. But I make money. I could buy out most of them—this McAllister, the Livingstons, even maybe Astor—

Fey smiled at him, got up from behind the coffee urn, and put her hand on his arm. "You will see," she said. "I don't promise the outcome, but I will at least meet this Mr. Mc-Allister."

Simeon bent and kissed the white parting between the two wings of shining black hair. "Be sure and tell him about your grandfather. And be careful, he'll ask questions. Don't want him digging up your past or—"

"Or yours," she finished, with a shrug. "I know what you want. You are distantly related to the Hingham branch of Towers. You are an orphan, it is very vague—" She shut her lips, burst out in sudden passion, "Ah, Simeon, you do not know what it is to be really an orphan, or you would not be ashamed of your parents!"

Dull colour seeped up his astonished face. "You don't understand," he said angrily. "They're very old, simple-minded. I provided for them liberally. They've never asked questions. I hated my home."

"Yes, well—" she said, quiet again. "It doesn't matter—" She reached over and picked a Gloire de Paris rosebud from the centrepiece, tucked it in his buttonhole. "Have a good day at the office, dear," she said, with her light tender irony. "Herd and prod your bulls and bears. Make lots of money for us and our new campaign!"

On the third day following, Fey ordered out the best brougham and directed that both coachman and footman should wear gala livery. Then she drove by appointment down to Ward McAllister's house on Twenty-First Street.

Fifth Avenue was lovely in the soft May air. All along the sidewalks the ailanthus and horse-chestnut trees were in bloom, every window-box glowed with geraniums and petunias. From Madison Square a German band blared out "Tales from the Vienna Woods" and the oompah-pa was exhilerating. Fey would have much preferred to walk. But fashionable ladies seldom walked, and her impressive equipage would be a desirable reinforcement. Her costume was also impressive, a blue shot-taffeta suit, lavishly garnished by mink tails and Mechlin lace, and further adorned by a seed-pearl and sapphire set of brooch and earrings.

Madame Loreste, New York's most expensive couturière, had made the suit to the accompaniment of admiring coos over

Mrs. Tower's perfect figure. So flat down here in front, which showed off the bustle in back—whereas many ladies—a bulge, alas!—And such a superb bust! No need for inserted ruffles—The only thing wanting was perhaps a little more tallness, but that was so easily remedied by heels and plumes on the bonnet. "Ah, Madame Tower is ravissante, is she not?" had cried Madame Loreste at the final trying-on. She had been born in Indiana, but she used French phrases with dexterity.

So did Ward McAllister, Fey discovered, as a white-capped maid ushered her into that gentleman's drawing-room.

"Enchanté! my dear Mrs. Tower. Enchanté!" murmured Mr. McAllister, rising from the armchair, where he was prepared to give audience, and touching her gloved fingertips.

Fey murmured, too, though not in French, and sat down with her usual composure while she considered him. Short, plump, medium colouring—waxed imperials à la Louis Napoleon. Not an unkind face, but a self-important one.

"It was good of you to see me," she said.

"Pleasure—" McAllister bowed. He guessed her errand. He granted fifty such audiences a year, mostly, however, to Middle-Western parvenus who had marriageable daughters. This was different. Since receiving Fey's note, he had been making discreet inquiry about the Towers.

"I will be direct, Mr. McAllister," said Fey, smiling and looking at him through her lashes. "You are the most important man in New York society. Your word is law. I wish that you would advise us."

A faintly gratified look came into his prominent eyes. "Dear lady, you greatly overestimate my—er—my powers." He crossed his legs, and placed his fingertips together. "Now let's see. You know the Delatones?"

Fey nodded.

"*Mrs.* Delatone is delightful, is she not?"

Fey nodded again and waited.

"But perhaps not quite—" He paused delicately. Joseph Delatone had not been invited to be one of the Patriarchs.

"You see," said Fey, "we have a daughter—"

"Ah—" They all had daughters. "And how old is she?"

"Almost four," answered Fey, laughing.

McAllister did not smile. "It was never too young to get them started, and for the second generation it's easier. Forgive me, ma'am, but is it true that you are well connected in England?"

"My grandfather was a Scottish baronet, Sir James Cameron."

Dios, she thought suddenly, how stupid this all is! Her smile became more brilliant.

"Indeed," said McAllister. "Oh, the happy days I've spent grouse-shooting with dear Lord Lansdowne! I remember once near Balmoral—but I mustn't reminisce. Mr Tower is from New England, I believe?"

Fey's square little jaw tightened. "Related to the Hingham, Massachusetts, Towers," she said quickly, "but an orphan from earliest years."

"Sad," said McAllister, pursing his lips and digesting this. He glanced out of the window at the magnificent brougham, then at Fey's dress and jewels. "Mr. Tower has been successful; his business ventures no doubt continue to be advantageous—"

"Oh, we're very rich," said Fey.

McAllister winced. "Dear lady—might I suggest that such frankness is hardly, hardly—"

"Sorry," she smiled. "I thought that was what you wanted to know."

After a moment McAllister accepted this with a wave of his plump hand. "A fortune is useful when one wishes to enter the best society, but it is not a passport, thank Heaven, or we should be swamped by an undesirable element. It is"—said he, drawing himself up—"my privilege to help guard the—may I say—inner sanctum from pollution."

"Yes, I know," said Fey sweetly, giving him the full benefit of soft admiring eyes. "You are a very wise man. That is why I came to you."

McAllister was warmed. He looked at her kindly. Stylish little lady; charming, too. Mrs. Astor might just possibly be induced to take her up eventually. But those things could not be hurried.

"I'll see what I can do, Mrs. Tower," he said, bowing. "At Newport it's easier. The move is wise. One word of advice, though. Have you a governess for your little girl?"

"Oh, no," answered Fey, surprised. "I have a nurse, but usually I take care of her myself. I love to."

"Charming. Maternal affection. Always charming. But might I suggest that a governess—English, of course, conversant with all the ways of British nobility—would be helpful. Or—it has just occurred to me—perhaps some poor relation of your own Scotch family—?"

I, myself, am the poor relation in my Scottish family, thought

198

Fey, wryly. Out loud she said, "Is a governess really necessary?"

"It is the thing to do," returned McAllister definitely.

That night Fey told Simeon of her interview, and he listened to the oracle with what seemed to her a pathetic earnestness. They must get an English governess at once, and a French chef, since Simeon had heard that they, too, were all the rage. He was anxious to do in everything exactly as "they" did. But I was like that once, too, was I not? thought Fey. What's happened to me that it no longer seems so important? I must take it seriously or it will not work, our campaign. That much, at least, I have learned from life; one gets what one goes after with single-hearted purpose, but otherwise not.

She went up to Lucita's nursery and the little girl bounced up and down in her crib, holding out her arms to her mother.

"Sing a song, Mama," she called. "Sing Lucy a good-night song!"

Fey lifted her out of the crib, hugging the squirming little figure in its long batiste nightgown. They nestled down together on the great polar-bear rug before the fireplace. This was their nightly ritual. Fey stroked the bright auburn curls, seeing the rose-flush of health on the child's cheeks, the straightness of the body, sweet-scented and powdered from the bath.

"You are to have an English governess, mi corazón," she said. "Won't you be elegant!"

Lucita chuckled, delighted always at the grave grown-up way her mother spoke to her. "El-e-gant," she repeated carefully, enjoying the new word. "Sing Lucy's song, Mama."

Fey gathered her close and sang an old Spanish lullaby. If Simeon were with them—and he sometimes joined them at this bed hour—she sang only English songs, "My Lady Wind," "Beautiful Dreamer," or "Hush thee, my baby." Simeon would sing, too, bumbling along in a self-conscious bass which delighted Lucita, who loved to clamber on his lap and play with his massive gold watch-chain. But Fey never sang the Spanish songs. Simeon would have hated them.

In the last week of June, the three Towers—for obvious reasons Lucita's last name had been changed to Tower—and the English governess, Miss Pringle, boarded the *Inveraray* and steamed to Newport Harbour, the French chef and ten other servants having preceded them by train. Two victorias and a dogcart for the luggage awaited the yachting party on the pier. They drove along Bellevue Avenue toward the ocean, passing increasingly sumptuous villas until, near Bailey's Beach, they reached their own. It was built of grey stone in the medieval manner and embellished with turrets, stained glass, and an edging of wooden fretwork. It was called "Kenilworth".

Simeon glanced at Miss Pringle, hoping to surprise some emotion of astonishment or even awe. As usual, she disappointed him. Her high-nosed, horsey face continued to show supercilious patience, its unvarying expression since, tempted by an enormous salary, she had joined the Tower household a month ago.

She had been governess in the Marlborough's ducal family until her charges grew up, then, moved by some unexpected urge for adventure, she had come to New York. The urge had rapidly expired. She despised America; she despised even the fabulous two hundred yearly pounds she received from Simeon, though her common sense had prevented her refusing it. She despised Simeon for being a self-made man, and Fey— whose connection with Scottish gentry did not impress her; after all, what was a Highland baronet?—for supinely living in this preposterous country. To Lucita she showed a chilly conscientiousness and the little girl was already picking up the best Oxford speech.

Miss Pringle was, in short, precisely the type of English governess which McAllister had had in mind. She added tone to the household. When she accompanied Lucita to the beach, she snubbed the other assembled governesses so thoroughly that they were impressed. This filtered back to the employers, of course, and some interest began to devolve upon the Towers. They made real headway when Ward McAllister, after long deliberation, invited them to one of his "fêtes champêtres."

This was a picnic at McAllister's harbourside "farm," for which occasions he always hired a flock of Southdown sheep and a half-dozen cows to give the place an animated and suitable look. His farm fêtes were carefully graded, and the Towers were invited to an inferior one. Mrs. Astor would not be present; the throne would that day be occupied by Mrs. Sylvester Bull.

Simeon was delighted. He had been growing bored and thinking of running down to New York to the office. But here at last was recognition.

"I suppose sporting clothes for a picnic?" he asked Fey

anxiously on the morning of the event. "And you'll wear muslin?"

Fey frowned. "I don't know—Lucita's been playing with the little Bull girl at the beach and she said her mama was going to wear lace and diamonds, but I can't believe it. Lucita must have misunderstood."

"Ask Miss Pringle if she heard?" suggested Simeon. "It wouldn't do to make a mistake now."

Fey giggled suddenly, a youthful mischievous sound. "You don't seriously mean me to ask the Pringle? And what would she answer?" Fey threw back her head and pinched down her upper lip—"I confess to great astonishment, madam, that you should expect me to listen to childish prattle."

Simeon gave an unwilling smile. "She's certainly hard to get along with."

"Only one way," said Fey airily, ringing for her maid. "Snub her first, and hardest. I'm learning. Simeon, you mustn't care so much what people think. You don't care in business, that's why you're successful."

"I don't care in the least what people think," he snapped. "You make me sound like a frightened schoolboy."

Fey gave him a quick, indulgent look.

They were slightly underdressed for McAllister's picnic. Fey, after the first discovery of this, forgot all about it. Simeon suffered and hid it by volubility and a return to his earlier manner of excessive geniality.

Fey heard the booming laugh and the beginning of the story about the insurance agent and the pink garter which had used to be so popular amongst Fisk's crowd. Oh, dear, she thought, for she saw Simeon's audience, a small group of frock-coated impeccable gentlemen—listening in polite astonishment.

But she was determined to enjoy herself. This was not difficult if one relinquished expectation of "picnic" and substituted "banquet" in a remote incidental outdoor setting. Long tables swaddled in pink damask were set on the lawn beneath awnings, an orchestra imported from New York played from a raised marquee. McAllister, a beaming host, tripped everywhere, personally frappéing the champagne, as he had previously concocted the twelve-course menu in which two white or two brown sauces must never succeed each other; the terrapin must come only from Maryland; and the fillets of beef might be covered by truffles, but never mushrooms.

Fey sat between Mr. Sylvester Bull and Mr. E. Templeton Snelling—exalted company, but she was completely successful with them. Her small talk was perfect: the comparison be-tween Christine Nilsson's voice and that of Madame Parepa Rosa, the pleasures of archery and croquet, the unseasonable coolness of June and consequent deplorable effect on the strawberries.

She turned gracefully from Bull to Snelling at the end of the fish course, reversing the process after the second entrée, and so on. She listened to them breathlessly and laughed at their gallantries. When the picnic was at last ended and before they all progressed to the marquee for the cotillion, she saw McAllister contemplating her with marked approval. Further accolade—Mrs. Sylvester Bull detained Fey as she crossed the lawn to their carriage, saying, "Dear Mrs. Tower, I hear from my Susie that you have a small daughter. Will you send her over next Tuesday at four—little birthday party—and her governess, of course?"

Fey accepted with the proper—not excessive—touch of gratitude.

"We're in!" cried Simeon on the drive back to their house. He put his arm around Fey's waist and squeezed her, his moustache pricked against her cheek. "You were wonderful, darling. I was proud."

"I'm glad that you're pleased," she said. She moved gently, imperceptibly, away from him. "We are not 'in' yet, but in time I think we will be."

"In time," she repeated, very low to herself. Time . . . The carriage had turned on to Ocean Avenue and her nostrils were suddenly filled by the wild smell of the sea. She heard the breakers crashing out there in the darkness and the shrill cry of a sea-gull.

She put her hand to her throat, where there was a thickness, a suffocation. Shut in like this in a black moving box gliding inexorably and blindly through the starlit night.

"Tell Briggs to stop the horses," she whispered. "I want to get out."

"My dear girl—whatever for? We're only ten minutes from home."

"I want to be near the sea," she answered, in a hoarse, un-natural voice. To be near the sea, lying face up on the sand alone and free, with only the waves and the stars.

Simeon was puzzled. "You're near the sea at Kenilworth; all you have to do is go down the road a bit to Bailey's Beach. Not tonight, of course," he added. "The Casino'll be shut."

"I want to get out," she repeated, so faintly that he had to bend over to hear her. The horses trotted on faster, sensing their nearness to the stable.

"Fey, dear," he said, stroking her hand, "you're tired. The excitement of the fête. You've exhausted yourself."

Exhausted! she thought, while I sit here crammed with bounding aching energy; when I want to dance, to shout, to beat upon the sides of this suffocating black box until I tear them down!

"What is it, Fey?" he asked sharply. The lamps from a passing carriage had for a moment illumined her face. She heard the note of fear in his voice.

She pressed her hands hard to her throat and then, relaxing them, put them in her lap. "Nothing, Simeon. A mood."

They drew up under the crenellated porte-cochère.

For the remainder of 1872 and the vexatious year of panic which followed, Simeon was too much occupied in trying to save his own skin to be able to divert much energy to social rise. Annoyance followed annoyance and threat followed threat.

Hard upon Grant's re-election and the reassuring defeat of Horace Greeley, trouble began with the explosion of the Crédit Mobilier scandal. The Crédit Mobilier had financed the building of the Union Pacific. The astounded and indignant public now learned that "every step of that mighty enterprise had been taken in fraud."

Simeon and the other railroad entrepreneurs retired into bleak, apprehensive silence while congressional investigation flayed the Union Pacific, and Oakes Ames, head of the Credit Mobilier, was terrified into reading the names of those who had profited. As these included the Vice-President, the Senator from New Hampshire, and a collection of Representatives— amongst them James A. Garfield—the nation's indifference to public corruption was finally punctured. And the great panic of 1873 had begun.

Simeon, and most of the other millionaires, warned by a dozen signs recognizable only to the initiates, put out sea anchors and survived the tempest.

Jay Cooke was one of those who did not survive. On September eighteenth, his bank, the biggest and best-known in the Western world, closed its doors. Five thousand commercial houses followed. For the ten days of acute crisis, while lights burned all night on Wall Street and grey-faced men stared at each other with the blankness of unceasing fear, Simeon scarcely left his office. He slept in snatches on the horsehair sofa, he sent Lemming out for pitchers of black coffee, and he spent hour after hour watching the ticker, agonizing, hoping, and even sometimes praying.

By Christmas the situation had settled and clarified itself for the rich men. Simeon, along with Gould, Vanderbilt, Carnegie, Morgan, and Rockefeller, had time to breathe once more and compute the damage, while two hitherto unknowns, Frick and Harriman, had already dived in and were profitably salvaging from the wrecks. The financial sea was still troubled, but to Simeon it once more seemed navigable.

"We'll manage now," he told Fey on Christmas morning "The worst is over. Here, my dear, is your present."

It was a sable cloak which reached from her chin to the floor.

"It's beautiful, Simeon," she said, kissing him, "but should you, right now?—I know you've lost quite a lot of money. Should we not economize?"

"Certainly not. This is just the time to splurge. Got to guard against the faintest appearance of embarrassment or they'd all be after me like a pack of hounds. Besides, I'll make back what I lost and more."

Now's the time to jump in and expand, he thought. Extend the Gulf and San Diego. Maybe even outsmart Gould and grab the Missouri Pacific.

But it was at just this time, too, that Jay Gould first turned his genuine financial genius upon the problem of acquiring Simeon's Gulf and San Diego for himself.

Life in the Fifth Avenue mansions rippled along as usual through that winter of 1874. On New Year's Day, Fey and all the other hostesses sat in flower-filled drawing-rooms and received the traditional calls from gentlemen who had enjoyed their hospitality. This year the silver basket in the vestibule of the Tower house contained the cards of Sylvester Bull, Templeton Snelling, and Ward McAllister, besides a hundred others. It was gratifying. The season promised very well now that the panic was subsiding. Fey, urged on by Simeon, ordered a new wardrobe from Madame Loreste, and made enthusiastic plans for little supper parties after the opera—they had, of course, taken a box for Monday nights at the Academy of Music.

This is really a most agreeable life, thought Fey, awakening on the morning of January fourteenth, to find her bedroom fire already sparkling and her maid standing beside the bed holding the breakfast tray. Fey yawned, and raised her arms for the swansdown bed-jacket. No plans until lunch, she thought lazily; I might take Lucita skating in the park.

"Please ask Miss Pringle and Miss Lucy to come here," she said to her maid.

The little girl presently came in with her governess. The child came up to her mother, holding her back stiff, toes pointed out, as Miss Pringle had taught her. "Good morning, Mama," she said, carefully enunciating.

Fey reached out and scooped the child up on to the bed. "Hello, sweetheart," she whispered, tumbling the tight curls, and kissing the plump neck. "It's a lovely morning—shall we go skating?"

Miss Pringle, watching the scene in cold disapproval—how was one ever to train up a little lady when the mother acted so undignified?—gave an audible sniff. "It is quite impossible, madam, for Lucy to go skating this morning. She has a piano lesson at ten and a fitting at eleven."

"Oh, of course—I forgot," said Fey slowly. "But what would you *like* to do, darling?" She looked down at Lucita.

"Might I suggest," said Miss Pringle, "that the child is hardly a judge, and that it seems to me unfortunate to influence her to skip obligations in favour of pleasure? She has plenty of amusement."

Dios, how I dislike this woman! thought Fey, but was at once checked by justice. The Pringle was right. Lucita must develop a sense of duty, and it was also true that the child was learning beautiful manners.

"Some other day then, dear," she whispered to Lucita, who had said nothing at all, but turned her head gravely from her mother to her governess as each spoke. The child slid off the bed.

"Curtsy to your mama, Lucy," said Miss Pringle.

Lucita curtsied. Miss Pringle took her hand, at the same time smoothing the ruffled curls not ungently. "Come, dear," she said. "We mustn't keep Professor Latoni waiting." Lucita came docilely.

Fey lay frowning at the closed door. But there was no real cause for complaint. Lucita seemed happy enough, and Miss Pringle was what they had wanted, conscientious, impeccable, and inordinately refined.

After a while Fey got up and commenced dressing. She would go and see Doctor Rachel on this bright winter's morning, and with this decision came the realization of how very long it had been since she had visited the Infirmary.

They weren't at ease with each other any more, she and

Rachel. After the first conventional inquiries, there never seemed to be anything to talk about. Fey continued to send cheques to the Infirmary, and Rachel acknowledged these by cordial notes, but the visits had ceased. Perhaps, thought Fey, she will enjoy going out for a ride with me, she works so long and so hard.

Fey dressed in a moss-green velvet afternoon costume, so as not to return home before attending Mrs. Sylvester Bull's luncheon. The meal was a new and fashionable importation from England, now that the dinner hour had gradually moved into the early evening. She topped the green velvet with the sable wrap and matching sable hat and muff. She put on pearl-grey gloves, dangling gold earrings, and a whiff of her frangi-pani perfume.

Then she paused before her rosewood cheval glass for the last critical appraisal. "Muy elegante, Doña Feyita," she whispered to her image, making it a tiny bow. Suddenly the richly furred reflection slipped and stood back; another took its place —a pale, dirty face between strands of uncombed hair, a torn camiza, a pair of shamed, resentful eyes.

Was that one, too, really me? she thought. Ah, Gertrudis— you would never believe this! But mixed with the triumph there was a formless discomfort.

"Bah!" she said violently, and, picking up her beaded pouch bag, she hurried from the room.

Last week's snowfall had levelled down enough to make sleighing delightful. Briggs, the coachman, was waiting on the street in the red-and-gold cutter. They set off down Fifth Avenue toward Eighth Street, and in the cold crispness the jingle of their silver bells harmonized sweetly with the tinkle of brass or tin bells on inferior sleighs.

Everybody was on runners; the milk and butcher carts, the heavy brewery wagons, family parties bound for skating in the park, fashionable cutters like her own headed for shopping at Stewart's or Lord and Taylor's. At Tenth Street they saw the Astor sleigh. Mrs. Astor herself, muffled to the chin, sat on the back seat in majestic splendour.

Briggs instinctively slowed his horses. Mrs. Astor inspected the Tower turnout, her sharp eyes reaching last of all Fey's hopeful, uncertain smile. Mrs. Astor hesitated, then, just as the two sleighs glided past each other, she nodded briefly.

Ah, thought Fey, glowing. Wait until I tell Simeon! Perhaps soon now she will even leave cards!

Exultation was still with her as Briggs slid up to the In-

firmary entrance, but it was replaced by astonishment at seeing a crowd on the sidewalk. A sullen, murmuring crowd of
ragged men and women. As Briggs nervously helped her from
the sleigh, two men carrying a stretcher walked around the
corner of the block. The figure on the stretcher was huddled
under a heap of burlap bags and it was moaning. The crowd
fell silent, making way for the stretcher to mount the Infirmary steps. Fey followed it.

The Infirmary hallway and the floors of the clinic rooms
were covered by injured women and children lying on sheets,
quilts, and old blankets. There was the smell of blood and
vomit. From the corner by the stairs came the monotonous,
mindless sound of a woman's sobbing.

Fey stood appalled in the middle of the hall. She saw two of
the nurses scurry upstairs, and return carrying basins. In the
semi-darkness by the basement door she saw Doctor Daniel
bending over something on the floor.

The front door opened and another stretcher came in. Its
bearers stared around helplessly and dumped their burden—a
child—on the clinic desk.

The dispensary door opened and Rachel came out.

"Oh, what's happened?" cried Fey, trying to slip her sable
muff under the head of the child on the desk.

Rachel looked at Fey, then she, too, bent over the child.
"Take back your beautiful muff," she said, handing it to Fey.
"It won't help the child. She's dead."

"But what's happened?" whispered Fey, her dazed eyes
moving from the child to Rachel's stony face.

Rachel knelt on the floor beside one of the quiet figures.
She applied her stethoscope, lifted the flaccid eyelids. "As a
result of the panic there are tens of thousands starving in New
York this winter," she said, in the patient tone of one explaining to a foreigner. "Yesterday the unemployed and the suffering poor had permission to hold a meeting in Tompkins
Square. The city government revoked the permission without
notification. The people didn't know. When they had all
gathered, the mounted police closed in on them. These are
some of those who have been clubbed, beaten, and trampled.
The other hospitals are filled, too."

Fey exhaled her breath slowly. "Let me help! I can help!"
she cried, kneeling beside Rachel and putting her hand on
the forehead of the unconscious patient.

Rachel turned her head. "In velvet and sables and grey kid
gloves?" There was a spark of amusement in her tired voice.

207

Fey flushed, seeing the grotesque pearly sheen of her glove against the bruised, swollen forehead. She snatched her hand back, began to unbutton the glove, and Rachel stopped her. "No, Fey. Everything is changed in the wards since you were here, and we don't really need help. See, they're getting them all upstairs." It was true, the halls were clearing. "We have many nurses now. Your generous cheques have helped," she added, smiling faintly.

Fey got up. "You don't want me—" Her voice trailed. She stood hesitant, still wrapped in her sable cloak from which drifted the scent of frangipani, delicate and seductive above the stench of the Infirmary.

"Run along back to your other world," said Rachel. She gave Fey's shoulder a swift farewell pat, walked quickly into the dispensary.

Fey went out and down the steps. The anxious muttering crowd stilled as she passed through them to the sleigh. They stared at her dumbly without hostility. Their agonizing anxiety for their injured, and even the senseless horror of injustice which they suffered, did not move them to resentment of anything as rich and glittering and safe as Fey. They gawked at her as they gawked at the lovely painted ladies in the Arcade museums.

"Where to now, madam?" asked Briggs, thankfully flicking the horses.

"I don't know," said Fey. "I don't know where—" Then catching his startled expression, she collected herself. "The park, I think, for a while. I'd like to just drive around."

CHAPTER

15

ON the Wednesday morning of Valentine's Day, 1877, the Towers were awakened by the distant bang of hammering and the subdued rushing of excited servants up and down the back stairs.

Fey ran from bed to the window, peered between the tightly drawn damask portières, jerked them open, and jumped back into bed again. "The sun's shining already!" she cried. "It will be a fine night for our ball."

Simeon turned heavily, opening his eyes with difficulty. The light hurt them; his brain felt thick and confused, as it often did now in the mornings. He had had another bad night. Vague nightmares, punctuated by hours of semi-wakefulness caused by the familiar gnawing discomfort in his stomach. Only food, rich creamy food, seemed to stop this periodic gnawing and burning.

"A touch of dyspepsia, my dear Mr. Tower," the doctor had said. "Mustn't work too hard. Take a long trip. As we get older, you know, the machine creaks a little. Anno domini, my dear sir."

" I'm only forty-seven," said Simeon irritably.

"To be sure," said the doctor. "Prime of life. But cut down on cigars and champagne, and I do recommend a long trip. Travel and change, you know." This was the unfailing prescription for rich people with vague, unclassifiable discomforts. When they came back from their long trips, they usually complained of an entirely new set of symptoms, but at least it was a new set.

"I can't take a trip now," Simeon snapped. "I'm a busy man."

A busy man, yes; that he had always been. But never before this an incessantly worried one. The luck which had supported him all these years seemed to be crumbling bit by bit. He had not, after all, made back the money lost in the panic, and there had been minor setbacks as well. The old wool mill on the Saugatuck had unaccountably failed, one of his best Transic Line boats had foundered in a Gulf hurricane. Insignificant losses in proportion to his capital, and once he would have written them off and plunged with grim fighting zest into recouping somewhere else.

But he could no longer recapture the zest, and the major fight which took all the shrewdness and energy he could muster was not a triumphant campaign leading to new victory, but a bitter secret struggle against Jay Gould for the retaining of what he already possessed.

Gould never showed his hand. The Mephisto of Wall Street sat like a small black spider silently enmeshing enterprise after enterprise. It was a web of railways that he spun, and his pattern was always the same; as for Erie, from which he had looted millions, so for the reorganized Union Pacific, the Missouri Pacific, and a dozen others.

He worked slowly and methodically; time and again by some dark alchemy he persuaded the public that he was an anti-monopolist, desirous only of the common good. And he

209

got what he wanted. Now he wanted the Gulf and San Diego, and his manœuvrings were spiralling nearer and nearer to the goal.

But I can fight him, he can't lick me, thought Simeon, floundering back to wakefulness on the February morning of the ball.

"You had a bad night again, Simeon?" asked Fey. She touched his head, gently smoothing the fair hair that was tinging to grey.

"I'm all right," he grunted. "No, don't stop. I love your touch, makes me feel better."

She smiled, and went on stroking. She looked very young and fresh in her ruffled nightgown, her eyes bright from sleep, her cheeks pink, and the two long thick braids of black hair flung over her shoulders.

"Business worries?" she asked. "I know there is something bothering you."

At once he closed up. She must be protected, and he must appear always the infallible, the miraculous provider of bounty.

"Nothing could ever bother me that I couldn't handle. I should think you'd know that by now." He waited, and she quickly complied.

"Of course I do. You're the smartest man in the whole United States. Why, yesterday at Mrs. Bull's, she was saying that her husband thinks you've got more vision and foresight than any other financier."

Simeon made a noncommittal sound, and she saw his frown fade.

Surely he would tell me if anything were really wrong, she thought. We're spending more money than we ever have. This ball tonight—but why worry! She gave an excited, pleasurable sigh. The ball was their pinnacle, their apotheosis. It had taken all this time, but at last they were really "in." Everyone was coming, even Mrs. Astor who, after months of suspense, had finally left cards. It was to be a domino ball in costume, the quadrilles organized by Ward McAllister. The papers had talked of it for weeks, and for this ball Simeon had built a huge ballroom, adding it on to the back of his house.

There was a discreet knock on the door and Fey's maid came in, carrying, besides the coffee and rolls, a square beribboned package. "Just come by messenger, mum," she said, presenting it to Fey, who started at once to untie the red ribbons.

"Wait," said Simeon, gesturing toward the maid. He looked

conscious, a little embarrassed. When the maid had gone out, he turned his back on Fey and fumbled for his slippers.

She gave him a puzzled look and opened the package. It was an enormous valentine, a froth of gold-lace paper, cupids, doves, and a plump red-satin heart on which was written, "For my dearest wife." The heart opened, and inside it on jeweller's cotton lay another heart made of little rubies.

"Oh, darling!" she cried. Her eyes filled. For days he would be grumpy, taciturn, or irritable, and then he would do something like this, the sentimental spirit-warming gesture that a woman loved.

She pinned the ruby heart on her nightdress, rushed around the bed, and kissed him.

"You're good to me—so good, Simeon."

"I'm glad you like your valentine," he answered gruffly, but he caught her tight against him, forgetting the throb in his head and the feeling of brooding menace.

He had sent Lucita a valentine, too, Fey later discovered. The little girl's red-plush heart contained a gold bangle, and she was delighted. Even Miss Pringle seemed less disapproving than usual. And I know our ball will be a success, thought Fey happily. For weeks Fey had been concentrating her natural executive ability on this ball; with the assistance of a social secretary and Ward McAllister she had checked and rechecked lists. Nothing was forgotten, the supper menu, the orchestra, the flowers, the roll carpet and canopy for the front entrance, an army of extra waiters, cotillion favours— all arranged. The only thing she had not been able to arrange was the weather, but Providence smiled. It was clear and not cold, an ideal February day.

At nine o'clock the first guests arrived. The long drawing-rooms began to spot with extravagant colour as the costumed figures bowed and greeted their hosts before drifting into the ballroom. There were giggles and genteel excitement, the release from propriety furnished by the carnival spirit and the partial anonymity of the dominos. There were a few home makeshifts, monks, clowns, and gypsy girls, but the majority of the costumes had been made to order by Mapleson's at a minimum cost of a hundred dollars.

Simeon and Fey were magnificent as King Arthur and Queen Guinevere, a resplendent 1877 version of the royal pair, vaguely derived, of course, from the extremely popular *Idylls*, and in no way handicapped by research into the sixth century. Mapleson's taste had run to velvet trimmed in brocade and ermine and plenty of gilt. Simeon had a gold crown encrusted with rhinestones, a gold leather sword belt and scabbard, and a hint of chain mail woven from gilded thread. He also had a wig of shoulder-length brown hair upon which the crown rested shakily. He was uncomfortable and he felt slightly ridiculous until the awed comments of the arriving guests restored him. The Louis the Fifteenths and the Henry the Eighths, the Venetian princesses and the Martha Washingtons, were also resplendent, but Mapleson had seen to it that the Towers outglittered them all.

Fey's gown was of red velvet edged with ermine, her crown sparkled even more dazzlingly than King Arthur's, and in her own black hair, loosely braided and reaching to her knees, were twined yards of imitation pearls. Here she had over-ridden Mapleson who had recommended a string of rhine-stones for her hair, and maybe a few red plumes "just here, to set off the crown. We must be truly regal, Mrs. Tower; the hostess dare take no chance of appearing insignificant at such a ball as this."

Now, standing beside Simeon, Fey knew that she did not look insignificant. In the rich red velvet, ermine, and pearls she looked exotic, a vivid woman on whom many startled eyes lingered. Little Mrs. Tower was always pretty and stylish, but she didn't usually impress one as a beauty. The costume suited her, that was it, thought the men. The women were puzzled.

"She doesn't look quite—quite American, somehow," whispered Mrs. Bull to Mrs. Carson behind her Madame de Pompadour fan, "but charming, of course, Mapleson's has done well," she added, for Fey had aroused no jealousies. She did not flirt with husbands, and toward powerful ladies like the Madams Bull and Carson she had always maintained an atti-tude of endearing gratitude and diffidence. She had made an ideal protégée. And now, in spite of her rather disturbingly foreign appearance, her behaviour continued to be punctili-ously correct. She smiled and bowed and she passed new ar-rivals on to her husband with just the right shade of dignified cordiality.

Even when there was a stir around the far door and an un-mistakable figure, not in the least disguised as Queen Eliza-beth, progressed past the line and stopped before the Towers, Fey did not lose her poise. "We are honoured to receive you. It was good of you to come," she said quietly, cutting across Simeon's overeffusive stammer of greeting.

"Well!" said Mrs. Bull to her friend. "So Mrs. Astor *did* come!"

"Oh, yes," answered Mrs. Carson, who was on more intimate terms with their leader and did not intend that anyone should forget it. "Carrie told me she would when I took tea with her last Wednesday. She says that we must be broadminded about widening our circle from time to time, especially when they give such delightful balls.'

Everyone agreed that it was a delightful ball, even before the opening grand march had ended. There was a Greek gods and goddess quadrille and a royal personages quadrille expertly directed by Ward McAllister, who was daringly costumed as the Huguenot lover of Marguerite de Valois. The cotillion favours were gorgeous—solid gold handkerchief holders or bonbonnières for the ladies, cuff links for the men.

By eleven-thirty the ball was in full swing. Fey excused herself from the general dancing for a moment and slipped into a rose-bowered cosy corner—one of several provided for couples who wished to sit out.

They were all waltzing—her guests, beguiled by Strauss's increasingly popular "Wine, Woman, and Song." The mosaic of glittering colour whirled past her. Beneath the tiny half-masks mouths laughed, jewelled and bewigged heads tilted coquettishly. The air was voluptuous with the scent of powder, of the garlands of La France roses which festooned the shaded gasoliers, of resinous floor wax.

Fey saw Simeon nervously manœuvring Mrs. Astor through the reverse. Her Elizabethan farthingale and famous diamond stomacher made these manœuvres risky. Simeon, being the host, was unmasked and his face glistened with heat. But he looked happy.

We've done it! thought Fey. Security at last and triumph. She sighed a little, drawing back into the shelter of the corner. She must go out and dance; she saw that Ward McAllister had discovered her and was edging around the room in her direction. I need some champagne, she thought; this has been a strain. But we've done it!

"Fair Guinevere, wilt thou trip a measure with me?" said McAllister in the high, whinnying voice he considered suitable for disguise.

"Most certainly, brave Huguenot lord," answered Fey. This sort of thing was part of a domino ball.

"Never did I see so goodly a company," he said, clasping her red-velvet waist in his plump arm and leading her toward the floor. And he added, in his ordinary voice: "A howling success, my dear. I'm so pleased for you. Mrs. Astor just told me she thought everything was very well done."

"I'm so glad," whispered Fey.

"I took the liberty of seeing that your servants were frappé-ing the champagne properly," he said. "It means so much." He waited for her thanks, and was surprised to get no answer, for Mrs. Tower was always extremely appreciative of his help. He glanced down at her face and saw on it a peculiar expression. She had grown very white and she looked dazed. Her eyes were fixed toward the end of the room near the orchestra, and, as she mechanically whirled with him, she kept her head turned in that direction.

"You're looking for somebody?" he asked.

Fey's eyes flickered and came back to her partner. "I'm sorry. No. That is, one of the costumes startled me. I hadn't seen it before."

"Oh, no doubt you mean that rather ghastly Mephisto-pheles," said McAllister, always delighted by feminine sensi-bility. "He *is* quite terrifying. I think it's young Tremont."

Fey smiled faintly, and let it go at that. It was not Mephis-topheles which had set her heart to a thick, frightened pound-ing, but the glimpse of an inconspicuous black suit, tight trousers, short jacket, and flat broad-brimmed hat, the ordinary dress of a Mexican caballero. To everyone else it would seem a costume, a sombre and uninteresting one amongst all the elaborate creations, but still a costume. To Fey it was a fami-liar memory, and her first reaction was one of amazement. Who had known enough to reproduce a suit so authentic? It was on the second glimpse that she examined the wearer. His face was distorted by the half-mask and it was too far away to see details. But there was something in the height, the length of back, and a flowing sort of grace— He was waltzing with a stately Martha Washington.

I'm loco, said Fey to herself, and the use of the blunt little Spanish word reassured her. It's impossible that what I for a moment imagined should be true. "Feyita la Loca." For here is our great ball, there is Simeon still dancing with Mrs. Astor. If I got near that man, I would see that there is no resemblance.

"I think, if you don't mind, a glass of champagne—" she murmured to McAllister. "It's so silly, but I seem to be a little tired. No, I'll come with you."

She did not look back at the ballroom, but walked beside

McAllister down the corridor that separated it from the rest of the house and the supper rooms. She sank on a gilt chair, accepting a glass from her escort.

"I shouldn't leave my guests, should I?" she said, giving a vague little smile.

McAllister was perturbed. Mrs. Tower seemed suddenly to have lost the poise and assurance which he had always admired. She gulped her champagne, and sent him for another glass. Her hands moved restlessly, her fingers twisted and untwisted one of the strands of pearls in her braid.

"The guests will expect to unmask at midnight. You really should be there, unless you are unwell," he said.

"Yes—yes, of course," answered Fey. But she did not move. I'm afraid, she thought, afraid. I don't want to go back to that ballroom.

Suddenly, to McAllister's relief, she got up, and looked at the gold and ormolu clock on the mantel. "It's time," she said. "We'll go right back, and will you give the order, please?"

At once propitiated, for he adored being master of ceremonies, McAllister bowed and offered his arm. They returned to the ballroom. He went to silence the orchestra, and Fey walked over to Simeon, who was now seated beside Mrs. Astor and fanning her. The great lady nodded graciously and made room for Fey beside her.

The music stopped, and McAllister waved his arms for silence, crying, "Our amiable host and hostess, King Arthur and Queen Guinevere, decree that everyone shall unmask!"

There was a flurry, a little gale of high-pitched squeals and protestations. The dominos were removed and flung into a corner, where two footmen gathered them up.

He isn't here, thought Fey, after a quick survey. I was dreaming. The shaking in her chest subsided. She turned full attention to Mrs. Astor, who was examining the company critically and commenting. "So that was Minnie Atkins all the time. Green is so trying for her.—Oh, yes, and there are the Lorillards." She paused. "A few faces new to me. So refreshing. One gets sick of the same ones, of course."

Fey smiled and nodded. Across Mrs. Astor her eyes met Simeon's and they exchanged a quick, exultant look.

"Oh, I see Mr. Clareforth, just going through the door. I'm most anxious to speak to him." Mrs. Astor smiled at Simeon. "Would you mind—?"

Simeon rose eagerly and made off through the crowd after

Clareforth. McAllister, who had been hovering, slipped into his place. Mrs. Astor's eyes roved again. "There's a tall young man in black, over by the last window. Really very handsome. Is he one of the Randolphs, I wonder?"

Ice flowed over Fey. The ballroom darkened and swung around her in wavering circles. She followed Mrs. Astor's gaze. Across a hundred waltzing heads she saw Terry, staring in her direction. As he saw her look toward him, he sketched a slight mocking bow.

"I don't seem to know him," remarked McAllister, puzzled. "But a few people asked permission to bring house guests, did they not, Mrs. Tower? He must be—"

"Of course," interrupted Fey sharply. "I believe he came with the Goodhues. Oh, the new cotillion is forming! And here are Simeon and Mr. Clareforth. Will you excuse me for a moment, please?"

She stepped down from the dais and she walked rigidly, deliberately, around the fringes of the crowd. Anger such as she had never known beat through her like a gong, but her mind had cleared, withdrawn itself to a pinnacle from which it issued directions.

She knew that Terry would follow her, and she walked to the corridor which led to the main house, waited in the deserted supper room until he came sauntering along. She threw a swift glance around. Nobody. They were all gathered for the cotillion. She walked down the hall and opened the door of a small anteroom. Terry followed her inside, and she shut the door.

"This is charming," he said, smiling, and extending his hand. "I'm used to conquest, of course, but I must admit I usually have to plot a bit longer than this before I can persuade a beautiful lady to—"

"Callate!" cried Fey, stamping her foot, and she hissed three other words.

Terry blinked and dropped his hand. Then he recovered. "Well! I'd never have dreamed the elegant Mrs. Tower still knew how to be rude in Spanish! . . . And you used to be such a cool little party. I used to kind of hope you'd get stamping mad. It's becoming."

Fey unclenched her hands. She turned her eyes from him. You're a fool, she said to herself. You're twenty-seven years old and you're acting like a child. This man has no power over you.

216

She moved over to a small chair and sat down. "Why have you come, Terry?" she said quietly. "And I might also ask, how did you get in?"

Terry grinned. He also seated himself on a brocaded settee. The long body was as lean and muscular as ever. There were a few lines across his forehead and around his bright hazel eyes, and his flaming hair was dulled a trifle from the sun, but ten years had scarcely touched him.

"It's like this," he said amiably, while she waited in a chill, resistant silence. "I got back to New York last month—first time since I left, by the way—and I went to Delmonico's for a decent meal. Who should I see at a distant table but a little girl I once toted out of Sante Fe with a mule team. Only I didn't know her right away, because she'd turned into a fashionable lady, drooling sables and diamonds. So I asked the head waiter who that was, and he said 'Mrs. Simeon Tower.' Then I went home and did a lot of thinking, and I read the papers."

"Go on," said Fey. "Hurry—I've got to get back."

"Well—in the papers I saw a lot about a masked ball to be given by these Simeon Towers. So I decided to go. Having just spent three years in Mexico on interesting but not very productive business, I dressed myself in the suit I wore there, added a domino, and when guests were streaming into the house I streamed in with them. Very simple."

Simple, yes, and melodramatic, the kind of thing you've always wanted to pull off, she thought, her anger rising again. But she controlled herself, and said: "Yes, I see. But now you must leave immediately. You owe me that much. Simeon mustn't know—no one must know who you are."

"Why?" he inquired with interest. "Didn't you ever tell Tower about me? Are you a bigamist, my little love?"

"I divorced you," she said acidly. "Besides, as you told me that morning in Mrs. Flynn's boarding-house, we were never really married."

Terry got off the settee. He stood near her, but not touching her. "I've regretted that morning, Fey, regretted it deeply." Sincerity in that caressing voice, the rare humble note which had always melted her.

"I was a fool," said Terry. "Underneath it's always been just you—mi corazón."

Useless to tell herself that he had learned from and doubtless practised this endearment on dozens of Spanish women.

217

It was the one she used to Lucita and it was warm with sentiment. Lucita! This is Lucita's father.

"Go away, Terry," she said, moving to the door. "I didn't want and I never do want to see you again."

"Ah but you do," he said. "I saw your eyes just then." He spun her around, pulled her to him and kissed her.

Her mind tried to get away, it called to her thinly—"See how practised he is, how well he knows how to rouse a woman, even more than he did then." But her lips remembered, they parted under his, and the thick sweet long-forgotten delight swept down through her body.

"Ah, my dear," whispered Terry. "You don't act like that with old Tower, I'll bet."

Fey could not speak. She looked at him with hatred and with passion.

"Do you remember," said Terry gently, "the park bench between the Marble Arch and the Mall where we used to sit that week we had together in New York? Will you meet me there tomorrow at three? I've got to talk to you again."

She did not answer.

He picked up his black hat, swinging it from the chin cord. "I'll worry you no more tonight," he said. "But remember, I love you, Fey, I always have." He looked at her yearningly and walked slowly out the door.

Cheap! she thought, shoddy dramatics as they always were. But suddenly she fell on her knees, her hands clasped, her head bowed—"Madre de Dios," she whispered, "help me, help me!"

Fey returned to the ballroom just before the cotillion ended. Simeon, who had been watching for her, but assumed that her absence had something to do with supper, noticed that her cheeks were flushed and her breathing rapid. Momentarily released from paying court to Mrs. Astor, he hurried up to Fey. "My dear, there's nothing gone wrong with the arrangements, is there? You look a bit strange."

She lifted her lids and looked at him. A little man in a ridiculous brown wig, a bogus empty scabbard dangling from a glittering belt which was buckled too tight around the middle. "Your wig's crooked," she said.

There was a silence. The cotillion had dissolved, the music stopped. Everyone was waiting for Mr. Tower to usher Mrs. Astor in to supper. Heads were turned their way expectantly.

"Why do you use that t-tone?" said Simeon.

218

Fey swallowed, pushing it down, trampling on it.

"I'm sorry. Excitement, I guess." She smiled, raised her hands and gently straightened the wig. "They're all waiting to go in to supper."

IN his small room at the Saint Nicholas Hotel, Terry whistled cheerfully while he dressed himself for the park rendezvous with Fey. He was almost certain that she would come, and it amused him to see how eager he was. In his experience old loves were always stale and flat when resurrected, but this was different. As evidenced by her response to his kiss, she was as receptive as ever, and her old attraction for him had returned. Though he had forgotten it for years, he now remembered that he had never had a woman quite so romantically and sexually satisfying as Fey had been during the first weeks of their marriage.

She's a strange little thing, he thought, brushing his hair before the mirror, adjusting the cat's-eye stickpin on the brocaded cravat, and look what an extraordinary success she's made of her life!

He admired this success and he was curious about it.

Curiosity and the pursuit of a new variety of amorous adventure were, as yet, the only motives responsible for his renewed interest in Fey. He wished her well and he had no intention of making trouble. He owed her that much certainly. If she didn't show up in the park today, he'd leave her alone and go on back to Chicago, as he had intended to.

Chicago suited him a lot better than New York. He had been doing well there until the great fire in '71. He and Maude had set up a high-class gambling house. But the fire wiped them out. They had then wandered through the Middle West working the river boats, holding medicine shows, and sometimes playing bit parts in local opera houses. Now and then they were flush, more often broke. They had got bored with each other at about the same time, and parted amicably in St. Louis. After that, Terry drifted down into Mexico, where luck and the tender interest of a politician's wife brought him to the notice of President Lerdo de Tejada, Juarez's successor. A pleasing and remunerative sinecure followed and lasted for three years. Unfortunately, six weeks ago Porfiro Diaz's revolutionary activities had coincided with a violent quarrel with the politician's wife, and Mexico had become too hot for Terry. He had shipped out of Vera Cruz on the first boat and it had carried him to New York. He had two hundred dollars in gold and undimmed optimism. Chicago by all accounts was nearly rebuilt and bigger and better than ever. This time he would really find himself some permanently profitable enterprise. But there was plenty of time to dally with Fey if she were so minded.

He flicked his cravat, sleeked his hair with scented macassar oil, adjusted his grey bowler, and set out by the Broadway streetcar for the park.

The horses were slow, and at Fifty-Ninth Street Terry was still further delayed by a young lady who needed help to cross the slushy street. The lady was pretty and appreciative, and it was only a surreptitious glance at his gold watch that startled Terry into bowing himself off. He hurried toward the Marble Arch.

She was already there, pacing up and down the walk. Her small figure wrapped in a furred and hooded cape gave an unmistakable impression of agitation.

Terry smiled to himself. He walked quietly so as to come up behind her and sang in her ear—

> *"Chula la mañana, chula la mañana—*
> *Como que te quiero ..."*

the gay New Mexican love-song.

Fey stiffened and stopped. He slid his hand under her elbow. "Do you remember how you taught that to me out on the Kansas prairie?"

She drew herself away. "I came only to tell you that you must leave New York at once!" But it was not the tone she had meant to use.

"I would have, darling," said Terry softly, bending down and smiling into her strained, tight face, "if you hadn't come today."

Fey gave him a frightened look. But it can't be true—he's lying! Oh, why did I come! Yet she had used logic and clear thinking in making the decision. When the last guests had left at five and she and Simeon were at last in bed, she had lain for hours staring up at the embroidered tester, not moving for

220

fear Simeon should speak to her. She knew by his breathing that he wasn't asleep either. He would want to talk about the ball, and for her the ball had blurred into a jumbled background to the scene in the anteroom. Again and again like an adolescent she relived the physical impact of Terry's kiss while her mind jeered at her. This conflict went on with slowly diminishing force until the clock on the landing struck ten and she decided to get up. She raised herself cautiously on her elbow and saw that Simeon was asleep. He had tucked his hand under his cheek and his unguarded face held an expression of anxious hopefulness. That is the way he looked as a little boy, she thought painfully. She kissed him on the forehead. He stirred and said "Fey"—but he did not wake.

She slid out of bed, determined to ignore Terry. She dressed and went downstairs, where exhausted servants were trying to put the great house to rights. She tried to busy herself in helping and directing them, but they did better without her and a lassitude swept over her. She lay down on a couch in her boudoir, and it was then that it suddenly occurred to her that she had better see Terry once more. So long as he did not know the circumstances of her marriage to Simeon, he was clearly a menace. For Simeon's sake, she must explain and appeal to him. But she would not mention Lucita. Obviously he knew nothing of the child's existence, and there was no reason why he should. She would speak but a few words to him; she would make him realize that last night meant nothing, and she would be back in the house in an hour. Simeon was still asleep when she ordered the carriage and had herself driven to Central Park's Fifth Avenue entrance. She told Briggs to wait and walked from there.

"Let's sit down here," said Terry. "It's quite warm and I can't see your face when you fidget about like that."

She hesitated, sat down on the corner edge of the slatted wooden bench.

"I can't stay," she said. "I just wanted to tell you—to ask you—"

"Yes?" he questioned lazily. He was watching her mouth. He lifted one of her gloved hands and put it to his lips. "What did you want to tell me, mi corazón?"

She snatched her hand back. "Don't call me that!" She went on crisply. "No one knows I've been divorced, of course. I can trust you not to say anything?"

Terry considered this. "No, I suppose all those swells you

had there last night wouldn't speak to a divorcée. Just how'd you get rid of me, might I ask?"

"Simeon arranged it through Judge Barnard in '68," said Fey, very fast. "We gave out that I was a widow, a Mrs. Dawson from the South."

"Why *Mrs.* Anything; much simpler for you to appear unmarried, I should think?"

"I couldn't because of—" She stopped. Fool, fool, what's the matter with you—

Terry sat up. "Because of what?"

She was silent. Two small boys skipped past the bench bound for the skating lake; their skates bouncing on their shoulders made tiny musical clinks and the runners flashed in the sunlight.

"You had a baby," said Terry.

Her lips tightened and she said nothing.

"Was it mine—or Tower's or somebody else's?"

"It was yours. A little girl. But Simeon has been her father. He's given her everything and he loves her."

"Why didn't you tell me—that day at Mrs. Flynn's?"

"Would it have kept you? And would I have wanted to keep you—out of pity? No, Terry, I have managed alone, as you told me to." She got up, drawing the cloak tighter around her. "Now good-bye."

"Wait a minute!" He jumped up and stood in front of her. "Please, Fey—I don't blame you for feeling the way you do, but think of me, too; this news is a shock. I'd like to see my child once. It's only natural."

He saw her eyes darken and shift from his pleading face, but she answered inflexibly. "No, it's impossible. It would hurt Simeon deeply if he ever found out. He thinks of Lucita as his own. And he's very conventional. We've been a long time reaching the place where—well, where we could give a ball like last night."

"Oh?" said Terry. He found it interesting, this hint of social struggle, not only for Fey, but Tower too, and he caught the faint whisper of a new idea.

"Look, honey—don't go yet," he said. "There's nobody about. Let's walk toward the Mall as we used to. I know I treated you badly, but I didn't know about the child, and I can't help wanting to understand a few things, can I?"

Go, said a voice clearly in Fey's head, go quickly. There's danger here. You've already said too much. But, on the other hand, what harm is there? A few minutes more—this man was my husband, the father of Lucita.

He felt her arm relax beneath his fingers, and he moved his hand under her cape to that he touched her bare skin above the glove. He heard her indrawn breath as they began to walk down the path.

"Tell me about Tower," he said. "How did you manage to meet him in the first place?"

At first she answered Terry's eager questions in monosyllables, but gradually as they strolled along she found that there was pleasure in reliving that far-past year-and-a-half of struggle, to the accompaniment of his sympathetic exclamations, and she told him about everything. The Arcadia Concert Saloon and her first glimpse of Simeon, the months at the Infirmary, her assault on Simeon's office and his quick and exciting capitulation.

"Smart girl," said Terry, laughing heartily. "The nerve you had diddling him into buying that old lump of Injun turquoise! I always felt sorry for you, setting such store by that thing, but, of course, you didn't know any better. You've come a long way, sweetheart."

"Yes, I have," said Fey, smiling. She had forgotten that Terry was an enemy, in the delight of sharing the carefully guarded secrets with someone, the sense of triumphant accomplishment reflected from his admiration.

The sun slanted over the low broken line of brownstones on Central Park West, a chilly wind sprang up, and the Mall became nearly deserted.

"Funny little thing you used to be," said Terry, squeezing her arm, "with your mind-reading and your visions. Used to give me the creeps sometimes when you'd stare right through me with those big grey eyes. Thank the Lord, you've lost all that nonsense."

"Yes," said Fey, "I guess I was quite ridiculous." She shivered suddenly, and Terry under the protection of her cape slid his arm around her. "Tienes frio, mi amor?" he inquired tenderly.

"Don't!" said Fey. "Don't talk to me in Spanish. It belongs to that other life. I don't want to remember it. Simeon hates it—that part of me."

Aha! thought Terry. He had begun to form a very clear picture of Tower's character from the many little sidelights she had thrown. He saw a rich man who was nevertheless insecure and morbidly anxious to appear conventional. A middle-

223

aged man in love with a young wife and jealous of her past. The new idea which had glimmered before began to take vague form.

"I'm afraid you should go now, darling," he said very gently. "I don't want you to get into any trouble."

She started and flushed. "Yes—yes," she said. "I must. It's terribly late."

"Tomorrow," said Terry, holding her closer, "you'll come here again and bring the little one? Yes"—he said against her quick protest—"if it's my child you can't deny me just once."

His hazel eyes were warm with entreaty.

It's only fair that he should want to see her, thought Fey, it's only fair.

"You won't tell her, Terry, don't say anything that would give her an idea—"

"Of course not." He looked hastily around, bent and kissed her on the mouth.

She broke away from him, running down the Mall, her furred boots slipping on the frozen snow.

Terry watched her disappear before he moved. Then he walked back toward the Broadway entrance. Upon his return to the Saint Nicholas, he went into the bar and settled in the corner with a bottle of whisky. After the third glass he began to hum "Chula la Mañana" softly to himself. It was a good world and still crammed with interesting possibilities.

The next day Simeon went to the office and it was simple for Fey to arrange her afternoon as she wished. After breakfast, when he kissed her good-bye, he asked her plans for the day, but on hearing that she proposed taking Lucita for a drive in the park Simeon nodded absently, and set off on foot down Broadway. Walking helped, it cleared the brain. The Gulf and San Diego stock was not behaving right. Gould and his new ally, Russell Sage, were manipulating under cover somewhere, but so far all efforts had not been equal to flushing them out.

But I'll get 'em, he thought, it'll be all right. I've done it before. He stifled the insistent murmur that never before had his position been so shaky, of the further colossal bank loan which he must somehow wheedle from the Continental Trust. Bluff would do it again, bluff and the confidence built up by his past glittering successes. Old Stevens at the Continental had hardly batted an eye when he granted the last loan, and he was close-mouthed as a pike, no danger of a leak. Publicity about the triumphant ball would help—the fifteen-thousand-dollar ballroom, the catering and orchestra—most splendid yet seen in New York—not paid for yet, of course, but they'd wait. Nobody ever doubted the Tower credit. Just a little more push, a little more fight. Get back that old certainty, that sure hold on a problem. This muzziness would pass, this uneasiness which seemed to unsettle the mind as it also reproduced physical sensations below the diaphragm.

Simeon walked faster. I'm as good as I ever was. Better. With an effort he effaced thoughts of the afternoon's coming negotiation at the Continental Trust and applied an antidote. The ball —everybody in New York worth having—and the hint given by Sylvester Bull. Simeon Tower's name would come up before the membership committee at the Knickerbocker Club, and Bull had smiled certainty as he mentioned it. The Knickerbocker!—most exclusive of them all, founded in 1871 because the Union and Union League Clubs were getting too democratic.

For a moment Simeon allowed himself a memory. Little Simon Turmstein, jeered at, hiding behind fences, rushing home early from school before the other children chose sides for Run Sheep Run and Pom Pom Pull Away. And those children now? Farmers, factory hands; not one of them worth more than a thousand a year.

Simon entered the marble doors of Tower, Slate, and Hatch, nodded in response to the flurry of respectful greeting, mounted the stairs, acknowledged Lemming's watchful bow, shut himself into his office, and awaited the market's opening quotations.

In abstracting Lucita from Miss Pringle's iron-bound routine, Fey had had to silence all the governess's stock objections, and had wondered, not for the first time, if it were really necessary to turn the care of her child over to another woman. It was so long since she had had Lucita to herself, because there had been the mounting social duties and the pressure of the ball; and now the child seemed to her a remote, polite little doll.

Briggs tucked the fur robe around them and the cutter started up Fifth Avenue toward the park. Fey gave her little girl an anxiously loving look. Lucita was so pretty, with her red-gold curls, her velvet bonnet and coat and buttoned boots, a replica of her mother's, so pretty and so quiet.

"See, darling," cried Fey, "I've brought your skates. We'll have fun in the park together."

225

"Yes, Mama," said the child. "It is most kind of you to take me."

"Oh, Lucita!" cried Fey. "It isn't kind of me—I love to have you. Now that stupid ball is over, we'll do lots of things together."

Lucita gave her mother a wondering look. "Miss Pringle says you and Papa are very busy. I mustn't bother you."

Fey's heart contracted. "But, of course, we're not too busy for you, darling. I'll tell you what. We'll plan a special treat soon. Just you and me and Papa. Would you like that?"

The child nodded. "Very much, Mama."

Fey hesitated, and took the child's mittened hand from the squirrel muff, held it tight in hers. "You love Papa, don't you, dear?"

"Oh, yes, I do. He is so good. He gives me lovely things."

The cutter whizzed past Saint Patrick's Cathedral, still unfinished, though the two tapering spires now pierced the clear air high above all the surrounding city. It no longer reminded Fey of the Parroquia in Santa Fe, and the familiar sight of the twin spires provoked no memory of nine years ago when it had given her asylum.

Her eyes passed it absently while each thud of the horses' snow-packed shoes increased her nervous excitement at the coming meeting.

When they crossed the open square at Fifty-Ninth Street, she glanced at Brigg's stolid back and said to Lucita, "I think we may meet somebody in the park, dear. A gentleman, a kind of —of cousin of ours I haven't seen for a long time."

"Will he skate, too?" asked the child politely.

Fey smiled, but did not answer. She stopped Briggs at the path, telling him to come back in two hours, and holding Lucita by the hand she set off toward the Marble Arch.

This time Terry was not late and he hurried to greet the two approaching figures.

Fey had braced herself for awkwardness, but there was none. Terry inspected the child, then picked her up and gave her a resounding kiss. Lucita looked astonished, but not resentful. When he had put her down, she smiled shyly up at the tall handsome gentleman.

"Mine all right!" said Terry, in a loud whisper to Fey. "Hair just like my mother's and the nose too."

"Hush!" cried Fey. "You promised to be careful."

Terry shrugged and laughed. He was in high spirits. "She can't understand, she's only eight."

"I'll be nine in June, sir," said the little girl, turning her clear blue gaze from Fey to Terry.

"You see?" whispered Fey, above the child's head. Eight, she thought; at that age one understands and knows more than people think. I was only seven when Father died and I knew many things. We *must* be careful.

But Terry would not be careful. It amused him to charm his daughter.

By all means they must go skating, he cried exuberantly, and, linking arms with Fey and Lucita, he swept them to the upper skating lake.

They arrived breathless and laughing, both infected by his animal spirits. He scarcely allowed Fey time to be sure that there was no one she knew amongst the swirling skaters, though indeed there was little danger; this was not the fashionable lake. He had buckled the runners on to his daughter's boots and rented skates for himself and Fey before she had finished her half-hearted protest.

"I'm not any good," she said, staggering on the skates and clinging to his arm.

"Neither am I," he laughed, catching her around the waist. "You'll have to show us how," he said to the delighted child. "You see, your mother and I grew up in a land without ice ponds."

The three of them floundered and struggled together. They fell down and they laughed. The other skaters gave them a wide berth, smiling sympathetically at the gay family party. Lucita was transformed, her cheeks crimson, her little voice shrill with excitement.

When they had had enough and were walking to the refreshment kiosk, she hung on to Terry like an affectionate puppy, and as soon as they were seated climbed up on to his lap, where he immediately cuddled and petted her.

"Get down, darling," said Fey sharply. "I know you like—Cousin Terry, but this is a public place."

"Jealous, my dear?" asked Terry, tightening his hold on the child and grinning at Fey. "What more natural than that I should fondle my—"

"Terry!"

"Ah—here comes our chocolate, I see," said Terry, sitting Lucita forward on his knee so that she might reach the foaming cup.

To Fey, who was still frowning, he said:

"It must be the Scotch part of you, in which I never quite

227

believed, by the way, that makes you so anxious and serious. Laugh, my dear, as you did on the lake. It makes you much prettier."

"It isn't the Scottish part," she answered angrily. "It's common decency."

"Ah!" said Terry. He bent over the little girl and added in a stage whisper, "We wouldn't know about that, would we, Lucita?"

The child looked up from the chocolate and inspected him earnestly. "No one but Mama calls me that—everyone else says Lucy."

Terry turned from the child and, leaning back in the chair, fixed his warm, lazy gaze on Fey's face.

"But you don't mind, do you? I used to know your Mama very well—and shall again." He weighted the last words with caress and meaning.

Fey tried not to answer his look as she tried to push down the heat she felt seeping across her face. This is a game with him, as it always was, she thought. I'm not an ignorant child any more, and I know this is not love. But her eyes of their own separate will responded to his.

And suddenly he spoke in Spanish—"Yes, it is true that we belong in each other's arms; you also remember the joy."

Fey jumped up and at her convulsive motion the chair grated on the restaurant tiles. "Come, Lucita," she said. "It's very late. We've got to go."

"Oh, Mama—" protested the child, and then, seeing her mother's face, she slid from Terry's knee with frightened speed.

"Good-bye, little one," said Terry, smiling at Lucita. "We've had fun, haven't we? And Fey, I'm at the Saint Nicholas, you know. I'll be waiting to hear from you."

Fey turned her back on him and hurried Lucita out of the restaurant.

The little girl gave Fey several apprehensive looks while her legs trotted as fast as they could to match her mother's pace; at last she said, "You look so funny, Mama; you aren't cross with me, are you?"

Fey stopped dead, leaning against a bench and trying to get her breath. "No darling, of course not." She managed to smile and saw the troubled face clear. "Lucita—I hate to—" She stopped and started again. "This meeting with Cousin Terry this afternoon—it must be a secret just for you and me."

228

"You mean I mustn't tell Miss Pringle—or Papa?" said the child slowly.

"Not anyone. Promise me."

"I promise, Mama. But shan't I see him again? He's so big and nice, and he looks like that picture of the Sun-King in my story-book."

"Yes, I know," said Fey bitterly, beginning to walk again. "But Miss Pringle taught you something you wrote in your copy-book. 'Handsome is as handsome does.' Do you remember?"

"Yes, Mama, but I don't understand it very well."

And I haven't learned it either, whispered Fey to herself. I haven't learned it either. Her jaw set, and for the next few days she directed her servants and attended to social obligations with a tense, chill efficiency.

CHAPTER

17

ON Tuesday morning at eleven o'clock Terry took the Broadway stage for Wall Street. He intended to do nothing decisive, particularly nothing which might jeopardize the satisfactory progress of his affair with Fey. This was to be merely a reconnoitring expedition. And for its outcome he trusted to luck. Luck, as usual, treated him very well.

He wandered in through the doors of Tower, Slate, and Hatch, admiring the veined marble pillars and cast-iron grilles, and before the first junior clerk had approached to ask his business, he encountered Noah Lemming. Lemming was temporarily downstairs supervising a bond transfer, and Terry's appearance interested him.

"What can we do for you, sir?" He bowed before Terry, smiling his tight smile and adjusting his glossy paper collar.

"Why—" Terry hesitated. "I had a little private matter to take up with Mr. Tower, but there's no hurry. I just thought I'd run in."

"Mr. Tower's out just now. Over in the Exchange. But I'm his secretary. Maybe I could assist you."

"Well—I hardly think—" began Terry, smiling with great friendliness.

229

He had no idea where or if this secretary might be useful, but he had no intention of making an enemy.

Lemming, far shrewder than Terry, instantly followed this reasoning. Something's up, he thought, and I'm going to find out what.

"Come up to my office and join me in a Havana, anyway," he said, and led the way upstairs.

Terry followed uncertainly. He had not the faintest notion of what he was going to say.

"Nice office you've got," he offered, sitting down in an armchair upholstered in red plush and accepting the cigar. "Must be fine working for a rich man like Mr. Tower."

Lemming's foxy face sharpened. "You're looking for a job?" he asked, disappointed.

"Hell, no!" returned Terry. "I couldn't stand office work for a second."

"So I should have imagined." Lemming permitted himself a thin smile. "My name is Noah Lemming, and what is yours, may I ask?"

Terry hesitated, but there seemed no reason for concealment. "Dillon," he said. "Xavier T. Dillon."

Lemming considered this, frowning. Something familiar about it, some teasing correlation just over the edge of memory that couldn't quite be fished out. He reached beneath his desk and brought up a bottle and glass. "Brandy?" He poured Terry a large glass and handed it to him with the utmost graciousness.

Terry nodded and took a huge fiery swallow. You won't catch me that way, he thought, amused. I could drink six of you under the table, you dried-up little weasel.

"Been in New York long?" asked Lemming.

"Why, no. As a matter of fact, I've just come. I spent the last three years in Mexico." And make what you can out of that, he added mentally.

But he was wrong. Lemming's eyes veiled themselves; beneath the edge of the desk his dry hands gripped each other as the lost correlation slid into consciousness. Mexico—Spanish. A woman with an accent, breaking into angry Spanish. Mrs. *Dillon*! Mrs. Simeon Tower.

He decided to clarify matters by a bold attack. "I think," he said, delicately setting down his glass and giving it a little half-twist, "that your call concerns Mrs. Tower—who was once, perhaps, Mrs. Dillon?"

"How the devil did you get that?" cried Terry, astounded out of caution. "Oh, I suppose you knew about the divorce."

Divorce. Lemming's face fell. He had hoped for bigamy. Still, far more clearly than Terry, he saw the possibilities.

"Let's be frank, Mr. Dillon," he said. "One can hardly deny that your appearance may embarrass Mr. Tower. Just how much did you think your—ah—silent disappearance was going to be worth?"

Terry was shocked. Lemming had at one bound jumped much farther than Terry's vague optimistic plans had reached. His precise voice had nailed down the gauzy moth, and now, no longer fluttering on ahead but starkly spread out on the desk between them, it looked crude and ugly.

"That's an extraordinary question," said Terry. "Nothing I've said has given you any such—"

"Let's not be childish," interrupted Lemming. He was now sure of his man, and moved by natural malice and the prospect of safe advantage, he saw the kind of guidance that Dillon required.

"I can help you, you know," he said, smiling. "You will find my—ah—advice invaluable, I assure you."

The smile did not reassure Terry. He was out of his depth, for after all this man was Tower's secretary and presumably would guard his employer's interest.

"I know what you're thinking," said Lemming, who did. He found that handsome, pseudo-sophisticated face very transparent. "Let me convince you, Mr. Dillon, that, though of course I am entirely loyal to Mr. Tower, I really see no reason why you should not profit a bit by this situation."

"And you?" said Terry, after a moment.

"Well—" Lemming again produced his pinched smile, he poured Terry another glass of brandy. "I'll leave that to you. You will find, I think, that my advice has—ah—value."

Terry emptied his glass and moved uneasily in the red-plush chair.

"Just what is your advice?" he asked sulkily.

Lemming glanced at the wall clock. Tower might drop back to the office from the Exchange on his way to Delmonico's for lunch, and it would be unwise for him to see Terry. "Come back at three," he said, rising. "He'll be well-fed and less irritable than at other times. Ask for ten thousand."

Terry jumped up. So much! The nebulous plan had never reached an exact figure, but no such sum as that had he ever aspired to. "He'll kick me out," he said.

Lemming shook his head, his eyes hardened into a fleeting expression of contempt. "Not if you handle the interview with finesse; no threats, of course. Keep a light tone. You will naturally in no way let him guess that you have talked to me." He paused and waited, until Terry nodded slowly. Then Lemming continued, "And in case you do run into trouble, you might just—ah—mention the name—Pansy Miggs."

"Pansy Miggs!" repeated Terry incredulously. For a moment he had the disagreeable sensation of riding a runaway horse through a tunnel, of having lost control while being rushed willy-nilly into darkness.

"Why, yes," said Lemming, in a light conversational tone. "A public figure like Mr. Tower always has several things in his past which he would prefer to forget. I see no reason why he should not pay for the privilege of forgetting them."

"By God, you're right!" cried Terry, laughing. The disagreeable sensation had stopped and the brandy had produced a haze of good feeling. He noted that Lemming's fingers trembled very slightly and that he glanced nervously at the clock. The little weasel was neither headlong nor dangerous, and if he, too, wanted to pick up a bit of cash, who could blame him? I can handle him all right, thought Terry, and it was lucky I met him. "Well, so long," he said cordially. "I'll be back at three and have a go at it. After it's over, you sneak out to the Saint Nicholas and we'll compare notes over a drink."

Lemming bowed, wincing a trifle, as Terry clapped him on the back. Terry went out to find some lunch, and the glow continued. He looked forward to the afternoon interview with relish. It would be fun, a good game, far more exciting than faro, and for higher stakes. It was amusing, too, to feel power over the great Simeon Tower, and he thought of him almost affectionately. Funny dumpy little man in a silly king's costume, such a rich little man with a few shady spots in his past. Jealous of Fey, too, thought Terry, grinning to himself, as why wouldn't he be when he had nothing but money to offer a woman? Terry squared his shoulders and threw out his chest, seeing the eyes that were being made at him from under a frizzy blonde bang across the room. There'd be a message from Fey in a day or two. He knew her; underneath she was the same dazzled girl he had met in Santa Fe. And in the meantime, thought Terry, consulting his watch, off we go to give her precious husband the shock of his life. He paid his check and walked back to 57 Wall Street.

Lemming had suavely arranged the interview. "There was a

man here, Mr. Tower, didn't give his name, but I've a feeling it's important. Might be—ah—that information you wanted. He's to be here at three again."

Simeon nodded, and his heavy eyes brightened a little. The leaks which had once been so helpful all seemed to have dried up. And today, though the market had been firm, Transic and the Gulf and San Diego both showed the effects of a stealthy ambiguous hammering.

Simeon sighed, letting himself down into his desk chair with a grunt. He had eaten too much lunch; the fuzzy dull discomfort was back, but not the gnawing pains. Food always helped them. But he was sick of eating at Berry's or Delmonico's. Pretty soon he could go to the Knickerbocker, though, he thought, relaxing. Have lunch with Bull and Van Vrandt, not as a guest, but as a member. Simeon lit himself a cigar, watched the wreath of fragrant blue smoke curling up toward the gasolier.

Lemming's discreet tap sounded on the door, which opened and shut again.

"Hello, Mr. Tower," cried Terry cordially from the door. "Enjoying your after-dinner cigar?" and he strode to the desk, grinning, and holding out his hand. "Good of you to see me!"

Simeon put down the cigar and his eyes congealed. He nodded briefly, touched Terry's hand, and indicated the chair. If Lemming's let a salesman in on me, he thought, and another thought—A "ladies' man," big! He looked at the curly reddish hair brilliant with pomatum, the ingratiating cocksure smile, the wide shoulders under the puce broadcloth coat.

"Why did you want to see me, and you have a name, I presume?"

"Oh, to be sure, I have," said Terry, sitting down and making himself comfortable, "but I doubt you'll like it much when you hear it, so let's chat a bit first. I've long admired you, Mr. Tower, and it's a fair treat to of met you at last." This was the way to do it, breezy, good-natured, and a bit of the brogue for charm.

"I think," said Simeon, "that we will have your name now." He did not move at all and his voice was quiet.

Terry's confident grin faded a trifle. "If you like. My name then, is Dillon. Xavier T. Dillon." And he leaned forward, watching eagerly.

"Indeed," said Simeon. There was a pause. He picked up the cigar and took a leisurely puff. "I thought you had died in the Chicago fire."

Terry moistened his lips, trying to stiffen his face, which he

233

knew was crestfallen. Still, he had seen the slightest flicker in the watchful eyes opposite him.

"You knew I was in Chicago?" he said lamely.

"Certainly. And when your gambling house burned, I was told you went with it."

"Sorry to disappoint you," said Terry, trying to recapture the light touch.

Simeon lifted one shoulder, compressed his lips, and waited. Get out of my office, he thought, *get out!* You were finished and done with. I haven't thought of you in years. She hasn't either. I can't stand this, too, just now. Get out!

He kept his eyes steadily on Terry, who felt a slow dull heat rising in him. The game had bogged down. This was the moment for teasing, a delicate baiting, watch the rich little man squirm, but good-humouredly.

"It's awkward having me turn up, isn't it?" he burst out.

Simeon shrugged again. The office was thick with silence. It clung to the damask draperies, it pressed on the maroon carpet, the massive furniture.

"You know damn well it's awkward, you know damn well it's ruinous—if I talk!" cried Terry, goaded into the open by that impassive silence. "What about your precious social position? What about Fey's position?" That's done it, he thought with relief, for at the mention of Fey's name an involuntary tremor showed on the compressed mouth.

"D-does Mrs. Tower know anything about this?" asked Simeon, still in the remote, bored tone, but Terry relaxed still further. Got him asking questions, at least; got him stammering a bit, for all he sits there like an image.

"Oh, of course not!" answered Terry airily. "No use upsetting Fey. I wouldn't hurt her for anything in the world. Nor would you," he added, with a charming smile.

"What is it you want?" said Simeon, and he heard his own voice, channelled, impersonal.

"Why—" said Terry, crossing his legs. "Let's just run over the situation, clear it up for both of us. People don't know Fey was ever Mrs. Dillon, and they don't know she was divorced, and if they did know, the public wouldn't stand for the kind of divorce she got; it must have been pretty phoney."

"How do you know?" said Simeon sharply.

"Oh, my dear Tower! I'm not a fool. I've searched the records; the divorce doesn't appear. I suspect you used one of the convenient little Tammany setups, and they're in very bad odour just now, aren't they?"

Got out of that one pretty neatly, thought Terry.

"What is it you want?" repeated Simeon.

Terry took a deep breath. "Ten thousand dollars," he said. "In cash, of course."

Simeon rose, leaning a second on the desk, and then straightening. 'That's preposterous. Get out!'"

"Oh, not preposterous at all. A millionaire like you. That's chicken feed. It's only fair that you should pay for the privilege of forgetting certain things in your past. I know quite a lot more than you think—for instance"—he paused—"Pansy Miggs."

Good old Lemming, thought Terry, watching; that was quite a tip. Tower's face turned a nasty colour like the dusty lace curtains in the window behind him. But you had to admire his control. His voice still wasn't higher or lower as he said, "I'll have to think it over, Dillon. You can come back Thursday."

"Oh, sure," said Terry, getting up. "There's no great hurry." He grinned at the silent figure behind the desk, feeling almost sorry for him. "Thursday," he said, and after leaving the office, he winked at Lemming, who sprang into the hall. Terry clasped his hands and waved them in the air, the sign of victory. "Going fine," he whispered. "See you later."

Simeon sat on at his desk, staring at the heavy bronze inkstand.

Why didn't I call the police? Why don't I call the police? Go to Commissioner Smith. No use; not like the old days. If Oakey Hall was still mayor—squash the whole thing and no one the wiser. Hustle that red-headed jackanapes out of town. Wickham no use. Don't know him. But money talks still— Don't dare risk it. Don't gab to the papers. Money—I haven't got it. Where could I raise ten thousand in cash by Thursday? —pay him off—get rid of him—get his receipt—scare hell out of him—get that crook from the investigation agency put him on a train for the West. I've handled things like this before— that little guinea back in '66 who smelled out the Transic figures—the Ring took care of him, buried in the Tombs for a year; when he came out he'd lost interest. But I can handle this alone. I'm a fool to get jumpy. He can't prove anything. Face him down. Let him go ahead. Say he's lying. He's not the type to go through with it. Bluff him. But where'd he get his facts? Pansy, too; nobody knew about Pansy. Somebody's talking. Lemming? Can't be; he didn't know, and why would he keep quiet all this time. Not Fey—she couldn't—she hated him—he said he hadn't seen her. Got to protect Fey.

If this damnable pain in my middle would stop, I could think. Not like me to get panicky. I've been in tighter spots. But he'll go to the *Tribune*. He's got enough brains for that. They'd tie it in with that old Ring business and Erie. All forgotten; Gould's got away with it. He faces them down and goes ahead, but it's not his private life, too. The Knickerbocker Club. I've got to go home, can't think here. They'd rally around, Bull and Van Vrandt and Snelling. They wouldn't believe scandal. They like me, they've become my friends—and Fey's. Let him go ahead, prepare a denial for the papers, maybe squash the whole thing yet. I'm Simeon Tower. Who's going to listen to that long grinning imbecile? But if I bought him off, he'd shut up. I'd see to that. Offer him five. He hasn't got the guts for real blackmail. Whatever happens, Fey mustn't know. She might try to see him. But she's loyal. There's no danger there. He deserted her and Lucy. And Lucy. Get rid of him quickly, hustle him out of town. Why didn't I get his address—fool! It would take until Thursday to get the agency to track him down. But maybe he said something to Lemming—

Simeon pushed the bell-button.

Lemming glided respectfully in. "Yes, Mr. Tower?"

"That man who was here, did he give you his name or address?"

"Why, no, sir. He wouldn't. I thought him a shade mysterious, but as I assumed it was about that—ah—information, I didn't insist."

"Yes. Quite," said Simeon. The secretary waited; beneath hooded lids he inspected his employer's face avidly.

"That's all," said Simeon. "I'm going to go home now."

"Indigestion bothering a bit?' asked the secretary sympathetically.

Simeon moved his lips in a smile. "A bit." He looked at the thin, sharp-faced man, and suddenly saw familiarity, the warmth of years of association. "Noah—we've—you've been with me a long time. Perhaps I haven't remembered to tell you that I appreciate your service—your usefulness and loyalty."

Fancy that, thought Lemming; fine words butter no parsnips, my lad.

"It's been a pleasure to work for you, Mr. Tower."

There was a silence. Simeon felt and suppressed in himself an instinct of appeal. Noah, tell me I haven't lost my grip, tell me I can lick 'em all as I used to. Childish.

"As soon as I get the G. and S.D. and Transic straightened out, we'll have to reconsider the matter of your salary," he said.

Lemming bowed. "That's good of you, sir." And a wait till Doomsday if I'm not mistaken, he added to himself. That was the catch; he wasn't sure yet that the little bulldog mightn't yet worry his way out or he'd take that tempting offer in Gould's office. But in the meantime one could look out for number one.

Simeon sighed. He gestured toward the closet and Lemming sprang to get the overcoat and hat, held the coat up with solicitous speed.

That night Fey was filled by a nervous gaiety. She saw that Simeon was low physically and she set herself to amusing him out of the heavy silences. She had put Terry out of her mind. He might hang around New York for ever, for all she cared; she would never get in touch with him again. She had spent the day alone locked in her little boudoir and she had been able to flood the problem with a noon light of practical analysis. The two meetings in the park had been foolish, perhaps, but justifiable, for they had established the fact that she did not love Terry. She could see him objectively, dispassionately. She was cured and strong once more. And that shameful resurgence of emotion was conquered.

She had dressed carefully for Simeon on that Tuesday night, a new green taffeta robe de toilette, with darker green overdress and bustle. It was disconcerting not to have him notice it. And yet several times she caught him watching her, but as she smiled in quick response, he turned his eyes away. He ate little, drank nothing, and her chatter about the doings of Astors, Bulls, or Ward McAllister, which before this never failed to interest him, provoked only absent-minded answers or none at all.

After dinner, when Miss Pringle sent Lucita down to the drawing-room to say good night, he roused himself and became more normal. He smoothed the child's curls and listened patiently to a rendition of "The Angel's Lament" on the Chickering.

When she had finished, Lucita sat on his lap and rang his chiming watch—a nightly ceremony. As she tucked it back in his pocket, Fey knew a second of terror, for the child said, "Papa, why don't you have an elk's tooth on your chain like—?" She stopped and looked at her mother guiltily.

"Like who, pet?" asked Simeon.

237

Fey got up and went over to the child. "Oh, I don't believe she knows anyone with an elk's tooth," she said, laughing. "Come, darling, time for bed."

Ignoble, thought Fey, and to force my child into it, too. I've never deceived Simeon. Why don't I tell him I've seen Terry? It means nothing now. I *will* tell him when I get back to the drawing-room.

But she did not. Simeon sat staring into the fire. He looked shrunken, hunched over, his back making an old man's curve; she saw this with pity and an unexpected prick of irritation. Like a monkey, she thought; why does he let himself look like a tired monkey? The doctor said there was nothing much wrong. All these men have indigestion at times. This she knew from the half-admiring plaints she listened to over the teatables. All rich men had dyspepsia; it was almost a mark of caste.

"You're tired, dear," she said briskly. "Would you like me to stroke your head?" So often lately he asked for this, drawing comfort from the magnetic vitality in her hands.

He straightened his back, moving to a more comfortable position on the mohair couch. Charter the yacht, he thought. Pembroke'll snap at it; won't ask questions. Only way to raise the cash, only thing won't cause talk.

"Sing something, Fey," he said. He gestured toward the piano. She continued to look at him. There was something—something more than dyspepsia or business. I used to know what he was thinking. Now he won't let me in. She gave a dissatisfied sigh. The evening had curdled; she had put on the new dress, piled her hair into an elaborate mass of ringlets for him. As a sign—I make myself lovely for you alone, I want only you. He should have known.

She walked to the piano on which she could play a few simple chords by ear. The guitar which she preferred had been forbidden. Fashionable ladies did not play guitars, which were foreign instruments, raffish, associated with street-singers.

Fey struck the D minor chord and began to sing, "Flee as a bird to your mountain, Thou who art weary of sin—" This was a favourite of Simeon's, a plaintive hymn whose words had been written by the poetic Mrs. Dana. It was a favourite of Fey's, too, though she had never told Simeon why. Mrs. Dana had appropriated an old Spanish melody for her hymn, and the music sent Fey back to a night twenty years ago in Santa Fe when she and her father had been walking along the Alameda in the moonlight and this tune had come floating, disembodied, from one of the shuttered houses. They had

238

stopped to listen, both hushed by the poignancy, the yearning question in that gentle song. She remembered the smell of earth and burning cedar, the look of the low adobes across the little river, and the feel of her father's hand. She had squeezed it tight as they listened, and when the song had ended, he had bent and kissed her. She remembered the joy of receiving his rare caress, and that momentary certainty of shared emotion.

The English words had always seemed meaningless interlopers; she had sung them automatically. Tonight the curtain of her resistance was abruptly raised. A sensuous tingle ran up her spine.

> *"Flee as a bird to your mountain,*
> *Thou who art weary of sin.*
> *Go to the clear flowing fountain,*
> *Where you may wash and be clean.*
> *Fly, for the avenger is near thee;*
> *Call, and the Saviour will hear thee—"*

She forgot Simeon. Her voice deepened and throbbed, her eyes misted. This was a message; this was awareness once more returned after the long dark night of the soul, the illuminating ray of secret wisdom, a ray of sound as well as light. "Listen—" it said, beneath the yearning music, beneath the trite words. "Listen. There is still time."

Her hands fell from the keys, her voice broke and stopped. Her fixed eyes stared unseeing through the pampas-grass bouquet on the piano, the still-life painting and pressed leather wallpaper behind it.

"What is it, Fey?" Simeon spoke sharply. He got up and came over to her.

She swallowed, reaching for his hand and laying her cheek against it. She gave a choked little laugh.

"Nothing. I'm silly. The music suddenly— Simeon, we must be closer to each other. Don't shut me out. Help me, darling, help me—"

His eyes had softened and come alive until her last unconsidered words.

"Help you?" he repeated. "How do you mean?"

She saw the suspicion, the guarded look. Oh, what is it? she thought; it can't be—he can't know about Terry!

"I don't know what I mean. I'm foolish. Women are sometimes." She looked up at him through her wet lashes, her small head tilted on the long white neck, her red mouth tremulous with a pleading smile.

239

He caught his breath and kissed her. She did not resist, she put her arms around his neck, but he felt her body shiver, and for the instant that he saw into the grey eyes the pupils contracted, as though they closed against repulsion.

His arms dropped.

Instantly she tried to make amends. "Don't let me go like that. I love you, Simeon."

"You're tired, my dear, I think." He moved heavily from the piano bench back to the fire. "Better get some rest."

"You'll come up soon?"

"Pretty soon. Don't stay awake."

She went upstairs, her head bent, her hand heavy on the banister, and as she reached the door of her room, Miss Pringle darted out. "May I speak to you, madam?"

Fey raised her eyes and sighed. "Certainly. In the boudoir." She led the way into the rosewood, velvet-and-lace confection Simeon had built for her.

"I think there's something you should know, madam," said the governess, sitting gingerly on a damask chair in response to Fey's gesture.

And why, thought Fey, sighing again, when people start that way is it never, never anything pleasant? She began to strip off her rings and drop them on the ring-stand.

"Yes?" she said.

"Yesterday afternoon I took Lucy to the park and a gentleman accosted us. I must say quite a handsome and pleasant-spoken young man."

Fey's hands stopped moving. She stood with her back to Miss Pringle, holding the last ring clenched in her fingers. The dry, clipped voice continued:

"He hailed her by name, the name you call her, 'Lucita,'" said Miss Pringle, with distaste, "and at first the child acted rather strangely, as though she didn't know him."

Fey shut her eyes for a second, dropped the last ring on the stand, and turning around, said, "Well, who was it?"

"A distant cousin of yours, a Mr. Smith, he told me. He was very civil. He begged leave to join us, and as Lucy soon stopped acting silly and addressed him as Cousin Terry, I saw no harm." There was the suggestion of a flutter in the spinster voice, of bridling.

So he got around her as he can any woman, thought Fey, with fury. How dared he bother Lucita! He promised. It was clearly understood—

"I know who the man must be," she said rapidly. "But I'm

sorry to say I think him most undesirable. I don't blame you, of course. I quite understand—"

Miss Pringle's nostrils dilated, she primmed her mouth.

"I trust I am qualified to judge of the desirability or undesirability of a given individual, certainly her Grace the Duchess of—"

"Yes. Yes. I know," cut in Fey. "Kindly tell me exactly what happened."

Speaking to me like that, like a servant, thought Miss Pringle, breathing hard. But she couldn't bully Fey and knew it. Too, in this matter of the gentleman in the park, she had some guilt. Quite flattering he had been, and she had enjoyed herself, obviously cause for guilt.

"He walked along with us to the lake, and then he took Lucy skating for a while," she said resentfully.

"He was alone with Lucita?"

"Never out of my sight, naturally. They seemed to have a very good time. I never saw the child laugh so much, too much for a little lady, as I told her later. She gave as excuse that he had told her a great secret."

Secret. Fey had the dream sensation of bottomless falling. But even Terry couldn't do that. He was heedless, mischievous; he had wanted to see his child again, perhaps had met her by accident.

"This must never happen again," said Fey, and as the governess looked both angry and startled, realized she was being too dramatic. She forced a smile. "I mean, I think you had better take Lucita to Madison Square or keep her in the garden for a while. The man is quite a gentleman, it's true, but a ne'er-do-well relation. We prefer to forget about him. I'm sure," she added, descending to diplomacy, "you understand these situations, Miss Pringle. You have had so much experience."

The horsy face relaxed a trifle. "As long as I am in your employ, madam," she said darkly, "I shall, of course, do as you say." And she stalked out.

Fey threw herself on the sofa, pressing her fingers to her temples. I must see Terry again! I must! Find out what he told Lucita. I can't question my poor baby. She must forget it. Tell him he's got to go away. I demand it.

Like the tinkle of a far-off music-box, she heard the song which had so moved her in the drawing-room. All that surge of feeling was gone, even the memory of it was thinned and vague. "Flee as a bird to your mountain—Flee as a bird—"

Silly words, draggy sentimental music in which to read illumination.

I must see Terry again. Have it out with him. This is intolerable.

She ran to her writing-desk, picked up her carved malachite pen.

CHAPTER

18

THE next morning, Terry was awakened at ten by a bellboy bearing Fey's note. "Three o'clock," it said. "Same place. F."

Terry beamed at it, admiring the clear feminine writing and the thick creamy paper emblazoned with a small crest. This latter was Simeon's idea. An accommodating genealogist had traced back, through the arrival of John Tower at Hingham, Massachusetts, in 1637, to the concoction of an impressive crest, a plumed turret complete with Norman motto. Simeon had come to believe it himself most of the time, his descent from an obscure branch of the Hingham Towers. He quite often alluded to it casually when mentioning Fey's Scottish ancestry. But he never did it in Fey's hearing after once seeing an amused indulgence in her eyes.

Terry was impressed by the crest and delighted with the note. He kissed it gallantly and then—following the traditional chivalrous rule in affairs like this—he tore it up and threw it in the fire.

Conditions for the rendezvous were scarcely ideal today, since it was snowing, but, as Terry's plans included only the briefest possible stay in Central Park, it didn't much matter. He breakfasted quickly, and then, hiring one of the new hansom cabs, set out for Schultz's Hotel way uptown on the East River at Yorkville to make arrangements. These satisfactorily completed, his spirits rose so high that they included the cabdriver.

He poked open the little door in the roof. "A fine town this, Paddy," he called up. "I like New York, don't you?"

"Yez wouldn't be likin' it so foine if you was hacking in all weathers like me," answered the man morosely. "And it ain't Paddy, it's Cadwallader."

"Holy Saint Mary!" breathed Terry, "that's beautiful. Come on, Cadwallader, let's have a drink. I'm celebrating."

"I ain't celebrating nothing," said the cabby, but he stopped the horse in front of a saloon.

When they came out again, they were arm-in-arm. The snow had stopped and Cadwallader had mellowed. He drove down the sparsely settled First Avenue, and sticking his face close to the trap accompanied Terry's exuberant songs in a diffident tenor. They sang "The Man on the Flying Trapeze," and "Captain Jinks of the Horse Marines," to the appreciation of the slaughter-houses' employees and a few hockey-playing urchins. They turned west on Houston, heading back for Terry's hotel, but paused instead at Duffy's Chop House, and, after a fortifying round, Terry invited Cadwallader to lunch with him there.

Over oysters, mutton chops, and beer, Terry grew confiding and a trifle sentimental. "Going to meet the most wonderful woman in the world this afternoon, Cadwallader," he said earnestly. "I can hardly wait. Eager as a boy with his first sweetheart, that's what I am."

"Indade, sir," said the cabby, gnawing on the chop bone and grinning. "And the grand upstanding gentleman that yez are, I'll be bound she's as eager as you." He would have said this, anyway, being grateful for Terry's drinks and fine lunch, but he was sincere. Without you counted Denis Shane, the ladies' delight at Wallack's Theatre, this was the handsomest gentleman he'd seen for many a day, and the warm Irish grin of him, too, the democratic manner.

"I'll be bound she is eager," said Terry complacently, "but she won't show it at first. Ladies don't, you know."

Cadwallader nodded. "O' course not. Even my old woman, she comes all over coy at times. 'Tis a virtue of the sex." He raised his beer mug. "It's luck I'm wishing you, sir. Not that ye need it."

The mugs clinked as the chop-house clock struck the half-hour. "Half-past two!" cried Terry, startled. "I must hurry. Tell you what, you're a discreet man, aren't you, Cadwallader? You drive me up to the park, we'll pick up the lady, and then back to Schultz's Hotel where we just were."

"Oh," said the cabby. He wiped his mouth thoughtfully. "It's like that, is it? I mean to say, sir, I thought when ye said "lady," I was thinking ye meant a genteel young female wot yez had honourable intentions toward. But I'm game for a bit of fun." He winked at Terry, who frowned.

"It's not a bit of fun," he said coldly. "It's just a question of

243

awkward circumstances. Damn it, I tell you, I'm in love with her. I wouldn't hurt her for the world." And that's true, he thought. Little Fey, lovely little Fey. My wife once, the mother of my child. Never been a woman meant so much to me. His eyes moistened, and he stared accusingly at the apologetic cabby, who said, "Sorry, sir. I don't know nothing about the ways of gentry. Hadn't we better be goin', sir?"

Terry flung a gold quarter eagle down on the table and they went back to the cab. It was snowing again, and there was no singing as Cadwallader hurried the horse up Fifth Avenue to the park. Terry, by no means drunk, yet was enjoying a nostalgic and sentimental haze. Lovely little Fey, he repeated to himself, so brave, so winning—and his thoughts moulded themselves as they often did into the theatrical speeches of his California days. Villain that I am, how could I have deserted the best, the truest of wives! I will make amends. She shall know love again, the tenderness, the forgotten ecstasy—

He saw her from the carriage drive hurrying along the path toward the Arch. He jumped from the cab and ran through the falling snow to catch up with her. "Darling—" and he pulled her back the few steps into the waiting hansom. "We can't stand out in the snow—" but she did not object. She said nothing at all. He pushed up the trap, nodded to Cadwallader, who flicked the horse, and nodded back. Terry closed the flaps in front of them, fastened the extra leather storm curtain, encircled Fey with his arm, and tucked the rug snugly around them both.

"How beautiful you are!" he breathed, looking at her averted profile. Her body had curved against his and he could feel the beating of her heart, but her head was turned and she seemed to be looking out of the side window with a curious effect of stillness. She had worn her sable wrap and little sable toque; on the rich dark fur and her darker hair there was a spangling of snowflakes. These and the colour in her cheeks gave her a fairy-like delicacy, though from the furs there rose the heavy perfume of frangipani.

His arm tightened. "I was so happy, Fey, to get your note." He bent his head, and his lips touched her cheek.

She did not move. It begins again, she thought, it begins again. She spoke without turning, her voice thick.

"You had no right to speak to Lucita. You promised and I trusted you. That's the only reason I've met you today."

Terry laughed. "You're a sweet hypocrite. You used to be honest with yourself, Feyita, mi amor."

She moved her head, the wide grey eyes stared at him helplessly. She appeared drugged—scarcely conscious of him or the hastening cab. He put his hand behind her head, and began to kiss her.

On Seventy-Ninth Street, Cadwallader peeped quietly through the trap, chuckled, and pulled the horse down to a walk. Ten minutes later they passed the old Gracie Mansion still standing in its park full of beautiful trees, continued four blocks up the frozen dirt road to the northern curve of Horn's Hook and Schultz's Hotel. This had once been an honest clapboard farmhouse with a beautiful view up the river toward Hell Gate. The view remained if one stood outside, but the Schultzes had embellished their purchase with so many porches and gables and scrollwork shutters and three pairs of shielding curtains to all the windows that the river was no longer visible from the interior. The patrons of Schultz's were not interested in the view.

The cabby drew up under the peeling yellowish portico. "Here y'are, sir," he called hoarsely through the trap.

Fey started, pushing against Terry. "Where?" she whispered. "Where are we?"

"Way uptown, miles from anywhere," he said reassuringly. "I've ordered tea for us."

"I can't. You know I can't. Take me back, Terry."

"Nobody'll see you at all. There's no harm in a cup of tea after a long ride." He could not help laughing as he said this, amused that even Fey should demand the conventional appearance of innocence.

"Come on!" he said, for he was impatient, and women at this point preferred to be commanded.

She got down slowly, drawing her sable cape tight around her and shivering on the wooden step. She gave the hotel's door a dazed, uncertain look. She was breathing rapidly and she had grown very pale.

"Here, my friend," said Terry, tossing a fifty-cent piece up to Cadwallader. "Buy yourself a drink and then wait over there in the livery stable until we call you."

The cabby gave him a fraternal salute and drove off. Terry pulled the bell-knob and the door opened. A fat German in a soiled apron bowed them inside.

"Just a cup of tea, that's all. A cup of tea before the ride back," said Fey faintly to both men.

Schultz bowed again without speaking. The women often made some silly remark like this when they first came in. He

245

looked neither at Fey nor Terry, but led the way upstairs to the end of a short hallway.

"I haf give you Turkish Room," he said in a low voice to Terry. "Is nice, is gemütlich."

He bowed them inside and shut the door. The Turkish Room was Schultz's conception of Oriental voluptuousness. A divan upholstered in red satin had been built in one corner, and an arrangement of curtains transformed it into an alcove. Round stuffed hassocks dotted the gaudy Turkish rug—made in Birmingham; on the walls were crossed scimitars, crescents, and pictures of extremely fat and naked houris gazing at pashas. Rose incense—from Chinatown—burned in a small brass brazier, hot air blasted from an ornamental register in the floor, and on a mother-of-pearl tabouret, carefully arranged, lay all the usual adjuncts to seduction—a decanter of whisky, a bottle of champagne, Turkish cigarettes, even a little dish of aromatic cachous for the breath.

Terry hung his hat and coat on a brass clothes-tree, divested Fey of her cape and toque without help from her. She continued to stand on the centre of the Turkey rug, staring at the room.

"Quite a place," said Terry. "Cosy. Come, Fey, sit down." He propelled her over to the divan, poured her a glass of champagne and himself a shot of whisky. She accepted the champagne glass, balanced it carefully in her fingers.

"Drink," he said. "Drink to our old love transformed into a new and better love."

"Do you believe that, Terry?" She put her glass, untasted, down on the tabouret.

"Of course I do." Terry checked irritation. Damn women, damn their eternal demand for the romantic approach! We'd passed this point. However— And he knew very well the note to strike.

"Darling—" he said very softly, moving a little away from her. He went on in Spanish. "Don't you remember, Feyita, the old days on the Trail? Was there ever happiness like that? The nights when we lay in each other's arms under the stars and our hearts spoke to each other as our bodies did? It's there for us now—waiting. You know it—you can't deny it, my little chula."

Her immobility shattered. She put her hands to her throat, giving him a blind, frightened look. "I can't see clearly. I can't think. Let me alone, Terry—"

He reached up to the chain which dangled above the divan and pulled off the light.

There was a discreet tap on the door at five o'clock, and a murmur outside. "It's the time you asked to be called, sir." Then vanishing steps. Fey was sitting at the foot of the divan, her hair recoiled, and she completely dressed.

"So you thought of that, too, Terry," she said.

He roused himself. "Didn't want you to take a chance of being late, honey. Old boy might get suspicious."

"Fortunately, Simeon trusts me."

Still sunk in an amorous drowsiness, he missed the intonation of her voice. "Sure, the old boy's an easy mark."

"Why do you say that?" She pulled the light chain and the gas flared up, while she contemplated Terry with steady, narrowed eyes.

"No particular reason, darling." He was startled. He had never seen that expression on anybody's face before, certainly on no woman's.

He sat up and reached for her hand. "You were wonderful, Fey, you're a wonderful girl."

She looked down at the big brown hand with its fine gold hairs.

"You mean, that I am a satisfactory mistress, no doubt?"

"Really, Fey, what *is* the matter with you! It was perfect, you know it was. Why, I feel—I feel—"

"Yes?" she said, with a small inclination of the head. She rose with precision, walked across the room toward the clothes-tree.

"Fey, listen. You're being silly. It isn't even like a real—uh—a real infidelity. Why, you were my wife once. I never thought you'd act this way—under all that coyness you were as—"

Again she gave a slight inclination of the head. "Certainly. I was as lustful as you." She pulled the sable cape around her shoulders and adjusted the little hat before one of the fly-specked scrollwork mirrors. "Good-bye," she said.

"Wait, Fey. You can't leave like that. I don't understand. It isn't fair," he cried passionately.

She turned to face him, one hand on the doorknob. "Listen then, Terry. It is finished at last, and I feel for myself a loathing. I was always a—an incident to you, as I have been now. I knew this. I even told myself this over and over, but I—Oh, what's the use! Perhaps it was necessary that by yielding to my body I might become free of it, and you."

247

Terry laughed, for this type of rationalization was familiar to him. To be sure, it was usually he and not the woman who suffered a backwash of boredom and revulsion after the event; still, Fey had always been different, and as he well knew, these moods were temporary.

So he spoke with a caressing assurance. "You may feel like this now, but you won't in a day or so. You know where to find me. I'll be waiting and eager."

"I tell you," she said, spacing her words, "that it is finished. I cannot in fairness blame you for not believing me, but it is finished, at last and forever."

And this time he did believe her, for he identified her expression with that of a man in New Orleans. A man who had caught him cheating at faro, but whose contempt for his own stupidity had prevented him from exposing Terry. The man's eyes had held this same pitiless finality before he had shrugged his shoulders, tossed a bagful of coins on the baize, and walked out of the gambling house.

"Yes," said Fey. "I see that you understand."

Terry flung back his head and spoke through his teeth. "And you have the audacity to pretend that, after going this far, after leading me on, after just now allowing me so signal a mark of affection as you have just conferred, you dare to think that—"

"I think, my dear Terry, that this very fine speech was written once by someone else. Can we perhaps simply say goodbye?"

He lowered his head, closed his mouth slowly. She twisted the knob and opened the door, giving him a small remote nod. "I ask you to leave town. But whether you do or not, I shall see to it that you never meet me or Lucita again."

She shut the door behind her, and he heard her light footsteps dwindle on the hall carpet. He went to the shrouded window, pushed the massed red curtains aside, and peered between the slats of the blind.

He saw a boy summon the hansom cab from the stable, saw the cab disappear under the porte-cochère and then drive off through the softly falling snow. He let the curtains drop, and they gave off a reek of stale incense. He walked to the divan and poured half a tumblerful of whisky. He drank it down and looked at the frayed rose-silk pillows which still showed two indentations. "You'll find it's not as simple as all that, my dear," he said. "Love goes, but money stays. Maybe that was written once by someone else, too. Little bitch!" But he was surprised to find that he wasn't particularly angry with Fey; he even felt for her a certain respect, and when he had finished the bottle, the sentimental mood returned. He thought with tenderness about Lucita. Pretty child, nice little girl. Certainly don't want to stand in her way. No, that wouldn't be right, he thought, shaking his head. Guess I'll pull out of town after the old coot kicks in with the cash tomorrow.

Suddenly bored with the dishevelled Turkish Room, he shoved the tabouret out of the way and eased himself into his hat and coat.

During the drive from Schultz's Hotel down Third Avenue, Fey passed a small church she had never seen before. Acting automatically and without conscious thought, she directed the cabby to stop, and she dismissed him.

She entered the dark, deserted church and knelt down in one of the pews. No prayers came. Her mind was numb. Gradually the enveloping numbness effaced the impulse which had brought her into the church. Her muff slipped from her fingers and the sharp edge of the prayer board bit into her knees.

At seven, the sacristan touched her on the shoulder, and said that he must lock up. She gave him a dazed look and, gathering her fallen muff, purse, and gloves, she hurried out of the church. She walked the twelve blocks home, and during the walk the numbness melted and she began to feel a sensation of comfort and release. The obsession for Terry was gone. The incident, sordid as it had been, was therefore not a sin. Things like that happened. Everyone suspected that the beautiful Mrs. Johnson had had several such episodes. Nobody knew for sure, of course, and nobody would know of this. Simeon could not be hurt in any way, and from this moment, now that the spell was lifted, she could make him happier than ever before, shelter him in her true and grateful affection.

See, she told herself, when she reached home to find that Simeon had not yet returned from the office, all is made easy for you. There is not the slightest danger of discovery, nor reason to feel guilt. That hour had no significance. One must be realistic nor ever look back. On that part of my life, too, the door is shut for ever.

The feeling of relief and comfort grew, and she dressed carefully for dinner. Then she played and sang with Lucita, and when Simeon finally arrived, heavy and silent as he had been the night before, she greeted him normally and even won from him a smile or two. It was not until she sat down to dinner that she found that her hands were wet and that the smell of food disgusted her, but this uneasiness soon passed.

At three o'clock on the following afternoon, Simeon paid Terry eight thousand dollars, and received in return an ambiguous paper which said, "For value received, I agree to remain outside of New York City, and that the name of Simeon Tower shall never be mentioned by me at any time or any place, either directly or by innuendo." And he signed it Xavier Terence Dillon.

"He'll make you sign something, of course," Lemming had said in a morning meeting. "That can't be helped, but there won't be much danger; he'll be no more anxious to put down the facts than you are." So Terry had signed, but not without an angry demand for the full ten thousand.

"You may believe it or not, as you like, but eight is all I can raise at the moment. And that's what you'll take," Simeon said, and he said nothing more, but looked out of the window, his face grey and set while Terry harangued and threatened. When Terry finally received the thick roll of bills, he took them resentfully, for with his usual optimism he had been so certain of the whole amount that this seemed like actual loss, and would Lemming believe it—Lemming, who expected ten per cent?

"There's a seven-forty for Buffalo leaves the Grand Central Depot tonight, from there you can make connections with Chicago," said Simeon.

Terry nodded sulkily.

"There'll be a man at the depot to be sure you get on that train. Now, get out!"

Terry went. In the outer office he whispered to Lemming, "I only got eight," and was at once sorry he had not said seven or six.

"You're a fool!" snapped Lemming. "I told you—" He glanced at the shut mahogany door. "Never mind now. Go to your room at the hotel and stay there. He's probably got you tailed. I'll be there later."

"But how about you—won't he find out?" And I hope he does, thought Terry viciously.

"I can take care of myself," said Lemming, but he smiled, for he saw that this big stupid tool of his needed managing. "I've got a new idea," he whispered. "We'll talk about it. It's good."

For ten days Simeon and Fey were happy. For both in their separate worlds fear retreated. The private detective reported that Dillon had duly taken the train for Buffalo and Simeon felt a relief so immense that it also reflected on his financial situation. The Huntington outfit in California were definitely interested in a merger, new feelers came through almost daily, thus providentially confirming the bluff offered Stevens at Continental Trust for the extraction of the last loan. And construction on the Gulf and San Diego was at last proceeding rapidly after the firing of the construction superintendent, who had evidently been enjoying a programme of monstrous graft and subtle inaction, dictated somehow, no doubt by Gould, though Simeon could not prove it. And a trip West was indicated. To Simeon in this new buoyant mood it seemed incredible that he had delayed this so long; that bogged down in that morass of muzziness and fear he had felt compelled to flounder in the four walls of his office—and the Stock Exchange—negotiating, worrying, accepting second-hand reports, pouring more and more money into his sagging stocks. Stop worrying and act! That was the secret. Start in two weeks, take the Transic to Galveston, inspect the G. and S.D. personally, then on to see Huntington. A couple of months would about do it. Fey wouldnt mind too much, being left. But he'd never left her before— His mind slid over and passed beyond an obstacle, the actual physical sensation of deadlock, never objectively examined. He floated high on freedom and certainty, and beneath in the structure none of Life's foundations were threatened, after all. Health much improved. Social achievement—more assured than ever. And Fey—tender and responsive. He upbraided himself for his recent brusqueness to her, and his brief incredible suspicions. She was, as she had always been, a perfect wife, and he loved her the more for having protected her from an ugly menace.

Both Simeon and Fey, therefore, followed the will o' the wisp, called a "fresh start," and their speeding feet were winged with a tenuous optimism.

On Monday night they attended a performance of *Aïda* in their box at the Academy of Music, and that tragic, lovely opera affected even the fashionable Monday night audience. Nobody had yet arrived in time to hear the "Celeste Aïda," of course, and the usual whispers, flirtations, and visiting back and forth between boxes continued during the next three acts, but the final duet of the dying lovers managed to silence them all. Mrs. Astor inclined her famous black wig and listened. The

251

Bulls and the Van Vrandts and the Snellings listened, Ward McAllister ceased checking the list of the Patriarch Ball which was to follow, and listened uneasily. "O Terra Addio," sang the poignant commingled voices of the eternal mystery of love and death, and Simeon, looking at his wife's rapt face, clumsily reached for her hand. She leaned back in her chair against his shoulder, her hand responding to his with an almost convulsive grip.

In their carriage on the way to Delmonico's for the ball, the emotions released by the music made him articulate.

"You're beautiful tonight," he whispered. "I'm so proud of you. D'you really love me, Fey? D'you love your old codger of a husband?"

"Oh, Simeon, you know I do. More than ever before."

"We do seem closer lately," he said. "I was pretty crotchety for a while, I'm afraid."

"Of course. You weren't well. Oh, we're going to be very happy, my Simeon."

She put her hand through his arm, looking up at him with a confiding sweetness.

She still looks so young, he thought, like an innocent girl. She *is* still so young. He straightened his shoulders and raised his chin.

"Fey—after my Western trip, shall we go off together this summer? To Scotland, say—look up your people. Would you like that?"

"Oh, yes! I'd love it. But Newport and the summer season— I thought you wanted to be there."

"We've reached the point where we won't lose ground if we aren't there for a couple of months." He spoke in solemn triumph. "Besides, I've let Pembroke have the yacht for the season. I thought we wouldn't be needing it."

She looked at him quickly. He never told her his plans until they were decided, and there was nothing strange in his chartering out the *Inveraray* if they were going to Europe. She must have imagined something strained in his voice.

They had drawn up before the canopy, and the doorman was running down the red carpet intent on reaching the barouche door and a tip before the Tower footman could get off the box.

"The first waltz with you, dear?" said Simeon, adjusting his muffler and opera hat.

"All of them if you wish," she answered, smiling. "I like dancing with you so much."

She means it, he thought, with a glow of gratitude. All these years she's never made me jealous, never looked at another man, though plenty of 'em have made sheep's eyes at her.

They progressed through the private entrance and up the stairs to the dressing-rooms to leave their wraps. Fey soon emerged, looking radiant in her moiré gown the colour of wood violets. It lent purple lights to her eyes and a blacker sheen to her hair.

He noticed the admiring looks from the little knot of tail-coated gentlemen awaiting their own ladies by the door, and he basked in the flattery of her indifference to this admiration. Amongst the group of men he saw Johnson and Haines, cuckolds both of them, for all that they were tall and young, cuckolds and everybody knew it. He looked at them with a contemptuous pity and led Fey into the ballroom.

CHAPTER

19

ON Tuesday, March the sixth, the Towers expected a small dinner party. The numbers were small, only three other couples, but their importance was great, and acceptances from the Sylvester Bulls and the Van Vrandts marked another upward notch for the Towers. That these people attended one's balls, or even teas and luncheons, conferred no such mark of intimacy as their presence at a small dinner party. The third couple consisted of Ward McAllister and a new protégée of his, the young widow of a southern aristocrat, a Mrs. Colefax.

"Do ask her, dear lady," McAllister had said to Fey. "You'd like each other, I'm sure. She has a background much like yours was, don't you know."

Fey laughed as she passed this on to Simeon. "The only difference being, of course, that she's a *genuine* Southern widow," she said, and then could have bitten her tongue out. Simeon was very angry.

She apologized and placated him, but she could not resist saying, "I never do make a mistake in public, and I should think sometimes when we're alone together we might let down and just be ourselves."

"That's a very stupid remark," he said coldly.

"Yes dear. I'm sorry. Forget it. Now the menu for this

253

dinner— Did you tell me that Mr. Van Vrandt can't abide oysters?"

Why is he still afraid? She thought. We're safe now. This very dinner party shows how safe we are. The memory of Terry and those days when she had seen Terry seemed months, years away. It was finished because she wished it to be finished. The little brown snake was once more locked in its box. It was easy to forget Terry, since the cure had been complete. Both the passion and its converse—the hatred which she had so long felt for him—had fused into a dead indifference. And nothing told her that this fusion had occurred too late. No sense of warning now, no confused dreams or intuitions. She skimmed along the surface, planned dinner parties for Simeon, and Punch and Judy parties for Lucita. She looked forward to the European trip in the summer, to the excitement of buying Parisian clothes, as much as to the pleasure of seeing her father's boyhood home. She slept well and she ate well, and she told herself that this was contentment at last.

By eight o'clock all the guests were assembled in the south drawing-room, the ladies making, as McAllister lost no time in pointing out, "A highly beauteous bevy." Fey was in golden orange satin. Sophie Bull had worn her Worth import, a silver plush trimmed with thirteen yards of swaying taupe fringe, the back drapery and overskirt tastefully caught up here and there by cut-steel bows. Sophie's blonde hair, too, was crimped, festooned, and braided with an ingenuity her maid could never have achieved. She had, therefore, called in Eglantin, the coiffeur, for the occasion, and Fey was duly flattered that a *diner intime* at the Towers' should call forth a *première toilette*. These phrases had, of course, been introduced by Ward McAllister, but now that more and more people ran over to Paris for a month or two, he sometimes encountered subversive competition.

He was encountering it now from Mrs. Van Vrandt, who remarked, "Our young hostess looks very well, I think, très soignée. Quite séduisante in that jaune d'orée gown."

"Indeed, yes," said McAllister hastily, twirling his imperials and wishing he might talk to that sweet little widow, Mrs. Colefax. But Mrs. Van Vrandt was an imposing matron, and she had been a Livingston.

"Rather bare, though, this drawing-room," continued the lady, reverting to English. "For people of wealth." She stared around disapprovingly. Only five pictures on the walls, and only one whatnot. No Rogers groups, no Dresden shepherdesses on the mantel beside the glassed-in-clock, no hassocks or tabourets on the singularly inconspicuous carpet.

This sparseness was Fey's fault. She tried hard to keep the house furnished like the fashionable ones she visited, but her early years in interiors so different continually defeated her. A welter of objects and colours made her miserable, and all Simeon's lectures on the beauties of obvious opulence did not convince her.

"One hears that it is becoming the fashion in Paris to have emptier rooms, dear Mrs. Vrandt, but of course you'd know, having spent last September there," said McAllister, neatly scoring.

Fey, Sophie Bull, and Mrs. Colefax were discussing children and servants, the age-old resort of ladies whose men have coalesced by a fireplace to discuss business, as Van Vrandt, Sylvester Bull, and Simeon were now doing.

Fey had long since discovered that she could contribute to the servant or child problem while thinking very hard about other things. Tonight she thought a trifle nervously about the coming dinner. She had a competent butler and chef, and she and Simeon had worked out the menu and wines, but these people and McAllister in particular were extremely critical. And the reputation for serving fine food was one of the chief ways of maintaining pre-eminence. Stone should be announcing soon. She gave a furtive glance at the clock.

"Quicksand years that whirl me I know not whither—"

Fey started, and gazed at the speaker in astonishment. Mrs. Colefax had said that, in response to a vague politeness of Sophie Bull's to the effect that the war had been terrible, and one did feel so sympathetic to all the poor rebels now, and how were things in Virginia?

"That's Whitman, isn't it?" cried Fey, remembering the thrill of excited discovery in Mr. Tibbins's bookstore, so long ago.

Penelope Colefax's eyes lit. "Do you read Whitman? I admire him so much, for all he's a"—she smiled—"a Yankee."

Why, she's different from these others, thought Fey, seeing for the first time intelligence and a kind of poised force beneath the pretty stylish surface.

"Mr. Bull would never, never let me read that Mr. Whitman; he's quite naughty, isn't he?" said Sophie roguishly.

Neither woman paid attention to her, though they smiled politely. Both were savouring that first rare moment of kinship, of recognition.

"Do you remember any more of it?" asked Fey.

"A little," Mrs. Colefax nodded, answering Fey's urgency, and sensitive at once to the unexpected deeper note. She said, in her soft Virginia voice,

" *'Quicksand years that whirl me I know not whither—*
Your schemes, politics fail, lines give way, substances mock
    and elude me,
Only the theme I sing, the great and strong possess'd soul
    eludes not . . .'

"I forget the rest, except the last line—

'When shows break up, what but One's-Self is sure?' "

There was a small silence. "Yes," said Fey, "thank you." And where was it gone, that triumphant certainty that had once sprung from these lines for her? Where was that crystal hardness, that passionate integrity, she had felt in response?

"Very pretty," said Sophie Bull, moving restlessly. Really Mrs. Tower and Mrs. Colefax were acting a little strange, staring at each other and reciting poetry about being sure of one's self. "I like Longfellow," she said. "So inspiring, 'Tell me not, in mournful numbers,' you know. Susie's learning it by heart to recite for her Papa's birthday. Really that child has the most remarkable memory, only the other day her governess was saying that she had never seen a child who could—"

"Dinner is served, madam," said Stone, bowing in the doorway.

Fey rose, with the other ladies. Be my friend, she said silently to Penelope Colefax. You're real, and I'm not any more. Be my friend, help me.

She gave a welcoming smile to Mr. Van Vrandt and accepting his portly arm followed her guests downstairs to the dining-room.

The dining-room was very warm, and odorous from the scent of massed violets in the centrepiece. On the twelve-foot table, shrouded in pink damask with Irish lace thrown over it, there were no bare spaces; each gilded and monogrammed service plate was surrounded by an archipelago of nut, celery, and relish dishes, of bonbonnières, a diminishing file of wineglasses, and ten massive silver knives, forks, and spoons. And six inches above each plate, coquettishly lurking in a bower of violets, were small hand-painted porcelain slabs where the guests might read the menu of the evening.

Fey saw McAllister consult his, squinting with his far-sighted eyes through a concentrated appraisal of each of the seven

courses from the consommé à la Sévigné through the terrapin
à la Maryland, the fillet of beef Renaissance, the salmi of
pheasant, the roast saddle of lamb accompanied by rum sherbets, the asparagus mousse, to the profiterolles au chocolat
garnis de fraises, the ices and the cheese.

Fey saw him nod, and surreptitiously unfasten the lower
buttons on his waistcoat before turning to his neighbour, Mrs.
Colefax.

The chef had surpassed himself. The wines were perfect,
the dry Montilla sherry, the Haut Brion '65, the Romanee
Conti, the champagne of '57.

The stately process of consumption flowed on. During the
fillet of beef, Fey asked Mr. Van Vrandt what he knew of Mrs.
Colefax, her interest in the young widow was keen. There was
a similarity between them of age and looks, besides that flash
of sympathetic awareness.

Van Vrandt ate a truffle, washed it down with the Haut
Brion, and said: "One of the very best old Virginia families,
but left quite destitute after the war. I believe she supports
herself and her little boy." He lowered his voice. "I've heard
that she *writes*, under another name, of course."

"Oh," said Fey. She watched Mrs. Colefax for a moment. "I
wonder she hasn't married again," she added.

"Oh, she's had plenty of chances." Van Vrandt poked under
the remains of his fillet in the hope of finding more truffles.
"They say young William Waldorf Astor proposed to her, but
she won't marry for money."

"I should think for the sake of her child—" Fey's voice had
sharpened into a sudden intensity. She bit off the rest of the
sentence, painfully aware that she had been refuting a critic-
ism never dreamed by the placid masticating gentleman on
her right. What's the matter with me tonight? she thought. She
looked down the table to Simeon. He was telling Sophie Bull a
Negro dialect story about 'Rastus in the chicken roost which
Sophie received with twitters of polite laughter. Simeon looked
happy. He felt Fey's gaze and their eyes met for a moment in
affectionate marital signal. The dinner was going off beautifully.

Fey sighed, smiled, and upon the arrival of the pheasant
salmi turned to Sylvester Bull. "Haven't we had an unusual
amount of snow this winter? Your family must have made
great use of your pretty new cutter."

Which launched Mr. Bull on his favourite topic—his stable.

At ten-thirty, having demolished the saddle of lamb and enjoyed the prescribed digestive pause furnished by the sherbets, they were well into the asparagus mousse, and Fey was listening to Mr. Van Vrandt's impressions of Paris when she heard, muffled by the swinging door to the butler's pantry, the ring of the front-doorbell.

She saw Stone glide out of the dining-room to answer it, decided that it must be someone's carriage arrived early by mistake, and continued to look brightly receptive for Van Vrandt's minute-by-minute account of a soirée where he had met the Count de Chambord.

When the butler reappeared, he seemed ruffled, and his clean-shaven cheeks were dully red. Puzzled, Fey watched him walk down to Simeon and whisper something, at the same time giving Simeon a folded paper. Simeon excused himself and stared down at the note in his hand. Fey gave up all pretence of listening to Van Vrandt as she saw the change in her husband. He started to his feet as though on violent impulse, looked at Sophie Bull, sank back in his chair again. He sat staring at his asparagus mousse, and as Sophie stopped speaking, gave a loud off-key laugh which made the nearest heads turn while Sophie, who was not observant, wondered if she had really said anything quite that witty.

Fey saw him lift his champagne glass, sip from it, and put it down. His hands had a controlled tremor. He continued to talk to Mrs. Van Vrandt and Sophie Bull, swaying his whole body jerkily from one woman to the other and apparently making little sense to judge from their expressions of well-bred perplexity. He lifted his glass several times, put it down before it touched his mouth. He stood up again, this time slowly. "Will you be so very kind as to excuse me? Important message. Please go on with dinner. I won't be long." He did not look at Fey, though she tried hard to catch his eye. He gave them all a vague smile and walked out of the dining-room.

The slight pause was immediately filled by accelerated murmurs of conversation, while everybody politely ignored this deviation from etiquette. Van Vrandt went on precisely where he had left off—"Paid Mrs. Van Vrandt and me marked attention, asking questions about America, very democratic, considering he's heir to the Bourbon throne."

"Indeed, he must be charming," said Fey, clenching her hands under the enormous pink damask napkin and watching the two footmen, who took an interminable time to crumb the table and change the plates. At last Stone bent over her with the platter of chocolate profiterolles.

258

"Who was it came?" she whispered.

"I don't know, madam. Very forward young man, insisted on my taking a message to Mr. Tower. I put him in the library."

Fey said "Thank you," and inclined her head once more toward Van Vrandt. The violet centrepiece, the littered table, the hissing lights in the gasolier, the six faces, all wavered and combined into a slow circling spiral. It can't be, she thought. It is something about business. There are many young men. There'd be no reason for him to come here like this and ask for Simeon. No reason. The words repeated themselves with a mechanical monotony like the sound of train wheels. No reason. No reason. No reason.

"He most kindly invited us down to his château upon our next visit to La Belle France—" Van Vrandt was saying, and it occurred to him that Mrs. Tower looked a bit strange. She was very pale and those big grey eyes of hers were fixed on his face with a sort of intensity of listening that made you feel she didn't hear a word. What's the matter with these people tonight? he thought irritably. Host rushing off like that in the middle of dinner. Hostess looking—well, you'd say frightened—if that wasn't so ridiculous.

"These mints are delicious, Mrs. Tower," said Sylvester Bull.

Yes, thought Fey, turning, now I must listen to you. I can't leave. I can't find out. Simeon would never forgive me if I left.

"I'm so glad you like them, Mr. Bull. Maillard's makes them for us specially." When we get up, I'll go to the library. I'll make an excuse. But it will be some man from the office.

"Dear lady," said McAllister, leaning forward across Mrs. Colefax and Sylvester Bull, "this delicious dinner will positively make history. With your permission I shall mention it in the little book on Society I am writing."

Fey smiled. "On condition that we may have an autographed copy to keep on our drawing-room table, Mr. McAllister." Madre de Dios, will they never finish eating! Why doesn't Simeon come back! It isn't Terry, it can't be. But with the actual inward voicing of his name, she knew that it was.

She stood up. "Forgive me—I won't be a minute," she said to them.

Only Penelope Colefax heard the note of fear, for only she was qualified to recognize it, and she sent Fey a look of concern. The others shared Van Vrandt's annoyance. One simply did not flit off from the table without explanation, and the ices, cheese, and dessert not yet served, either.

They watched Fey go out. Mrs. Van Vrandt shrugged her fat

shoulders, a gesture repeated by her husband. They sat back and waited.

When Simeon entered the library, Terry had been standing by the desk examining a carved carnelian paperweight. His back had been turned to the door, the long broad-shouldered back, which even in that position gave the impression of swagger. His bright head with its close curls was bent possessively over the paperweight.

Simeon, whose whole being had been concentrated on control, rushed across the room and snatched it from Terry's hand. "How d-dare you touch my things!"

Terry grinned with perfect good nature. He had been drinking all day since arriving in New York. It hadn't seemed easy this morning, this new plan, but it did now. Easy and a magnificent joke, too. They were giving a swell dinner party, he'd seen it through the window. Tease the stuffy old codger, give him fits, while Fey and the nabobs sat across the hall in the dining-room.

"You signed an agreement that you were never to bother me again. You went to Chicago," said Simeon, more quietly. He walked behind his desk and stood there, holding the little paperweight.

"Sure I went to Chicago. But I came back again—by way of Danbury. I spent the last few days in Danbury looking up your folks." Still grinning, Terry cocked his head and watched.

Simeon's breath made a sound; otherwise he didn't move. A short heavy man in black-and-white evening dress bulwarked by the wide rosewood desk.

"I found lots of things in Danbury that people don't seem to know," said Terry. "I laughed myself silly. Maybe they would, too."

The library gathered itself into a listening stillness. The gas fire sputtered softly. From across the hall came the sound of Sophie Bull's high laugh.

"So it occurred to me," said Terry, "that for that two thousand you held out on me, and maybe a few extra thrown in, I might sign another agreement."

For the first time a faint unease penetrated Terry's alcoholic euphoria. The little man didn't move at all; not even his lids, and the eyes behind them looked like black pits.

"Come on, don't take it like that," said Terry, making a placatory gesture. "You're a rich man. You can afford to keep things quiet. And think of Fey."

"Have you seen Fey?"

Terry relaxed. So now the old boy was coming off his high horse. Why not tell him the truth? thought Terry, with a muddled spurt of irritation. Why should he think he had everything, money, Fey, Lucita—

"Sure I've seen Fey," he said. "Lots of times. And she was mighty glad to see me, too. Just as loving as in the old days."

"I d-don't believe you." Simeon put down the paperweight. His right hand moved slowly to the brass knob of the desk drawer.

Terry threw back his head. "You don't believe me!" He showed his teeth and his laugh rang out. "Why, what have *you* got besides money to hold a woman with—little t-t-t-Tombstone?"

Simeon opened the desk drawer and, taking out a small loaded revolver, aimed it deliberately at Terry's chest and pulled the trigger.

Fey had reached the hall when the sound of the shot hurtled through the house. "No!" she whispered; "no—no! No!" She opened the library door.

On the carpet Terry lay, his hand clutching at his breast, and a foolish, astonished smile on his face.

Simeon still stood behind the desk, holding the revolver, from its muzzle floated a pendant of acrid blue smoke. He looked at Fey.

"Is he dead?" he said. "You'd better find out if he's dead."

She did not move. She stood beside Terry's body, looking at Simeon, and behind her in the doorway crowded the appalled faces of the dinner guests.

CHAPTER

20

RACHEL MORETON had finished her morning rounds through the Infirmary wards before she retired to her own room to eat a late breakfast and glance over the *Chronicle*.

She saw the name Tower in the headlines. "Frightful Tragedy at Tower Mansion. Simeon Tower Under Arrest."

Rachel gathered up the paper and carried it to the light, grimly straining her far-sighted eyes on the column of small type. The paper obviously had imperfect knowledge of the facts, and even these were reported cautiously with due regard to the financial and social importance of the Tower name. It was plain, however, that an unknown young man had been shot in the Tower library, and that Simeon Tower had been held.

Rachel folded the paper and put it on the bed. She went to her cupboard, took out her brown satin bonnet and thick woollen cloak. She hurried down to the dispensary and found Doctor Daniel pounding camphor in a mortar.

"I'm going out, Annie," she said. "I don't know for how long. Can you manage the wards?"

Doctor Daniel nodded. "You're upset?" she asked, in surprise. In all these years of association, she had seldom seen Rachel's serenity ruffled, and then only by the loss of a patient.

"Yes," said Rachel, and did not explain. She knew that Doctor Daniel had long ago forgotten all about the strange girl who had lived with them at the Infirmary for some months eight years back. Nor would she connect Fey with Simeon Tower if she did remember. As far as the Infirmary went, Fey had vanished for ever on the day she and the baby had moved to Eighteenth Street.

Rachel hailed a passing hack and drove to Fifth Avenue and Twenty-Ninth Street. Several people stood in the street in front of the brownstone house, gaping up at the shuttered windows. A bewhiskered policeman lounged against the iron railing at the foot of the steps. He straightened up as Doctor Moreton approached him, saying, "Is Mrs. Tower inside? I should like to see her."

"Guess she's there all right," said the policeman, fingering his badge. "But I don't know—I've got orders not to—"

"I am a physician," said Rachel. "And also her friend."

"You don't say so—a lady doctor! Was one of those helped my Maggie last year and—"

Rachel gave him her kind smile and mounted the steps to the front door. It was opened at the third ring by a frowzy and terrified little kitchenmaid who was the only servant left in the great house. The rest of them, infected by mass hysteria, had bolted like rabbits at the termination of their formal questionings by the police. Molly, the little kitchenmaid, would have bolted too, but this was her first job since landing and she had no place to go.

"I would like to see Mrs. Tower," said Rachel.

"Oh, mum—ain't it 'orrible—" cried the girl, gulping. "The 'earse just took 'im away, the poor young gentleman. 'E was that 'andsome. To think of Mr. Tower doing an orful thing like that! I can't stop me teeth chattering, I'm that frightened."

"Go and make yourself a cup of tea and lie down for a while," said Rachel, in a soothing voice. "Where is Mrs. Tower?"

Molly pointed a shaking finger. "Upstairs in 'er room. She ain't seen nobody since the perlice went."

Rachel went upstairs, noticing even in her distress the magnificence of the marble balustrade, the gold leather-embossed wallpaper, the imported stained-glass skylight, and the silver-gilt gasolier which hung down three stories in the stair well. She reached the second-floor landing and stood uncertainly, confronted by a row of shut mahogany doors. "Fey!" she called. There was no answer, but from the corner of her eye she saw something small and white move in the darkness at the end of the hallway.

She investigated and discovered a little figure with red-gold curls huddled on the back-stairs landing. Rachel's heart contracted, but she said, in a brisk matter-of-fact tone, "Why, hello! You must be Lucy. What in the world are you doing here in your nightie, dear?"

The child looked up at her dully. Her mouth was pinched and bluish, her pupils enormous.

Shock! thought Rachel. Can she have seen something? "Come, dear, get up and show me your room. I'm going to put you to bed."

Lucita got up and walked to a door across the passageway. "Miss Pringle's gone," she said. "She packed all her things in a box and went. She said she was going to take the first boat back to a decent country."

"Well," said Rachel, straightening the unmade bed and lifting the child into it, "I expect that was sensible of her, if she's that kind of person." She smiled at Lucita, at the same time feeling the little girl's pulse. "I want you to drink this." She poured a few drops of ammonia spirits into a glass of water. It had not occurred to her to bring her medicine bag, but she kept a small emergency kit in her old-fashioned reticule.

The child drank docilely. She lay back on the pillow, looking up at Rachel. "Why did Papa hurt my real papa?" she said.

Rachel, for all her self-control, could not hide her dismay. "What do you mean?"

"I saw it," said the child. "Last night there was a terrible lot of shouting and people running. I got out of bed and went downstairs. There wasn't anybody seemed to see me, not even Mama. I saw Cousin Terry, my *real* papa, lying on the floor in

263

the library. There was blood on him. And everybody was saying Papa had shot him."

Rachel took Lucita's hand in her strong warm grip, and she shut her eyes for a moment.

"Lucy," she said, "did you ever have a bad dream? A nightmare?" When the child nodded, she went on, "Do you remember how it's only real for a second after you wake up, and then it fades away into nothing?"

Lucita nodded again earnestly.

"I want you to think of everything that happened last night as a bad dream. It will fade away. You're going to sleep now. And when you wake up, I want you to think hard about the thing you like best in the world to do. What is that, dear?"

"Swimming—I guess," said the little girl. "Playing on the beach."

"Exactly. Think about sand castles, the golden sunshine, and the sea."

Rachel poured a sedative into the glass and held it to the child's lips. "I'll leave the door open and keep an eye on you," she said. "I want to find your mother. Do you remember what I told you to think about?"

"The sea and the sand," said Lucita. "I'll try. But—" She turned her head away, and whispered, "I *hate* Papa for hurting my real papa."

Rachel pulled up the bedclothes and drew the curtains. How could this horrible thing have happened, and how was it that the child knew?

Nor did she understand more clearly after she had found Fey, who was sitting in a chair by the window in the huge bedroom she had shared with Simeon, and was still dressed in the golden satin evening gown.

"Doctor Rachel!" she whispered as the door opened. She got up in a dazed way, came over to Rachel, and laid her head against the strong shoulder. "It couldn't be anybody else but you, could it?" she said. "Because I haven't any other friends at all. You should have seen the way they looked at me last night—afterward. At me and Simeon. They were so frightened, and they ran so fast to get away—like the servants, too."

"Fey," cut in Rachel, "I want to know exactly what happened. You're strong, and I've seen you handle many emergencies. I know you're exhausted and suffering from shock as Lucy is, but I want you to pull yourself together and give me a collected account."

"Lucita!" cried Fey, the vague stare focusing. "She's with Miss Pringle. She doesn't know anything about this. She was asleep. I've been afraid to go to her for fear she'd guess from my face."

"Miss Pringle has gone like the others," said Rachel dryly, taking off her bonnet and shawl. "And that poor child was not asleep last night."

"She saw—?" whispered Fey.

Rachel bowed her head. "No, don't go to her now—she's sleeping."

And she continued, in her carefully unemotional tone, "The papers didn't say so, but I assume, from what Lucy says, that Mr. Tower shot your first husband, and the child knows it."

"She doesn't know who Terry was—that he was her father—"

"She does," said Rachel.

Fey sank down in the chair again. "He told her," she said, half-aloud. "He did tell her. I'm glad he's dead."

"Fey! You mustn't talk like that!"

"He was blackmailing Simeon. He betrayed me. He betrayed Lucita."

Rachel frowned. There was something here that she did not understand, some obliquity anterior to and outside even the ghastly fact of murder. She knew the dead man only through Fey's descriptions, but she had thought to recognize the type, a drifter and a scamp, wholly graceless, but easily influenced and not vicious. And there was Lucy's attitude; when and how had that come about?

"How does it happen, Fey, that Terry came back into your life and managed to gain such an influence? Tell me from the beginning."

After a while Fey talked in nervous, jerky sentences. She told the bare facts. Terry's appearance at the Valentine Ball. The three clandestine meetings in the park. Then she stopped, raising her eyes to the wise, listening face in front of her. She got up from the chair and, walking to the centre table, straightened a magazine which had slipped askew from the rest. "That's all," she said. "Everything of any importance."

Rachel frowned, watching the small white hands levelling and smoothing the pile of magazines. She saw that Fey had not faced the tragedy yet, nor its inevitable consequences; that she was still groping through some protective mist of compromise and self-deception, as she had been for years. A child or a weakling might shield itself behind the excuse of shock, but Fey must not be allowed to.

"Where is your husband—Mr. Tower—now?" Rachel asked sternly.

Fey turned from the table, the hardness, a defiance so subtle that Rachel was not certain of its nature, left her strained face. "They took him away. He wouldn't speak to me. I tried to tell him—to tell him—" Her voice broke, and for the first time she began to cry. The tears ran down her face, staining the golden satin bodice. "The dinner party was going so well—it meant so much to him—how could he have—"

Rachel made a sharp sound of pity and impatience. She went to the girl and held her by the shoulders. "Fey!" It was a command, and she waited until the grey eyes raised reluctantly. "Wake up!" said Rachel. "You've drugged yourself long enough. This is real. You've got the strength. Now use it! For the salvation of your own soul and your child's and Simeon's—you've got to find the Inner Truth!"

A quiver shook the shoulders under Rachel's hands, response flickered and was gone.

Rachel compressed her lips, and released Fey. But her voice was very gentle. "Take off that dress, child. Wash your face and hands, and then we'll go look at Lucy."

For the next weeks of confusion and cumulative disaster, second only to the tragedy itself, Rachel stayed on in the Tower mansion. Even her strength was barely able to withstand the blows which battered down the house of cards so hopefully erected by Simeon and Fey. With the withdrawal of the guard on the third day, the house was besieged by panicky creditors. And two days after that, the newspapers trumpeted forth new headlines. Simeon Tower was bankrupt! His entire stockholdings had been put up as collateral and he owed enormous sums to most of the merchants in town. Gulf and San Diego and Transic broke in half. Gould, who had been waiting, though anticipating no such fortuitous assistance as this, quietly negotiated with Stevens at the Continental Trust, with whom unknown to Simeon he had an understanding—and stepped into control.

Neither Fey nor Rachel knew anything of finance, but they did not need the headlines to tell them that the Tower fortune had crashed as deafeningly as the social scaffolding on which the Towers had precariously balanced—simultaneously crumbled into a heap of dust.

With averted eyes and a terrified unanimity they closed ranks—the Van Vrandts and the Bulls, Mrs. Astor and Ward McAllister; indeed, all the guests who had attended the Valentine Ball. Van Vrandt and Bull would have to appear as witnesses, witnesses in a murder case! Admit that they had been dinner guests of the murderer! Had Simeon or Fey been one of themselves, born and bred amongst them, they might have rallied around, they would certainly have exerted their power and resources to muzzle the press. But as it was, each morning's paper brought new revelations which proved how duped they had been. Murder! Bankruptcy! And that was not all.

All the papers, but particularly the *Chronicle*, which had made the case its own, speeded ravening young reporters hotfoot on the scent of the alleged blackmail. It was not long before they encountered Lemming.

Noah Lemming had been momentarily aghast at the murder. His first instinct had been to fly as far away as possible and hide. Saner reflection showed him how silly this was. No one now living knew of his connection with Dillon, and he told himself that he was in no way responsible for the unfortunate outcome. So he received the reporters suavely, and presented the perfect picture of a loyal and distressed employee. He parried their questions with extreme subtlety, denying any knowledge of Dillon. And inadvertently, as it were, to provide them with a red herring—he set them on the Danbury trail. The *Chronicle* spent three days in tracing Simeon's remote past, and blazed out with the result. Simeon Tower had no connection with the Hingham Towers at all. He had been born Simon Turmstein, son of a mill hand and a Jewish peddler. The old parents were still living, and, said the *Chronicle* quite untruthfully, were bitterly hurt by their son's desertion. What manner of man was this—cried the *Chronicle*, trying the case in the newspapers—that would murder a man because he was going to disclose humble parentage? "The gallows alone can atone for this ignoble crime," said its editorial. And the other papers—with more or less vehemence—agreed.

Lemming sat outside Simeon's empty office listening to the hue and cry and waiting for the summons from Gould, for which he had now indicated that he was ready. But Gould had not and had never had the remotest intention of employing so disloyal and devious a man. All the flattering little conferences and marks of interest stopped. Gould looked through him on the street. And Lemming, frenziedly busying himself with the dolorous tag ends of the Tower interests, would not recognize that he was sinking as fast and as inexorably as the man he had helped to ruin.

Through all this, Simeon had made no statement except the one sentence he had uttered to the first policeman who rushed into the library. "He was blackmailing me," Simeon had said, in the harsh, toneless voice which all the reporters later emphasized, and he had handed over the little pistol which he was still holding.

He had been taken to the Tombs and put on the second tier of cells, the so-called "Murderers' Row," next door, as it happened, to the cell once occupied by Fisk's assassin, Edward Stokes.

As counsel Simeon had designated the firm of Williams and Day, who had been handling his affairs, but when old John Williams, the senior partner, visited him on the morning after the crime, he found an unco-operative and baffling client.

He entered cell Number 6 to see Simeon, coatless and unshaven, but still wearing the black trousers and white ruffled shirt with diamond studs of the evening before. He was crouched on the iron cot, staring at the noisome slop-bucket, and he did not change his position as the guard unlocked the grilled door, then locked it again behind the lawyer.

"Dear, dear! Tower—this is dreadful!" said the old man, pushing aside the sleazy grey blanket and seating himself gingerly beside Simeon. He dealt in corporation law, and since his salad days had neither handled nor wished to handle criminal procedure.

"I was appalled, simply appalled when I heard," he said, waggling his grey head irritably. "Whatever made you do a thing like that?—I suppose you *did* do it?"

Simeon lifted one hand, let it drop again palm upward. "He was blackmailing me."

"Yes, I know. But what about? And who was he?"

Simeon raised his eyes from the slop-bucket; they rested with the same vagueness on the lawyer's grizzled whiskers. "I won't tell you."

"But man—that's ridiculous! I'm your counsel. How can I help you if I don't know the facts?"

There was no answer. Simeon hunched his shoulders.

"Do you want to be hanged?" cried the old man; then controlled himself, for the look on his client's face jolted him out of exasperation to a reluctant pity. He had never particularly liked Tower, though he had very much liked such of the Tower fees as came his way. He had thought the financier pompous and not nearly as shrewd as many people supposed. But like or dislike had nothing to do with this matter, for the man was clearly abnormal at the moment and presented such a picture of bleak suffering as would disturb anyone.

"We must make you more comfortable," he said, looking with disgust at the verminous cot, the worm-eaten stool, and the tin slop-bucket. "I'll arrange to have some furniture sent in, and some decent food. By the looks of you, you need a doctor, too. Who's your own man?"

"I'm all right," said Simeon. "Leave me alone." He turned his back on the lawyer.

John Williams shook his head, dusted himself with his gloves and called the guard, who let him out and followed him along the narrow open portico which surrounded the four sides of the central skylighted well.

"Ain't had such a big bug in here since MacFarland or Stokes," remarked the guard complacently. "Millionaire, ain't he? I seen the papers."

"Yes," said Williams, for nobody yet knew of Simeon's bankruptcy.

"What's he want brought in?" asked the guard, his eye gleaming. "I know a firm'll fix him up mighty cosy, bed, desk, carpet, even a lamp. Doylan's 'll do the food and wine at ten per day, and I can take care of the other little accommodations a gent might be wanting."

"He doesn't seem to be wanting anything right now," answered Williams, gloomily buttoning his greatcoat, for the fetid air was dank.

"De-pressed like," assented the guard. "They often are at first. I'll order him a good strengthening dinner—ersters and a roast."

"Go ahead," said Williams, and he dropped a gold eagle into the eager hand. "I'll be back to-morrow."

He descended the iron stairway to the ground tier. I don't want the firm to handle this, he thought wearily. Tower ought to call in someone like John Graham or Webster. With all Tower's money they'd jump at it. But he was reluctant to split the fees, which would certainly be colossal, and he temporized for a while, each morning visiting Simeon, who each morning refused to speak. Then, by the end of the week, Williams along with everyone else discovered that there was no Tower money. And this shocked him even more than the murder had.

He and his partner, Day, held many uncomfortable consultations, and finally came to the conclusion that they would withdraw from the case, suggesting to Tower that he call in one of the best trial lawyers in New York, such as Thaddeus Webster, "and hope," said old Williams gloomily, "that Tower'll do it, for he seems to have lost all sense of self-preservation, and I don't know whether Webster'll touch it either, unless he thinks the publicity'll make up for the lack of fee. The defence stinks, anyway. Client won't talk, nobody knows anything except the damned newspapers, and they've got the whole thing tried and Tower convicted before anybody can get started."

After three weeks the newspapers had temporarily exhausted themselves, and turned their attention to the mysterious death of a baby in Brooklyn. The district attorney's office was silently and meticulously beginning to assemble the evidence for the prosecution.

In cell Number 6 of the Tombs, Simeon's special perquisites had ceased. Doylan's countermanded the flow of oysters and roasts and champagne, which Simeon had hardly touched, anyway. The new furnishings remained for the present because Williams had paid the first month's rent from his own pocket, but Simeon seemed indifferent to them, indifferent to everything. For three-quarters of the time he lay on the bed with his eyes closed, and the prison doctor, who had forcibly examined him, gave it as his opinion that there was a touch of brain fever—a convenient and popular term which covered all shades of mental abnormality. The doctor also recommended a suicide watch. The prisoner was deprived of tie, handkerchief, and belt; his eating implements were reduced to a wooden spoon; and the disappointed guard, naturally exasperated that this millionaire had turned out to have less ready cash than most of the other inmates, emphasized his hourly inspection by curses and furtive kicks.

And at the end of this three-week period, Doctor Moreton moved Fey and Lucita from the Fifth Avenue mansion to a small brick house on Thirty-Sixth Street at Kip's Bay. Since it was obviously impossible for Fey and the child to return to the Infirmary, and equally impossible for them to remain in the enormous, servantless house which had been taken over by the trustee and was in process of forced sale, Rachel had found the solution in one energetic morning of search. The little house on Kip's Bay was old and inconvenient, and it was so far uptown and out of the way that nobody wanted it. The owner had been delighted to rent it and its sparse furnishings.

Rachel returned to Fey and told her to pack, though the few personal belongings released by the trustee scarcely filled a small trunk. Most of the jewels and furs had never been paid for, Madame Loreste's bill alone ran into thousands, and

270

earlier purchases to which there was clear title must be held for the final adjustment.

Fey obeyed without question. She had been living in a shifting maze of shadows. But she had had Rachel, and she had depended on her quiet strength as blindly as Lucita did. At first people came and went incessantly; detectives, reporters, creditors, even morbidly curious strangers. Fey saw some of them and Rachel handled others, but both of them gave the same answer to all questions. "I don't know." This was Rachel's decision—arrived at after painful heart-searching. It was not entirely true, for they did know the real reason for the blackmail and the victim's identity, but with a man's life at stake, and conscious as she was of ignorance of all other facts, Rachel decided as best she could. She was exhausted by responsibility, and feminist though she was, dismayed by the extraordinary lack of a strong masculine helping hand. There seemed to be no one. The faces which did appear were all hostile or indifferent, and Rachel realized that, during those years of feverish self-aggrandizement, the Towers had made no real friends.

Rachel moved them to Kip's Bay on a Monday morning, Fey and Lucita, and they took Molly, the little housemaid, with them. The hackney cab held all of them and the one Saratoga trunk was lashed on the roof.

As the horse trotted off toward Madison Square, Fey looked back at the house. Two carpenters were already busy boarding up the windows, but otherwise it was the same bulky brownstone pile which she had stared at nine years ago: stared at with longing and fixed purpose. Nine years ago there had been someone else on that sidewalk, who also gazed up at the house with a very different longing. Pansy Miggs . . .

Fey made a muffled sound and jerked her head around.

"What is it, Fey?" said Doctor Moreton from the other corner of the carriage. "Memories?"

"Memories," repeated Fey. Lucita, who was sitting between the two women, gave her mother a frightened look and shrank toward Rachel. This had happened several times lately and added pain to the confused nightmare. Fey bent over the child. "Darling," she said, "won't it be fun to live in a new little house by the river?"

Lucita's big-eyed tenseness did not change. "Aunt Rachel'll be there too, won't she?" she said anxiously.

"Of course," said Rachel, patting the child's hand, but she shook her head. Somehow the child was identifying her mother with Simeon's guilt and repudiating her, too. But Lucita had never again mentioned the tragedy, and Rachel was afraid of doing more harm than good by trying to straighten the confusion in that child's mind.

She sighed, and so rare was any sign of discouragement from her that Fey was startled into awareness.

"Doctor Rachel!" she cried. "But how *can* you stay with us? What about the Infirmary?" She looked at the calm big face, really seeing it, and she saw the age and the tiredness. "You're worn out. I've let you do everything. We've needed you so."

"You still do, I'm afraid," smiled Rachel. "The Infirmary can do without me for a while. I'm taking a vacation."

"Vacation!" said Fey bitterly. "You ought to go South, or to the country—"

"The brick cottage will do for a substitute, you'll see," said Rachel, and when the cab crossed First Avenue and stopped before a rusty iron gate, Fey and Lucita both gave cries of surprise.

This section two hundred years ago had been the site of Jacobus Kip's farm, "a goodly estate covering one hundred and fifty acres, and comprising meadow, woodland, and stream." The section now was a chaos of squatter shanties, goats, and an occasional block of brownstone tenements, interspersed with a few dilapidated farmhouses left over from the eighteen-forties, when gentlemen like Horace Greeley and Francis Winthrop had here their country estates. The little brick cottage was as shabby as everything else, but it had been built in 1800 of honest Haverstraw brick, its lines were still pure and its colour mellowed to a rosy tan. There was half an acre of weeds around it, two chestnut trees, and a syringa bush enclosed by the rusted and twisted iron fence; but it was not the unexpected trees or the bush or even the decayed picturesqueness of the little house which surprised Fey. It was its location not fifty yards from the glinting and majestic East River. Seagulls circled by the roof uttering their lonely mewing cries and returned to a clump of rocks on the shore, while behind the gulls a side-wheeler and a sloop, both battling the time, glided softly toward Blackwell's Island against Brooklyn's backdrop of church spires.

The air smelled sharply salt, and the March sun glittered off the ruffled wavelets.

"I didn't know there was any place like this in New York!" cried Fey, standing in the mud of the road and breathing in the air.

Rachel snorted. "There are a great many things you don't

know about New York, child." But she was pleased. It would be good for them all to be here; perhaps with the help of the river, they might at last get perspective on the black insoluble problems.

There were five rooms. Downstairs a big, old-fashioned kitchen, with Dutch oven and set-in cookstove; a low-ceilinged parlour whose gay French paper was stained and peeling a little, and the furnishing consisted of a rickety sofa, two Windsor chairs, an excellent Sheraton desk, and straw matting on the floor—nothing else. But the two unshaded windows looked directly on to the river so that the room appeared to be filled with moving water and light.

Upstairs there were three small bedrooms, each with a bed, washstand, and chair. That was all, except a lean-to backhouse connected with the kitchen porch. "Hardly what you're accustomed to, Fey," said Rachel, thinking of the silver tubs and the central heating of the house they had just left. They were all shivering, for the unaired cottage was damp and chilly, and she watched Fey carefully, wondering how deep the decay of luxury had eaten.

"For the first eighteen years of my life, I had no such comfort as this," replied Fey, looking out of the parlour window at Lucita, who had run down to the water's edge and was talking to the startled gulls. But the transition back to hard work and sparseness was not so easily accomplished.

Molly remained only three days, during which time she grumbled incessantly. The brick cottage was too much like home; she had no use for the " 'orrid damp river air, and I 'ad me fill o' lugging in nasty coals and pumping every drop of water back in Stepney—" So she disappeared on the second afternoon, and, having found a new job, left them the next day.

"And just as well," said Rachel. "We really couldn't afford her."

This problem of money was the minor but equally baffling one with which Fey had begun to wrestle, as her soft pampered hands struggled through a dozen long-unfamiliar chores. For they were dependent on Rachel's own modest income.

Each night, exhausted by work, Fey slept a few hours on the lumpy mattress, then awoke as the grey dawn light sifted through the coarse muslin curtains from the river, and lay listening to Lucita's breathing from the little room next door. Each morning, as the narcotic shock-born haze of the first weeks lifted, she awoke to a more hopeless anxiety. Again and again her brain reeled off those moments in the library. She saw the figure on the floor with its foolish, surprised smile, she saw Simeon behind the desk holding the little gun as one might hold a glove, heard him say, "Is he dead? You'd better find out of he's dead."

But the voice was thin and tinny, the figures had no more reality than if they had flashed on a stereopticon. The scene had no essence or inner meaning, nor did the concept of Simeon in the Tombs. In this concept, too, there was confusion and uncertainty. He refused to see her, she had twice applied through the police and been told of his violent refusal. The relief this had given she had instantly suppressed. And, after all, what could she do?—he had competent counsel, they told her; the case would not come to trial for months probably, and until she heard further from the district attorney's office or the defence lawyers, there was nothing to do but wait.

CHAPTER

21

DURING those days at the brick cottage, the three of them—Rachel, Fey, and the child—spoke seldom and only of domestic matters. The inescapable household tasks kept them busy, and to Lucita these were a delightful novelty. For her some of the shadow had lightened, and in consciousness she forgot the reason for their escape to this interesting place. She forgot the cause, but she continued to treat her mother with a nervous constraint which hurt Fey, and would have hurt her bitterly except that no emotion seemed quite to pierce the thin shell which surrounded her.

They all lived in a state of suspension, even Rachel, who was blunted by domestic labour and responsibilities, though she loved these two and never ceased praying for them.

In April her prayers were answered in a most unexpected way.

It had been drizzling for days, the cold, disheartening rain of the dying winter, but it had melted the last patches of snow at the north side of the cottage, and today suddenly spring had come. Sparrows chattered on the branches of the two budding chestnuts, and the strengthening sun drew up the fecund odour of moist black earth. The river water lapped at the warmed rocks, and at four-thirty, when the Boston boat steamed by, her decks swarmed with gay hats and parasols. The ship's band played on the afterdeck and the enticing strains of "The Blue Danube" floated into the kitchen of the brick cottage where supper preparations were under way.

"Might I go out, Mama?" asked Lucita eagerly. "I've peeled all the carrots." She addressed Fey, who was trussing a roasting chicken, but she looked at Rachel.

"Where do you want to go, darling?" said Fey, holding the chicken with one hand, but putting the other arm around the child.

Lucita's sturdy little body did not resist, but Fey sensed the impulse of withdrawal. She put the chicken quickly on the roasting-pan.

"I want to go see Benjie," said Lucita. "Aunt Rachel knows."

"That sick gull she's nursing down on the rocks," explained Rachel. "I made a splint for its leg. Let's take Mama down and show her Benjie. I smell spring and it won't hurt this supper to wait."

Fey nodded, trying to smile. Rachel continually urged the little girl to include her mother in her activities.

"I'd love to see Benjie," said Fey, and all three moved at once for the door.

Neither Fey nor Rachel paused to take off their enveloping aprons; the nearest neighbour was a block away and no one would see them. Fey's cheeks were flushed from the stove, and the coarse net into which she had bundled the masses of black hair had slipped askew and hung over one shoulder. Her sleeves were rolled up to the elbow, and, as they walked toward the path to the rocks, she dabbed at a floury smooch on her thin arm. It is a lovely day, she thought, feeling the sun on her back. Spring again. Again.

And what have I to do with spring? She saw it embodied as a golden globe into which she might look, but not enter, and behind her, where she would not look, was a dark and shapeless chasm.

It was Lucita who heard the thick clops of horses' hoofs approaching on the muddy road, and she raced back to her mother and Rachel.

"Look, someone's coming here in a cab!"

The two women stared at the approaching hackney and then at each other, dismayed. Lawyers, they thought, more police —the approach of trouble, yanking them again from the recent abeyance.

The cab stopped before the rusted iron gate and a man got out. He was fairly tall and he was muffled in a plaid Inverness cape, a trifle incongruous against the rest of his clothes which were soberly dark.

A stranger, thought Fey. As all the recent callers had been strangers. She started to remove her apron, then let it be. The man opened the gate; but, seeing the two women and child, waited until they came up to him. He doffed his stiff black hat. "I'm looking for Mrs. Tower-r."

"Yes?" said Fey, dully resigned, but aware of a thin splinter of surprise. His voice, that slight burring of the "r," made her think of something.

It was Rachel who gave an exclamation. "But surely—" She frowned, staring at the amiable rugged face, the peculiarly clear grey eyes, the dark stubborn hair. "Haven't we some-where—"

He turned his gaze from Fey, whom he had been examining with such intense interest that she was annoyed.

The years had made a difference in Rachel as they had in him. Her hair was now entirely white, and all youth had left the big-boned face, also the last time he had seen her she had been chastely resplendent in dove-grey satin under soft lights. But suddenly he smiled, the quick crooked smile which she remembered. "Why, it's the Infirmary doctor! I've not forgotten our conversation in the elegant Misses Carys' drawing-room."

"MacDonald!" cried Rachel, recovering the name. "I'm glad to see you again, Mr. MacDonald. But whatever brought you out here?"

"My cousin," said Ewen, indicating Fey gravely.

"I don't understand," snapped Fey, certain that this was one more trick, a new way of prying, of making her talk. She turned around and started through the gate to the house.

Rachel gave a troubled smile which indicated apology for Fey's behaviour. "I don't understand either. But please come in."

"I will," said Ewen, and he paid off the cabdriver. Lucita had been watching round-eyed. Now she stepped forward from behind Rachel. "Would you like to see my sick sea-gull?" she said.

At once he bent toward the child and gave the question due consideration. "I would, bairnie, and I will. But first I must talk to—" He indicated the house where Fey had disappeared. "It *is* your mother, is it not?"

Lucita caught her underlip with her little white teeth, and her pupils dilated. She nodded without speaking.

"You and she have naught to fear from me," he said, answering her expression. "I'm your kinsman. Do you know what that means?"

The child shook her head.

Ewen smiled. "We'll teach you then soon." He fished in his pocket and brought out a soggy little package wrapped in brown paper. "Here's a bit o' Dundee cake I brought all the way from Glasgow. Maybe your sea-gull'd relish it, if he's convalescent, and you can share it with him."

"Oh, Benjie'd love it." The child smiled, and Rachel, who had been listening, thought how seldom Lucita smiled. Her initial liking for MacDonald increased. But she was profoundly puzzled.

Rachel led the way in to the parlour, left MacDonald seated on the slippery horsehair sofa, and went to find Fey, who was in the kitchen rubbing lard into the chicken, her burned, reddened fingers moving in nervous stabs.

"Has he gone?" she said, pushing the loosened hair out of her eyes with the back of her arm.

"No. He wants to see you. Lord 'a' mercy child—he's a very nice man. Don't act like that. Aren't you curious to find out what he means? I am. Why, I'm just beginning to remember— the story he told—that day at the Carys'—" Rachel stopped. She took the roasting-pan from Fey and put it decisively in the oven. "Tidy yourself up, child, and come down to the parlour."

When Rachel spoke in that tone, people obeyed, and Fey left the kitchen and went upstairs, half-ashamed of the reluctance she felt to seeing the stranger again. She took off her apron, rolled down her sleeves, unpinned her hair and brushed it, and each homely act was sheathed in hostility. She braided and rolled her hair into its enormous coil, then leaned toward the tiny fly-specked mirror. "Let me alone!" she said, out loud, and for a moment she looked deep into her own eyes. The other, in the mirror, struck back at her like a snake. She lowered her head, flung the brush and comb into the drawer and banged it shut.

She went downstairs, placing her foot softly and carefully on each step. She entered the parlour with the same careful tread, her head high, her face expressionless, and Ewen, rising, thought, She's a true Cameron except for that heather-white skin and that she's smaller than our women.

She sat down on one of the Windsor chairs. Rachel already had the other.

"I'll clear the mystery at once," said Ewen, smiling at Fey. "My mother was a Cameron, your grandfather, old Sir James's youngest sister. I searched for you once, ten years ago, and did not find you. I have found you now, and I've come to help."

Rachel leaned forward, her voice ringing with astonishment. "But she was with *me*—that night, when you told me of your search, if I'd only known— Fey, if you'd only come with me! So near a thing—"

Rachel stopped, overcome by the blind frustration of chance. Ewen, though very much startled, kept his eyes on Fey, puzzled by her immobility and the guarded enmity he saw in the grey eyes so like his own.

"Yes, I was with Simeon," she said. Her voice was a small flat stone dropped into a waiting pool. The concentric ripples reached the edge of the room, then vanished into silence. Compressing her lips, she turned her head and looked out at the river.

It was Rachel who asked the questions which explained Ewen's arrival there that day.

He told of the cable long ago from Simeon Tower, of his answering letter, and Simeon's final reply, giving neither Fey's name nor address, and making it clear that he wished no further connection with Scotland. Ewen had retained a great liking for the United States, and subscribed to a New York Sunday paper. There, from time to time, he had seen mention of the Towers. There, too, he had read of Simeon's financial ruin, but the tragedy and Simeon's arrest had been cabled abroad and he had seen it first in a Glasgow paper. "I knew she needed help," he said. "And that's a kinsman's duty. Moreover, my conscience has given me no rest for having failed to find her before Sir James died. I dislike loose ends."

They both glanced at Fey, who had bent her head to rest her chin on her hand, which half-concealed her face. She seemed not to be listening, but they knew that she was, and that, too, she was engulfed in a peremptory inner turmoil, which neither of them understood.

"How did you find us now?" asked Rachel, thankfully, for no matter what Fey's reaction, Rachel felt the first relief she had known since the day she had discovered Fey and Lucita deserted in the Fifth Avenue mansion.

"Well," answered Ewen, "when I read the paragraph in the paper, I wound up my affairs as best I could—I'm a barrister, you know— Last Tuesday week, I caught the *Anglia* from Glasgow, we docked this morning. I knew that the police would have Mrs. Tower's whereabouts. After I convinced them of my respectability, they gave me this address, and here I am."

"And I thank God for it," said Rachel. "For we badly need advice, there has been nobody."

Ewen made a sympathetic sound, then grew grave. His eyes became shrewd and attentive. When he was not smiling—the quick sideways grin which had in it an endearing touch of self-ridicule—he looked older than his thirty-three years. The furrows across his forehead were deeply cut, and in his black hair there was some grey, mingled in like course white threads.

Not a handsome man, thought Rachel, but an attractive one, strong, intelligent, wiry, virile, perhaps a little like one of his own Scotch Airedales. He would be a tenacious fighter, and he would be infallibly loyal. He had more than that, though. She felt a sensitive intuition, and in his behaviour to Lucita and now to Fey, who was certainly as ungracious and inexplicable as possible, he showed extraordinary tact.

"Tell me the whole story from the beginning," he said, crossing his lean legs. "That is what I've come for."

"Yes," answered Rachel. "But it's Fey's story. And it is she who must tell it."

They both saw Fey stiffen and a tremor run across her averted back. They waited.

Suddenly she jerked around and looked at them. "No!" she cried violently. "I won't go through that again. Let it alone. What's done is done. What difference how or why!"

There was silence.

Fey got up, groping for the chair-arm. "Tell him what you like," she said to Rachel, and walked rapidly out of the room. They heard her steps ascend the stairs.

"So," said Ewen, after a moment, "she's hiding something?"

"Perhaps," answered Rachel, "but I think not so much from us—from herself. I don't know exactly what it is."

Ewen accepted this and dismissed it for the time being. Then he began to question Rachel, who told all that she knew.

Ewen had ample time for thought as he walked back to his hotel that evening, and the next day, when he translated these thoughts into action, he was dismayed at the results of his investigation. He had a stiff, uncomfortable interview with old John Williams, who resented inquiry and indicated that a Scotch barrister could not hope to understand American law. To this Ewen agreed, but he refused to be dismissed and continued his cool questions until he understood the situation. Williams and Day had no intention of defending their unfortunate client themselves, and Thaddeus Webster, whom they had requested to take the case, had not definitely done so. He had been away, his health was precarious, he was still "considering."

"In short," said Ewen, puffing on his briar pipe, "he's afraid he won't be paid, and he's afraid he can't win."

Williams shrugged his skinny shoulders and looked at the ceiling.

"There are other barristers—criminal lawyers in New York," said Ewen.

"Webster would be best—for a thing like this." The old man stood up, fingering his watch-chain. "I hope you understand our position, Mr. MacDonald. We really aren't qualified, and now these bankruptcy proceedings, too, we have our hands full—"

Ewen bowed, took his leave, and went to see Thaddeus Webster. He found an enormously fat man whose spaced, explosive speech rose from him like sluggish bubbles sighing to the surface of a kettle of boiling mush. He slouched in his mammoth office chair which he overflowed, but his little eyes, peering like currants from between the flesh, were steady and watchful.

"I cannot beat about the bush," said Ewen, "there's been too much of that. I'm related to Mrs. Tower, and I've come to find out if you will defend her husband. I myself will guarantee your fee."

"In-deed," said Webster, on two soft aspirations of the breath. His pudgy, surprisingly small hand made a gentle arc through the air.

"Come, Mr. Webster, I wish to settle this thing. The district attorney's office is not also bogged down in vagueness and indecision, I'll be bound."

"The *prosecution*," said the sighing voice, "has a case. I don't like defending a man who won't help himself. I don't like"—the plumb lips curved in a soft apologetic smile—"to lose— And the accused is unpopular, for what he represents. The city still smarts from memories of the Tweed Ring."

"Yes. Yes, I know. But Tower doesn't deserve to hang because he's unpopular. There *is* a defence—a strong defence." Ewen stopped, thinking of Fey, who would not talk, and of little Lucy. It was to protect Fey that Tower would not talk either. I doubt that she merits this protection, he thought angrily, ashamed of his kinswoman.

"There is a strong defence," he repeated, "but we can't use it. We must find something else. Temporary aberration caused by—the blackmail, perhaps?"

Webster hunched his fat shoulders.

"The blackmail rests on Tower's unsupported word, and its cause—either theory produced by the newspapers, that he feared discovery of lowly parents and Jewish blood, or that he feared discreditable financial exposure—will never move the jury to tolerance."

Ewen knew this to be true. He had had time now to overcome the first distaste for the mountain of flesh across the desk, and to sense embedded in it authority and a shrewd intelligence. The thick, sighing speech fastened attention, and once one was used to it produced a feeling of confidence. It would so impress a jury, decided Ewen, from his own considerable experience.

"The complete anonymity of the victim is a puzzling point," continued Webster softly; " "simply a red-headed young adventurer—who appears from nowhere, and registers at the Saint Nicholas Hotel as Xavier T. Dillon—"

The sentence floated through the room in the form of a question. Ewen nodded, and made up his mind, at the same time berating himself for hesitation.

"That was his real name, and he was Mrs Tower's first husband."

"Ah-h." The fleshy lids dropped over the little eyes. "One has wondered, of course, if the young wife were not involved. But in the face of obstinate silence—"

"She must not be dragged into this!" cried Ewen. "We must find some other way."

"The prosecution," continued Webster imperturbably, "have probably not discovered this relation. And it would not be to their advantage. Of all things, they dread the effect of 'the unwritten law.' And if there was adultery—"

"There's no question of that!" snapped Ewen.

The little black eyes shifted to rest on the Scot's worried frown with consideration, even kindliness. "You may trust to me a good woman's reputation, Mr. MacDonald."

"Then you'll take the case?"

The massive head nodded. "And my fee will be three thousand dollars—half now, as a retainer."

Ewen translated that into pounds, and concealed a mental start. This represented a quarter of his entire estate. But it was not in him to flinch. He had come to help Fey, and, as it now appeared, to try to save her husband from the gallows as well.

"I wish to have a talk with Mrs. Tower as soon as possible," said Webster. "Oh, I shall be most grateful, I won't embarrass her—just a few questions."

"To be sure," answered Ewen, getting up. "I understand she's been in a rather dazed state, not communicative, but, of course, she'll come. I'll bring her tomorrow."

But this Ewen found that he could not do. When he drove out to the brick cottage on the following morning, Lucita greeted him on the stoop.

"Mama's sick," she said importantly. "Real in-bed sick. Aunt Rachel says she has a big fever."

"I'm mortal sorry to hear that, bairnie." He laid his hand on her bright curls, amazed at the shock her news gave him. A shock as strong as though it came from anxious love. "Will you please to call Doctor Moreton for me?"

When Rachel came downstairs, he skipped all greeting. "What's happened, doctor? What ails her?"

Rachel sighed and motioning him to the sofa sat down beside him. "I don't know. She acted strange yesterday, weak and listless; she went to bed early, and this morning I found her very feverish. But don't be alarmed. I think it's not any of the infectious diseases."

"But what is it, then?—what is it?" he cried.

Rachel stared at his face and shook her head. To conceal a swift-piercing dismay, she got up from the sofa and walked to the window, instinctively seeking the comfort of the bright flowing water below. Was it possible that he was falling in love with Fey? And this hint of yet one more complication discouraged her.

"I think," she said at last, from her position by the window, "that the body sometimes reflects the health of the soul. Fey has a fine strong body or it would have given in before this."

"You mean brain fever?" he asked sharply.

Rachel sighed again, still looking out at the water. "Brain fever, mind fever, soul fever—not any of them terms we understand. I'm caring for her body. God will do the rest. God *must* do the rest," she added slowly.

She stood outlined against the light, a gaunt ageing woman in a faded alpaca dress—and as Ewen looked at her his initial admiration was touched by awe. He forgot his anxiety for Fey, startled by the recognition of a kind of beauty his natural cynicism had denied. She openeth her mouth with wisdom, he thought, and in her tongue is the law of kindness.

"Did I believe in papacy," he said, with the ironic tinge which hid emotion, "I'd make you a saint, doctor."

Rachel stirred and laughed. "Nonsense. Come into the kitchen and have a cup of coffee while I brew Fey an herb tea. I want to hear what happened yesterday."

Upstairs on the narrow white bed Fey had wandered into a desolate country whose climate was fear. This bleak shadow land was at the same time suspended in remote space and yet interpenetrated by the little attic bedroom which swelled and shrank in a monotonous ghastly pulsation. When this pulsation stopped, it was replaced by discordant sound—jangling bells clanging no melody and yet producing one senselessly reiterated which Fey, lying with her hands clenched against her ears, knew to be the little Spanish song which carried the hymn, "Flee as a bird to your mountain—" The bells beat at her with phrases from this hymn. "O, thou who art weary of sin. . . . Haste, then, the hours are flying, Fly, for the avenger is near thee . . ." These phrases swelled in deafening clangour until the terror could no longer be borne and seemed to crash down like a huge breaking wave, and, while she held her breath, suffocated, it seeped slowly outward, leaving her alone on a melancholy strand. Then the first faint chiming would commence again, and the sequence repeat itself.

There were never any people woven through the anguish of this experience. Only the fear was personalized, and it at times separated itself from the bells and the wave and became a dark veiled figure towering in the corner of the room. Sometimes, when it made a gesture as though to uncover its face, the terror grew so acute that she cried out.

When this happened, Rachel was always there. "Hush, dear. Quiet." Changing the cold cloths on her head, forcing her to drink. Fey obeyed, but she was not conscious of Rachel and spoke to her in Spanish. "Gracias," she would whisper, and add fretfully, as she tried to throw off the covers, "Hace calor, calor del infierno." And Rachel, who knew enough Latin to understand the last word, would be filled with pity.

A night came when Rachel was really frightened. As nearly as her experienced fingers could judge on Fey's pulse, the fever was no higher, but the girl was exhausted, drained. Her stomach rejected all food and the delicate bones of her face showed too clearly the modelling of her skull. And she whispered to herself, no longer in Spanish, but in the Scottish tongue of her earliest childhood. That this backward penetration in time was a bad sign, Rachel knew all too well.

When she talked to Ewen, who had come every day, she could not hide her anxiety. "She's in no immediate danger, but the battle in her spirit is destroying her. I don't know how more to help."

Ewen swallowed and his lips tightened. Silently he went upstairs behind Rachel and they looked at the small figure on the bed.

Fey seemed to hear them; she turned the hollow grey eyes in their direction.

"I have lost it," she said distinctly. "The donsie heathen gaud. I do not wish to find it. I sold it—"

Ewen understood the words, but he attributed this talk of a baleful heathen trinket to delirium; Rachel did not understand, but she went to the bed and took Fey's hot hand. "What has thee lost, child? I'll find it for thee."

Fey shook off the soothing hand and sat up; her fever-brilliant gaze pushed past Rachel and rested on Ewen's face with sudden recognition. "Why didn't you come before—my love?" she said to him plaintively, and she held out her arms to him. But at once they dropped; she twisted her head and, looking up at Rachel, answered the previous question—"You cannot find it—" she muttered sullenly. "And I do not *wish* to, it'll give me pain." She fell back on the pillow and closed her eyes.

Rachel and Ewen looked at each other in sharp fear. He had felt a great leap at his heart when Fey held out her arms to him, but he had not needed the doctor's quick, forbidding headshake to stop him from running to the bed. That flash in Fey's face and her words had made plain to him his own feelings. He stood rooted in appalled realization, then turned and went heavily downstairs.

In the sick-room, Rachel sponged once more the inert body on the cot, straightened the bedclothes, and adjusted the shutters while she endeavoured to hold off panic by steady, confident prayer. She went to Lucita and tucked the covers around the little girl before going to her own room, where she lay down on the counterpane, fully clothed, listened awhile to Fey's rapid, uneven breathing, and fell into an exhausted doze.

For Fey the bells began again. But now the terror they brought was muted and in its place an anguish of loneliness. This desolation, softer and more hopeless than the fear,

284

wrapped her in dense black folds in which there was no shadow or movement. Beneath the stifling blackness her heartbeats slowed, and tears oozed from between her lids.

Early that evening there had been fog on the river, but with the coming of a fresh night wind it lifted and a cool moon shone. None of its light fell through the attic window, but to Fey there came gradually a lessening of the anguish. Words formed themselves on her lips. Words learned long ago with her father and never again remembered.

"Save me, O God; for the waters are come in unto my soul. I sink in deep mire, where there is no standing. Deliver me out of the mire and let me not sink. Draw nigh unto my soul and redeem it."

The denseness and the blackness pressed down harder, but now there was motion in them, and a compulsion. The compulsion grew, and she whimpered a little, turning her head from side to side on the hard pillow. At last she opened her eyes. There was dim light from the lamp burning in Rachel's room. Fey pushed herself up from the bed. A clammy sweat broke out along her back; she put her feet to the floor, and, supported by the footrail, dragged herself three steps across the matting to her trunk. She stumbled forward and fell against the trunk.

At once Rachel ran in. "Fey!" her cry thin with fear. She tried to lift the girl.

Fey shook her head. "Open the trunk," she said, and to Rachel's amazement the voice, though weak and gasping, was rational.

Rachel lifted the unlocked lid and held Fey, who pushed aside layers of garments and underclothes to fumble in the corners at the bottom.

"What *is* it, dear?" cried Rachel. "What is thee trying to do?"

"I know I brought it," answered the girl fretfully. "I threw it in here somewhere the day we packed and left the house, I did bring it—" She gave a sigh, and, drawing her closed hand from the trunk, slumped against Rachel, who supported her back to the bed, then ran for the lamp.

By its light she saw the gleam of blue between the thin fingers, and turning Fey's hand recognized the turquoise which the girl used to wear nine years ago. For a moment she recoiled at this evidence of superstitious attachment, at the same time excusing it as a symptom of the strange illness. But Fey looked better. Her pulse had slowed, and even while

Rachel watched her, she fell into a profound sleep.

The next morning Rachel knew that the illness was over, and the problem now chiefly one of physical convalescence. Fey was weak and very quiet. She gave an impression of bewilderment, but the self-preoccupation and a certain hectic defiance which she had shown since the tragedy—these were gone.

Somewhat to Rachel's disapproval, Fey braided silk threads into a chain and once more wore the turquoise pendant. "Thee's too intelligent to need a fetish, Fey," objected Rachel, who now again used the plain speech to her two charges. "I know it helped thee that night thee was so sick, but it's a childish crutch."

Fey smiled, the gentle vague smile which was new. "Perhaps. But I need it. You can walk alone. I can't."

Rachel was silenced, thinking that Fey referred to the murder and Simeon's situation; these, since Fey was not strong enough to take action, Rachel had avoided mentioning. It was not entirely that which Fey meant.

During these days of convalescence, she felt without understanding that that terrible problem was a part of something else toward which she was groping. And the sense of unreality persisted. There was, however, a change. And she showed this on the first day that she came downstairs and saw Ewen.

She was already tucked up on the parlour sofa when he drove out to the brick cottage, bearing a bunch of daffodils and a bottle of port wine.

He opened the front door and, walking in without ceremony, was so startled at seeing her downstairs that he stood by the parlour door tongue-tied as a schoolboy, clutching the bouquet and wine against his Inverness cape. "It's good to see you about again," he said stiffly, and he wondered if she remembered that passionate gesture she had made toward him on the night of her crisis.

Fey did not know that she had externalized the emotion, but its aftermath remained as a memory. Instead of antagonism, she now felt yearning and a dependence, and a sensation of deep understanding. Upon first meeting him, she had thought him ugly and insignificant. Now she did not. She wanted him close to her, yet she did not even hold out her hand. This impulse, too, drifted to nothing, extinguished by the impression of deferred crisis which had since her recovery been her only certainty.

"What'll I do with the posies?" said Ewen, smiling, and dumping them on the table beside her. "I need not ask what to do with the wine. If ever a lass looked in need of good rich wine 'tis you."

"Do I look as bad as all that?" said Fey, smiling. "My skin is always pale."

"You show your Highland blood only in your eyes, and maybe that square little jaw," agreed Ewen, uncorking the bottle and fetching two glasses from the corner china cupboard. He had made up his mind that this visit must be one of trivialities. Her thinness and paleness shocked him, while it moved him to a fierce protectiveness. The illness into which she had escaped still shielded her. It can wait, he thought, torn as he had been for days between his love for Fey and pressure from the outer world, where Thaddeus Webster was grimly and pessimistically trying to marshal a defence.

Fey surprised him. She sipped her port, frowning a little into the garnet glass. "I'll be strong enough in a day or two," she said. "I want to try to see Simeon."

Ewen sat up, staring at her. This semed to him an oblique and astonishing way of opening the subject at last. She did not ask what was being done, what had been found out; she asked nothing about the trial, nor even her husband's health.

"I thought he refused to see you."

Fey lowered her head. "I think I should have gone, anyway. He might have seen me." She moved her eyes to Ewen's face, but continued in the same groping way, "But I didn't want to see him, or think of him—"

"Well, that's natural. You were dazed. It's not surprising that the mind would—would try to reject such horrible circumstances. And the tragedy had nothing actually to do with you, you were an unfortunate pawn."

He broke off as she gave him a strangely frightened and bewildered look. "No, there was nothing I could do," she murmured. "Nothing."

He checked his desire to comfort her at the expense of fact and said brusquely: "But now you must do something to help your husband—when you're stronger. Thaddeus Webster has undertaken the defence. You must tell him the whole truth, about Dillon's identity and everything you know— Oh, you won't have to appear," he added quickly, for her pupils had dilated until the grey vanished—"you'll be protected in every way."

"But Simeon's in no danger!" she cried. "Terry was blackmailing him. He said so. That's enough. I'm sure there's no danger."

Ewen shook his head. "You don't understand, Fey! You're not refusing to talk to Webster?"

She pushed distractedly at the afghan around her knees "No, no—not if you want me to, of course—but" Her face crumpled. She seemed to shrink into an imploring child.

He jumped up, starting to go to her, to gather her up against him, and already on his feet he checked himself. And she checked her tears. They looked at each other and, while her jaw tightened and her mobile face became controlled, the resemblance between them was strong.

The muscles of his legs relaxed, he sank back into his chair, They were silent. From the kitchen they could hear Lucita's voice calling to Rachel, and the distant clatter of saucepans. Ewen's neglected daffodils made a splotch of tender gold on the rough pine table by the head of the sofa. Fey picked them up and held them softly against her breast. In this there was no coquetry, but they both understood. Their eyes met again in poignant affirmation, then relinquished each other.

"Tell me about Scotland," said Fey, after a moment. "Always for me it has been the land beyond the horizon—it seemed that I felt it in my blood, the mists over the grey waters of Loch Fyne, the purple shadows on the fairy Isle of Skye, the smell of the heather and the gorse and the peat smoke. As a child I longed and longed to go there—then I forgot."

"You will go," he said quickly. "You will."

Her lips curved in a faint smile. "Once I might have gone with you—"

He blackened, and a sudden anger seized him. "It was the De'il's own doing that I did not find you! Stupid savage Fate!"

A heavy curtain fell sharply across her mind. Her eyes went blank. "Tell me about your house in Inveraray, Ewen. Is it big? Is it near the Loch? Can you see the moors?"

He told her a little about his home, and she listened, her eyes half-closed and fixed on the reflections from the river, while she breathed in the scent of the daffodils.

22

FOUR days later, Fey had grown strong enough to stand the dual expedition—to Thaddeus Webster's office and to the Tombs.

When Ewen called for her at two, she was ready, dressed as he had never seen her, as a rich and fashionable woman. She wore her one suit, bought three years ago, but even this out-of-date spring costume—grey moiré banded in taupe velvet—was unmistakably luxurious, and it changed her. She appeared older and more remote, and at the same time the touches of cream lace at throat and wrists, the perfumed rustle of her skirt, the sleekness of her black hair beneath the plumed grey hat, and the coral salve on her lips, all combined to give her a sophisticated beauty which he had not suspected. Her manner confirmed her appearance; it, too, was cool and remote. She sat beside him in the hackney and answered his efforts at re-assuring conversation with polite monosyllables, beneath which he felt a guardedness, almost the earlier hostility.

When they reached the lawyer's building, she preceded Ewen through the indicated doors and greeted Webster in the same remote manner.

After brief civilities, she sat down, drew off her long grey gloves, and, laying them across her lap, sat composedly waiting.

"Now, Mrs. Tower, just tell me the whole—story, as you know it. The main facts, that is—I don't want you to fatigue yourself." The thick, sighing voice soothed and coaxed, but the little eyes were watchful.

"I am anxious to do everything I can to help my poor husband. Everything!"

The sudden throb of emotion in her voice moved both men. She raised her eyes to the lawyer's face, caressing eyes full of troubled appeal, and his own lost their sharpness. Fey looked down again at her hands and the thick gold wedding ring.

"Mr. Dillon forced his way back into our lives on Saint Valentine's night," she said. "We were giving a ball . . ."

She rehearsed the facts exactly as she had told them to

Rachel. The meetings in the park, her remorse at having allowed Terry to see Lucita, and his own encounter with the little girl and Miss Pringle. She told of the note she had sent him, explaining that she had still foolishly thought that an appeal from her might bring him to reason. All that she told was the strictest truth, and in the minds of her listeners there developed a picture of a suffering persecuted woman who had made brave efforts to handle a disagreeable situation without distressing a touchy husband.

Ewen saw that she had won the lawyer, who had been suspicious. Webster's chivalry was roused. More than chivalry, perhaps. For his questions now were softened by a protective tenderness, and once, when she leaned toward him, the fat small hand moved slowly on the desk, toward her arm.

She can't help it, thought Ewen, instantly denying anger at this atmosphere of sexual magnetism which did not include him. It's entirely unconscious, she's but appealing to him for help as a child would. At Webster's next remark, he realized that the lawyer was not so bemused as to forget the point at issue.

"It clarifies, dear Mrs. Tower—yes, it clarifies; but will it help Tower's defence—materially? That is what we must consider— If possible, we must spare you the—the embarrassment of having the divorce—the—ah—somewhat equivocal divorce, I'm afraid—become public."

"You can't!" cut in Ewen. "Dillon's identity must be brought out. It explains the blackmail. Mrs. Tower understands that."

Fey threw him a quick look, then her eyes returned to Webster's face. "Of course," she agreed. "It doesn't matter what the public thinks of me. We must save Simeon. And I have been very much to blame. I must share in the—the punishment." Her voice wavered as she finished and Ewen saw her hands clench on the grey gloves.

"Indeed, you are not to blame!" cried Webster warmly. "You were the innocent victim of two men. You may safely—trust me—to imbue—the jury with my own admiration and pity—for you."

Fey's hands unclenched. "Thank you," she said, and she gave Webster a smile in which he saw only a tremulous sweetness. Ewen, anxiously watching, saw more. He would not let himself doubt her; he had felt from the beginning her essential honesty, yet he was uneasy.

This she partly dispelled after they had left the lawyer's

office and were driving uptown to the Tombs. "All that I told him was the truth, Ewen," she said, breaking a long silence.

He answered with relief the implication. "But there was some further circumstance you did not tell?"

"It has no bearing. It concerns nobody now." She turned her head and gave him the same look of feminine appeal she had given Webster. Ewen put his hand over hers. "If you're sure of that, there's no reason to fret about it. It isn't good to fall into a bog of self-questioning and doubts. Even in a tragedy like this we must have common sense."

She looked down at his thin sensitive hand as it lay reassuringly over her gloved one. "I've always been very truthful," she said. "Simeon used to laugh at me. Even Doctor Rachel. We did have to tell some lies at the time of our marriage, but Simeon thought—" She stopped.

"To be sure," he said quickly. "It's but natural for a true woman to follow her husband's lead," and he smiled, adding on a lower, earnest note—"Dinna fash yoursel', Fey—"

She let out her breath in a long shaking sigh. "My father used to say that—" She swayed toward him, looking up into his face, and her lips moved in a whisper—"Ewen—I need you so—"

He made an inarticulate sound, and gathered her to him.

For them both a thousand lamps were lit. The wideness of enchanted seas flowed through the stuffy carriage. The April winds blew, and the two in the carriage, listening to the ecstatic song, felt themselves timeless and set free.

"My own Fey," he whispered—"we *will* go together. To Scotland. As soon as—" He kissed her shut eyelids. "Ah, my love—my love! You've suffered enough. It's nearly over—we can be together as the Lord meant it."

"Yes. Yes." She clung to him with a greater urgency. "We will go. It's not too late. This other—it isn't real. It doesn't touch me. Nothing has touched me until now. I can hide in your love until it's over."

His arms tightened. He held her exultantly and with defiance. "We will do everything we can—in justice, in decency. And then—whatever the outcome—you shall be free."

"Yes," she whispered again. "Free and forget—"

The rhythmic clop of the horse's hoofs diminished and stopped. The carriage drew up at the entrance of the Tombs. Neither of them was aware of the dingy pseudo-Egyptian façade. They mounted the narrow steps littered with droppings from the innumerable pigeons circling amongst the eaves or perched on the crude lotus capitals of the thick columns. They entered through the heavy iron door past the first guard, and then, as they had previously arranged, Ewen left Fey in the central hall, while he went off to interview the warden and obtain permission for the surprise visit to Simeon.

Fey, still moving in the timeless dream, was oblivious to the guards' curious stares, nor for a moment, after she had seated herself on a dirty wooden bench at the far side of the hall, was she aware of the barred wall near her. Behind the bars in shadow was the receiving pen, where newly admitted prisoners awaited allocation. They were quiet, as Fey sat down, gaping with an animal-like intensity. Little by little the whispers began again. The mass shifted. The stench of whisky and sour sweat and vomit assailed her.

She looked at them now, quickly, and from a great distance. They were disgusting, sub-human, a hydra-like beast joined into one body of filth and corruption.

She drew her skirts tight around her, and moved as far along the bench as possible.

Five minutes passed, and the prisoners, seeing that the guards were all busy at the other end of the hall, became noisier. There were muted guffaws, snatches of sing, hoarse bawdy comments on Fey. Her revulsion increased, and her loathing. And now the atmophere. stifled her. It is unendurable, she thought, and with this came its corollary, why should I endure it? I've done nothing. Her muscles tensed for escape. She felt them in her knees, her thighs, her stomach, stiffening propelling, urging her to rush through the iron door into the sunshine, back into the April wind. And she could not move. Her hands grew cold as the damp cement wall beside her, her breath came shallow and rapid and her chest constricted under the vicelike pressure of anticipation. Fear again! A paralysis of nameless fear as it had been during her illness.

In the pen an altercation had started. There were two voices, one accusatory and one apologetic and maudlin. Both were drunken. Of these two voices Fey had distinguished nothing, accompanied as they were by a dozen other noises, the distant shouting of the guards, the monotonous cooing of the pigeons outside, the flapping of a newspaper, the uneasy, disconnected sounds from the pen. And then a phrase, no louder than the rest, exploded in Fey's consciousness.

It was the lighter, whining voice. "Gawd," it said. "I wisht I could go back. Start over. I kin look back all right. But I can't go back."

The detonation shattered through her mind with the violence of physical agony. Her blood vessels pounded and a lightning pain filled them. Together her body and mind resisted, lashing out with denial. Then all pain eased. She became a void into which there seeped a bitter resignation. So it has come at last, she thought, I can no longer hide. But as yet there was no meaning. She leaned her head back against the wall and waited.

The prison faded and vanished, her consciousness gathered itself into a small flame, infinitely detached. From its steady centre she watched a scene unroll. She saw herself on the starlit hillside at Raton Pass, and the dark figure of Natanay outlined against the sky. She heard again the words to which she had not then listened. "Pobrecita—" and the melodious Spanish continued sadly, inflexibly: "A few are born for true greatness, and when these stubbornly deny the voice of the Spirit, it is their punishment that later they must look back and see the wrong turnings when they can no longer go back."

The Raton hillside shimmered and changed into a smaller, more familiar mountain which gave off a white light. Against this cold, relentless light scenes like living tableaux gleamed sharply and replaced each other in swift progression. Fey saw herself and Terry that first day on the plaza in Santa Fe, she saw them in Wootton's cabin. She saw the Arcadia Concert Hall and the first glimpse of Simeon. As she watched helplessly, the detachment lessened and a horrified intensity began to reach out toward her. She saw herself in Simeon's office and the proffering of the turquoise. She saw the interview with Pansy Miggs. The scenes accelerated and ran together through the Valentine Ball and Terry's return, the meetings in the park. Then there was an instant of blankness, and the final picture glided into place—the Turkish Room at Schultz's Hotel.

The white light was extinguished, there were no more scenes, but their full significance penetrated her consciousness with annihilating truth. *You are responsible, you!* All denials, all justification, had been wrenched away by that moment of vision, and she saw them naked at last—the swathed and secret purposes. It was she, primarily, who had been responsible for the elopement with Terry, and when that train of misborn consequences reached inevitable extinction, it was she who had initiated the new one with Simeon. When Terry returned, it had been she who held him and by carelessness and weakness impelled them all to the final tragedy.

At every step, every moment of choice, there had been warning to which she had been deaf. The other path had always been there.

I can't bear it! she cried. I'm not strong enough to bear it. But there was no pity. In the interior darkness the realization continued. She saw that she must accept the moral onus for Pansy's death, for Terry's—and so nearly for Simeon's. Heavy and solid as granite she saw them embedded in her soul, the motives which she had never turned to examine—the stubborn materialistic self-seeking, the lust, and—largest and most menacing of all—the continual compromise with hypocrisy.

It's not fair! she cried to the accuser. The others were to blame, too. The guilt is not all mine. And the accuser answered, You are not asked to be responsible for more than your share. But your guilt is greater because your strength was greater. And you were partly aware. They were not.

She listened and knew at last. She bowed her head and the desolate waters of humility flowed through her soul.

She sat there motionless, on the visitors' bench in the Tombs, and the prisoners forgot about her. Their four-o'clock supper had arrived. A tin bucket of coffee with a dipper—loaves of bread. They fell upon them gluttonously and became quiet.

Fey raised her head and gazed toward them. She got up and walked to the bars. They looked up from their food, some resentful, some amorously inviting. But even the stupidest of them grew silent as she stood there. Hydra-headed beast, yes, but the body is not corruption. The single heart that beats through them is mine, too. One heart for us all, and its life-blood is charity.

After a moment she walked away, back to the bench, and the little man whose words had been the instrument of realization was the last to munch his bread again.

"Gawd!" he said plaintively, "that one's got the saddest face I ever seed in my born days. What call's *she* got to look so sad?"

Nobody answered him.

As Fey reached the bench, Ewen hurried up. "I had quite an argument, but finally convinced— Fey! what is it? You look ill."

"I'm all right. Is that the pass?" she added, as he started to lead the way toward the stairs. "No, wait for me, please. I must go alone."

He watched anxiously while she mounted the winding iron stairs.

At the second tier she presented her pass to the guard, who looked dubious. "He won't see no one, that Tower. Ornery cuss."

"Yes. I know. Kindly show me to the cell."

The guard got off his stool with involuntary alacrity. Fey followed him down the open corridor past other cells and other visitors. The four tiers of cell blocks were built around a narrow enclosed quadrangle, and lit from the roof by inadequate skylights. Above each barred cell door hung a little slate with the prisoner's name and number inscribed on it in chalk.

They reached the far end of "Murderers' Row" and cell Number 6. Simeon in trousers and shirt was lying as he usually was on the cot. He showed no interest in the sound of the guard's key in the lock. "Leddy to see you, now be'ave yourself," said the guard. He swung the bars open.

Simeon sat up, and looked at Fey. His dull expression changed. It became the face of her premonition on the Christmas Eve so long ago—haggard, defeated, and the bleared eyes staring at her with an accusing hatred. "Get out!" he said, lying down. "I never want to see you again."

"I told you, mum," said the guard. "Carn't do nothing with 'im."

"Leave us alone," Fey opened her pocketbook.

"I'll give you ten minutes," he growled. "Watch yourself. He's a bad 'un." The barred gate clanged shut.

She stood at the end of the little cell, looking down at Simeon. He had turned his face to the wall, and, despite the new grey in his hair, there was a childishness in his crouched position. And he had grown so thin. Beneath his shirt she could see the angle of his shoulder-blades.

She walked to the cot and knelt down beside it. She stretched out her arms and pulled his stiff body wordlessly against her. For an instant she felt the resistance give, then he pushed her violently away. "Get out! I told you to get out!"

"Simeon, look at me!" she cried. At first he would not, and then he slowly, compulsively obeyed. And she knew. "Oh, my dear," she whispered. "Forgive me."

He drew a harsh breath and an ugly line thinned his mouth. In his eyes she saw the look which she had once cured, but stripped now of all defence.

"Get out!" he repeated. "Let me alone."

Panic caught her. There was death in his face. Desire for death weighted the stagnant cell. She fought against it with the blunted weapons of terror and despair and knew that they could not conquer.

Then she saw his hands. They were gripped on a fold of the prison blanket, but as she looked at them, they trembled. Her panic vanished like night in a flood of protective love. Love such as she had never felt, impersonal force, freed from self and needing no outward response to augment its steady glow. And while she knelt beside the cot, as motionless as he was, the long forgotten certainty came back to her. The awareness, and the first shimmer of the annunciatory light. On the prison blanket near his hands, a scene began to form. Not the retrospective vision of the past which had come to her below in the hall, but the true sight which she used to have.

She saw a dingy courtroom crowded with faces, and her own amongst them, set apart—alone. And she saw herself speaking. The scene faded, and she knew what she must do.

"Simeon," she said to his averted head, "you must believe two things. I will never leave you until death parts us. And I'm going by means of the truth to save you, whether you wish it or not."

Her voice pierced for an instant through the black sheath which encased him. The tremor moved from his hands and shook his whole body, then it was controlled. "I prefer the gallows," he said.

Tears blinded her, but she rose and sat on the cot beside him. She placed her hand on his, holding it firmly, giving him of her strength.

He did not speak again, but he sat beside her on the cot until the guard returned and ordered her out.

She went back along the cell block and down the winding stairs to where Ewen waited in the dark hall by the head guard's desk. As silently as they had come in, they left the Tombs, but Ewen knew the profound change in her. My love has gone from me, he thought. And while they waited on the kerb for a cab, he did not so much as touch her arm.

A hackney drew up, and as they entered, he started to give the driver the address of the brick cottage. She stopped him. "No, Ewen. Go back to Thaddeus Webster's. I must see him again."

He changed the address and got in beside her. She lay with her head against the cushions. There were bistre shadows beneath her eyes, but their grey beauty shone with a calm translucence.

"Will you tell me, Fey?" he asked at last.

She turned her head wearily on the cushions. "Back there in the prison I saw myself as I am. And I saw what I must do. It's a hard, hard thing."

He frowned, wanting to refute, to tell her that she was over-emotional, in a strained state, and must distrust whatever revelation she might have experienced. He could not speak.

They were silent as the cab re-traversed the way they had come so short a time ago. They had turned off Broad Street on to William before Ewen spoke again.

"What are you going to say to Webster, Fey?"

She touched his arm as though to comfort him, but she answered instantly. "I am going to tell him that I committed adultery with Terry, that Simeon knew it. And I am going to tell him that I insist upon testifying in my husband's defence."

CHAPTER

23

AFTER that second visit to Thaddeus Webster's office, Fey and Ewen never again discussed the case. Nor did Rachel, after she understood and had conquered her first protective impulse to dissuade Fey. Her strict ethical code, which she would never have relaxed for herself, was weakened by affection, and she protested against the public pillorying which would make of Fey an outcast for ever. "Dear child— There must be another way—"

"There is no other way," answered Fey. "I see clear at last, and I know what must be done, now and afterward—"

"Does thee mean thee knows what's coming?" Rachel was startled and hesitant.

"Some things I know. The pattern."

How she has changed! thought Rachel, looking at the thin calm face. It held a radiance, the subtle aura of mastery and steady purpose. Strong will there had always been, but now it was outgoing—purged of self-interest. Rachel recognized the integration and the strength she had longed to see in Fey nine years ago. But not like this, she thought sadly. Why did it have to come like this?

She never questioned Fey again. And she channelled her

efforts as they all did toward enduring as normally as possible the weeks of waiting. With a helpless pity she watched Ewen and Fey, who loved each other, dedicate themselves to the salvation of the obstacle which stood between them. She knew through Ewen that Simeon's health was poor, that he had developed a racking cough, and the prison doctor suspected consumption. Rachel was guilty of hoping that an all-merciful Providence might yet vouchsafe compromise—and release.

Fey knew better, and on a June evening, when Ewen came, she took the step for which she had been nerving herself little by little.

He had been out to the brick cottage almost every day and by tacit consent they had stayed near Rachel, or they had kept Lucita with them. They had not touched each other; there had been no word of love since the day they had visited the Tombs.

On this June evening, at the sound of the hoofs in the lane, Fey came out of the cottage alone to meet him. He watched her come down the steps and so close now was their understanding of each other that he knew what she was going to say.

The blue challie work-dress hung on her loosely; she had recovered no weight, and the rounded youthful bloom was gone. She had become a grave woman. But there was a new beauty —of sadness, of sweetness and austerity mingled. And the light within seemed to burn through her flesh. The lover in him resented her growing spiritual detachment, while his own spirit responded to hers with sympathy and an ever deeper love.

"Let's sit on the rocks awhile," she said. "It's a beautiful evening."

He followed her down the path to the water. It had been well worn by Lucita and it led them to the small ridge, tufted with sea-gull down, which the child called her castle. They sat down together and watched the river slip by. The setting sun warmed their backs and reddened the windows across the water on the Brooklyn shore.

He waited quietly and after a while she spoke. "I want you to go back to Scotland, Ewen."

He expelled his breath, picked up one of the gull feathers and smoothed it over his tweed-covered knee. "I want to be with you when the trial comes."

She shook her head. "It's better not." She leaned forward, resting her forehead on her hand. "We both know what's in our hearts."

He clenched his fingers around the feather, then released it.

It floated to the pebbles by their feet. "I cannot leave you, Fey. We belong to each other." With anger he heard himself use these threadbare words, so tattered in meaning by a thousand trivial usages.

"Yes," she said. "We will never be truly mated, nor could be with anyone else. And you must suffer, as I've made all those near to me suffer."

He drew back, staring at her. "That's morbid! That's not true! Just because you yielded once to your former husband—"

Fey, turning, silenced him, her lucent grey eyes seeking his face with a yearning sadness. "That was only a part of the whole— Dear love," she added softly, "believe me. There is only one way now."

His mouth tightened and he stared at the eddying water. Renunciation, atonement. Bitter cold words. Empty words, fitting only to mewling preachers! Male fury spurted suddenly through him. He wanted to beat her, to subdue her, and to claim her there on the rocks in the setting sun.

"Ah, Ewen," she said, watching his face and smiling a little, "I'd give myself to you if that would help us. It wouldn't. And we're so close that you know it as well as I."

The shining windows across the river darkened. Dusk sifted down over the rooftops. High above the church spires the evening star flickered with a chill, indifferent light. Together they looked up at it, and Ewen said, "What will you do, Fey— afterward?"

She answered him slowly, searching to explain to herself, as well as him, the certainties which had come to her. "If we could go back—both of us to that morning ten years ago in Santa Fe—if I had gone with Doctor Rachel to the Carys' that Sunday—I had two chances, and I would not listen or see. I chose wrong. Now there is no return. Only forward—stumbling as best I can under the burdens I made myself."

She hesitated, and he remained silent, but he reached for her hand and held it gently.

"There is one step I can retrace," she went on after a moment. "Once long ago, I went in to Saint Patrick's Cathedral— I went there again last week, I found a priest. He was wise and kind. I could talk to him. I'm going back to my Church, Ewen."

"It will bring you comfort?"

She considered this, her brooding eyes on the dark river before them. "Comfort—I don't know. Maybe not the comfort Doctor Rachel gets from her faith, or the power a Navajo shaman got from his. *He* said, the Navajo, 'There are many trails up the mountain, but in time they all get to the top.' I only know what is the right trail for me."

Ewen accepted this sympathetically, though for him it had no emotional significance. He believed in God, and for his temperament, as for Fey's, the mystical approach was congenial, but since maturity, and escape from the narrow dogma of the Kirk, he had thought little about religion. Now he reverted mentally to the problem of her material future, which she had not clarified, and his troubled love made him fearful that she was unable to grasp it. He had repeatedly tried to foresee the result of the trial. Webster was now fairly confident of reducing the verdict to manslaughter, with the help of Fey's testimony. This would mean for Tower three to five years in Sing Sing at best. Webster refused to be more optimistic than that.

And it seemed now that Fey might be certain of a tiny income, when the bankruptcy proceedings should be terminated. Ewen had already told her of his wish to supplement this as much as he could, and been refused.

He moved suddenly—relinquishing her hand and crying passionately, "How *can* I leave you, Fey—and I'm speaking now as your kinsman, not your lover—when every bit of the future is so uncertain? You cannot dree it alone!"

"I can," she said, very low. "I'll have Doctor Rachel. And Lucita."

A shadow crossed her face. The barrier between herself and her child had not been lowered.

"I've a plan, Ewen. I can't talk of it yet." She sighed, listening to the faint chime of the hour from the church across the river. Even to Ewen she could not describe the growing sense of dedication which had come to her. The sense of Self overflowing at last the rigid channels of personal love to merge with the infinite ocean which touched all shores at once. She was not yet ready to define to anyone the concrete direction which she knew the dedication would take. She told him only the first step. "But I'll stay with Doctor Rachel until the trial. I'm going to work in the Infirmary for a while."

"Fey—you mustn't!" he cried. " 'Tis no work for you. You're not strong enough."

She made a small sound in her throat and gave him a smile full of tenderness. "Hush, ma braw laddie," she said. "Dinna fash yoursel' about me"—and with the saying of it her smile died and tears stung her eyes. Full circle, she thought, and this is the end. They looked at each other through the twilight.

"You'll go back to Scotland, Ewen."

He bowed his head. A small breeze whispered down the river. The lights upstream on Blackwell's Island glimmered on like fireflies. And Fey spoke again. "You'll get married, Ewen. I want you to."

"How can you—" he said bitterly, turning from her.

"You will," she continued quietly. "To Rose, I think. Who is Rose?"

He started, astonished out of his bitterness. "Rose? I know only one Rose, a lass in Inveraray. She's nothing to me. What in the world made you think—?"

Fey nodded. "I saw the name clear. She's near you in thought. It's come back—the 'sight,' " she added, half to herself.

He frowned—accepting that and angrily dismissing it. "Fey, how can you believe that I could replace you—?"

She stood up, and held out her hands to him. "I don't. I know that for neither of us can there be anything like this. But Ewen, there are many kinds of love—"

They stood silent on the rocks looking into each other's eyes. They turned together and walked up the shadowy path toward the lights of the cottage.

Ewen sailed the next week for Scotland, and Rachel, Fey, and Lucita left the little brick cottage by the river for a house on Stuyvesant Square near both Infirmaries—the old outgrown one on Second Avenue and the new one at 5 Livingston Place. Rachel resumed her work, but not as resident physician. There was a young graduate ready to fill her place, and Rachel decided that the time had come for a partial break. She became consultant for the Infirmary, she took on some of the home visiting work, and she started to handle a little private practice. And throughout the summer months Fey accompanied her on most of her rounds, assisting, watching, learning.

It was because of Fey that Rachel had made the change in her life. Fey—and Lucita. Both these women who loved the child knew that there was a hidden festering sore to be healed, though now the outward shape of Lucita's life was more normal than it had ever been. An ex-patient of Rachel's, a sweet-tempered German girl, had been hired to look after her while Fey and Rachel were out, and though Lucita no longer had the river at her front door, she had the pleasant Square, shaded by elms and ailanthuses, where she met the children of the neighbourhood, and in a week was as proficient at hop-scotch and jump-rope as any of them.

It was on a pleasant evening near the end of August that Lucita's trouble came to a head. At seven o'clock, Fey and Rachel were sitting in the cool front parlour relaxing after a hard day. Supper was finished and the little German girl could be heard carolling "Ach du lieber Augustine," while she clashed the dishes in the basement kitchen. Lucita had pleaded for one more romp in the Square, before going to bed. The two women listened for a while to the babble of happy childish voices from outside and smiled at each other.

Rachel picked up the evening paper, stifled a yawn, and laid it down again. "Early bed for us both, I should think," she observed to Fey. "It's been a strenuous day, but we've pulled Maria Sacrone through the worst."

Fey who was mending a tear in one of Lucita's pinafores, laid down her needle. "You mean *you* have. I only followed directions."

"Thee underrates thyself, Fey. Does thee not know how the patients love and trust thee?"

Fey gave her an affectionate smile and drew nearer to the lamp, bending again over the pinafore. Rachel, unable to be idle, reached for the wicker mending basket and pulled out a sock and china darning egg.

"At first," she continued, "I thought thee unwise to want to go back to the West, but now I think thee's right. Nobody could do the work there as well as thee, and here there are many—and for *him* it would be best, too."

The front door was open to catch the evening breeze, and neither of them had heard light footsteps on the hall carpet.

Rachel adjusted her glasses and her needle wove across the hole with sharp, swift strokes. "I'll miss thee and Lucy," she said quietly.

Fey bent her head lower over her work. Once she would have rushed to Rachel, impulsively expressing her love and gratitude. Now there was no need for that, they understood each other, and Fey had learned the value of a serene control more expressive than impulse.

Rachel finished the darn and began on another sock. "How was thy husband today?" she asked, after a moment. She always asked this after Fey had made one of her visits to the Tombs in case Fey wished for the release of speech. Usually Fey did not. She was undergoing the twin disciplines of re-

302

adjustment and suspense, best endured in inner stillness. To-night she answered more fully.

"He's really better. The prison doctor has had him out in the yard for exercise. He acted almost glad to see me this after-noon. He never says much to me, and if I stay long, he drops back to that dreadful black brooding, but this time was more normal."

"Good," said Rachel heartily, and meant it. She had con-quered the weakness which had made her hope for Simeon's death as an easy solution. She knew that life seldom allowed its knots to be untied easily and magically. They must be un-ravelled bit by bit in gallantry and faith, as Fey was doing.

Fey folded up the pinafore and gazed down at the blue-and-white checks. "I told Simeon the trial was finally set for September tenth."

"What did he say?" Rachel waited.

"Nothing. His eyes took on that blind, wary look. Once, when I was little, I went to the mountains with the Torres boys. They had trapped a cougar. I remember its eyes as it glared up at us from the pit, before Domingo shot it." She paused, forcing herself from painful remembrance. She had cried over the cougar, and the Torres children had jeered at her.

"I told Simeon, too, that I was going to testify. He said, 'I can't stop you,' in that harsh, sneering voice. But underneath I feel him clinging to me. After I left, I turned suddenly, and his face was pressed against the bars, watching me go."

Fey's mouth quivered, she pushed her chair back, clenching her hands. "He's lost everything he wanted so desperately—money, position, power—and he thinks he's lost me. But he hasn't—he hasn't!"

Rachel swallowed. She took off her glasses, wiped them, and put them on again briskly. The grandfather clock on the land-ing struck the half-hour.

"We must call Lucy. It's her bedtime," said Rachel, and then they both heard a rustle in the hall, and running footsteps on the stairs.

The two women looked at each other, dismayed. "I didn't hear her come in," whispered Fey. They had been so careful to keep everything from the child, all newspapers, all reference to Simeon.

Fey got up. "I'll go to her." Rachel nodded.

At the top of the stairs, Fey listened, and heard the sound she had dreaded. Stifled, racking sobs. She opened Lucita's door. The child was lying on the bed in the darkness, her face buried in the pillow. She started when she heard her mother's step, pulled herself into a defensive little ball on the far edge of the bed, still hiding her face.

Fey walked to the gas bracket, lit it and turned the flame low. She went to the bed and sat down beside the crouching child. "What is it, darling?" she said evenly.

The little girl's shoulders quivered. She shook her head, and, as Fey touched the tousled curls, she felt a shrinking. She took back her hand.

"Tell me, Lucita. Tell me the truth. There's nothing you could say would make me love you less. You must never be afraid of anything. Tell me the truth."

Still there was no answer. Fey got up from the bed.

"Shall I call Aunt Rachel, dear?"

"Yes. Yes," whispered the child. Fey went to the head of the stairs and came back. When Rachel stood by the door, Lucita began to speak, incoherent, the words tumbling upon each other—"I heard what you said, Mama. You're going some place—with him. I hate him. I hate him. He killed my Papa. I know where he is—he's in *prison*." Her voice rose hysterically.

"Hush!" said Rachel. She came over to the bed beside them. "Thee's only a little girl, Lucy. Thee cannot understand. Now control thyself, and we'll listen."

The child slowly obeyed. She looked at the strong, kind face and her body relaxed. She turned to her mother. "Mama—I do love you, I do—but I don't want to go any place. I want to stay here with Aunt Rachel. Please let me stay with her always—please, please—"

Fey gathered the little body close against her breast. And she looked up into the face of her friend. My child loves her better than me! A bitter jealousy twisted through her heart. Not this, too, she cried—I can't do this, too. She held the child tighter and turned on the bed, shutting out Rachel's compassionate eyes.

The curly golden head lay trustingly against her breast as it had done in babyhood, but as Fey bent her lips to it, she heard the muffled, unchildish sound. She closed her eyes and inexorable pictures began to form in her mind. A litle girl freed from all shadow, from the repression of hostility, spared the necessity of continual choice. A little girl secure in a normal childhood, protected always by steady wisdom and serene affection. And for Rachel, too, whose sacrifice and selflessness asked nothing in return—the greatest gift, the recompense. The gift of a happy love to both of them. *But what about me?* It seared

through her again, shrivelling her. Madre de Dios! help me—
The invocation used so often in triviality, and never truly
answered. Until now.

She raised her head from the child and looked up at the still
face beside the bed.

"Will you?" she whispered.

Rachel bent slowly and kissed her. "Yes, dear, with God's
help. And I believe it's best."

CHAPTER

24

THE case of the people against Simeon Tower came to trial in
September in the brownstone courthouse on Chambers Street.
The summer recess had delayed it and postponements by the
district attorney, Charles Norton, who suspected the line that
the defence might take, but had no proof. The secret of Terence
Dillon's identity had been kept. The canny prosecution had
been able to trace Dillon no farther than embarkation in
Mexico; from that point back it was hopeless.

Mr. Norton, in his opening address, slid over this very
cleverly. He implied that knowledge of the victim was irre-
levant. Whether Dillon was linked with Tower's remote—and
unsavoury—past, or whether he had recently appeared, possessed somehow of an awkward secret, made no difference.
There had been murder committed, a foul and cowardly
murder of an unarmed man, and one undoubtedly premedi-
tated—witness the loaded pistol in the library desk drawer.
Perhaps there had been some suggestion of blackmail—he was
well aware that Mr. Webster, his capable opponent, was going
to stress the alleged blackmail. He did not deny that there
might have been extortion of a sort, though even this rested
upon the defendant's own word and an ambiguous little paper,
belatedly produced and allegedly signed by the victim. Mr.
Norton would for the moment waive the doubt that it was
signed by the victim at all; if necessary he would produce two
handwriting experts who doubted that the signature was
authentic after comparison with Dillon's signature in the Hotel
Saint Nicholas's register. But concede for the present the possibility of blackmail, where then did this lead us?

Straight to the defendant's own black and guilty character. What sort of secret, what secret so ghastly, so incredibly shameful, would seem worth a man's life to hide?

Ah—he did not suggest, averred Mr. Norton, carefully watching the jury, that the secret might be merely concealment of humble parents. That would be too monstrous for belief. And yet—Simeon Tower *had* concealed his parentage, as Mr. Van Vrandt and Mr. Bull would testify. And here Mr. Norton drew a heartrending picture of the old folks, waiting, hoping, pathetically submissive to the unnatural callousness of a dastardly son. No, repeated Norton, he did not suggest that that was the secret; he suggested a far more sinister probability. And then the jury were bombarded with phrases which awakened unpleasant connotations in every one of them, despite Thaddeus Webster's initial care in examining the talesman. For public opinion, so long apathetic, had now hardened into disgust and fear of the corruption which had for so long exploited the people.

"Tweed Ring," "Erie War," " Fraudulent oppression of the poor," "Barefaced plunder and pillage," "Our fair democracy stabbed, bleeding, writhing in anguish," "Ill-gotten wealth wrung from the souls of the poor"—all these produced the desired effect without the necessity for specific proof. And the defence could not deny Simeon's association with Tweed.

This, then, was the gist of the prosecution, and all through the week from Monday, September tenth, Norton subtly and successfully built up a damning case. When the prosecution rested and Court adjourned on Friday afternoon, Norton was inwardly jubilant. The jury had glared at the prisoner with undisguised loathing which Tower's attitude did nothing to mitigate.

Day after day he was hustled into the prison van at the Tombs, carried to the courthouse, and shoved into the dock, where he fixed his sullen eyes either on the courtroom window or the floor, and showed no emotion at all except in his mouth, which was twisted into a light, perpetual sneer. He presented the classic embodiment of the public's conception of a typical murderer. An idea seldom coinciding with fact, as Norton well knew, who had prosecuted many gentle, ingenuous-looking slayers. But Tower's behaviour was undoubtedly helping the prosecution. Too, Thaddeus Webster had been astonishingly unaggressive. Time after time he had waived cross-examination, to sit on—sluggish and impassive as behemoth—in the outsize chair which had been provided for him. That he had a surprise up his sleeve, Norton could not doubt, but on that Friday night he was certain of being able to handle it.

On the Monday morning, when Court again convened, Norton, upon looking over the witness bench, saw with dismay that which he had nevertheless half-expected. The presence of a small, pale woman attractively dressed in grey. Mrs. Tower! There was sensation also at the press table, and a buzz of murmurs. The pencils hissed across pages.

Thaddeus Webster lumbered to his feet at last and addressed the Court in the sighing voice, so soft and unassertive that the jurors, frowning, had to strain forward to hear.

"The worthy district attorney," said Webster, with a sadness, a commiseration, which brought the furious colour to Norton's face, "has moved us all with his oratory—his truly masterly line of attack. Alas-s, he has not—had access to the facts." There was a pause. Everybody waited. Webster continued, a trifle louder. "Before I present those facts—there is a point—only one point raised by the prosecution—which I must clarify for you— I refer to the matter of the loaded pistol."

Here he produced Stone, the Tower butler, who testified that in the two years that he had been in the Tower employ there had always been a loaded revolver in the library drawer, on account of the gem collection. He went on to say that in his opinion gentlemen always kept a loaded firearm about the house, because of burglars, was promptly shut up by Norton and the Judge, and this matter of opinion stricken from the record, but it had made its point.

Norton jumped in and tried to shake this testimony; he went as far as he dared in hinting that Stone was untrustworthy, that he had been bribed.

Webster sighed and called the little gunsmith who had sold the revolver to Mr. Tower five years ago.

Norton was beaten for the moment. He settled down again.

Thaddeus Webster waited until everyone had resumed his seat, and the courtroom grew still. He stretched his small fat hand toward the district attorney. "Mr. Norton has a brilliant creative imagination—to which I pay tribute—I'm sure we all do—"

Norton moved and the Judge scowled. Webster continued gently. "He has provided the defendant with several supposititious motives—but I give you the true one—through the mouth of one who alone is qualified to tell it—Mrs. Simeon Tower."

Fey stood up. She put her pocketbook on the bench beside Rachel whose brisk murmur of encouragement she did not

307

hear. She walked steadily to the witness stand, and while the clerk administered the oath, she looked down at her hand as it lay on the Bible. The Bible reminded her by its size and shape of the Bible from which her father had taught her to read. She considered this coincidence with detachment while she answered the routine questions as to her name and address.

A hundred pairs of eyes were fixed on her, and none of them were indifferent. The least emotion a greedy curiosity, hostility from Norton, encouragement from Webster and Rachel; and Simeon, at whom nobody looked, had at last changed his attitude. He had twisted in the dock, so as not to see her, and bowing his head had covered his face with his hand.

"Now, Mrs. Tower—" said Webster.

She nodded slightly and her mouth moved in a peculiar smile, which some of the papers later described as brazen and some as touching.

Fey sat down, fixed her gaze on the back wall of the courtroom and began clearly and slowly—"Ten years ago in a mountain cabin on the top of the pass between New Mexico Territory and Colorado, I—"

Norton jumped to his feet in violent objection, demanding that the witness present facts and not flowery biography.

Webster moved across his path. "I beg that the Court will permit this witness to tell her story in her own way. Believe me, it is pertinent."

The Judge hesitated, nodded, and said, "Overruled." Norton, perforce subsiding, saw that he had lost ground. In that little interval, during which Mrs. Tower waited as for the bickering of foolish children to subside, she seemed to have grown in stature. She continued in the same clear voice—"Ten years ago, I was married to Xavier Terence Dillon, the man whom my husband shot."

She waited again, while the Judge rapped and the attendants quelled the explosion of murmurs.

"It was not a good marriage, either for him or me, nor a true marriage, since we were both Catholics. It was not even dignified by real love. Though I pretended to myself that it was."

Norton half-rose and sat down again, abashed by a sudden recognition of a quality which courtroom experience had long ago banished from his expectation. "This woman is really trying to tell the truth . . ."

Fey continued tersely and without self-pity to speak of

Terry's desertion. "And being the sort of man he was and I knew he was, that was inevitable."

She told of her job as a singing waiter-girl at the Arcadia Concert Saloon, and again there was a sensation. "Perhaps you will not believe that in such a place I kept my body untouched," she said, in the same remote manner. "I did, however, not from a virtuous ideal, but from pride."

It was here that she had first seen Simeon Tower, "though he did not know it, and would never have married me had he known. I was attracted to him at first because he represented power. I did not clearly see it then, but I wished for power and a kind of revenge more than anything in the world. I came to love him later, for he loved me and he was so good to"—for the first time she hesitated, but went on at once—"to my little girl."

She went on to tell of the deceptions surrounding her divorce, her reappearance as Mrs. Dawson, and the two religious marriages.

This is appalling, thought Norton, incredible—but he leaned forward, breathless like everyone else.

"We built, little by little, a good marriage, Simeon and I, we understood each other—and trusted. Perhaps our aims—our ambitions—were wrong, but we shared them— Then Terence Dillon came back."

She moistened her lips, and the attendant handed her a glass of water which she drank, while the silent courtroom waited.

Fey rehearsed yet again the story of Terry's reappearance at the Valentine Ball, of her interview with him there and her subsequent meetings in the park, but now every intonation and every word she used coloured the bald facts with their true emotion. It was she who had kept him in New York, while begging him to leave, and it was she who had—no matter how unconsciously—given him the first idea of blackmail.

"I knew that there was danger somewhere, I knew what sort of man he was or could be," said Fey, "but I went on, anyway; talking too much, indulging myself in the luxury of confession —to the wrong person. Against my conscience. Against"—she stopped, added on a lower note, "against all loyalty."

The jurors looked at each other, puzzled, and Norton's spirits rose. This sort of stuff was too tenuous, much too subtle, to influence that body of twelve practical business men. He crossed his legs and, though he sent Fey a look of reluctant admiration, he followed it by one for Webster—of malicious amusement. If this was all the defence the fellow had been able to rig up—the soul-searchings of a woman quite naturally trying to save her husband and therefore, like all good women in such cases, willing to share moral blame! A fine pathetic picture, no doubt, but it wouldn't soften the verdict. He settled down complacently for the rest of the testimony.

And Fey's next words galvanized him.

"Then on the twenty-second of February I sent Terry a note, asking him to meet me again in the park. I pretended to myself that I wanted only to persuade him to leave New York. That was not my real reason.

"When I met him that last afternoon in the park, I knew what would happen. I wanted it to happen. But I pretended to myself that I didn't. To *myself*," she repeated. "That was the greatest sin. Do you understand that?"

They did not. They stared at this small pale woman who did not look at them, and it was as though she had erected a barrier around the witness stand; from its protection only her voice, cool and remote, reached over to them.

And as she continued her testimony, giving both fact and emotion in the same level tone, the jurors' puzzled expectancy shifted to astonishment and then to horrified recoil.

She spared herself nothing. The ride to Schultz's Hotel, the dingy lasciviousness of the Turkish Room, her own desire and subsequent disillusionment. Before they had had time to adjust to this, she added monstrous words—"I don't believe that adultery in itself is always bad, sometimes a great love must be bigger than moral law. I had not that excuse, but I pretended again. I told myself that what had happened was unimportant, even justified—" She stopped. For a second her face dissolved, her eyes slid to the left toward the dock where the motionless figure sat hunched against the railing. "I was wrong," she said, and bowed her head.

The courtroom was locked in an appalled silence, then motion swept over them. Webster lumbered forward to the witness stand and, holding out his hand, helped her down. "Splendid," he whispered, but Fey did not hear him.

Norton was trying frantically to rearrange his attack, while every juror and even the old Judge stared at Fey with the some hostility which they had previously given to the prisoner.

She had invoked shibboleths far stronger than Norton had. Even "Ill-gotten wealth" and "Fraudulent oppression of the poor" were pale beside the "Chastity of women" and "The Unwritten Law." For the next house Norton followed the only

310

course left to him. The attempt to prove that Fey's adultery was a fabrication, invented to save her husband.

Whereupon Webster called two witnesses. Schultz, the hotel proprietor, and Cadwallader, the cabdriver, and Norton knew that now it was hopeless.

The jury fidgeted during his summation, hardly listening to him, and the Judge's charge, verbally impartial, nevertheless quivered in every sentence with sympathy for the prisoner. The Judge himself had a young wife, and a fervent personal interest in the sanctity of the home.

The jury were out for an hour. At five o'clock they returned. And they acquitted Simeon Tower.

He stood up for the verdict, supported by the two guards, and for the first minutes of subsequent pandemonium it was not observed that, though the wooden gate had been swung open, he continued to sit in the dock, his face shielded by his hand.

All interest was concentrated upon Mrs. Tower, who had been immediately surrounded by shouting, gesticulating reporters, though the massive figure of Webster and a tall elderly woman in brown both tried to shield her.

She did not, however, need protection. She looked at the dock and then at the avid, mouthing faces which barred her way. She drew herself up, and her grey eyes gave out a power so icy and compelling that the startled reporters were silenced. "You will kindly let me pass," she said.

They fell back—watching.

She walked through the enclosure to the dock, where she put her hand on the bowed shoulders. "Come, my husband," she said, in a voice gentle, but so clear that the suddenly quiet courtroom heard.

Simeon Tower got up. He did not look at her. Yet, as she slipped her arm under his, it seemed that he leaned against her. They moved together down the long courtroom to the door.

EPILOGUE

In the last quarter of the nineteenth century, Santa Fe had not yet been discovered by tourists or Eastern artists. And the residential beauties of the Barrio Analco across the river had as yet attracted no Anglos.

Its physical appearance had changed little in fifty years. The poor still lived in their constantly crumbling adobes near the walls of San Miguel's Chapel, and the ancient Cañon Road still led north into the high mountains until at last it narrowed and became the old Indian trail to Taos. The Analco dwellers changed sometimes. During the 'seventies many, like the Torres family, left for Las Vegas and Cimarron, attracted by high wages from the advancing railroad. And sometimes there was bad sickness which killed others, like La Gertrudis and her Manuel. The houses did not stay empty long. There were always many villagers from the districts beyond the mountains who were eager to move near the capital.

South of the Cañon Road, near the foot of Atalaya Peak, there stood an isolated four-roomed adobe house, its rose-tinged mud walls indistinguishable at a little distance from the reddish piñon-tufted earth of the hills behind it. The Anglos across the river in the town knew nothing of this house's inhabitants, neither did the rico Spanish families. To the others —the Mexican people and the Indians—the house was known and beloved as far north as Santa Cruz and Truchas, as far south as Galisteo, and sometimes the piercing shriek of ungreased axles heralded the arrival of an ox-drawn carreta from distant Jemez or Mora.

At first they called this house La Casa de la Bruja, but when calling the woman who lived there a witch, they stripped the term of all opprobrium or fear. It was simply an affectionate nickname. They did not know her real name, and they were not curious. They knew only that she understood their speech and their ways, and that sometimes, when one of them became involved with some inexplicable ruling or restriction imposed by the Anglos, she could understand that, too, and make it clear to them. They came to her for things like that because she had wisdom and patience, but usually they came to her to be healed. She had a healing power that came from God. They knew it came from God because, quite a while after she first arrived and turned the back room of her house into a resting-place for the sick, a woman from the Analco, María Gonzalez, had become frightened at seeing her sick baby stripped naked, scrubbed all over with warm water and Anglo soap, and then at seeing a little knife plunged into the angry red boil on the baby's buttocks. María had seized her child and run all the way to Padre Antonio at the Cathedral.

The padre had listened very carefully to María's story and then had himself gone to visit the house by Atalaya. Quite a crowd had followed him anxiously. He had stayed inside a long time talking to La Bruja. Several people had looked through the window and seen the padre examining, one after the other, the medicine chest, some large books, and the three clean-sheeted mattresses which lay in the room for the sick.

It was during that visit of the padre that many of the people first realized that there was another inhabitant in the house, a small old man who coughed a great deal and lay on an Anglo bed high up from the floor in full sunlight from a southern window. They were too polite to stare at him as they circled the house to watch what the padre was doing, but when he saw them he turned his face to the wall with an expression of anger.

At last the padre came out of the house and smiled at the little crowd which waited for his verdict. "She is a good woman," he said solemnly. "She wants only to help you and start a clinic for you such as the Americans have back in the States. You may trust her. And she is one of us," he added. "This is her home."

They did not understand that very well, but they were re-lieved to know that her healing power came from God. The padre, too, was relieved. His people would not go to the few available American doctors, nor, unless they were dying and too weak to resist, would they go to the hospital where the Sisters of Charity were already overworked.

He had not, then, asked many questions of this strange señora. He knew only that she had been born here and had now come back with an invalid husband whom she tended with unvarying gentleness and skill. She had much medical know-ledge and she had an almost miraculous intuition as to what ailed the sick bodies or souls which came to her. As time went on, this power grew and they began to regard her with

313

semi-superstitious reverence. They no longer called her La Bruja, but now they spoke of her as La Santa instead. There was nothing remarkable about her. She was small and thin, her hair streaked with white, but people remembered her eyes. They were calm and grey and infinitely wise. They made you feel that, though you could hide nothing from them, neither would they ever be shocked or repelled by any secret they might read. Many thought she got her strength from the lovely image of the Virgin of Guadalupe which she kept in a niche by the hearth.

Once in a while Indians came to her from the near-by pueblos, and they thought differently, though they never discussed it. They thought that her power came from Atalaya, the ancient sacred mountain near whose foot she dwelt.

She healed and comforted many people throughout the years, and it could be seen that it was a source of great sorrow to her that she never completely healed her husband. His body gradually grew better, but his mind was clouded. Perhaps this was for the best, though, for in the beginning he had not treated her with the love she gave him. He had been surly, and had looked on everyone with a disagreeable, sneering contempt. But after his memory grew dim and his thoughts confused, his nature had softened. Then he began to follow her about like a small child, and he helped her with household tasks and he responded gently to her.

One day a strange thing happened. It became known because Frasquita Romero was convalescing from fever on one of the clinic beds and both heard and saw some of it. She understood English, having once been cook at the Palace for Governor Lew Wallace.

As Frasquita later told the story, it was on a brilliant June day that the beautiful young lady arrived at the house of La Santa. It was very surprising because one could see that she was most fashionably dressed, an Anglo-American from outside, and she came in a carriage from the station. The driver was very angry at having to go as far into the country over a miserable cart road, but he turned and drove off again without a word when he saw the meeting between the young lady and the couple at the Casa. The three of them stood and stared at each other for a long time, and then La Santa gave a cry and opened her arms and suddenly the tears were running down her face.

This had startled Frasquita very much, for La Santa had always seemed too calm and strong for tears. Then she heard

314

the young lady say "Mother!" in a tone of great feeling and the matter had been plainer. Still puzzling, however, was the behaviour of the old man, even granted that his mind was not clear. He had turned a very bad colour like a tallow candle, and he had walked out of the house alone, making a queer and dreadful noise like a child that is frightened.

The two women had fetched him back before he had stumbled very far, and the young one had kissed him on the forehead. "It's all over and done with long ago," she said, "and I've learned at last to forgive and not to judge. I came to tell you that and to bring you both back."

Frasquita felt sad to hear this, for suddenly she realized how badly they would all miss La Santa. But La Santa had not gone. The young lady had stayed a few days, she and her mother had talked in English for hours and hours on end. Far into each night Frasquita had heard their voices rising and falling from the next room. Voices very much alike, rich and soft, but with an undertone of certainty and power. Like the new organ in the Cathedral.

Finally the young lady went away again. Little Jaime Ruiz drove her to the station in his ox-cart, lovely silk dress, big diamond ring, parasol, and all. La Santa and El Viejo stayed behind in the little house by Atalaya. Frasquita thought maybe the mother would cry again, but she did not, and much of the sadness which had always lain in the back of her eyes vanished.

There were never any more visitors from the outside. The clinic went on and in time the cart track up to the house became beaten into quite a wide road.

Then one day the old man died, and La Santa did a strange thing. She had Jaime and his ox-cart carry the body across the river into the town, and she went with it to the Presbyterian Church on Grant Avenue for a Protestant burial. Jaime was very much shocked, and so were many others when they heard, but she never explained, and, though she went often to the Protestant cemetery with flowers, and they saw her walking lightly across the footbridge into town, dressed in the black dress and shawl that they all wore, they soon accepted this and forgot the reason.

She continued to work for them and heal them for a long time after that, and it was Padre Antonio who first realized that she was growing very weak. He mentioned this to one or two and at once there was a rush of sympathy and contrition from the many she had helped. Frasquita and María Gonzalez overrode her protests and stayed with her to care for her. The finest wine and delicacies flowed to the little house. Over and over again in the Barrio Analco they pooled their pennies and went to the plaza stores to buy special food for her. And the Indians heard. They came from Tesuque and Nambe and Santo Domingo to bring her gifts.

One evening María Gonzalez sent for Padre Antonio. He administered the last rites, and after that La Santa lay very still on her colchón, raised up a bit as she wished it so that she might see Atalaya through the window. Her eyes were continually seeking the mountain, and always the sight of it seemed to give her peace, even when she was in great pain.

At dawn of the next day she ceased to breathe, and while the two women sobbed, the priest, who had stayed with her, bowed his head with a sharp feeling of sorrow and personal loss.

She was buried as she had wished to be in San Miguel Cemetery at the nearest point to Atalaya. Buried in a simple black dress and around her neck a magnificent roughly cut turquoise pendant on a gold chain. María Gonzalez and Frasquita had been shocked to find that the chain did not end in a crucifix as they had always supposed. And they had rather timidly mentioned this to the padre.

"Is it not strange that this devout woman, whom we have considered as almost a saint, should wish to be buried like the heathen Indians with a lump of turquoise on her breast?"

And the padre answered: "Is it not strange that you, María Gonzalez, whose baby she twice cured, and you, Frasquita, whom she nursed for five months through the bloody flux, should dare to question her now? The soul, my daughters, may have many symbols with which it reaches toward God."

And the women were silenced.

Though he alone of all those who knew her had had many talks with her and learned something of her history, it was not until he opened the letter of instruction which she had prepared that he learned her real name.

Santa Fe Cameron, he thought in amazement; she was named for this town of her birth, for whose people she had done so much, and they have all these years unknowingly and against my wishes been calling her by part of her baptismal name. And this realization gave him a sense of mystical contentment, for it seemed in that moment of illumination that there was here a glimpse of the underlying pattern and meaning for which we all seek, and he pondered often on the woman's story.

She had once repudiated this place of her birth and spirit, fled from it with passion and a clamouring of the senses, as she had misused the vision with which she had been born. And because she was strong and had latent in her the possibilities for true greatness, even perhaps for the beatification she had here transiently and but semi-seriously achieved—because of this strengh she had involved others in her tragedy.

But there had been atonement, patient day-by-day self-sacrifice back here in the place which she had once despised. Ah, yes, thought the priest, it makes a pattern. And the pattern is God's.

When a new generation grew up in the Barrio Analco, she would be forgotten, her untended adobe house was already crumbling, the wooden Mexican cross on her grave would last no longer than all the others throughout the land, but something would endure. Something in the pure and exalted air on the summit of the mountains, in the fragrance of the junipers and piñons, in the warm shadows of the portales, and in the still sunlight and the gold-flecked dust of the far-reaching roads.

THE END

KATHERINE

Katherine was born the daughter of a humble herald, was betrothed to an obscure knight but was loved by a prince. She became the mistress of John of Gaunt, then his wife and the ancestress of the Tudor Kings of England. The dramatic and brilliantly told story of her love and her life is set against the superbly recreated pageant of fourteenth-century England.

"Miss Seton's enthusiasm for both character and period is infectious. Katherine emerges a glowing, vital figure who played no minor part in one of the significant periods of English history."

The Daily Telegraph

ORDER THESE BESTSELLING NOVELS BY ANYA SETON ON THIS FORM OR THROUGH YOUR BOOKSELLER

☐	15701 1	Katherine	40p
☐	15693 7	Devil Water	40p
☐	01401 6	My Theodosia	35p
☐	01951 4	The Winthrop Woman	40p
☐	02469 0	Dragonwyck	35p
☐	02488 7	Foxfire	35p
☐	02713 4	Avalon	35p
☐	15683 X	The Mistletoe and Sword	30p
☐	15699 6	The Hearth and Eagle	35p
☐	17857 4	Green Darkness	50p

All these books are available at your bookshop or news-agent, or can be ordered direct from the publisher. Just tick the titles you want and fill in the form below.

CORONET BOOKS, P.O. Box 11, Falmouth, Cornwall.

Please send cheque or postal order. No currency, and allow the following for postage and packing:

1 book – 10p, 2 books – 15p, 3 books – 20p, 4–5 books – 25p, 6–9 books – 4p per copy, 10–15 books – 2½p per copy, over 30 books free within the U.K.

Overseas – please allow 10p for the first book and 5p per copy for each additional book.

Name..

Address..

....